P9-BYH-756

THE MEMORIST

THE MEMORIST

M. J. ROSE

MIRA®

ISBN-13: 978-0-7783-2584-0
ISBN-10:   0-7783-2584-9

THE MEMORIST

www.MIRABooks.com

Printed in U.S.A.

For My Father

Memory is then the key word
which combines past and present, past and future.
–Elie Wiesel

Chapter 1

The souls must reenter the absolute from where they have emerged. They must develop all the perfections; the germ of which is planted in them; and if they have not fulfilled this condition during one life, they must commence another...until they have acquired the condition that fits them for reunion with God.

—Kabbalah (Zohar)

Vienna, Austria
Thursday, April 24th—5:00 p.m.

Beneath a dome nature had carved out of limestone, David Yalom circumnavigated the rim of the underground canyon without once glancing into its black crevasse. Nothing about his measured footsteps suggested he was aware of how dangerous the drop was even though only minutes before his guide had thrown a stone into the abyss that they'd never heard hit bottom. Finally, after four hours of rock climbing and trekking through the gloomy network of tubes and channels, wading through subterranean streams, crossing still pools studded with stalagmites and boiling lakes, he saw what he'd come here for. Up ahead on the right, exactly as Hans Wassong had described it, was a crude but massive arch cut into the rock, a cross roughly etched in the stone like some kind of religious graffiti.

"So this place you told me about really does exist." David laughed, but it was a bitter sound that, instead of suggesting humor, suggested there was none left anywhere in the world.

"I told you that you could trust me." To converse, these two men—the Israeli journalist and the Austrian felon—each spoke English with different but equally heavy accents. "This entire area is part of the larger tell site," Wassong continued.

"Tell site?" David's irrepressible curiosity got the better of him. He wasn't there as a reporter, but a lifetime of digging deep into every aspect of every story was a habit that died hard.

"A tell site," Wassong said, showing off, "is one that builds up in layers over time. A Jewish ghetto on top of a medieval city on top of an ancient Roman city. You'd have to raze all of Vienna's streets to chart this underground world of sewers, cellars and catacombs."

The area up ahead glowed in the beams of light streaming from the halogen lamps affixed to the men's helmets. Everywhere else fell off into shadow and interminable darkness; each step they took vanished behind them. The last few feet of the dangerous ledge rose steeply until finally they reached the entrance. Wassong walked under the low-hanging arch but David had to stoop to follow him into the crypt.

At the sound of their footsteps a rat, its red eyes flashing, vacated an infant-sized skull and darted off, disappearing into a pile of age-bleached bones.

The noise alerted David and he pulled his gun.

Wassong reached out and lowered the weapon for David. "No, you could set off an avalanche. We could be crushed to death and I prefer to be buried where my relatives can come visit."

All around them, intact skeletons rested in dozens of alcoves scooped out of the walls. Looking around the secret cemetery, David tried not to superimpose his own family's features on these bones—but failed. All dead had become his own dead, victims of his country's enemies' relentless efforts to commit genocide and the abysmal failure of those in charge to protect the innocent.

"Listen to these acoustics," Wassong said, and pointed to the ceiling as if it were possible to see the music filtering down. "Astonishing that the sound reaches down this far, isn't it?"

As the sour notes split the dank air, instead of violins tuning up, David heard an air raid siren before his brain acknowledged it was only an auditory mirage. He would kill to quell this constant onslaught of memories, except without them what would sustain him long enough for him to carry out his plan? Memory was a mystery. Why did he remember some moments—was even haunted by them—when others, desperate as he was to remember them—like the smell of his wife's hair—still eluded him?

"We're directly under Vienna's greatest concert hall now," Wassong explained as he took off his glasses and wiped them with a navy bandana. David had used the mannerism to characterize the man in the first article he'd written about him. After putting the glasses back on, Wassong pointed to the north wall, which had several fissures in it.

"This area abuts an ancient shaft that leads up to the building's subbasement. The music is traveling through grates that were once part of an old heating system."

"And you're sure this area isn't mapped?"

A clash of cellos, horns, flutes and oboes struggled but was unable to settle into harmony. One instrument dominated, then another and then another, all together creating discordant aggregates the same way David's mind threw up distinct and separate memory snapshots. His wife's face a mass of bloody, unrecognizable horror. Then Lisle's face years before, laughing at one of his pathetic attempts to tell a joke on a lazy afternoon at the beach. His son, Isaac, at five, insisting on taking his bicycle to bed with him the first day he got it. Then the raw stump where Isaac's left foot used to be. And on and on. David counted each memory as if that proved something. But what? That he had once been a sane man living a purposeful life? Or that he had valid and palpable reasons for what he was planning?

Hans was still explaining: "From the middle ages on these caverns were mostly used as burial chambers until they became so unsanitary that in the 1700s Emperor Joseph the Second shut them down. Who would map tombs?"

"That doesn't look like an artifact from the 1700s." David pointed to a crushed olive-drab metal pail half buried in a corner of the grotto. He'd learned when he was a rookie reporter that details told the truth even when people lied.

"During World War II the government reopened a few sections as bomb shelters. When the buildings above them were hit, some of the caves collapsed. Hundreds of people were crushed to death, and our underground city was once again abandoned, considered unsafe. Except, for some of us, it's safer down here than up there, isn't it?"

David ignored the conspiratorial wink in Wassong's voice. "But there *are* people who know about this place?"

"There were, yes, but judging from the signs, no one has been here in decades. You can trust me on this, David. And you can also pay me. I believe that was our agreement. I deliver your site, you deliver your fee."

Ten years ago, while writing a story about the Eastern European illegal arms market, David had met Hans Wassong, who'd been on Interpol's watch list for decades, suspected of kidnapping, manslaughter and trafficking of both weapons and explosives. Over the years, the journalist had gained the criminal's trust and used him as a source. Now their positions were reversed. David wasn't reporting on a story this time; he was going to be the story and Wassong was the one who could expose him.

Unzipping his dark green knapsack, David pulled out the thick envelope and handed it to Wassong, who opened it, counted through the pile of two-hundred-euro notes, then wordlessly stuffed the envelope inside his jacket pocket and patted it down. "So tell me, when will you have everything arranged?"

"By Monday or Tuesday."

"You'll move down here then?" Wassong's question sounded like urging.

"What have you heard? Is there any new chatter?"

"Tangentially. Ahmed Abdul has been spotted in Serbia."

Serbia was slightly more than 500 kilometers away. Two thousand kilometers closer to Vienna than Palestine. Was it a coincidence? David had covered every International Security and Technology Association conference since 1995, and it would have been simple for the terrorist to confirm David was reporting on ISTA again this year and follow him to Vienna.

"You know you're still on their list, don't you?" Wassong asked when David didn't respond.

"Of course." The tone he used to acknowledge he was being hunted was the same as the one he would use to acknowledge his profession as a reporter.

The orchestra finished tuning up and launched into the stormy and heroic opening of Beethoven's Fifth Symphony.

"Fate is knocking at the door," Wassong said.

"What?"

"One day Beethoven pointed to the opening of the first movement of this symphony and said to his secretary—'Thus Fate knocks at the door.'"

"You surprise me, Hans. An arms dealer, cartographer, spelunker and now I find you're a Beethoven scholar too?"

"It's difficult to live in Vienna and not soak up the musical lore."

For a few minutes the cold stones turned into plush red chairs, gilt molding edged the rock walls and the crypt became a concert hall as two men listened to a symphony, lost in its sound. David's wife had especially loved the Fifth. Shutting his eyes, he allowed himself the indulgence of memory.

"Are you all right?" Wassong asked.

The music rose to a crescendo that filtered down to the bowels of the earth, reaching his core. David didn't hear Wassong's question. *At least,* he was thinking, *next week, when they were all ushered out of this world it would be on the wings of music that belonged to the angels.*

"How far down are we?" David asked, back to business.

"Twelve or fourteen meters," Wassong said. "Too deep for ground-penetrating radar to find you and the perfect place to plant your explosives. Right here, right where we are standing. Nothing—not the building, not the audience—will survive the attack. You have to admit, it's an excellent spot, no?"

Chapter 2

Meer ran down the steps of the Natural History Museum on Central Park West, scanning the street for a cab even before she reached the sidewalk. When she didn't spot one, she decided it would be just as fast to walk the six blocks to the Phoenix Foundation. She shouldn't have agreed to leave work in the middle of the morning but Malachai Samuels wasn't an easy man to say no to. Part shaman, part therapist, part confessor, even when he'd been unable to find answers he'd always been there to help her through the dark nights and lonely days, to soothe her fears and assuage her sadness.

On the phone, Malachai had assured her the meeting wouldn't take more than an hour and that really was all she had to spare. Tonight's fund-raising event was critical for the success of the Memory Dome project: a permanent study and exhibition space devoted to the exploration of memory. As the project's associate curator she had too much to do to give up even an hour.

Eight minutes later she was listening to the ticking of the nineteenth century ormolu clock on the marble mantel that seemed to slow to creeping as if preparing to stop and then go backward. Impossible, except Meer knew that in Malachai Samuels' office time didn't always move in the same direction as it did everywhere else in the world.

"This is for you," the reincarnationist said, placing a badly weathered and over-stamped envelope on the table between them. She recognized her father's handwriting.

"So now you're playing messenger? Did my father tell you why he sent this to me care of you?"

"So you wouldn't be alone when you opened it."

"Like a child." Her smile was resigned.

"No matter what your age he'll always be your father." Malachai's refined British accent made the sentence seem like a pronouncement. He looked refined, too: his suits were always pressed, his nails always buffed. A hundred years ago he would have easily passed as a member of the aristocracy.

"Do you know what this is about?"

"He didn't enlighten me."

Picking it up, she ripped it open and pulled out the contents.

Unfolding the coarse yellowed paper she looked down on a little girl's drawing done in gold, orange, red and brown crayons. The lines didn't stay straight, didn't meet at the corners, but still managed to represent a box. Not just any box but the illusory treasure chest she'd been morbidly fascinated with as a child. When her parents asked her why she kept drawing it over and over she didn't know. When they asked where she'd seen it she could only tell them "before."

Then they asked what else she remembered from "before" and she told them. It was like a very bad dream, except she only had it when she was awake and it was always the same. She was in a forest, during a storm, being chased by a man trying to get the box away from her. In the background, mysterious music played like it did in movies. And sometimes when she came back to "now" as she called it, she was crying.

The colorful details on the page her father had sent were just scribbles but they illustrated what she'd so clearly seen in her memory—dark polished wood with elaborate silver fittings and a large silver medallion engraved with birds, leaves, horns, flutes, harps and flourishes. Once she'd told her father that the strange music she heard in the bad daydream lived inside the box but she couldn't ever keep it open long enough to hear the song all the way through.

Rejecting what her father and Malachai believed, that the storm and the music and the chase were her past life memories, Meer had spent years trying to understand what she perceived as an affliction. The search eventually led to her getting a master's in cognitive therapy along with a subspecialty in memory—and an acceptable explanation. Meer maintained she suffered false memories: as a young child either her unconscious had distorted actual events, or she'd confused her dreams with reality.

"It's just one of my old drawings," she said with relief as she offered it to Malachai.

His dark eyes widened slightly as he inspected it for a few seconds. Then he removed a paper clip in the upper right-hand corner, and examined a second sheet of paper. The clock ticked away the seconds as it had done for over a hundred and fifty years. "I think you missed this," he finally said as he handed it to her.

It was a tear sheet from an auction catalog. Under a block of text was a photograph of a dark wooden box with elaborate silver fittings and a large silver medallion engraved with birds, leaves, horns, flutes

and harps and a cursive letter elaborately woven into the design—
something a child would only see as flourishes but as an adult, Meer
had no problem identifying as the letter *B*.

"Well, now we know the box did exist," she responded quickly in
a dispassionate voice as she dropped the tear sheet on the table.
"That means somehow, somewhere, I must have seen it before I had
any cognitive memory of seeing it. Maybe my mother was looking
through a book of antiques that included a photo of this box. Or it
was in an auction. She used to take me with her to auctions all the
time." Meer shifted back in her chair, moving away from her drawing.
Away from Malachai.

There are dividing lines in everyone's life. Meer knew the deepest
depressions are the ones that define us, but the same way that the
earth's topography is easier to see from above, those lines are viewed
most clearly from the distance of years. Only looking back can you
pinpoint the moment a crack turned into a breach and a breach
became a border. Meer was seven when she'd heard the strange
music and told her parents about the box and the chase in the forest
for the first time. Before, there had been no terror, and after, she was
afraid of looking to the right or left for fear of seeing an oncoming
disaster. Before, she hadn't questioned the promises her parents
made, and after, she knew none of their whispers that everything
would be all right held any weight.

"Don't you realize this could be proof that you've been having past
life memories all these years?" Malachai's ebony eyes gleamed. He
reached for the auction catalog tear sheet again, and as he did Meer
glimpsed his shirt cuff peeking out of his handmade suit jacket, revealing a white-on-white MS monogram. This was a man educated
at Oxford, who quoted Aristotle, Einstein and Carl Jung to her, who
enjoyed showing off his collection of playing cards that dated back
to the fifteenth century, who had written an important monograph

on the psychology of Victorian England's preoccupation with the occult. When he discussed regression it never suggested psychic parlors with ruby-beaded curtains; he imbued the concept of soul transmigration with a scientist's gravitas, making it hard to dismiss his words as anything less than the truth. Nonetheless, she didn't believe what he believed. Or what her father believed. When she was younger she'd wanted to, tried to, even had been willing to be their guinea pig, but they'd never proved their theories to her satisfaction. The leap of faith they'd required of her was too great. Like her mother, Meer was a pragmatist.

"The description says the object is an early eighteenth-century gaming box that belonged to a woman named Antonie Brentano, who was a friend of Beethoven's," Malachai read aloud.

A metallic taste filled her mouth and made her teeth hurt. Her shoulders tensed and her jaw muscles tightened. A ripple of shivering shook her. She heard something, far away. Distant but distinct. Deep in her back, where she'd broken her spine when she was nine years old, the fused vertebrae throbbed. Suddenly, she felt sick. And even though she was no longer a child, but a thirty-one-year-old woman, she wanted to get up and run away.

She'd been running away that day too, trying to escape the haunting music that scared her because it always preceded the memory of that terrible chase through the forest. Her problem obsessed her parents. Had changed them into two strangers who argued about what kind of help she needed. The endless visits to various kinds of doctors kept her out of school, made her different and ruined the family's plans.

That afternoon she and her father had been in Central Park flying her kite. It had been winging its way higher into the sky than she'd ever imagined it could go when storm clouds suddenly rolled in, and with them came the awful, beautiful music.

Letting go of the kite she took off, running wildly, trying to escape.

Calling out for her, begging her to stop, her father ran after her, even managed to catch up to her and was only a moment away from pulling her to safety when a bike rider came around a bend too fast to stop. The impact sent Meer flying into the air and she landed on her back on rocks near the road.

"Meer? Are you all right?" Malachai leaned toward her, pulling her out of her thoughts.

"When I was a little girl, I used to sit here and think about all the other kids my father told me came to you for help and how they must have sat on this same chair and heard this same clock ticking and how they must have all gotten better because I never saw any of them in the waiting room. I thought you'd cured them all. I was sure you were going to make me better too."

Now on Malachai's face, Meer saw sympathy. She much preferred his default expression: the arched eyebrows and aloof gaze of the objective observer. Compassion wasn't what she wanted or deserved for succumbing to her old affliction. She knew how to fight the onslaught of an episode and keep it at bay. She knew her triggers and had avoided all of them. Yet, she could hear that old faraway music again...vague and indistinct, coming from beyond this room, this town house, this street, this city, from beyond this time. She felt the freezing anxiety that threatened to take her breath away and the terrible sadness that made her want to weep for something or someone lost to her now. It had been years since she'd been visited by this devil.

Gripping the couch's arm, she tried to focus on taking deep, even breaths and hold on to the present, but the mystery flooded back with ferociousness she was unprepared for. Not all the years of Malachai's help or numerous hypnosis sessions or the scientific theories about pseudomemories that she adopted like a creed were a match for the enigma's power.

"Are you all right?"

"Fine," she said, not wanting to admit—especially to herself—that the ghost of herself as a child had risen up and that the child's secrets were sucking the present out of the air, making breathing laborious, and that the haunting fears that used to encircle her, reach out with their sharp claws, pick her up and fly her away to a distant dimension, were reclaiming her again.

Malachai put a glass in her hand. Until she drank the water, she hadn't known she was thirsty, and then she couldn't drink enough. Finally, she placed the empty glass down beside the manila envelope and the drawing.

"What's real is now," Malachai said in a familiar cadence. "What's real is now."

Nodding, she concentrated on that. It was one of the prompts they'd worked out when she was just a little girl. *What's real is now. What's real is now.* She used the mantra to regulate her breathing. Shaking her head as if the motion would dislodge her memory, she pounded her fist into the palm of her hand. "I haven't gone near a piano. I'm not writing music. I haven't in twelve years. Why isn't that enough?"

"Meer, you are being too hard on yourself, this isn't something that's your fault. We come back in this life to work out what we didn't complete in our past lives and no matter how much we wish we could avoid our karmic debt we—"

Among his other talents, Malachai was an amateur magician who could turn a scarf into a white dove or a problem into a bouquet of possibilities but she wasn't in the mood to hear him offer up his outrageous explanations.

"No matter what's happening, I'm not going back on medication again to live in that fog." Her voice stretched as tight as the muscles in her long neck.

"What is it? What's happening?"

"The dreads are back," she whispered, using the childhood name for the pervasive anxiety and terror she used to feel and the dissonant, conflicting chords she used to hear.

Chapter 3

For almost three hundred years experts had entered this same private viewing room to pore over treasures soon to be auctioned off. But how many of them had felt their hearts pounding as fast as Jeremy Logan's was? Closing the door behind him, he turned the brass key in the lock and listened to the tumblers click into place. The inlaid parquet floor he crossed had been restored and the antique desk he sat at had been refurbished many times over but time hadn't erased the pentimento of the important discoveries made here. Would his efforts today be added to that history?

At sixty-five, Jeremy was not only the head of the Judaica department of the auction house but the man they called the Jewish Indiana Jones. Over the last thirty-five years he'd recovered hundreds of the thousands of Torahs and other religious artifacts hidden or stolen during World War II. Some he'd dug up like buried treasure, others he'd smuggled across the borders of Communist countries or secured through brokering deals with dangerous operatives who only cared about the money he offered. Even with all these finds to his credit, the one treasure he'd been searching for the longest still eluded him: the solution to his daughter's distress.

And now here was a possibility that he'd found a clue to that puzzle.

In addition to the whist markers, cribbage board, checkers and chess pieces and playing cards that he could see inside the box, an X-ray of the rosewood gaming case had shown a one-inch-deep false bottom containing a rectangle of either thin cloth or thick paper that even with their sophisticated equipment the technicians hadn't been able to identify. Now, secluded behind the locked door, Jeremy Logan was about to find out what it was.

Taking off his oatmeal-colored cardigan sweater, he threw it on the chair and pushed up the sleeves of his navy turtleneck. He plucked his reading glasses out of his tousled salt-and-pepper hair, settled them on the bridge of his nose and examined the box. Now that he knew what he was looking for and was using a magnifying glass, Jeremy could see that behind the letter *B,* there was a constellation etched faintly into the background. This was the only aspect of the box that Meer had never included in her drawings. Studying it, Jeremy was astonished to realize he was looking at the Phoenix constellation, named after the ancient mystical bird that symbolized reincarnation. Along with Malachai Samuels, he'd always thought reincarnation was at the heart of his daughter's crisis, maintaining that she was haunted by bleeds from a previous and troubled life.

He passionately believed in reincarnation and that circles of souls reincarnate with each other over time, which both makes it more difficult to come into contact with people we've had problems with before and easier when we reconnect with those we've loved. Family, friends, lovers and those you work with were all part of your soul group; he wished that he could convince Meer to have faith in those around her, to lean on him and Malachai and let them help her find her karmic way. But she was as stubborn a nonbeliever as he was a believer.

He picked up the box, which, like a recalcitrant child, had held on to its secret for all these weeks, and laid it on its back on a felt pad. Inlaid circles of various sizes, carved from different kinds of rare fruitwoods, were set in a random pattern.

The expert he'd met with yesterday in Prague had shown him a similar chest made by the same designer in 1802. It had looked equally enigmatic—a puzzle without a solution—until he'd pointed out the Taurus constellation etched into that box top's medallion and demonstrated how, when the circles on the bottom were manipulated to match the star pattern, the hidden drawer opened. As if by magic.

Judiciously, Jeremy worked the circles on the Brentano box, as it was referred to in the auction catalog. The first glided easily into place. By nature impatient, Jeremy struggled to go slowly, moving on to the next circle and then the next. He'd been studying the Kabbalah for the last twenty-four years and one of the most important lessons he'd learned was that his impatience resulted from his not being able to tolerate what the present moment had to offer. In the Kabbalah, every letter of the Hebrew alphabet has several layers of meaning. In life, he had learned, every moment did, too. And in every past life.

Taking a deep breath, Jeremy moved the last piece into place and heard a tiny mechanical click as the box's false bottom slid open. What had been impenetrable before was offered up without quarrel now and as he looked down on a folded sheet of paper that had likely been hidden there for almost two hundred years he was both exalted and, suddenly, frightened.

Chapter 4

The intercom buzzed to life and Special Agent Lucian Glass frowned at the interruption as he looked over to check the building's closed-circuit monitor. People thought nothing of ringing random apartments to get into the building because they didn't want to search for their own keys, were trying to leave takeout menus on every welcome mat or were hoping to get in so they could roam the halls and look for unlocked doors. Even in New York it was surprising how many people were burgled due to simple negligence. But this time Lucian recognized the heavyset man standing in the vestibule peering up into the camera.

The rented fourth-floor studio was sparsely decorated with a battered card table and four chairs but overwhelmed with surveillance equipment, and while Lucian walked his way through it all to reach the intercom, Douglas Comley, his supervisor and the bureau's

Director of the Art Crime Team, or ACT as they all referred to it, pressed the buzzer again.

Within seconds of activating the downstairs door, the droning stopped and Lucian went back to what he had been doing before: listening to Malachai Samuels' cultivated voice broadcasting from the Phoenix Foundation, across the street, via a state-of-the-art ultradirectional microphone. Since last summer, the FBI, Interpol and the Italian carabinieri had been investigating the so-called reincarnationist in an effort to prove he'd masterminded an international robbery that resulted in the brutal deaths of three adults and the kidnapping of one child. The stolen objects, a set of precious stones, were purported to be the legendary memory tools dating back to the Indus Valley in 2000 B.C.E. There was no question Malachai Samuels was obsessed to the point of fanaticism with finding absolute proof of reincarnation, proof he might have hoped the stones would yield, but neither Lucian's team nor Interpol had yet been able to conclusively tie him to the crime. Half of the stones had been recovered by the NYPD and returned to the Italian government but the other half were still missing. Lucian believed Malachai either had the walnut-sized rubies, sapphires and emeralds in his possession or knew where they were. All they needed was for him to slip up, just once.

"I think seeing the photograph triggered the music." Malachai was speaking. *"As for what happens next—that's your choice. You can cross the threshold or turn away."*

"You mean go to Vienna and see this thing?" the woman asked in a frightened voice.

Lucian had only seen her in a blur for a few seconds—jean-clad legs and leather jacket that looked supple even from across the street, perfect posture and wavy auburn hair framing her face—before she opened the door to the maisonette and vanished inside, but in that short time he'd sensed both her strength and loneliness. If he were going to paint wind, he'd choose this woman to stand in for the invisible power.

For nine months, Lucian had been listening to Malachai's conversations and phone calls and reading his e-mails. He'd heard dozens of children embark on strange journeys without leaving the Foundation's nineteenth century Upper West Side building. Astonishingly, they arrived in distress and left soothed. But the woman in the office today wasn't a child and the conversation was different from any Lucian had heard before.

"I've accepted the mystery of my memories," Meer Logan's tremulous voice whispered over the electronic equipment.

Lucian's ability to quickly grasp someone's emotional and psychological makeup had started before his FBI training but Quantico had helped hone his intuition. Listening to this woman, he wasn't sure why but he was worried for her.

"You think that but look at how much of your life, your ambition and your passion you've surrendered. You're being held hostage, your talent is being held hostage by the fears and sadness you carry around," Malachai said with a new urgency.

Without conscious thought, Lucian grabbed his sketchbook and started his third or fourth drawing of that hour, this one of Meer as a child. The pencil moved rapidly and a little girl emerged with dark hair, eyes wide with terror, tearstained cheeks and—

The doorbell rang and Lucian put down the book to let in his boss as Meer's voice came over the speaker. *"How can you honestly believe that if I see the box it could make a difference?"*

"Triggers work the same way, whether we're talking about past life memories or false memories, you know that. Here, I want you to read something..."

Comley walked in, heard Malachai's voice, nodded in the direction of the equipment and asked: "Did I interrupt something important?"

"Not to our case, I don't think so."

Looking around, Comley grinned. "Like what you've done with the place since the last time I was here."

"I've got some soda and there's coffee—can I get you something?"

"The hostess with the mostess. Sure, I'll take a soda." Comley sat down at the table and noticed the sketchbook. He was glancing at the drawing of the little girl when Lucian put the soda down in front of him. "Who's this, Mr. Painter Man? One of his clients?"

All the agents in ACT had law enforcement backgrounds but Lucian also had art school training: he was used to the nickname.

"An ex-patient, from what I've been able to decipher."

"Do you ever wonder if you should have stuck with this?" Comley continued examining the drawing.

"My mother asks me that every once in a while, too."

"And you also cleverly avoid answering her?"

Lucian didn't dwell on his past but neither did he hide it. His art background helped him in his job and in his uniform of black jeans, black T-shirt and black blazer, he still dressed enough like a member of New York's art scene to pass at a gallery opening. But that didn't mean he talked much about his life before the agency.

He'd been nineteen years old, an art student at Cooper Union majoring in painting the year his future changed its direction. The Met stayed open on Friday nights and Lucian and his girlfriend, also an art student, had plans to see the new Zurbarán exhibition. He was meeting Solange at her father's framing store, uptown, near the museum at six o'clock after the store closed, and they were going to walk over together.

The express train hadn't been running so Lucian took the local and that made him fifteen minutes late. When he got there, no one was in the front room, which was unusual, and no one answered when he called out. Without stopping to think whether or not it was smart, he opened the door to the workroom and walked in.

Solange's body lay on the floor, inside a large, empty frame, her blood splattered on its silver arms. As he stared down at the horrible arrangement, a flash of movement reflected in the polished metal warned him that someone was there—someone was behind him, moving toward him—but he wasn't fast enough. Lucian was only a skinny kid studying to be a painter. He didn't know how to defend himself.

When the paramedics found him, Lucian had lost six pints of blood from four stab wounds and been left for dead by the thief. Except he was still alive. Or was, until in the ambulance, on the way to the hospital, he died.

It took the paramedics ninety-two seconds to bring Lucian Glass back to life and although he'd never discussed that minute and a half with anyone, he had experienced it. He didn't allow that the near-death experience had changed his life or affected him in any way— if the world didn't look the same to him after the attack, he blamed it on losing Solange in such a violent way. But within months he went from a boy who'd never been in a fight, to a man fixated on retribution and revenge, and the FBI was the sanctuary where he turned that desire into a career. Art changed from something he wanted to create, to something he wanted to protect and rescue. Yes, he filled sketchbooks with unfinished portraits of people he came across during his cases, but how different was that from the way other agents took notes?

"You didn't come all the way here to talk to me about my latent talents, did you?" Lucian asked.

Comley turned the book over to get away from the child's sad face in the drawing. "I don't like being the bearer of bad news but we're shutting the case down. We can't—"

"Why do you and my father keep trying to convince me this is all part of some great cosmic plan, that it's my damn destiny?" Meer's strained voice

came over the microphone and Comley broke off, unable to ignore the plaintive tone.

"Destiny just puts us on the path that leads to opportunities. What we do with those opportunities is up to each of us," Malachai answered.

"Yes, I know that's what you think, but I think I'm too busy at the museum right now to go to Vienna."

Lucian heard a child's stubbornness in the woman's decision. With an angry twist he turned down the volume knob and shut out the conversation going on across the street.

"I can't justify keeping your team on this any longer without a break. You know how small our department is."

"Let me work the case alone." It was a request but Lucian said it more like an order.

"You're not *working* this case anymore, my friend, you're haunted by it, and that's not good for either of us. No. I'm sorry. I'm shutting you down."

Lucian walked over to the window and stared at the Phoenix Foundation. He'd been with the FBI for ten years, starting in the Art Theft Program and then being assigned to ACT when it was formed in 2004 in the aftermath of the Iraqi looting after the fall of Saddam Hussein's regime. Since then, he and his team had successfully recovered over a dozen precious works of art worth more than thirty-five million dollars, including a Michelangelo drawing and a set of rare coins from ancient Greece. He'd succeeded time after time and had known that sooner or later he would fail. But he didn't want it to happen on *this* case.

While he continued watching, the Foundation's front door opened and Meer exited. Pulling up her collar, she stood impossibly straight, facing into the wind coming off the park as if she were gathering strength from the gusting air, and then walked down the steps and away from him.

"What's the date on my eviction notice?"

"Two weeks from today," Comley answered.

"Two weeks," Lucian repeated with determination, as if making both a bargain and a promise.

Chapter 5

*Has it occurred to you that transmigration is at once an explanation
and a justification of the evil of the world? If the evils we suffer are the
result of sins committed in our past lives, we can bear them with resignation and hope that if in this one we strive toward virtue our future
lives will be less afflicted.*

— W. Somerset Maugham, The Razor's Edge

Vienna, Austria
Thursday, April 24th—6:20 p.m.

If anyone walking down one of Leopoldstadt's narrow cobbled
streets had glimpsed Jeremy Logan hurrying up the steps to Number
122 Engerthstrasse they wouldn't have given him or the artless
building identified as the Toller Archäologiegesellschaft—the Toller
Archaeology Society— a second glance. Not even the front door
with its decorative lock in the shape of a peacock attracted attention.
In Vienna, a lack of decoration would have been more noticeable.

Seconds after ringing the bell, Jeremy disappeared inside and went through a second door invisible from the street. As he passed under the carved letters on the entranceway's frieze that revealed the brotherhood's true name, the change from ordinary exterior to extravagant interior was drastic.

The Memorist Society, on whose board of directors Jeremy sat, had been secretly founded in 1809 to study the work of Austrian Orientalist Joseph von Hammer-Purgstall, one of the men responsible for the greatest dissemination of Eastern knowledge in late-eighteenth-century Europe. Of specific interest to the Society's founders was reincarnation—a belief common to the newly discovered Hindu Shruti scriptures, the teachings of the Kabbalah, the mystery schools of ancient Egypt, Greek philosophers and Christian doctrine prior to the fifth century C.E.

The then undesirable land near the Prater parklands, in the midst of the Jewish ghetto, had been chosen as the Society's location to both accommodate its many Hebraic members and keep curiosity seekers away. The architect had been given two specifications: the building should attract no undue attention and it should have at least one hidden entrance and exit.

Entering the sanctum sanctorum, Jeremy stepped into the vast assembly room where columns stood like sentries. An Egyptian mural illustrating the story of Isis and Osiris swept over the walls, and a gem-toned carpet covered the floor. The cupola ceiling was painted the cobalt of a night sky and stars—tiny mirrors that caught and reflected light from below—twinkled above. Every corner of the room was crammed with gleaming spiritual objects and artifacts, but Jeremy ignored it all as he headed purposefully toward the library and the board members meeting he'd called.

"*Guten abend,*" Fremont Brecht said as he put down his newspaper. Seated in a club chair as if he were a potentate and it was his throne, with thousands of leather-bound books behind him, Austria's ex-minister of defense and head of the Memorist Society was a commanding presence.

Few members greeted Fremont as warmly as Jeremy did, but men didn't make Jeremy cower; only mysteries he couldn't explain.

"Will we still be able to make the concert or will this meeting take too long?" Fremont asked.

"We should be fine. And I have my car here."

"Good, because I cancelled an appointment regarding next week's security and technology conference for tonight's performance of the *Emperor Concerto* and would hate to miss it after going through all that trouble." He gestured across the long room to the middle-aged woman with auburn hair seated at a card table, busy scribbling notes. "Erika's waiting for us." Fremont was spry, despite his seventy-eight years and almost three-hundred-pound frame, and stood with surprising ease. Only a slight limp as he crossed the room suggested any concession to his age and rich diet.

In a niche, an ancient quartz Coptic jar sat on a plinth, a pinlight illuminating it with an almost iridescent glow. In a church, an object this precious would be in a gold-tooled reliquary but the Memorists' relic had no power and promised no magic and the members took the jar for granted. But tonight, Jeremy stared at it as if he could see through the alabaster to the scattered ashes and grime that lay on its bottom.

"Does this meeting have something to do with our spy?" Erika asked when they joined her. Her amber eyes swept the room as if she was looking for someone who didn't belong there.

"No, but I think you'll be just as interested in what I have to say. Maybe even more so," Jeremy answered.

One of Central Europe's leading authorities on near-death experiences—NDEs—Erika's personal goal was to have the scientific community take her Memorist-funded research connecting NDEs to reincarnation seriously. No matter that sixty percent of people in the world believed in past life regression, the establishment was not only suspicious of it, they were disdainful. Recently Erika had made some headway but believed someone inside the Society was spying on her when, for the second time in a year, rumors of her research were ridiculed in the press. Since then she'd been actively lobbying for Fremont to hire a detective.

"What's on your mind, Jeremy? I really don't want to miss the concert." Fremont tapped one fingertip on the leather-topped table.

"Three months ago I was contacted by a woman who asked me to appraise a Torah that she'd discovered hidden in her grandmother's apartment in the hopes our Judaica department would be interested."

Jeremy explained how he'd walked into Helen Hoffman's grandmother's living room to view one treasure and literally lost his step when he noticed another, a dusty afterthought on a side table. Despite never having laid eyes on it before, he recognized the carved wooden box right away. For so many years, through long empty nights and wandering days he'd searched for this phantom, driven by the memory of his daughter as a small child with brown satin curls and doleful pale-green eyes drawing a facsimile of it over and over, exhausting herself and wearing down crayons as she struggled with the details while silvery tracks of tears stained her cheeks.

Jeremy had been astonished to stumble on an actual antique that was identical to the box his daughter drew but that had been a synchronicity he'd been able to grasp. It was the information in the letter he had discovered inside that box this morning that was unfathomable and that he was there to divulge.

"The box belonged to Antonie Brentano," he explained.

When Erika couldn't place the name, Fremont explained she was one of Beethoven's closest friends, and possibly his Immortal Beloved.

"Beethoven was also a friend of two of our founders—he knew

both Caspar Neidermier and Rudolph Toller," Jeremy added. As the Society's historian, he'd studied all the records stored in the underground vault. "In the process of preparing the chest for sale in the upcoming auction, I discovered Beethoven gave Antonie the box."

"While I admire the labyrinthine paths you traverse in your investigations and enjoy hearing about them, I really don't want to be late. You said something was hidden in the box?" Fremont asked. "What was it?"

"A letter written by Ludwig van Beethoven."

In the hearth, a log cracked and hissed. Jeremy looked toward it and then over at the recess that held the Coptic urn before continuing. They all knew that in 1813, Caspar Neidermier died after finding an ancient bone flute in India. In 1814, his partner, Rudolph Toller, gave Ludwig van Beethoven that same flute and asked him to find the song believed to be encrypted in complicated markings etched on its surface.

"According to our records, that urn contains the pulverized fragments Beethoven returned…all that was left of the memory flute after he destroyed it."

"But the letter says something else?" Fremont prodded.

"Beethoven wrote that he only *told* the Society he'd destroyed the instrument—that what he gave us back was an animal bone, dried out and smashed with a hammer. He kept the real flute, believing it to be too valuable to destroy and at the same time too dangerous to entrust to anyone. He wrote that he hid it. *For the protection of us all, and all to come* were his exact words."

"Is the letter authentic?" Fremont asked.

"I'll have an expert opinion by Monday."

"Did he say where he hid the actual flute?" Erika asked.

"Not exactly."

"Nothing is ever that easy," Fremont said.

"Some manners of death," she responded with a sad laugh.

"Beethoven wrote that he sent each of his closest friends one piece of information, a clue if you will, so that if it ever became necessary they would be able to pool their knowledge and find both the flute and its song."

"You're saying he figured out the music?" Erika held her breath.

"He says he did, and before you ask, yes, I've checked—without being specific—with two scholars about any finished or unfinished compositions for the flute that might be relevant and have the right dates on them. There's nothing."

"To go to all that trouble, what he found must have really frightened him...or...was Beethoven just paranoid?" she asked.

"He was cautious, easy to anger, but no, not irrationally paranoid," Fremont, the musical aficionado among them, explained. "Although we can assume Herr Beethoven had heard the rumors that circulated when Mozart died only six weeks after his *Magic Flute* debuted. Conspiracy theorists suggested the young composer had been poisoned because of the Masonic secrets he'd revealed in his opera. It's possible Beethoven could have worried that if Mozart had been poisoned for revealing a secret legend about a flute with unusual properties connected to the cycle of life and death, maybe he should stay away from another one." Fremont took a sip of his brandy.

Erika's forehead furrowed again but this time there was a light in her eyes. "What if Beethoven found out the memory flute worked? What if the people who listened to its music and heard its vibrations remembered their past lives? That could have been what he meant by dangerous," she suggested breathlessly.

Fremont set his snifter down so hard on the marble end table a fragment of glass chipped off and the sound resonated ominously. "Until we know if Beethoven actually wrote that letter, this is all just speculation."

"The timing was right too." Erika was too far into her hypothesis to stop.

"Right for what?" Jeremy asked.

"The genesis of Heinrich Wilhelm Dove's discovery of binaural beats in 1839—"

"Erika!" Fremont interrupted with a laugh. "This is useless speculation."

But Jeremy didn't think so. The possibility of binaural beats—low frequency tones, stimulating brain wave activity—prompting past life regressions was something he'd first looked into when Meer had started hearing music inaudible to everyone else and Erika's recent work suggested the possibility was a probability. More than half the people in her NDE studies had heard music during their journeys, and when asked to pick out music from a dozen samples that came closest to what they'd heard, one hundred percent of them chose the sample imbedded with binaural beat frequencies.

"It's not speculation. There's a great deal of scientific data demonstrating the results of religious chanting, music, drumming and other sonic phenomena on the mind and the body." Erika spoke more quickly now, racing ahead, intoxicated by the connections she was making. She believed frequencies similar to the ones people with NDEs heard could open the portal and induce the states of consciousness necessary for them to remember previous lives.

"If we found the flute and it proved that past life memories could be stimulated through sonic manipulation, we would revolutionize reincarnation theory. Not just reincarnation theory," she insisted, "but time-space theory too. It would be a huge scientific breakthrough."

"All thanks to our conquering Jewish hero here." Fremont gestured to Jeremy.

"Jewish? How does that connect?" Jeremy asked.

"You'd be vilified as a twenty-first-century Pontius Pilate for proving that man alone bears responsibility for his eternal rest and it is within each person's own control to get to heaven. The Kabbalah will be reviled. Jewish mystics everywhere will become ostracized again." Fremont stared into his glass, swirled the liquid once, twice and then, lifting the snifter to his lips, drank the rest of the brandy down as if it were as smooth as caramel.

"The Kabbalah is hardly the only religious doctrine that supports reincarnation," Jeremy said. "Why assume Jews would take the blame just because—"

"Fremont," Erika interrupted, "are you actually suggesting we give up our inquiry because of a possible religious argument?" The scientist was aghast.

"Of course not," Fremont responded. "I'm just saying that so much is at stake we need to take one step at a time, quietly and carefully."

"Well, if the letter turns out to be authentic—" her voice regained its hopeful, yearning tone "—then the box itself might be a clue to where the flute is hidden. Shouldn't we be prepared to buy both the gaming box and the letter at next week's auction?"

"But the letter was hidden," Fremont said. "No one even knows about it. You're not announcing its existence now, are you?"

"Of course not. I had no intention of announcing it," Jeremy answered. "Helen Hoffman has agreed to let me have it authenticated but hasn't made any decision past that."

Erika wasn't paying attention to what they were saying; she'd moved beyond the auction to what would come next. "If what the letter says is true and the flute wasn't destroyed, there might be a memory tool hidden here in Vienna. We have to find it. A memory tool..." she intoned reverentially. "It's almost unimaginable."

But they were all imagining it. And so was another member of the Society who, unbeknownst to them all, had been sitting in one of the darkened corners of the chamber since before the meeting began and had been listening intently to every word.

Chapter 6

David Yalom tugged the gray life raft from behind the stalagmite where he'd stowed it after coming across the subterranean lake two hours ago. Something was wrong; it was completely deflated. Flipping it over, he saw four short parallel rips on the underside. "How the hell did that happen?" He gestured to the mutilation.

Wassong bent down and inspected the slashes. "The rocks are sharp here. When you pulled it up out of the lake you must have ripped it."

"No, I remember, I lifted it up. I didn't drag it, precisely for that reason." David stared at the rips. "Besides, these cuts are too clean to have been made on the ragged edges of these rocks." Frantically, he scanned the cavern, his halogen beam flashing wild streaks of light on the rocky walls. "Someone did this. Someone is down here with us, Hans."

"Impossible."

"You're sure? What if someone followed you here?"

"No one followed me," Wassong insisted. "Me? Think about what you're saying."

"What's going on then?"

"Maybe it was the rats."

David's light beam shined right into Wassong's light brown eyes. In an article, he'd once described them as surprisingly kind, and he thought of that now.

"Rats, Hans?"

"There are thousands of vermin living in these tunnels, you've seen them for yourself. These marks certainly could have been made by a rat's claws. There's no reason to worry. You are overreacting—understand, I don't blame you—the stress you are under would make anyone overreact. But we still have my raft. If this were some kind of suspicious activity, my lifeboat would have been attacked also. We have enough rope to rig my raft so that I can go across and then you can pull it back and use it."

There was no other choice. The water was thirty percent hotter than the human body's temperature thanks to the geothermal heat under the lake's bed. If you tried to swim across you'd be boiled to death.

"Did you look? Are you sure your raft isn't damaged too?"

But it wasn't.

Wassong pulled a coil of rope out of his knapsack and knotted it through the die-cut plastic ring in the raft's rubber edging.

"This will work fine," he said, tugging on it to make sure the knot would hold. Done, he took his glasses off, wiped them on his bandana, then wiped the bandana across his forehead and finally put his glasses back on.

"Once I'm on the other side and give you the signal, you'll be able to pull the boat back." He picked up the rope and tossed it to David.

Watching Wassong paddling across the water, the steam mist

shrouding him, David thought about the likelihood of a rat ripping through the PVC. As if he were attempting to reconstruct it so he could write it up for the newspaper, he ran through his and Wassong's earlier actions once they'd reached the shore and stowed the boats. Did Hans have time to sabotage the raft? And if he had, why? Sweat dripped down David's back. He had already taken off his jacket. Now he unbuttoned his work shirt and mopped his brow with his sleeve. Reaching into his knapsack, he grabbed his last bottle of water and drank down what little was left. They'd only brought supplies for the day, and the day was over.

He listened to the even splashing of Wassong's oars.

When they'd come through this section earlier they hadn't lingered. Just inflated the rafts, unfolded the oars, paddled across, stowed the boats and then continued on. No, he suddenly remembered, they *had* stopped. David had needed to record directions for the oral map he was keeping so he could find his way back on his own next week. What had Wassong been doing while David had made his notes?

He tried to remember. He thought back a few hours ago but what came to mind was another night. The last time he'd used the recorder before today was almost a year ago. He'd been fast-forwarding through an interview he'd taped, rushing to file a story about an uprising in the Gaza Strip, trying to find one last quote. He'd looked up at the clock. It was 6:02 p.m. and he'd thought, *I'm going to be late. I'd better hurry*, not imagining that by then everyone—*everyone*—in his family was dead. Killed when an explosive was thrown into his house during his middle son's eighth birthday party. A gift from Ahmed Abdul in exchange for David just doing his damn job.

Two weeks earlier he'd filed a story on the PPLP—Palestinian People's Liberation Party—breaking the news that the terrorist organization was on the verge of collapse and that the head of the group, Nadir Abdul, Ahmed's brother, was going to be ousted. Nadir had committed suicide twenty-four hours after the story ran. Twelve hours after his burial, the threats on David's life had started. Taking no chances, the newspaper had hired a top security firm to protect him and his family.

Only David, who was late getting home that night, survived. Sparing his life was the sadistic trick of a god he no longer believed in. What kind of life could it be, would it ever be, when every minute of every day the slow motion imagery of finding the remains of that blast ran on an endless loop in his imagination, becoming more terrible with each replaying? That wasn't how time was supposed to work on memory. It should be smoothing the edges and filing down its rough rim.

And it wasn't just what he'd personally lost. The endless pattern of violence, reprisals and more violence continued. Baghdad, Mogadishu, Tel Aviv, Sadr...

David had covered terrorism since the mid-1990s. As he infiltrated sleeper cells, interviewed suicide bombers and their families, chronicling their methods and madness, he'd also covered the systems in place to trap terrorists and disrupt their plans. Over the years he'd seen hundreds of new mousetraps and heard all the promises of how each was better than the system before. But that wasn't true. And the deaths of his wife, two sons, daughter, parents, aunts, uncles, sisters and brothers were just one small fraction of the awful proof.

A fellow reporter named Louis Rene Beres had once written that facing an assault on its own survival, Israel should reject being a victim. "Instead," he wrote, "it has the regrettable but clear corollary right to become an executioner. From the standpoint of providing security to its own citizens—" he concluded in the article "—this right has now become a distinct obligation."

It was David's obligation, too. Not just as a reporter. He'd seen the writing on the wall and it was written in his family's blood: the time for building a better mousetrap was long past. There would always be a way to outsmart a new system. It wasn't about mouse-traps anymore but about changing the way both the mice and the trappers think. And it was about punishing the men who'd built the systems that failed him and his family. In five days, those men would be in the crowd, sitting a dozen meters above these caves, enjoying the gala performance of the Vienna Philharmonic at the end of their annual ISTA conference. All they'd given him was an apology, and that was so little.

The splashing ceased. Wassong had reached the opposite shore and climbed off the raft onto solid ground. As he bent over, the beam from his helmet created a spotlight around him and shined on some-thing that glinted cold and bright in his hand.

Like every Israeli citizen, David had spent two years in the army and was trained to quickly size up dangerous situations. As soon as his mind formed questions, he searched for answers. Instantly, he knew Wassong held a knife and guessed that he planned on using it to cut the rope and leave David stranded.

Wassong had never had any intention of sending the raft back to David, had he? This was all planned. But why go through the charade of bringing him here and showing him the crypt? For the money? It had to be. David's money first and Abdul's money after.

Instinct took over with the kind of strength only fury provides; David jerked on the rope and started pulling it back as quickly as he could. The unexpected lurch yanked it out of Wassong's grip before he realized what was happening. Dropping the knife, he reached out with both hands to grab hold of the raft. Wassong was trained too; he'd been a warrior all his life but David was younger and stronger and the raft was already moving away from the shore toward him.

Wassong misjudged its speed and, arms outstretched, fell forward, screaming in anticipation even before he plunged into the water. Instantly, reacting to the pain, his body recoiled, lurching up, arching back.

For a second David wondered if Wassong could somehow make it out. No, he knew that was impossible. He knew, because Wassong had warned him—no one survived the firewater. Wassong was splashing wildly, displacing a circle of water around him. He continued thrashing for fifteen seconds, thirty seconds, forty, and then all movement ceased. Hans Wassong lay still, floating facedown in the boiling lake, his glasses bobbing beside him.

Chapter 7

New York City
Thursday, April 24th—6:00 p.m.

It had started to drizzle but Malachai Samuels still decided to walk back to his office. He'd just left a meeting with his lawyer, who'd assured him the police were close to exonerating him—there simply was no evidence that he had been involved with the theft of the memory stones last summer, although it was anyone's guess when they'd formally close the investigation. It had been the end of a trying day but the walk uptown through Central Park was gratifying. Forcing the bastards who were keeping him under surveillance to trail him in the rain was one of the few pleasures he could take from the ignominy of his situation.

Strolling through the relative tranquility offered by the 700 acres enclosed by rough-hewn rock walls was part of his daily ritual. Although it was a vital part of the city, what Malachai appreciated was how little the park had changed since being designed in the mid 1800s when, just blocks away, his ancestors were founding the

Phoenix Foundation to study reincarnation and transcendentalism. Being in Olmstead's masterwork gave Malachai the illusion he was living in that other era.

When he allowed himself to think about it, it tortured him that he couldn't access his past. He'd spent his whole adult life watching children bear the burden of memories they didn't invite, and yet no matter how much effort he exerted, he couldn't access a single forgotten thread. But he'd come so close when the memory stones had been found. Damn, he'd come close.

Exiting through Hunter's Gate on 81st Street and Central Park West, Malachai continued north. His destination was just steps off the avenue—the Queen Anne style villa with gables, scrolled wrought-iron railing and a dozen gargoyles. Cast in the early evening shadows, the Phoenix Foundation—still housed in the same maisonette as the original nineteenth century club—took on a grave appearance, as if overwhelmed by the weight of all that had gone on inside its walls: investigations into births, deaths, and murders; the synchronicity and parallels of lives lived and lost; and the complicated issues raised because of them.

On his way to his office, he glanced into an empty waiting room, relieved to see his assistant had been able to clear his calendar. He couldn't send home a child in distress. To date, Malachai and his aunt, Dr. Beryl Talmage, the director of the Foundation, had seen over three thousand children suffering past life memory trauma and had helped almost all of them to some degree. Both trained psychologists, they believed their search for psychic DNA deserved serious attention and fought hard to keep their work free of populist faddism. Over the years, they'd seen the healing power of past life regression therapy with patients resistant to other forms of treatment. Seventy-five percent of the children who had come to the Foundation left within six months, their conflicts resolved. But it was the children he'd let down who plagued Malachai—like Meer, who was one of his greatest challenges and most disturbing failures.

He'd just sat down at his desk and was checking his messages to see if Jeremy Logan had called, when Beryl Talmage appeared in his doorway.

"So you're back," his aunt said. "How did the meeting go?"

Afflicted with MS, Beryl had been in a wheelchair off and on for the last two years but tonight the only sign of her illness was an ivory cane.

"You're looking well," he said.

"No news still? How can this investigation just go on and on?"

To a stranger, her comment might be interpreted as commiseration, but Malachai knew it for the indictment she'd intended it to be. Even though she believed completely in his innocence, she nonetheless blamed him for getting too involved in the search for the memory stones and bringing a scandal to the front door of the Foundation. The possibility that her co-director might be a thief and murderer had tarnished the reputation Beryl had nurtured for years.

"It's not your life that's been laid open. You're not the one who—"

Beryl's fingers tightened on her cane. "Are you asking me for pity?"

"I've surrendered my passport, opened my files, my correspondence, my bank accounts, virtually my entire private life—to men in badly cut suits and polyester shirts who are getting an inordinate amount of pleasure keeping me under their thumbs." Rising, he walked to the window and drew back the edge of the heavy silken drape and wondered if one of them was sitting in one of those parked cars right now watching him. "Being under surveillance feels as if someone's performing constant surgery on my soul."

"Don't be melodramatic."

"I'm past needing your approval, Aunt Beryl, but that doesn't mean I wouldn't appreciate your support."

"You have my support. You know that. For as long as you need it, both in public and private, but what I can't do is pretend that—"

The phone rang, interrupting her.

Looking down at the caller ID, Malachai recognized Jeremy Logan's number. "I'm sorry, but I've been waiting for this call all day."

With a sad good-night and favoring her cane, Beryl left his office. Relieved to be going, he thought, and he couldn't blame her.

"Did you meet with Meer? What happened when she saw the actual photograph of the box?" Jeremy asked in a rush once the two friends had exchanged greetings.

Malachai described Meer's reaction.

"How upset was she?" Jeremy asked.

"You know how well your daughter controls her feelings."

Like too many children of divorce, Meer had a strained relationship with the parent she blamed the most for the breakup—her father—and Malachai recognized the vestige of guilt he always heard in Jeremy's voice when he discussed his daughter.

"Giving up her music, studying memory science, taking on this Memory Dome project—why?" Jeremy asked. "She's devoted her life to proving that what she remembers about the music and the box is nothing but a false memory, and the harder she tries to deny—"

"Jeremy, this isn't the way to work through how—"

"I hoped if she understood that the box was real, she'd finally let us help her. Couldn't it be therapeutic if she came here and saw the gaming box for herself?"

"Of course. It could be the trigger we've never found. But she has to want to work on it and she's long past that. Besides, she has an excuse—in a week construction begins on one of her exhibitions."

"Work is always her excuse."

"Give her time on this one. Seeing the photograph was a shock."

"As was finding it. Along with the rest of what I found," Jeremy said, and then told Malachai the stunning news about the letter that tied the chest to Beethoven and one of the lost memory tools.

"Are you saying the flute might still exist?" Malachai asked after he'd heard the whole story. "That it could still be where Beethoven hid it?" He tried to keep his voice composed, not wanting anyone, not even his old friend, to know how much this news meant to him.

"Extraordinary, isn't it? I obtain information about a musical instrument purported to prompt past life memories from a letter hidden in an eighteenth-century gaming box. A box identical to an imaginary one my daughter's been drawing since she was seven."

"It's serendipity…" Malachai said by rote. It was how he began the standard lecture he gave to every baffled parent whose child was haunted by past life memories, but tonight he was the one bewildered by the connections Jeremy had just laid out for him.

Extracting an antique deck of French gilt-edged cards from his desk drawer, he cut them once, then again, and then a third time. They were worth thousands of dollars; most collectors would have kept the treasure behind glass but Malachai liked to play with his toys. Usually it relaxed him. As he shuffled, the corners slapped against each other, making a sound that typically soothed him. Then, while asking Jeremy questions and taking note of his answers, Malachai performed a little sleight-of-hand for an invisible audience: he hid the king of diamonds in the center of the pack and with his next move revealed it at the top of the deck.

Although a technical success, the trick had failed him. Malachai was still tense. He'd lost one of the memory tools. He was not going to lose another. And Meer was going to be his insurance.

Chapter 8

Vienna, Austria
Friday, April 25th—10:30 a.m.

Two hours after being hired via a cryptic phone call, Paul Pertzler walked toward one of only two empty tables at the Café Mozart on Albertinaplatz. Passing a young woman sitting alone, drinking a cup of coffee, his eyes dwelled on her extraordinary figure. At least the parts he could see from the waist up. Pertzler himself was very ordinary-looking, a man of medium height with light brown hair, dark brown eyes and ruddy skin—and she didn't look up. Which was wonderful. It gave him more time to ogle the cleavage exposed by her black V-neck sweater. Focusing on it so intently, he didn't notice that his newspaper had slipped from under his arm.

"Excuse me—" The man holding out the paper wore a blue jean jacket and mirrored blue aviator sunglasses. "You dropped this."

Slightly chagrined, Pertzler thanked him, took it and continued on to the empty table. After he ordered a beer, he lit a cigarette and inspected the passing parade. The Ringstrasse was always crowded no matter what the season, the time of day or the weather. Today was no exception. Across the street the town hall took up the whole block. It was a fine architectural objet d'art, except once you got over the grandeur of it you realized how dirty it was. A century of soot. Vienna had a perverse desperation to hang on to the past even when it proved toxic. World War II had ended over sixty years before, but secrets about Vienna's involvement kept cropping up all the time, exposing more Nazi crimes.

When the man in the jean jacket left, Pertzler barely noticed, but when the woman in the low-cut sweater walked off, he watched every step of her exit. A few minutes after her departure he glanced at his watch, dropped some coins on the table and got up.

Entering the Rathaus Park he took his time strolling through the well-kept gardens that included a wide variety of woody plants and unusual trees. Stopping to examine a Japanese pagoda and then a very old ginkgo, he showed great interest even though, for all he knew, he might as well have been looking at common maples. But before he opened the newspaper under his arm he had to make sure he wasn't being followed.

Landlines were too easy to tap, cell phones too easy to intercept, e-mail was relatively safe but left a trail, and while message boards worked well, he preferred old-fashioned methods. Pertzler had remained under the radar for twenty-five years for one reason only—he was exceedingly careful and didn't give anyone any reason to notice or suspect him. That's how he managed to deliver each and every time. This wouldn't be an exception. His client was paying triple for this job to ensure it was done fast and right. And triple sounded three times as good.

Certain he wasn't under surveillance, Pertzler sat down on a wooden bench, unfolded his *International Herald Tribune* and scanned the front page.

Rare Beethoven Letter Found After 200 Years
By Susan Essex—Vienna, Austria

Hidden inside a concealed false drawer in an antique gaming box, an expert at the Dorotheum auction house here has discovered a two-page letter possibly written by Ludwig van Beethoven. If the letter's provenance is validated and the handwriting guaranteed, the find could be worth more than 750,000 euros.

The information was delivered to this paper's office by unnamed sources. Jeremy Logan, curator of the Judaica department and the man who found the letter, could not be reached for comment but the auction house confirmed the letter's existence.

Experts agree that, considering the gaming box belonged to Antonie Brentano, a well-known friend of Beethoven's and possibly his "Immortal Beloved," there is a good chance the letter will be authenticated.

The gaming box, which was given to Brentano by the composer, will be sold at auction next week but the letter will not be included in that sale.

Estimates place the value of the box at approximately 100,000 euros.

Millions of people who read the article would all glean the same information from it but in his version a few dozen characters were underlined. Once Pertzler decoded them they'd spell out everything he needed to know about the job he'd agreed to take on from the caller who'd given him a name he was certain wasn't half as real as the antique letter he'd been hired to steal.

Chapter 9

I did not begin when I was born, nor when I was conceived. I have been growing, developing, through incalculable myriads of millenniums. All my previous selves have their voices, echoes, promptings in me. Oh, incalculable times again shall I be born.

—Jack London, The Star Rover

Vienna, Austria
Saturday, April 26th—7:30 a.m.

At the very front of the carousel, waiting for their baggage to appear, a man and a woman huddled together in the midst of a tense conversation.

"Well, then, what time do we get access to the concert hall?" The speaker was a very tall man wearing a gold Rolex watch, blue blazer with bright gold buttons, white shirt, jeans and lizard boots. Despite the casual clothes and easygoing Texas drawl, his voice was stressed and his eyes continuously swept the area around them, assessing everyone he saw as if they might be a possible threat.

"We're set to go there tomorrow—" The woman's drawl was softer than her companion's and while she was dressed as casually, her clothes weren't as expensive as his. Interrupting herself, she reached over to grab a piece of luggage. A silver cross on a thin chain fell forward and swung in the air, catching the light. By the time Tom Paxton reached out to help, she'd already lifted the large piece and dropped it at her feet.

On the luggage tag, circling a stylized gold globe insignia, were the words Global Security Inc. And below them was the woman's name in bold: Kerri Nelson, Web site URL, phone number and address in Houston, Texas.

"Tomorrow? Are you serious?" Tom ran his hand through his sun-bleached hair and did another survey of the area. "What's the holdup? The concert is in five days. You've read the reports on the building. It's a security nightmare. We can't wait."

"Our team has been living there for the last four weeks straight and there are no surprises left that we haven't—"

"Even if we had a hundred men here for a hundred days, it wouldn't be enough. And I don't care about the team right now. I want to see the area." The edge in his voice sharpened. "Everyone in the industry is watching us…investors are watching us. Terrorists are drooling over this concert. Heads of government security agencies all over the world, hundreds of VIPs and experts who—"

"What do you think? That I plan for us to go sightseeing at the Vienna Zoo?" Her expression was like that of a mother with a two-year-old in the throes of a tantrum. "We're working today. We're just not going to the concert hall. A driver is waiting to take us to the hotel where we're meeting with ISTA's head of security, then the concert hall's security team, who are coming to us, and finally we're meeting with the head of the police department who—" Kerri spotted Tom's luggage tumbling down the ramp and circling toward her.

This time he noticed her reaching for it and beat her to the bag. "Okay, let's get going."

As the two of them headed toward customs, he continued scanning the crowd, even though he knew that the only people to fear were the smart ones—and the smart ones never stood out in a crowd.

Chapter 10

Saturday, April 26th—8:17 a.m.

In the back of an impeccably clean taxi heading toward her hotel, Meer was at the same time tired and nervous. It had been an uneventful flight but she hadn't been able to sleep. She'd come to Vienna on the spur of the moment despite serious misgivings, not because she believed, as Malachai suggested, that seeing the gaming box would trigger past life memories but because she hoped seeing it would spark a present life memory. Maybe touching the box and being able to inspect it would offer up some clue as to when she really had seen it and where.

Looking out the window at the scenery, there wasn't much to capture her imagination until the cab reached the city's inner limits where centuries-old buildings were crowded together on her right and the Danube flowed on her left. Familiar with the music that extolled the river, she wondered if modern-day pollution had changed its color from blue to a dark brownish-green or if Strauss had employed artistic license.

At the hotel, she learned her room wouldn't be ready till the official check-in time at one that afternoon. She left her luggage, walked back outside and asked the doorman for a taxi. Giving the new driver her father's address, she was aware how foreign it sounded. He'd been living in Vienna for twenty years, but she'd never visited, seeing him instead in New York once or twice a year when he returned for business. Over dinner he'd probe her personal life for clues to her well-being and she'd give him perfunctory answers about her job and whoever she was seeing and then get him to tell her stories about his latest treasure hunt. She loved listening to those stories. She always had. When she was a child, all Meer had ever wanted was to go with him on his quests, frightened and at the same time excited about the idea of being been shot at, run over, attacked by guard dogs or arrested for smuggling.

Only a few minutes from the Sacher Hotel, the ride got suddenly bumpy and she looked out the window.

"Cobblestones," the driver said, speaking passable English. "I can always tell the tourists. As soon as we start to bang around on these streets, they look confused. We've entered Spittleberg, a very old part of the city."

Meer found the uneven rhythm oddly welcoming, as were the two- and three-story residences that graced the narrow streets. All painted fanciful colors, almost every house had window boxes overflowing with flowers. The area reminded her of an older, more genteel version of Greenwich Village in New York. The taxi driver pulled to a stop on the left at 83 Kirchengasse, a pale blue three-story building with dark green shutters—her father's house.

Meer rang the bell. A wreath of dried bay leaves hung in the middle of the door and as she listened for her father's footsteps, she counted the leaves. When she got to twelve she rang the bell a second time. At twenty-two, she assumed he wasn't home.

Since she'd only decided to come yesterday and had booked via a travel agent at the last minute, she'd had little time to let her father know she was coming. Calling him last night from the airport while she waited to board, she'd reached his machine and left a message telling him she'd go to the hotel first and come here about eleven o'clock as long as the plane was on time. She was early, but would he have gone out so close to the time she'd be arriving? Not unless he had something he couldn't cancel at such short notice. But then wouldn't he have left her a note...or called on her cell? Except in her rush Meer hadn't remembered to call and activate the overseas option so she couldn't check.

Maybe her father hadn't heard the bell because he was in the shower and was just getting out. Ringing for what she determined would be the last time, she listened to the slightly off-key chimes again—that flat should have been a sharp.

When Meer was a child she'd invented a language made of musical sounds; whole ideas and phrases expressed by series of notes. Living inside of sound, Meer was used to everyone else living outside it but her father had learned how to speak that language and it had been a special bond between them. She'd have to translate his chimes for him, she thought now, and almost smiled.

When the vibration stopped Meer put her ear up to the door. She could hear music playing deep inside but no footsteps coming this way. She checked her watch: 9:50 a.m.

The sound of a bee buzzing around the window box distracted her. Plump and slow, it was melodic in its own annoying way as it flew from the window box on the left to the one on the right, dipped into a red begonia then hopped onto a sprig of lavender and finally flew into the house through the open window.

The window was open? Why hadn't she noticed? Bending over the flowers, she stuck her head inside the house and shouted hello.

No response.

Meer was frustrated and tired, and this was her father's house so it wasn't trespassing, she thought as she raised the window and climbed inside. After the strong sunlight, it took a few seconds for her eyes to adjust to the darker interior. There was a pile of books by the couch and a closet door was ajar. Torn between following the music or the scent of coffee, she chose the music first and wound up in her father's crowded library. The floor-to-ceiling shelves were crammed with so many books that if they all came down at once she was sure she'd be crushed beneath their weight.

A large pile of papers was spread out on the desk and one of the drawers gaped open like a screaming mouth. Her father was always slightly disorganized but this seemed excessive. By now the background music had worked its way into her consciousness and her right hand automatically fingered the notes. Maybe everything was fine and she'd simply fallen under the symphony's foreboding spell. It was a fascinating mystery how humans emotionally responded to majors and minors on a level that bypassed consciousness. At the Memory Dome, one of the exhibits already underway explored Jung's theory of the collective unconscious applied to musical memory. How a tribe of African Bushmen who had never heard a violin listened to a concerto intended to convey sadness, and started to weep. How a fifteen-year-old girl in France who'd never been to India, heard a sitar for the first time and entered into a deep meditative state without any instruction. Or how a child heard ghostly music no one else could hear and became so frightened she tried to run away from it. Over and over. Was running still.

Johannes Brahms' *Tragic Overture* took on an even more ominous tenor.

"Dad?" Meer yelled out, surprised her voice sounded so panicky. Only the music answered. Melancholy clarinets giving way to a rushing and loud finish.

"...*Wien Philharmonics geleitet von Simon Posner.*"

Meer spun around but no one was there.

"*Die Zeit ist neun dreißig——*"

Then she realized the voice was coming from a radio announcer via the stereo system nestled in the bookshelves. But why was the stereo on if no one was home? There had to be someone she could call to find out where her father was...maybe someone at the auction house. Or perhaps she would just go back to the hotel and wait for her father to call her.

In the hallway she took a right instead of a left. An open door revealed a bedroom where everything appeared orderly. Perhaps she'd overreacted. Stravinsky's *Firebird Suite* played on the radio now. She stood and listened to the less foreboding music for twenty seconds, a minute, and just when she finally felt slightly more relaxed, the scent reached her. Verbena. Her father's cologne for as long as she could remember. Not a whiff but an intense cloud of it. Stepping over the threshold, she saw a pool of golden liquid and shards of broken glass on the dresser top. Something really was wrong here.

Turning, she headed back in the direction she thought would lead to the living room and the front door but instead found herself in the kitchen where a steady and rhythmic drip attracted her attention. Meer couldn't explain why but it seemed imperative she shut off the faucet before she left the house. On her way, she tripped and glanced down, expecting to find a chair leg in the way but instead saw a shoe. She reached down to pick it up and move it out of the way. Except it was still on a foot. Someone was lying under the table. Her father?

Meer swallowed her scream, felt her breath coming in furious gulps, got down on her hands and knees and peered under the table.

No, not her father, a woman she'd never seen. About sixty. Short gray hair curling around a sweet face. Meer noticed so many things at once: a huge purple bruise on the woman's right cheek, a zigzag of dried blood starting at the corner of her mouth, her left leg—obviously broken—lying at an impossible angle. Could the woman have fallen this way? But why would she have crawled under the table? No. From the way the woman's shirt and pant legs were bunched up, she'd been dragged there. A gold watch gleamed on the woman's wrist.

"Don't worry, I'll get help—" Meer said to her while at the same time processing the pallid complexion, the unblinking eyes and the immovable form. Meer quickly reached out and pressed down on the woman's outstretched wrist. Her skin was cold. As cold as Meer felt a few minutes ago. No, colder. Was she dead?

The doorbell rang and the off-key chimes broke into her consciousness. And then a man shouted out: "Hello, hello," in a deep voice with a German accent.

It wasn't her father's voice.

Chapter 11

Geneva, Switzerland
Saturday, April 26th—10 a.m.

"I appreciate you bringing me the original letter," Dr. Karl Smettering said as he leaned over his worktable, scanning the spidery script in slightly faded black ink on parchment.

"The quality of the copy was near perfect," Jeremy said regretfully.

"But still a copy. You've never been concerned before, why now?"

"Didn't you hear about the substitution made at Sotheby's in London last month just days before a sale? A forged signature sold for thousands. No one's figured out how it happened but it's made us all more cautious. And then yesterday a story about this letter was leaked to the *Tribune…*"

"You didn't tell me. How did that happen?"

"Confidential information with news value commands a nice price. I logged it into the system at the auction house, which is password protected, but someone must have breached protocol to access my report. It's happened before but I thought we had new fire-walls in place so it couldn't happen again."

"Technology." Smettering spat the word.

"Yes, but our privacy is sacrosanct. We owe our customers discretion."

"Well, I'm sorry but working with a copy is like looking at a photograph instead of the painting itself. The answers I'm looking for are in the nuances." The expert positioned the letter under a microscope and peered at the individual characters. "It's not just the handwriting I need to see but how the ink holds the lines, seeps into the paper, the pressure the nib made, if there are rips, spills. Clues, Jeremy, they are all clues."

"I know that. Still, traveling with an original is a risk." Which was why he'd driven here rather than taking a plane; he wouldn't travel with the document and without a gun.

"For a scholar, you've always been courageous. What's going on? A letter from Beethoven to Antonie Brentano is definitely a breathtaking find, but there has to be more to this to explain your reaction."

"You'll understand once you read it."

"Worth killing for?"

"You and I both know how little people will kill for."

Smettering swung the scope out of the way and read the letter. When he finished he glanced over at Jeremy, shook his head slightly and sighed as if a burden had just settled on his shoulders. Without saying anything, he hunched over the letter again, this time reading not from left to right as the sentences had been penned, but from right to left, and not from top to bottom but bottom to top. It was critical for the expert to look at the words out of context because sometimes peculiarities were more noticeable with the change in focus.

Jeremy began to pace and take inventory of the room. In all the years he had been visiting the "master"—as he called Smettering—

this Bauhaus clean and spare room had never changed. Not a painting or a plant had been added. There were only two objects on the blond wood desk: a black microscope and sleek black table lamp that offered six levels of halogen intensity; the other tools of the trade were in drawers.

Smettering had been working for over a half hour and still hadn't offered up an opinion. Jeremy was once again struck by how much patience was required of him. He glanced at his watch. Meer was probably at his house by now and Ruth would be making her something to eat. Maybe he should step out into the hall and call and see if—

"This is a major find for you, congratulations," Smettering said as he walked around to where Jeremy stood and patted his colleague on the back, drawing him away from the desk area over to the couch.

"It's authentic?" Jeremy asked.

"I have no doubt." Taking two snifters from a side table, he poured an inch of brandy into each and handed one to Jeremy. "I know it's early in the day but you deserve a moment to enjoy this accomplishment."

Accepting the glass, Jeremy thanked his friend.

"Although it is a very complicated accomplishment, isn't it?" Smettering continued. "Beethoven very clearly admits he was involved in both a robbery and a forgery."

"Which will make me the man responsible for exposing Beethoven as a criminal."

"There will be dedicated Beethoven enthusiasts and scholars who'd rather destroy you, than let you destroy their hero's reputation."

Jeremy shrugged.

"Not concerned? You'd better be. This is Beethoven, the iconic master we're talking about. Your revelation will be a powder keg."

On the lawn a robin landed in the birdbath and the movement distracted Jeremy, who watched through the window as the bird put its head down and drank, concentric circles rippling out from where its beak broke the surface. While he watched, he saw a reflection in the window of someone walking in the room behind him and heard, almost instantly, an angry shout from Smettering.

Jeremy spun around.

A man wearing a black wool mask pointed a snub-nose revolver at Smettering's chest.

"Stay where you are," he snarled at Jeremy. "Don't move away from the window."

When Jeremy hunted for Torahs he always carried an Austrian-made Glock 17A that right now was locked in the glove compartment of his car outside in the driveway. Why hadn't he brought it inside? He had to do something. Quickly. Estimating the distance between where he stood and the desk, he judged whether or not he could reach the man and force the gun out of his hand without risking Smettering's safety.

Then, miraculously he heard footsteps approaching from the hallway. Footsteps coming closer. The man threatening Smettering didn't seem to notice. Maybe this would be the distraction Jeremy needed. Once the man turned to see the intruder, Jeremy could rush him and wrest the gun from him.

"There's nothing here of any great value," Smettering stammered, lying, Jeremy thought, unconvincingly. "There are some books... there...that pile...first editions. Take them."

The man in the mask eyed the parchment on the desk. "What's that?"

Smettering didn't answer.

Pushing the gun deeper into the elderly man's chest, the gunman repeated his question. "What is that?"

Despite the gun, Smettering put his hand down on the Beethoven letter.

The footsteps were coming closer. Whoever it was was almost there.

"Let him take it, Karl," Jeremy said. His friend was old and frail and he was worried for him.

Smettering didn't lift his hand.

"Karl! Let go."

But Smettering didn't release the letter.

The footsteps finally reached the door. Jeremy watched, ready to shout out a warning that hopefully would also be a cry for help. His heart raced. The man stepped over the threshold—damn. Jeremy should have anticipated this possibility. Damn his optimism. This second man was also wearing a black wool ski mask and he too held a gun that he pointed at Jeremy while the man at the desk used his revolver to force Smettering's hand up. The Beethoven letter, streaking like a lightning bolt in a zigzag across the tabletop, was the last thing that Jeremy saw.

Chapter 12

Inspector Fiske, who had sad, basset-hound eyes and a full mustache, asked Meer yet more questions she couldn't answer. One after the other. No, she didn't know where her father was, and no, she didn't know the woman whom she'd found in the kitchen. No, she didn't know if anything was missing. No, she'd never been at the house before; she'd never been in Vienna before.

Finally he gave up and left her in her father's living room. She sat there for a minute, not sure what she should do next while she watched police swarming through the rooms, making their way around the small house; taking photographs, dusting for fingerprints, peering into corners, closets and behind doors. It seemed an intrusion her father would have resented but she couldn't stop them.

"I just talked to the inspector. He said you're free to go."

Meer looked up. It was the man she'd opened the front door for right after she'd found the woman on the floor.

"She has no pulse. I don't know what to do" was all she'd said to him, and he'd taken over, calling an ambulance and then starting CPR and sticking with it until the paramedics arrived. Maybe it was Meer's fault the woman had died. If she'd started CPR in those critical seconds when she first found the woman perhaps she'd still be alive.

"It was too late even by the time you found her," the man said to her now.

He was an uncomfortable paradox: a familiar stranger. She didn't recognize anything about him: not the soft-spoken voice, high forehead, golden brown hair waving over the collar of a pale yellow shirt or slightly cool blue-gray eyes and not the mouth that either hinted at a secret or the capacity to be mean. She was certain she'd never seen him or met him before today—except she knew him. And he knew her. Hadn't he just answered a question she hadn't asked out loud?

Two policemen walked with an empty stretcher in the direction of the kitchen and the man moved so that his body blocked her from seeing it. "There's no reason for you to stay here. Is there somewhere I can drop you off? Your hotel?"

"Thank you—" she started, then stopped. "I don't even know your name. Or why you showed up." She lifted her hands and let them drop in a helpless gesture. "Or anything."

"I'm sorry." Now the corners of his mouth moved into a smile and the secret was gone. "Sebastian Otto. I'm a friend of your father's. He phoned me early this morning and said you would be arriving before he could get back. He told me his housekeeper would be here to let you in, of course, but since she doesn't speak English, he asked if I would mind making sure you were all right and explaining his absence."

"Making sure I was all right? His words?"

Sebastian nodded.

"The inspector wouldn't tell me, do you know if the police have any idea what happened here? An arbitrary burglary gone awry? Or more complicated than that?"

"I wish I did, but I don't. Except your father's so smart—and he certainly knows how to protect himself…I'm sure wherever he is, he's fine."

"Do you have children?"

He nodded, and she thought she noticed a flash of pain in his eyes. "Why do you ask?"

"The way you're reassuring me, you sound so paternal."

"I think I was trying to reassure myself as well."

"My father, he's fine. He's impervious." That was how she used to see him: an adventurer who vanquished dragons, a swashbuckling pirate who stole stolen treasure. She had to remember he was a sixty-five-year-old, very religious, slightly eccentric curator who was far too comfortable taking chances. She was making herself nervous.

Coming from the direction of the kitchen, the two policemen re-entered the living room with the gurney. Even with Sebastian in the way, Meer could see, under a sheet, the outline of the woman she'd found in the kitchen. She shuddered.

"I've got a car outside. Is there somewhere I can drop you?"

"The inspector said he'll be going to the auction house when he's finished here to see if they know where my father is. Could you take me there?"

Police cars crowded the narrow street in front of Jeremy Logan's house and it took Sebastian a few minutes to maneuver his Mini out of his parking space.

At the end of the block, Meer looked back. "Did you know her?"

"Only to say hello when she answered the door. Or to thank her when she brought in tea or served dinner."

"What was her name?"

"Ruth…" He hesitated. "I don't know her last name."

Meer looked at the fine blond hairs on the back of his hands on the wheel, noticed the long fingers and hard veins that stood out in relief and questioned her immediate sense of intimacy with this man she'd never seen before today. Not at ease with most people, never comfortable with small talk, instant simpatico with a stranger was alien to her. And yet, that's exactly how she would describe her reaction to Sebastian—as if together they'd traversed the same treacherous shadows.

"You've been in my father's house before. Did you notice if anything valuable was taken?" Then she amended the comment. "Nothing could be as valuable as that woman's life. I didn't mean—"

"It's all right. I know you're not heartless." His accent wasn't heavy but it was enough to make everything he said slightly inscrutable.

"How would you know that?"

"I would have seen it in your eyes."

"That's impossible," she said, because if it wasn't, then the pain she saw in his would be hard to bear.

He looked away from the road to face her and the connection when they made eye contact unnerved her.

"I'm sorry," he said, and she wasn't sure why he'd apologized. For the discomfort he'd just caused? The lack of pretense in their exchange? People didn't meet for the first time and talk like this, even under extenuating circumstances.

He negotiated the traffic and Meer examined the sights. Her father's residential neighborhood had given way to a more commercial part of the city where the past mixed with the present. An occasional neon sign or familiar brand name emblazoned on a building did nothing to mar the sense that here, history was vitally alive.

From the car's stereo, strains of Beethoven's Sixth Symphony filled the silence, but something was wrong with the sound, as if two separate tracks were playing over each other, one slightly slower than the other. The overlaps created jarring contrasts that corrupted the piece.

"Would you mind shutting that off?" Meer asked. She opened her window and let the cool breeze blow on her face.

He turned off the stereo. "Are you all right?"

"Fine."

He hesitated, then: "Your father told me."

"Told you what?"

"About your childhood. Your memories. The music you heard but could never remember. The accident. How close you came to being paralyzed when you broke your spine and what a trauma it was."

Meer was exposed in a way she wasn't used to and didn't know how to respond.

Again, as if he could read her mind, Sebastian apologized. "Please understand, he only told me because of what my son, Nicolas, is going through."

"How old is he?"

"Almost ten."

"What's wrong with him?"

"At first..." Sebastian shrugged. "We don't know. Dozens of medical doctors have confirmed it isn't anything physical. My ex-wife is a psychologist and believes it's a psychotic break but I don't agree. Not anymore."

Meer knew what was coming and wanted to stop him from telling her. She didn't want to hear about another child who was lost the way she'd been lost, who suffered with the mystery and isolation that she'd endured, but Sebastian was already explaining.

"My research led me to past life trauma and the Memorist Society. After I described what had happened to my son, your father shared what had happened to you."

Unused to discussing her private hell with anyone, Meer didn't respond. Forgetting to be worried about her father for a minute, she was instead angry with him. Who was Sebastian to him that he'd shared all this?

Either not noticing her hesitancy or choosing to ignore it, Sebastian continued. "My son is now in very bad shape and is living at the psychiatric hospital where my ex-wife works. He can't even talk to me anymore." Anguish scarred his voice.

"I'm sorry." Meer was filled with empathy for him but even more for his child.

"Thank you. It's horrible. Not for me, for Nicolas, for every day that he loses. And what's making it all worse is that Rebecca and I don't agree on what the next steps should be…she's a rational woman who looks at things one way only. I went along with her and the other doctors at first but too much time passed with no improvement…there are other things we can try and I want to try them all. We *have* to try."

"You mean regression therapy?"

Sebastian nodded and made a right onto a wide street. Taking the corner too hard, his wheels screeched in revolt. He turned the stereo back on. Mozart's *Prague Symphony* filled the car with its rich complexity. "I'm sorry. You have enough on your mind right now. I should be distracting you, not depressing you. Why don't I tell you something about where we are instead of my problems." His voice was slightly forced but determined as he launched into a detailed description of the area. "This is the Ringstrasse, the boulevard that circles the inner city. It was built in 1857 when the Emperor ordered the thirteenth-century walls that were here to be torn down."

It was strange, given the circumstances, but also a relief to pay attention as Sebastian pointed out the large twin museums—one art, one natural history—and Emperor Ferdinand's palace.

"A personal tour," she said lightly. "How lovely."

"My mother ran a travel agency and gave tours. Over the summers, when the tourists descended, I was often drafted to help out. It comes naturally."

"I spent those same summers in my mother's antiques store. You probably had more fun. At least you were outside." She looked out the window. "It looks so much like somewhere I've been before. Paris maybe?"

"Yes, a lot of the Emperor's Vienna was based on Parisian design. For a European city, much of what you see is relatively new, built in the 1800s. It was this rebuilding and the fortune the Emperor spent that led to his losing popularity with the people. And now, we're entering the inner city," he said as he steered the car down yet another twisting street.

"That building looks out of place here." She pointed to an art deco bank on the corner. "Too new."

"Funny. It's from the thirties…not so new. It's difficult in a city with so much history to find a balance and keep Vienna's architectural integrity…"

Meer had stopped listening. Up ahead was a café with large plate-glass windows framed in carved, weathered wood. "I know where we are. I've seen this street before. The auction house is only another half block from here."

"How do you know how far it is?"

"I must have seen it in a movie. There have been so many movies shot here. Isn't this a famous area of the city?"

Sebastian parked the car and came around to the passenger side, opened the car door for her and offered his hand to her to help her out. The gesture surprised her for its old-fashioned sweetness, which made the intense shivering that overtook her and the sense of foreboding that flooded her all the more unusual. Within seconds, the people passing by, the car, the reality of the moment, all shimmered and seemed to become translucent. A metallic taste filled her mouth and made her teeth hurt. Her shoulders tensed and her jaw muscles tightened. A ripple of pain shook her. Deep in her back, where she'd broken her spine when she was nine years old, the fused vertebrae throbbed. And then she heard the beautiful and terrifying music and disappeared into remembering.

Chapter 13

As the music began, Major Archer Wells, resplendent in his crisp blue uniform with his rows of gold medals and insignia, extended his hand to Margaux and she allowed him to escort her onto the over-crowded dance floor. Waltzing was the last thing on her mind but Caspar would be disappointed if she sat at home and worried. *You can do this,* she could hear him say in his deep voice that always seemed to reach out and embrace her. *You can do anything.*

Looking around the ballroom it seemed as if all of Europe was in Vienna for the Congress and that most of them were at this gala affair being given by Austria's foreign minister, Prince Klemens Lothar Wenzel von Metternich. Reapportioning Europe after Napoleon's devastating wars was hard work but it was also an excuse for Vienna's hosts and hostesses to show off to the sixteen thousand dignitaries and delegates who'd taken up residence in the city, bringing not just their wives, mistresses and servants but their own spies as well. Surely with so many people here, she could find a way to raise the money she needed to put together a search party to find and save her husband. There had to be a way. Her heart had been frozen until yesterday, and now there was hope. She was finally living again because of that hope.

"I'm pleased to see your mourning period is over," the British officer said as he expertly led her in a dance.

Tonight, for the first time in nine months, Margaux Neidermier wore her emerald-green ball gown. Yesterday's news had caused her to fold up the black frocks and put them away.

"You've been misinformed, Major. I'm not a widow."

"Forgive me but even in England we followed your husband's explorations. We all heard about his tragic death in the Himalayas."

Margaux hesitated, wondering if there was any reason to keep her news a secret. "That was what I also believed but just yesterday I received correspondence that's convinced me Caspar is very much alive and being nursed back to health by a group of monks in the mountains. I'm determined to raise funds to send a search party to bring him home. That's why I'm here tonight."

"How wonderful. Congratulations, Madame. While you're working so hard you will need some distraction. Let me seduce you."

"I'm afraid I'm old-fashioned about faithfulness."

"Faithfulness is no more valuable a currency these days than the coins Napoleon had minted."

Despite herself she smiled; there was no denying Archer was charming but for Margaux, a liaison was out of the question. He was right; taking a lover was no more serious a diversion than a game of whist and of course she was free to do what she wished. She always had been. Caspar had taught her about free will: a woman's not a possession. His ideas were revolutionary, a word that was tarnished in these post-war days. When they'd traveled across the continent after their wedding, during the worst of the Wars, he'd insisted that for safety's sake she dress as a young man in his employ and then had been delighted when the freedom exhilarated her. Margaux was in the unfortunate position of being very much in love with her husband. That's why it didn't matter that the British major held her too close as they waltzed. If with each one, two, three, one, two, three, memories of what it was like to be a woman in a man's arms returned, it was only because she was imagining her husband's hand on her back.

Caspar, hold on, I'm coming.

She had to close her eyes lest the major see them filling up with tears.

"If you won't let me seduce you, then perhaps you'll allow me to help you raise the funds you need. If what I've heard is correct, there may be something that belongs to you that would be of value to some friends of mine. It's rumored that while in India your husband found an ancient flute, is that true?"

"Meer?"

Whose name was that? Whose voice?

"Meer?"

She looked around in the shimmering air and found the face. A different face, a different time. The metallic taste dissipated. She wasn't as cold anymore. But the sadness…the sadness was unbearable.

"Meer?"

Meer knew what had just happened to her: she'd experienced a detailed but false memory her mind had manufactured to cope with the stress of her father's disappearance. It was similar to the way the unconscious translates actual incidents into symbols and far-fetched actions in dreams. Except if that was all it was, how could the grief and passion some unknown woman felt be lodged so deeply in Meer's own heart?

Chapter 14

The black sedan came careening toward him, and for an instant David contemplated taking a step forward instead of back and putting himself in its path. But instinct took over and he jumped back. He watched the car as it disappeared and memorized the license plate number. Had he just avoided an accident? Or a hit? How far had Wassong gone in selling him out? Dying didn't scare him but being locked away in a prison remembering for the rest of his life did. He'd been a journalist for twenty years and had seen enough men in prison to know that just breathing and eating and shitting and sleeping wasn't living. When he got back to his hotel he'd e-mail his Interpol contact and have the number checked. If the car was owned or rented by one of Abdul's men it would be unlikely David could track it back to the PPLP. He could, however, eliminate certain other possibilities.

Crossing the street, David had just entered the museum grounds at Maria Theresien-Platz where formal gardens were laid out in geometric certainty when his cell phone vibrated. He checked the number and answered. It was Tom Paxton's assistant, confirming the interview with the head of Global Security Inc. for the next afternoon. David assured her he'd be there.

Continuing on as a journalist after the tragedy made it easy to obtain all the information he needed without raising suspicion. Terrifyingly easy, really. Once the posthumous story he was writing revealed his duplicity in compromising his position and his sources, other reporters would likely suffer, but for the first time in his life something was more important than the ramifications to the fourth estate. Missing family occasions, working on holidays, putting everyone second while he chased the lead, he'd given his job everything it had demanded of him—for what in return?

As years of reporting on terrorism and global security had taught him: no new and improved mousetrap would ever solve the problems facing the world and men like Paxton had to stop pretending they would.

And that was why he worried about who'd been driving the car. David wasn't only hiding from Abdul and his thugs but from the police and the security firms like Global who were attending and protecting the ISTA conference. Even if they didn't know it, they were searching for him—not for David Yalom—but for the nameless, faceless threat lurking in the shadows, intent on disrupting the conference. He knew how men like Paxton ran their firms: they didn't wait for danger to show itself, they invented hundreds of hypothetical attacks and planned how to circumvent them all. Frequently over the next five days, people would be looking for him even if they didn't know his name or have his picture, and he had to be more prepared than they were. And that was why he was at the museum.

Walking toward the grand staircase, he fought his inclination to turn and see if he was being followed. If he was, the last thing he should do was let on that he was aware of the surveillance. Looking down instead, he noticed the slightly depressed center of each marble step, worn by the millions of visitors who'd passed this way.

At the landing, David followed the museum's map to the library where he had an appointment and presented his credentials to the younger of the two librarians sitting at the front desk. After studying his papers for a few moments she looked up and smiled. "So you are working on an article about the author Hermann Broch," she said, and the research facility opened to him like Ali Baba's cave.

"Yes," he said, lying. "In his correspondence he mentioned using this library to do some of his research and I'd like to see the material he refers to...here's the list...mostly historical prints, books and maps."

There was no such correspondence but the fabrication passed muster and within fifteen minutes all the materials David requested were brought up from the stacks. For the next hour he sat at the end of a long wooden table working his way though each item, taking notes in a spiral-bound notebook. Finally he reached the one piece of ephemera he'd come to inspect: an antique map of the city of Vienna, circa 1750, detailing excavations of Roman ruins. Wassong had insisted no drawings or diagrams of the underground crypt existed, but with sick satisfaction David had tracked this one down from an obscure reference in the Vienna City Cartography Archives.

The drawing was faded, worn down the crease line, frayed at the edges, but definitely problematic since it showed chambers under the exact area where the Musikverein concert hall was now located at Bösendorferstraße 12. If anyone at Global had already found this map, the existence of the labyrinth David had turned into his personal ground zero would be exposed and he would fail.

Getting up, he walked through the narrow aisles between tables and chairs to reach the front desk. "Excuse me," he said to the librarian who'd helped him when he first came in. She was by herself at the desk now.

"Yes, Herr Yalom? How may I assist you?"

"Do you have records that would show me how often these papers and books have been requested? It would be helpful for me to see their popularity."

It turned out to be exactly the sort of literary treasure hunt that appealed to her but instead of just looking them up on the computer and giving him the most recent dates, she invited David into a dusty, windowless storage room, filled with dozens of wooden file cabinets.

"We can start here." She pointed to a section on the back wall. "And work from the past forward. What year would you like to start? Our records go back more than two centuries."

"1930. Right around the time Broch looked at them."

It was certainly further back than necessary. David only cared about anyone asking to see the map in the last couple of years but that request wouldn't have jibed with his research.

As it turned out, the map had not been requested since 1939. And from 1930 to 1939 it had been examined only once. So it really was relatively unknown.

Now David had twenty-five minutes before the library's early Saturday closing time to figure out how to ensure no one else found this map if they came looking for it. Stealing it, he knew, was out of the question. The library was too well-guarded; everyone's bags were inspected when they left.

Sitting at his table again, making a show of searching through the books spread out before him, David took more notes he didn't need until the librarian announced closing time in ten minutes. He didn't get up during the ensuing flurry of activity at the front desk as scholars returned their materials. Instead, he picked up the map that showed the area under the concert hall. He checked its call

number, then checked the call number on the archival box closest
to him. He put the map in the box. Then he put away the next map
and picked up the third—

"Was tun Sie?"

David didn't understand the words but the tone was sharp and accu-
satory. Looking up, he found the middle-aged librarian he hadn't inter-
acted with pointing to the map he was about to return to its case. He
also noticed that the guard by the front door had come to attention.

"I don't speak German," David offered diffidently.

"You are not supposed to be putting away those maps. We are
supposed to do that."

The guard took a step closer and David's adrenaline surged. The
librarian held out her hand and David gave her the last map. She
picked up the last archival box, checked the number to make sure it
corresponded and slipped the map inside.

"I'm sorry, I didn't mean to—"

"I'll take care of the rest of your materials," she interrupted. "The
library is closing now."

The guard waited for him at the door. "I will need to look through
your papers, please. Just a precaution."

David nodded, handed over the spiral-bound book and watched
as the man inspected it. Nodding, he offered it back. "We have to be
careful, you understand. There are many valuable papers here."

"Yes. Of course." David took his notebook and left without
glancing back.

Descending the marble steps, he again focused on the slight depressions and wondered if his efforts would prove successful. First,
it depended on whether or not the librarian checked to see if he'd
correctly put those first two maps away in their corresponding cases.
He was counting on the fact that it was a lovely Saturday afternoon
and the end of the workweek and she'd be in a hurry. If he'd passed

that hurdle, his plan required that no one request either of the two maps for the next five days since the box supposedly containing the map of the cave under the concert hall now held a map of the Lur-grotte cave beneath a pine forest near Graz, two hours from Vienna. And the box that should have contained the 1894 Lurgrotte cave map now held the map of the area under the Musikverein at Bösendor-ferstraße 12.

Crossing the lobby again, he glanced at the extravagant murals, taking mental notes of the splendor for the last set of articles he'd be doing, unassigned but certain to be published.

Outside he caught a whiff of flowers in the air and knew instantly there were lilacs blooming nearby. Spying the thick bushes he walked the other way, avoiding the flowers his wife used to put in their bedroom. He thought about what he'd accomplished in the last few hours, wondering if it had just been a lot of extra work for nothing. Global Inc. had a state-of-the-art GPR system so would they even need to search out old maps? Well, if they did, it was unlikely they'd be able to find the one he'd just hidden by Thursday when he planned on turning Beethoven's Third Symphony into a referendum, a warning call and his own requiem.

There was a better chance they'd find him first.

Chapter 15

Inside the Dorotheum auction house Sebastian pointed past the main rooms toward a staircase. "The offices are up here."

Meer was still distracted by the disturbing daydream she'd had outside when Sebastian offered her his hand. Her father and Malachai would have insisted what had happened was a full-blown memory lurch—a fragment of a past life bubbling up to the surface of her consciousness. What they'd always suggested her storm/chase/forest memories were. But based on her own studies, she'd merely experienced another pseudomemory—episodic rather than solitary this time.

She'd read enough about Europe in the eighteenth and nineteenth centuries to have conjured this little scene out of her imagination, just the way she'd come to believe her childhood daydreams must have stemmed from a story someone had read to her—a fairy tale that she had morphed into her own nightmare. Inflated imagination, scientists called it. It even made sense that her mind had manufactured this falsity now. She hadn't slept much on the plane, was over-tired...in shock over finding Ruth and worried about her father...

They'd reached a suite of offices where there was already a fair amount of chaos. A dozen people Meer assumed were Dorotheum employees were crowded into a small reception area along with several policemen she recognized from her father's house.

Sitting at a fortresslike desk, a carefully dressed young woman with pearls around her neck and dark hair in a bun stopped Sebastian and Meer and asked them something in German. After he responded, the woman stood and walked around to Meer. "Please, come in. It's very confusing right now. The police have just arrived and are asking to see your father."

"Is he here?"

"Herr Logan always goes to temple on Saturday mornings—but you know that of course. He should still be there..."

Meer didn't know her father went to temple on Saturdays but it didn't surprise her.

"Could he have been on his way to temple when he called you?" Meer asked Sebastian.

"No, he only told me it was business related and—"

"Does he usually come here after temple?" Meer asked the receptionist before Sebastian finished.

"On Saturdays before a big auction, like the one we will be having on Wednesday, he would, but I think you should talk to Enid, she'll know more," she said and disappeared.

Seconds later, an imperious woman, dressed impeccably in black slacks and a caramel-colored jacket, her hair coiffed into a smooth gold helmet, offered a manicured hand and an introduction.

"I'm Enid Parnell, associate curator of the department. I recognize you from your photo in your father's office." She spoke with a clipped British accent.

Before Meer could respond, Inspector Fiske approached, nodded at Meer and Sebastian and asked Enid something in German.

"*Sprechen sie Englisch?*" Enid asked him.

"Yes, I do."

"Then if you don't mind, I'd prefer to speak in English—it will allow Mr. Logan's daughter to understand what's going on."

"Yes, fine. There has been an incident at Mr. Logan's home and we are looking for him. Can you tell us where he is?"

"An incident?"

"Is he on his way here? No one seems to know." Fiske wanted to get answers, not give them.

"Yes. We expect him later today."

"Do you know where he is now?"

She hesitated. "What kind of incident?"

"Miss Parnell, this is very serious. If you know where Mr. Logan is, please tell me. We need to be in touch with him."

"I can give you his cell phone number."

"We already have that. Mr. Otto gave it to us at Mr. Logan's home. He isn't answering. So we return to where we started. Full circle, I believe is the English expression. Where is Jeremy Logan, Miss Parnell?"

"Is he in danger?"

"Is there a reason to suspect he would be?"

"There is always the chance of it because of the objects he works with—all of us who work here are vulnerable." She played with her watchband, opening and closing the gold clasp in an uneven rhythm.

"You're interfering with an investigation."

The metal snapping accelerated. "He's in Geneva meeting with Dr. Karl Smettering, a graphologist."

"Geneva?" Meer turned to Sebastian but he just shrugged.

The inspector asked for all the pertinent information about Dr. Smettering, including his phone number and address, and Enid reeled them off from memory. As she did a junior officer who had been hovering stepped away from the group and opened his cell phone.

Enid turned to Meer. "Why don't we all wait in your father's office? It's this way." As an afterthought she turned back to Fiske. "It's all right with you if we wait in there, isn't it?" Even though it was a question, from Enid's tone it was clear she was informing, not asking, and he didn't raise any objection.

Like his home library, Jeremy's office was filled to capacity with books and catalogs heaped on top of every conceivable surface. Photographs of religious artifacts and maps of Europe were tacked to corkboards covering the three walls. His desk was organized but there was little empty space among stacks of thick files, catalogs, a computer, exotic-looking glass paperweights and a jug of pencils. Sebastian picked up a silver-framed photograph of a woman with dark hair bending over a five-year-old child whose hand was raised to touch her mother's cheek. The pose was a reversal of the expected— the child was trying to comfort the mother, not the other way around.

He offered it to Meer, who took it and studied the informal portrait, instinctively putting out her hand to touch her mother's cheek. What the photograph didn't show was how in the very next moment, Pauline had taken Meer's little hand off her face, unable to accept the sympathetic gesture even from her own child. Despite the rejection, Meer had never stopped trying to find a way to drive that lonesome look from her mother's eyes. And when she was finally grown up enough to try a different way, it was too late.

Meer had been eighteen years old, a freshman at Juilliard, the afternoon her father had picked her up from class and took her for a walk in the park. They sat on a bench outside her old playground and as the sun set, he told her about her mother's illness. Even though her parents had been divorced for six years by then, he'd come back from Vienna to take on this burden, offering his open arms and a fresh handkerchief to his stunned daughter. That Pauline had hidden her leukemia from Meer and then allowed her ex-husband to tell her about it was a bitter disappointment but not really a surprise. And afterward, in those last months, as Pauline continued to expend her energy and attention on the china and glass, the mirrors, rugs, chaises, armoires and étagères in her store, she shunned her daughter's efforts to expend any energy on her. Pauline never admitted during all the weeks of treatments that anything was wrong or that she was suffering or was afraid, and then, without warning, she slipped into a coma and two weeks later was gone. Too late for mother and daughter ever to have the conversation that might have made a difference.

"You look like her," Sebastian said. "So much like her."

"Not really. She was beautiful—"

Sebastian began arguing when Inspector Fiske walked in. "There has been an accident," Fiske said, looking right at Meer, who held to the picture frame more tightly as she listened to the news.

Chapter 16

Cyberspace
Saturday April 26th—12:25 p.m.

The screen saver was an infinite universe of navy blue dotted with stars swirling in a slow-moving circle. Only the e-mail icon was static. And that was worrying. According to the plan, the information should have arrived by now, winging its way through the fiber optics and—finally, the expected icon popped up. A double click of the mouse and the e-mail opened. A quick perusal. Just a banal description of a family vacation. No reason to read it in detail. Instead, it was cut and pasted into a decoding program, and forty-five seconds later the narrative about a week at the beach morphed into a letter written by Herr Beethoven to Antonie Brentano.

A first read.

A second.

The words tantalized but were inconclusive. Was that sentence true? What did this one mean? Beethoven named Stephan von

Breuning and the Archbishop Rudolf and said he'd given them clues, but what clues? Was the gaming box itself a clue? This was a treasure map. It needed to be read again. More slowly this time. Starting with the salutation that in itself was a great find. A newly discovered letter written by Beethoven to the woman who many historians believed was his one true love would be worth hundreds of thousands of euros. Perhaps a million. But the monetary value was insignificant compared to the information it contained because ultimately this was about power and faith. About possibility and impossibility. It was about legends and myths and conjecture and hypothesis come to life. And it was about a flute that might prove to be a forerunner to a device using alpha and theta harmonics created in the 1970s by Robert Allan Monroe. What if there was an instrument that produced binaural beats that really could help people access past life memories? What would that mean?

All in time. All in time. All in time. Now he needed to read through the words again and work on a mystery that had eluded mankind for so many hundreds, no, *thousands* of years.

Chapter 17

Vienna, Austria
October 25th, 1814

Dear Beloved,

You may never find this letter, my Antonie, but as I write it, I can picture you visiting your cousins at their country house in the Vienna woods and your surprise when my boy delivers this gift. I imagine you opening it and seeing the note in my handwriting and hope it made you smile fondly and remember the sweetness of our times together; the words we spoke, the music I played, the deep abiding emotions we shared.

I can picture one of your children coming in and interrupting you and you putting the box on a side table in the drawing room and attending to your family—perhaps even showing them the gift and suggesting you all might want to play some of the games.

You wouldn't have wondered at my odd choice of a gift because you are not a suspicious person. You take the moment and make love to it and live it the way I live my music. But ask questions? Be curious? Not really. That's why

I have chosen you as its recipient. That and because more than anyone I trust you, if the day comes, to do the right thing with my most important secrets.

Did you try playing any of the games inside? Most of them would not have given you pause. Except for one of them. What did you think? That my gift was defective? And what did you make of my request that you keep the token for remembrance's sake even if it did not please you? Romantic that you were, romantic that I trust you still are, I'm certain you did as I asked.

Now you will understand the true reason for my request.

If you are reading this, it is because I have died unexpectedly.

My friend and longtime patron, Archbishop Rudolf, has a sealed letter he has sworn he will only open if my death is suspicious. In it I have told him to come to you and ask to see the gaming box. My other most noble and trusted friend, Stephan, has a letter with similar instructions—to read only if my death is suspicious. His missive contains instructions on how to open the false bottom that contains this letter but without telling him where the box is. Only telling him to go to Rudolf and trust him.

So here, my friends, now that you are all together, now that you have opened the box, here is what I have done.

I have hidden a flute and its music. The flute was given to me by the Society of Memorists in hopes I could decipher the song that they believed would open a passage to the past and show us our previous incarnations. Having been able to decipher the music and having experimented with it, I've seen firsthand how extremely dangerous it is. Much too valuable and dangerous to put in the hands of men who want to use it for nefarious gain. At the same time too valuable to mankind to be destroyed. So I have chosen to tell you three, lest the secret be lost forever.

Herewith are the clues to where the flute is hidden.

The gaming box holds the heart of the puzzle, and the key to that puzzle is yours, Rudolf, to find.

Once found, Stephan, you will be able to unlock the treasure because it is already in your possession.

As for the music, Antonie, you alone will understand this. I've done the only thing I could with the music and have given it to our lord and savior. The same who sanctified and blessed our love.

One more note. Antonie, if you find this letter by happenstance, please put it away, forget you read it and don't try to decipher it or attempt a treasure hunt on your own at any cost.

Know that I take pleasure in the memory of everything we have been to each other. Those memories bring me solace. I miss you still. I think of you always with my very heart and all of my soul. And I do believe in the soul. More now than I ever imagined. I have looked into mine and I have seen a great many things there: joy and sadness, opportunity found and lost, but the greatest gift is that I've seen your soul there. I know now that as humans, we don't even begin to know what we know, and if we did, we would be so burdened with it, our very future would be at risk.

LVB

Chapter 18

"Your father is fine," Inspector Fiske reported to Meer.

"Where is he?"

"At the trauma hospital in Geneva. There was a robbery. From what your father told the police there and what they reported to me, it appears chloroform was used to render both your father and Dr. Smettering unconscious."

"But he's all right?"

"Yes, please, don't worry. He was taken to the hospital as a precaution and has recovered fully. Not so with Dr. Smettering. He's in very serious condition."

"What's wrong?" Sebastian asked.

Fiske shook his head. "We need to speak to his family first."

"What was stolen?" Meer asked.

The inspector shook his head again. "I'm sorry, but I can't discuss anything about the case with you."

"Did you speak to my father?"

"No, to the police officer who accompanied him in the ambulance. I have a phone number if you want to call. My associate will put your father on the phone."

"Thank you, yes." Meer took the slip of paper he offered.

"One last thing we overlooked at your father's house. I need your address in Vienna, along with a phone number where we can contact you." He opened a notebook.

"You can't suspect her—"

"I don't, Mr. Otto—" Fiske cut him off "—any more than I suspect you, and I am going to make the same request of you."

He offered Meer the pad and pen and waited while she scribbled the name of her hotel and a series of numbers. "My cell isn't turned on yet but that's the number," she said.

"That's fine. Now, Mr. Otto, shall we take care of this in the hall and give Miss Logan some privacy to call her father?"

A man answered on the second ring. She asked for her father and, during the long silence, Meer imagined the policeman getting up and walking over to her father who she tried but failed to picture in a hospital bed—

"Meer, I'm sorry you were the one who found Ruth. Are you all right, sweetheart?"

She had an instantaneous visceral reaction to his voice that, like a giant breeze, blew away all other sound and she bit the inside of her mouth to keep her emotions in check. It had been a long time since she broke down and cried and she wouldn't let it happen now with the police and Sebastian and her father's coworkers waiting for her outside.

"Me? Yes, I am. Are you? What happened? The police said it was a robbery?"

"Yes, but I don't want you to worry. The doctor tells me the thieves knocked us out with chloroform. I have a slight headache…but it's nothing at all."

She could hear his efforts to hide his weariness from her. Picturing him, she imagined he was wearing the mask, her name for his default expression, taught to him, he'd told her, by his own father. A legacy from Hitler's troops. *Never show the depth of what you are feeling. Don't give yourself away. Don't give the enemy ammunition.*

Jeremy wore the mask too often when it came to Meer. Donning it, she knew, to spare her pain. He'd hidden or tried to hide so much from her—his worry over her dreads and the doctors' failure to help assuage her anxiety, then his concern during the weeks she was in the hospital, uncertain what kind of mobility she'd have once her spine healed. Later, he'd worked so hard to conceal why he and her mother were separating, and then divorcing. But she knew what had broken their relationship. The same thing that had broken her spine.

"Sweetheart, my friend Dr. Smettering has had a stroke. He…the stress was apparently too much for his blood pressure… The hospital is trying to find his son, who is traveling. I should stay here until we can find him, except I'm very concerned about you and don't want you to be there alone."

Her mother tried to keep her out, her father tried to keep her safe.

"There's no reason to worry about me," she said in an eerily calm voice, using the same words she had said to him hundreds of times before.

"I can't help it."

"Please. I'm staying in a lovely hotel that has room service. I'll be fine."

"I wish I'd been there. Wish more than anything that you weren't the one to find Ruth. Poor Ruth…"

Meer heard the sadness and guilt in his voice. Staring down at the picture of her with her mother she recognized that even though she'd tried, she'd never been able to ease anyone's pain. "I'm so sorry."

"Did Sebastian find you?" her father asked.

"Yes. He did. He got there a few minutes after I did. He's still here."

"I'm glad. If you need anything, please ask him, all right?"

"Yes, but I'm fine."

"Meer, the doctor's asking for me, I have to go now."

"Wait. Why was Ruth killed? Does it have something to do with what happened to you in Switzerland? Dad, what are they looking for?"

She heard him suck in his breath.

"I'll tell you tomorrow…tomorrow when I see you," he said. "Hopefully, I'll be back by the morning. The doctor needs to talk to me now. I'll call you later."

"One more thing—" She needed to know.

"What, sweetheart?"

"It's connected to the gaming box, isn't it?"

Chapter 19

Lucian Glass and ACT's supervisor, Douglas Comley, sat behind a two-way mirror watching NYPD Detective Barry Branch talk to Malachai Samuels. On the scarred table between them was a slim, navy leather booklet approximately five inches square. On the front, stamped in gold letters, was the word *Passport,* the eagle insignia, and in smaller type: *The United States of America.*

Malachai hadn't reached for it or looked down at it once. Lucian knew that because he'd been sketching the myriad expressions that had been passing over the reincarnationist's face.

Over the past several months he'd seen Malachai almost every day, but there had been few opportunities to study his subject this closely. Now he was mesmerized by the man's inscrutable gaze and self-possessed manner. Malachai was too calm. Even the innocent were nervous when the police questioned them. Was it possible that

Malachai had hypnotized himself to sustain this level of equanimity? He was, after all, a master hypnotist who used the technique regularly when he regressed his young patients.

Lucian turned a page and started a new sketch.

"And so we're officially closing our investigation." Detective Branch sounded annoyed, as if he blamed Malachai for this. He pushed the passport ferociously over an invisible halfway line on the table.

Unhurriedly, Malachai pocketed the booklet without once looking at it. "So, you've finally found your villain? Who did it turn out to be?"

For months Lucian had listened to Malachai's mellifluous voice and still found something unsettling in the slow, measured way the doctor spoke. It was too premeditated. Like the man's relaxed manner, it was designed to conceal. The way he sat there, he could have been a seventeenth-century Spanish nobleman painted by Van Dyck, all authority and aristocracy. Lucian was convinced that everything about Malachai was a deliberate and elaborate smoke screen. What people saw was what Malachai wanted them to see: a dedicated psychologist and an iconoclastic researcher. Behind the self-assured, pretentious facade Lucian saw a troubled man desperate for…what? Lucian could only see the desire, not what was desired.

"I can't give you that information until the suspect has been arraigned," Detective Branch said.

"He deserves the worst punishment you can mete out. This man was responsible for several atrocious crimes."

Lucian was riveted by the compassion that flared in Malachai's black eyes, so sincere, no one would ever suspect this important renowned psychologist and scion of a prestigious old New York family was capable of ordering anyone's death.

Branch, who was in his late fifties and had the physique of someone with a desk job, put his hands on the table and gave himself a boost up. "Let me show you out, Mr. Samuels."

On the other side of the mirror Douglas Comley also rose. "You'd better not be wrong about this, Mr. Painter Man. I'm supposed to be shutting you down in ten days, not approving additional funding. I'm going out on a limb for you. Again."

"How often has that proved a mistake?" Lucian asked.

"But you've always had something for me in exchange. Something...dare I call it evidence?"

"I know this man. I've watched him and listened to him for months. Malachai won't be able to resist the promise of tracking down a second memory tool."

"He won't? Or you won't?" Comley asked skeptically.

There was no time to protest. Malachai had his walking papers and would be leaving the building soon, and wherever Malachai went, Lucian followed. At least for the next ten days. And right now hopefully that meant getting on a plane and flying to Vienna.

Chapter 20

Vienna, Austria
Saturday, April 26th—3:03 p.m.

"You must be exhausted. Let me drop you off at your hotel," Sebastian suggested when they were back on the street.

"I can't imagine that I'd be able to go to sleep. I think I'll just walk around for a while."

"When was the last time you had something to eat?" He pointed to the café up ahead that she'd noticed when they'd parked earlier.

"Thanks, but you've done enough. I can't take up any more of your time."

"Your father would never forgive me if I let you go off alone on your first day in Vienna. Let me at least buy you a cup of coffee. It will do you good."

The idea of coffee did appeal to her and the truth was Meer was far too anxious to go back to an empty hotel room.

As they walked to the corner, Sebastian described the café society of Vienna, keeping up a steady monologue she was sure he offered as a distraction. "Everyone has a café they frequent either near their home or their office. It's a daily routine. One is almost expected to sit at a table and linger for hours over a single cup of coffee and a piece of strudel."

Sebastian held open the door and Meer stepped inside Café Hawelka. Immediately the fragrant atmosphere enveloped her. It was a scene from another century. Waiters in black frockcoats with white aprons bustled about carrying silver trays, reflecting ad infinitum in the large wall mirrors that expanded the small space. The heavy rust velvet drapes with white lace half curtains underneath gave the room a sense of both intimacy and opulence.

Once they were seated at a marble-topped table, Meer looked around at the reddish-brown ceiling and smoke-stained walls. Taking it all in, she felt wistful for an era she never knew.

"What would you like?" Sebastian asked.

"An espresso."

"Nothing to eat? Well, at least we have to order Mrs. Hawelka's homemade *buchteln*. They are wonderful little jam-filled pastries, and you need to eat something."

"You're doing a very good impersonation of my father."

Sebastian smiled and nodded toward the waiter, who came over and took their order in a very officious manner.

"He's very formal," she noted after he left.

"All the waiters are. They go to school and train for years before they earn the title of 'Herr Ober,' 'Mr. Waiter,'" Sebastian explained. "There are actually twenty-seven hand motions required to prepare the tray correctly with the glass of water, coffee, sugar, napkin, spoon, etcetera."

Meer's fingers brushed the velvet upholstery. "How old is this café?"

"Usually there's a history and a list of luminaries who frequented each café on the back of the menu." He reached for it and read out loud: "There's been a café or bar operating at this address since the 1780s."

While he read, the waiter returned with the coffee, glasses of water and cookies, making a show of dressing the table with the refreshments. Sebastian thanked him and then continued where he'd left off with the history of the café. Sipping her coffee, Meer listened while she watched the patrons interacting and the waiters moving around the room almost like male dancers in a ballet. Snippets of conversation filled the air but instead of the foreign language reminding her she was an outsider—a stranger far from home—it was welcoming.

"There's a timelessness about this place," she said when Sebastian finished. "Not just this café, everything about Vienna."

"I travel a lot with my work and Vienna is special that way. Maybe it's that the love of music, theater, art and philosophy remain alive here in ways it hasn't in other cities."

"Listening to you, I feel like I'm back at school."

Sebastian raised his eyebrows. "Compliment or criticism?"

"Compliment," she said a little uncomfortably. What was it about him that confused her? "You mentioned work, what do you do?" she asked, trying to find some neutral ground.

"I am the principal oboe for the Vienna Philharmonic."

He was a musician? Before she responded, Sebastian voiced exactly what she was thinking.

"Your father told me you played piano and were going to be a composer before you left Juilliard. He said you haven't written music in years."

"Is there anything he didn't tell you?" She backed her chair away and stood up. "You know, I think I'm going to take a walk. Thank you for everything you did today. Can I pay you for the coffee before I go?" She opened her bag.

"No." Sebastian took his wallet out, pulled out some bills and put them on the table. "You'll get lost. I'll take you."

"I won't." She wasn't thinking, just trying to escape. "I'll be fine, I know where I am."

"You do?"

She was confused by her own words. "We're on the same street as the auction house and since I know where that is on my map I'll have a landmark. I'll be all right, really. You're not my warden."

"No, of course not. You're certainly not in jail."

But he followed her out into the street anyway. God only knew what her father had asked of Sebastian but clearly she wasn't going to be able to shake him until she was ready to go back to her hotel room.

He walked with her to the corner and out on the Graben and explained that this same wide avenue had been Vienna's main shopping street for centuries. Lined with popular boutiques, the array of stores bewildered her. Narrowing her eyes, she tried to see something that wasn't there.

"You are disappointed? Is it because you have all these stores back in New York?"

"No, it just looks too new."

"Would you rather walk to see some of the older sights? There are so many. Especially for music aficionados. Mozart's house, or Beethoven's. Or Strauss's or Mahler's."

"Beethoven's house is still standing?"

When she was seven, Meer had been playing in her mother's antiques store one afternoon after school when an elderly man who spoke with an accent brought in a clock that played Beethoven's music and she'd fallen in love with that song. But when she started piano lessons, curiously, the only pieces she couldn't play were Beethoven's. As soon as her fingers executed more than a few bars of the maestro's music, her dreads attacked.

"Yes, would you like to see it?"

Suddenly all she wanted to do was get away from this street and all the shoppers and Sebastian's kindness and go back to the hotel and sleep. "I would, but not today. I think my jet lag just caught up to me."

"And the shock, I'm sure. Let me drive you back to the Sacher."

Chapter 21

Saturday, April 26th—3:36 p.m.

David Yalom walked into the big, splashy, modern hotel where, along with many ISTA members and the press corps, he was registered. Since it was one of the conference hotels he recognized several people as he walked through the bustling lobby toward the elevator bank. He nodded to them but didn't slow down to invite unwanted conversation. Entering the first empty elevator, he quickly pressed the button to shut the doors so there'd be less of a chance that anyone would get in with him.

Getting off on the fifteenth floor, he checked that the hallway was empty, walked to the staircase, opened the door and listened. When he didn't hear the sound of footsteps he hurried down to the fourteenth floor where he repeated the exercise of checking the hallway before proceeding to his room. Once more he glanced over his shoulder to check that no one was in the hall, slipped his key into the lock, opened the door and entered his room, pulling out a small gun from his shoulder harness and holding it in front of him as he did a quick inspection of the room.

It was a lucky thing—no, a smart thing since the last thing he had in his life was luck—that he'd arranged to buy the gun from someone other than Hans Wassong. Otherwise it might have been defective. But David had thought through every step of this mission, separating each from the other. This ensured no one had any more information than was absolutely necessary. He'd made a mistake with Wassong— trusting someone who was untrustworthy—but there was no more reason to dwell on that than anything else in his life. Thinking about the past was futile. Memories instigated pain, that was all.

The drapes were half drawn and the light that came through the gauzy under-curtain was enough for what he needed to do but he turned on the beside lamp anyway. And even though he wasn't interested in watching it, he clicked the television on and found the all-news channel. Standing by the desk, he called room service, ordered and asked that his meal be rushed. He wasn't hungry. Didn't much care about eating anymore. But a car needs gas even if it can't taste it.

With a yank, David pulled the bedcovers down and roughed up the pillows. He sat down on the edge of the bed but not for long. Opening the minibar he grabbed a bottle of water, twisted off the cap and carefully placed it on the bedside table. After swallowing half the water in one long gulp, he put the bottle beside the cap. Next, he picked up the British thriller novel by David Hewson he'd bought in the airport but not yet read a word of. It had been facedown and open to page 120. Now he turned to page 144 and replaced it, facedown once again.

He made sure that the bathroom was in some semblance of disarray, as if he'd spent time there, and then David sat down on the edge of the bed to wait for the food to arrive.

Fifteen minutes later, he heard the knock, checked through the peephole, put his gun in his waistband, pulled his shirt out to hide it and met the waiter at the door. He signed for the sandwich and soda, added a healthy tip and watched the man leave. David put the tray on the bureau, picked up the ham-and-cheese sandwich and wrapped it in a piece of newspaper. He popped the tab on the soda, poured half of that into a glass, took one gulp, and then another, and wiped his mouth with the napkin.

Next, David called a random number and while it rang said: "This is David Yalom. I'll be in my room for the next hour and a half if you want to come up. I've got some work to do. I won't leave before hearing from you."

Finally he changed from his navy sports jacket into a tan windbreaker, making sure to move all the hangers around in the closet, stuffed his green backpack into a red-and-black gym bag, threw the sandwich in, zipped it up and looked around the room, surveying it carefully, before opening the door very slowly and checking the hallway. It was empty.

Instead of the elevator he took the stairs but this time down to the tenth floor. There, he used the elevator to go to the hotel's lower level, which opened to a busy subway stop. You couldn't get up to a room floor without using your key from inside the elevator, but you could get down and out into the train station. It was a convenience for the businesspeople who frequented the hotel.

The station was busy as usual and David hurried out into the crowd. Chances were if Abdul's men were watching they were also listening, and the phone call he'd made and the food he'd ordered had bought him enough time to get out of the hotel undetected.

The subway ride involved changing trains at the art deco Karlsplatz station and then taking a second train to the Schwedenplatz station on the other side of town, an area filled with small jazz clubs, inexpensive boutiques and restaurants that nestled up to the river and were always crowded with teenagers and tourists.

Twenty minutes after David left the large first-class hotel where he'd never spent more than two hours at a time since arriving in Vienna, he walked into a rundown one-star pensione. The manager behind the desk, who wore ripped jeans and a dirty white sweater, didn't look up as the man who was registered as Michael Bergmann walked in, head down and shoulders slumped, and took the small elevator that stank of body odor and garlic up to his room where he would spend another sleepless night.

Chapter 22

After Meer had checked in and unpacked she'd lain down and tried to relax but she kept remembering Ruth on the floor and how cold the woman's skin had been. At home whenever she was restless, she walked. So Meer went downstairs, got a map from the concierge, and took off.

The giant Ferris wheel gleamed in the setting sun and the cables that tethered the gondolas looked like fragile gold threads instead of strong steel capable of withstanding thousands of pounds of pressure: the distant landmark was as good a destination as any other.

Vienna, like many other European cities she'd visited, was a medley of architectural styles, occasionally dissonant, often harmonious. A baroque bell-domed Italian-style church peacefully coexisted between two simple Biedermeier town houses next to a fanciful gilt-and-bronze Secessionist apartment building. But now she reached an area identified on the map as Leopoldstadt, which had a more cohesive feel, with narrow cobbled streets and houses, theaters and stores crowded on top of each other. Most of the signage was in German but occasionally she'd see Hebraic letters on a storefront. Even though, like her mother, she wasn't religious, Judaism was her heritage and the familiar symbols were reassuring.

Suddenly, Meer heard shouting—a woman's voice and then a man's—and turned, searching out the noise, but twilight had descended on the street and she couldn't see anyone in the shadows. Scanning the three- and four-story buildings that leaned into each other, she searched for the open window where the noise might be coming from. One of the buildings drew her attention precisely because it didn't have any windows. Nondescript except for two columns on either side of the door, it was set back slightly and shrouded in even more obscurity than the others. The shouting resumed and Meer became certain this was its source. As she stood there listening, she felt a chill that came from inside her, not from the night. Shivering overtook her as the air started to shimmer and her surroundings became translucent. Her shoulders tensed and her jaw muscles tightened as a metallic taste filled her mouth. Her spine began to throb. The dreads were back, and with them the music and more memories.

Chapter 23

As the twilight deepened around her, Margaux walked the half block to the nondescript gray building, climbed up the wide steps between the two columns, lifted the doorknocker and let it fall.

The door opened a crack and candlelight from inside the foyer spilled out on the landing as the servant peered into her face with surprise. "I'm sorry, Frau Neidermier, but you can't come in, it's against the rules for women to visit," he said once he'd realized who she was.

She walked past him, striding into the anteroom with feigned bravado.

"Can I help you?" he asked, completely unsure of how to handle her forced entry.

"I'd like to see Rudolph Toller," she said, naming her husband's business partner, hoping she sounded stronger and braver than she felt. So much depended on the outcome of this meeting.

Staring up at the elaborate domed ceiling Margaux tried to calm her nerves by concentrating on the hundreds of tiny mirrors that twinkled like stars. Caspar had told her there was no more elaborate building in all of Vienna, and she was certain it was true. What a spectacle her husband and his partner had created. What a treasure trove. Tables inlaid with lapis lazuli, carnelian, tiger's eye, onyx and malachite. Gold fittings and gilt moldings glinted in the firelight. Glazed oil paintings of ancient Egyptian scenes added dimension to the boundaries of the room. And the smell! Burners in all four corners of the room scented the air with the same Cassia incense her husband had given her when he'd come back from his last trip. Being here was like being inside her husband's mind, seeing though his eyes. Feeling her own eyes brimming, she blinked back tears.

"If Caspar were here now, he'd remind me that it's a mistake to ever underestimate you," Toller said as he came out to greet her. "He used to say you were like your homeland's Mistral—an unrelenting wind. And he was right. You've broken all our rules coming here, Margaux. I was going to respond to your letter in time."

Despite the fact that her husband had trusted Toller enough to include him on his Indian expeditions, the man's cadaverous countenance frightened her. As he bent down to kiss her hand a whiff of his stale scent reached her nostrils: he smelled as if he were spoiling from the inside out.

"But I don't have time."

"Did you come here in your own carriage?" he asked suspiciously.

The three gold keys dangling from the chain around his neck shone in the firelight. Even though Margaux knew he'd replaced Caspar as the Anibus, it pained her to see the necklace on him. As head of the Society, her husband had worn it under his shirt for their entire marriage. When Toller had come to tell her he'd returned home alone from India and she'd seen the keys hanging from his neck, she'd had to hold herself back from ripping them off.

Margaux straightened her shoulders, adding another inch to her slight form. "Yes, I came in my carriage." It took effort but her voice didn't waver.

"Is it waiting outside?" Toller asked.

"No. Of course not. My driver is in the park, down the road. I know better than that."

"Did you tell anyone you were coming?"

"Why are you interrogating me?"

"Forgive me, but we're more concerned than usual about drawing attention to the Society with all of Europe here in Vienna for the Congress. Thousands of dignitaries and delegates and every one of them with a spy in tow. Despite the supposed enlightenment of our times, the Emperor's laws make our existence here a crime punishable by law."

"I know that. Caspar explained it all to me long ago. I wouldn't—"

"Come, Margaux, let me take you back to your carriage." Toller took her arm.

She wrested it away and stood resolute. "As Caspar's wife, by Austrian law what belonged to him now belongs to me. I'm here to claim what he found on his last trip."

"Those items belong to the Society."

"No, in fact, they don't. My income funded every one of my husband's explorations, Herr Toller. Now, please. Would you be so kind as to give me what I've come for?"

"What the devil!" Toller lost his patience. "I most certainly will not."

Margaux and Major Archer Wells had discussed what would happen if Toller refused, so she didn't falter. Without waiting for him to accompany her, Margaux crossed the foyer and quickly walked into the inner sanctum as if she'd been there a dozen times before and knew where she was going. It was heady being inside the actual rooms after so many hours of studying their architectural plans with Caspar.

"You're trespassing," Toller called out as he chased after her into the library.

Opening a door at the far end, Margaux walked into a closet. Caspar had been so proud of the building's puzzles and had told her—yes—here was the handle—invisible unless you knew where it was. She pulled on it and a section of the wall swung open and a *whoosh* of cool air wrapped around her.

"He shared this too?" Toller was behind her, breathing heavily, his voice thick with anger. Grabbing Margaux's arm again, he tried to pull her back. Surprising herself a little and him more, she kicked him hard enough to hurt him. Caspar had taught her how to defend herself using whatever she had available: her fists, her boots, a pistol or a sword. They lived in dangerous times and he'd wanted her to be safe while he was gone.

With the seconds she gained, Margaux rushed down the dimly lit staircase that circled back on itself as it descended into the catacombs. At the landing, the cavern opened up before her. Dozens of niches were carved into the walls, each one containing a dusty skeleton. A shocked *O* escaped from Margaux's lips. Although her husband had described the old Roman burial ground to her, the reality of these long-dead was deeply shocking. Shadows flickered and moisture dripped down the stone walls. The mold was heavy and the scent of decay filled the air.

Holding a lantern, Toller came up behind her, leering. "What's the matter?"

Margaux started to breathe through her mouth as she proceeded toward the far end of the room toward the crude cell with iron bars: the Memorists' vault where she expected to find the treasure her husband had found in India: the treasure Major Archer Wells had offered to buy for a sum that was more than enough for her to fund her husband's rescue. Only the cell was locked.

"What do you think is down here besides our records?" Toller asked.

"The engraved flute Caspar wrote about in the last letter he sent me."

Toller's laugh was more sickening than the smell of the dungeon. Stepping up to the rusted iron door, he used one of the keys from the chain around his neck in the lock. "It's not here. Look for yourself."

Chapter 24

The six-foot-three-inch-tall Texan poured what must have been his sixth cup of coffee of the day. He didn't blow on it or sip it. If it burned, he didn't let on. There was a china plate of fruit and another of cheese and a basket of bread on the table in front of him, but they remained untouched. Caffeine was the only fuel Tom Paxton needed, even if it was too hot.

Seated opposite him in the suite's dining room, now outfitted as a makeshift office, were the architects of the plan that had won Global Security this contract. Kerri, his personal assistant, sat next to him as she always did, her laptop open and her fingers flying over the keys. Paxton felt reassured by the constant tapping.

Bill Vine, who, along with the other two men at the table, had been in Vienna for the last month overseeing the "symphony job" as they'd dubbed it, was bringing his boss up to date when Paxton interrupted.

"If I read you right on that last point, you're saying there are *still* access control issues? You haven't resolved all of them? Do I have to remind you the concert's four days away? What the hell is going on?"

"There's only one issue we don't have locked down. That's all. And we're close to solving it." An ex-army guy, Vine never lost his cool. He'd seen enough death and had enough bad memories stored up to haunt him for the rest of his life. While he knew every job was a matter of life and death, not much rattled him. Certainly not a demanding boss, which was one of the reasons he still had this job. "Let's go over what we've got squared away first. The traffic issues are taken care of. We have the city's agreement to close the street outside the concert hall on the night of the performance. Even VIPs will be let off a block away and required to walk. Access to all entrances and exits of the protected area will be handled with a Zenith biometric access card and mantrap and we're up to speed on all that. Everything's in top working order and we have backups to our backups. The locals are being very cooperative."

Vine had been with Global since Desert Storm. His PTSD would have incapacitated a less determined man but he kept his demons under control. Even so, every once in a while, like this morning, just to be safe, Paxton searched for evidence of them deep in the man's eyes. He didn't see them. If he ever did, Vine would be out no matter how close the two men had become or how much Vine had done for the company.

"Can you can show me the card setup?" Paxton asked.

"You bet." While Vine typed commands into his computer to bring up the right program, Paxton shifted his focus to the other members of the team, checking them for alertness, signs of tension, weariness. Being at the ISTA conference in the catbird seat, he couldn't afford any screwups. It had taken him too long to get there.

Every year the noteworthy body gathered in a different country to share the latest developments in security products and procedures, see demonstrations, debate policy and discuss challenges. Attended by the top brass from every major security company, hundreds of analysts, VIPs and officials from most governments' security agencies, the International Security and Technology Association conference was a giant bull's-eye: a sweetheart target for a showy terrorist attack. And on Thursday night it would be his responsibility to prevent that from happening.

Since ISTA's inception in 1958, individual firms competed for the honor of providing the conference's security each year. Several companies were usually chosen, depending on how many venues there were. This year there were six. One to handle the conference center where most of the activities, meetings, panel discussions and exhibitions would take place, and one for each of the four hotels where the attendees were staying. Those five firms would do little more than provide backup systems since the venues themselves were chosen based on the state of their security.

But the site the sixth company would be protecting was not as secure.

The systems in place in the one-hundred-and-thirty-nine-year-old Musikverein concert hall at Bösendorferstraße 12, off the Kartner Ring were mediocre at best, so the company awarded that contract inherited the biggest opportunity along with the biggest challenge. And that company was Global Security Inc.

"You want all the gory details?" Vine asked his boss.

"You may think we all know every step of this system as well as our own names but—"

Vine cut him off, finishing the sentence for him. No one else on the team had the nerve to do that but Paxton actually cracked a smile as Vine intoned the company mantra, mimicking his boss's voice: "But repetition is a small price to pay to ensure everything goes smoothly." And then he launched into a monologue illustrated by dozens of 3-D visual displays on the laptop. "The holder will activate the card by placing his or her thumb in the left quadrant. The thumbprint will need to match the chip implanted within the card. The chip will have specific information about the cardholder…" Vine looked up and over at Paxton. "You know that drill, you set it up. Am I right in assuming you want me to keep going anyway?"

"Yeah, I like hearing your voice."

Vine offered Paxton the closest thing to a smile he could manage: the right corner of his mouth lifted very slightly. You didn't notice what was off about Vine when you first met him. Square-jawed with a full head of dark brown hair, he was a good-looking man, just past his prime but holding his own. And then you noticed how little his face moved and how few expressions he could manage. Twenty-two separate surgeries had put Humpty Dumpty together again. Well, almost put him back together again.

"Each cardholder's name, organization, age and weight will be entered along with a picture, passport and driver's license information. The maintenance crews, catering crews and concert hall employees have agreed to comply. We're almost done collecting their data."

"How far from being done?" Paxton asked.

"With those groups, another twelve hours."

"Good. Go on."

Around the table, there was a subtle restlessness. Paxton didn't care that he was boring the bejeezus out of them. He wanted to hear the details again. And again. Like a lover telling him over and over how good it feels. Not that he was sure he'd remember what that was like but this was no time to reflect on the dried-up, hostile battlefield he used to call a marriage.

"The card will work only when the thumbprint matches the database on the chip. We'll have proximity readers read the cards. Enough so we don't cause traffic at any of the entrances, which could be used as diversions. If the information given to the reader matches the original database in the access control computer, the mantrap access gate will allow entrance into the building. If the information doesn't match, the gate will lock, allowing neither entrance nor exit. Of course there's an override protection so that the guards at our monitoring point can allow access in cases of emergency. The concert hall isn't happy about the gates."

"Why?" Paxton asked as he got up and poured himself the seventh cup of coffee.

"Aesthetics."

"Aren't we using bulletproof plexi? They should be thankful we're not bringing in metal bar gates."

"The building's an historic treasure and they—"

"Fuck 'em." Paxton dismissed the concern. "How many pounds leeway are you building into the sensor pads in case the weight on the access card isn't exactly the same as the weight entered into the database? I don't want to have a repeat of the incident in Washington last month." A Supreme Court judge had gained six pounds since his access card had been created and the mantrap had locked him in.

"Ten pounds. Should be fine."

Paxton sat back down and ran through it all again in his mind, then looked at Vine with an expression of bewilderment. "So all that's left is the orchestra. That's where the snafu is? With the fucking musicians?"

"I'm getting to it."

"Or avoiding it."

"I'm waiting for a phone call and was hoping it would come in while I was briefing you. We're at a standstill, Tom."

"Why are they giving us a hard time?"

"The concertmaster doesn't want to submit the members of the orchestra to the 'ordeal' as he insists on referring to it. He's saying that these are world renowned artists and he won't have them treated like criminals."

"We need this solved ASAP." Paxton was about to belabor the point but stopped himself. There was no reason to lecture Vine. Instead, he turned to his number two. "Alana, time for your song and dance."

Alana Green, a science and math whiz who had graduated from MIT at eighteen, had been with Global ever since. Now, at twenty-four she was still the youngest employee and only one year older than Paxton's daughter. About to launch into her presentation, she stopped when Kerri's cell phone rang. Paxton's assistant looked at the display and then answered it. "David Yalom is on his way up," she said after taking the call.

"Let's wait," Paxton said to Green. "We might as well put this show on for the press."

"And one other thing," Kerri continued.

Paxton looked back at her.

"I just got word that, schedules permitting, we might have a few extra guests at the concert."

Paxton raised his eyebrows.

"Don't keep me in suspense."

"The Vice President of the United States and Secretary of Defense will be in Eastern Europe toward the end of next week. It seems that both of them are Beethoven fans."

Chapter 25

David Yalom had interviewed Global's top exec several times before and Tom Paxton greeted him warmly, if awkwardly, when he arrived. He hadn't seen Yalom since the explosion that wiped out the journalist's entire family and while he'd never met a man on death row, that was the first thought that came to his mind when he shook the Israeli's hand and looked into his dead eyes. Yalom was pale and his face was drawn. He'd lost far too much weight. The man was walking wounded.

"Would you like some coffee? Something to drink?" Kerri asked.

"Coffee," David said, and then as an afterthought, added, "that would be great." Pulling a notebook from the pocket of the dark green knapsack, he opened it to a clean page. "Congratulations on winning the competition," he said to Paxton. "This is a big job."

"And a big job requires big plans. Ready to get started?" As he briefed him, Paxton watched Yalom carefully. There was something off about the reporter; it was as if there was a one- or two-second delay between thought and deed. But as Paxton ran through the major initiatives Global was putting in place and would be using to protect the hall, Yalom had no trouble keeping up and interrupting every few points to ask intelligent and probing questions.

This was the fifth or sixth time Paxton had worked with Yalom, who'd been covering the ISTA conferences for quite a few years. The players knew him as a fair reporter with a reputation for doing impeccable research. Paxton wasn't concerned about any of David's probing questions; his company was operating at peak and he knew the reporter wouldn't be able to find anything damaging to write.

"The first thing we're going to show you is a demonstration of the main security program. Sorry, we have no popcorn," Paxton joked.

Yalom chuckled and Paxton thought it seemed forced. Green hit the start button and, as promised, the show she put on for the assembled group via her laptop rivaled any thriller movie any of them had seen. Shadow intruders infiltrated the concert hall in various scenarios: including invading via the backstage loading area, landing on the roof of the building and burrowing through a wall in an adjacent building. In each case a series of guards, alarms and security systems went into high alert and the animated intruder was always captured.

"Now watch what happens if it's not an intruder, per se, but someone with limited access to the concert hall who tries to get to the VIP boxes…"

Except for David Yalom, the people sitting around the table all knew how everything worked, yet each was mesmerized by how the simulation, complete with disturbingly lifelike avatars in a perfectly recreated concert hall played out on the screen. There was even a soundtrack to underscore the tension.

"Like watching a damn James Bond movie, isn't it, Yalom?" Paxton asked, unable to disguise the pride in his voice.

"It almost makes you want to send someone through for real and see it all go into action," Green said wistfully.

"You scare me when you say things like that," Paxton said with a laugh. "Especially in front of the press." Turning to Tucker Davis, another longtime Global employee and member of the top tier, he said: "Your turn, Mr. Engineer. Tell us about the infrastructure of the building itself."

"It's old. It's drafty," Tucker said. "Its corners have corners, but we've been at it 24/7 and I'm confident we know all of them. We even know the names of the rats climbing up through the pipes."

"You sound positively gleeful." Paxton was confused. Tucker was usually taciturn and annoyed when there was a reporter in the room, anxious about letting the press in on a job prior to the event. "What's going on?"

"Angela called last night." Pause. "She's pregnant."

The couple had been trying for several years, and the news was greeted with congratulations all around, Kerri going so far as to wipe away tears. Paxton was struck by her gesture. She'd been working for him for five years, and he'd never seen her get emotional before. Even more surprising was how her emotion stirred him, which in itself was an out-of-place, unexpected and undesirable reaction. He didn't mix business and pleasure. Never had and never would. Suddenly restless to get to the concert hall, he stood up. "I'd like to go to the site now and see it for myself. Yalom, would you like to join us?"

"Sure would. That would be helpful at this point."

"Kerri?" Paxton asked, glancing over her shoulder down at her laptop. "Is there anything we need to worry about before we head over to the hall?" It was his signature closing line. The one question he asked before he wrapped up any meeting, and he knew that to this woman who prided herself on never missing a beat—in fact, to all of his team—his inquiry was like fingernails on a blackboard.

"Nope, nothing."

Paxton didn't doubt her but he never entirely trusted her, either. Or anyone else. Everyone was capable of forgetting and of making mistakes. When you were dealing with security, with life and death, no one could forget anything. Nothing could go wrong. Ever. Especially not on this job.

Paxton had spent each vacation of his adult life mountain climbing successively more difficult peaks. He had to assume he couldn't trust anyone when it came to checking his gear or to being there if he slipped and yet at the same time, he had to trust the people on his team if something did go wrong. The ultimate conundrum.

He'd brought his company to a similar apex. At least when he climbed, only a few other climbers were with him. In Vienna, the entire industry, government agencies, VIPs and every potential client would be watching. If this job went well it would make Global shine so brightly everyone would have to wear sunglasses when they dealt with him. The contracts would flow like icy water from those snow-capped peaks. And he needed them to flow. Paxton was overleveraged, overmortgaged, overinvested in his own company and in the midst of an ugly divorce that was going to cost him money he didn't have and wouldn't get unless this conference did for his reputation what he expected it would.

He'd never been in a better position, or a worse one. This was his own personal fucking Everest. Up till now Global had been pure potential. After the 50th ISTA conference concluded Thursday night after the gala concert, he would have either exceeded expectations or lost his goddamn shirt. And to kick up the pressure a notch, he knew every important member of ISTA was hoping for the lost shirt scenario. They were dying to see the bad boy of the industry bested. But Paxton planned to be anything but vanquished.

"The cars are downstairs. We're meeting the engineers at the Musikverein. I'm itching to see how our new GPR systems are working."

"New systems?" the reporter asked. "How do they differ?" He seemed even more focused.

"Most GPR systems are designed for aboveground detection in a fairly open environment as far as thirty meters away. When using them for underground detection we normally can't go farther than nine or ten meters. But we've snagged some ground-penetrating radar models that are still in trials that can get down at least a meter deeper," Paxton bragged.

"One extra meter. Doesn't sound like much, David, but it's enough room for a man to crouch in, hiding, waiting," Vine explained further.

"I'm assuming you'll give me a demo?" the reporter asked.

"You bet," Paxton said, and continued showing off. "We should also tell you something else we're doing that's a first. We're spending a hundred thousand dollars to track terrorist activity in the area."

"The local authorities take care of that normally, don't they?" David asked.

"We're not leaving anything to the local authorities on this job."

David's pen was poised. "What kind of activity? How big an area? What kind of system are you using to do that?"

"Now if we told the press that then everyone reading your article would know how to avoid our traps." Paxton laughed.

"Embargo the information till after the concert," David suggested.

"Not this time," Paxton said. "Not this job. Once we're on the other side of the concert I'll fill you in on some of the initiatives we've invested in. Now, let's get over to the music hall."

They left the room and were headed toward the elevator when Kerri stopped and turned back.

"Something wrong?" Paxton asked.

"No." She shook her head. "I just forgot something."

"Good, because nothing's going to go wrong. Not this week. Not this job." He turned to David. "Am I making you nervous?"

"Nervous?" The reporter looked confused.

"When security systems work," Paxton said as he jabbed the elevator button, "there's not a great deal to report. I was just wondering if you're afraid you're not going to get much of a news story out of this effort."

Chapter 26

As we live through thousands of dreams in our present life, so is our present life only one of many thousands of such lives which we enter from the other more real life and then return after death. Our life is but one of the dreams of that more real life, and so it is endlessly, until the very last one, the very real life, the life of God.

—*Count Leo Tolstoy*

Outskirts of Vienna, Austria
Sunday, April 27th—12:05 p.m.

A shaft of sunlight filtered down through the blue-green trees and splashed on Meer's hands and face. They'd been driving through deep woods for the last quarter of an hour talking about music. It was an easy drive and an easy conversation that had led to Sebastian putting on the Mahler symphony they were listening to now.

As the road twisted she caught a glimpse of redbrick and white stucco structures and beyond them, a shining gold dome, and then Sebastian took a right turn and the vista disappeared. She was finally tired, so tired she thought if she closed her eyes she might be able to sleep.

Last night, after her strange experience on the street in the old Jewish section, she'd gone back to her hotel almost in a trance. How could a fabricated story have affected her so deeply? She felt as if she'd absorbed the imaginary woman's fears and anxieties...and all her awful responsibilities, as if someone she herself loved was in danger and it was urgent she help him. Meer wished there was a way to shut down her mind, to prevent her unconscious from spinning any more tales.

She was picking at a dinner of soup and salad she'd ordered from room service when Malachai called to tell her he was no longer under investigation and would be arriving on Monday. With the gaming box connected to a possible memory tool, he wanted to see it for himself and perhaps bid on it at the auction on Wednesday.

She told him how relieved she was for him. No matter how desperate the police were to find someone to blame, how could they have suspected Malachai had been involved in a kidnapping? He *helped* children. Had all his professional life.

Because of her jet lag, she hadn't been able to fall asleep until well past two in the morning and then it seemed only moments later when she got another call that woke her up at seven. Her father's voice was rutted with grief for his friend whose condition, he told Meer, had worsened overnight. Smettering's son was scheduled to arrive by noon and Jeremy would be back by that evening. Unfortunately he had his car with him and had to drive. Was she all right spending another day alone?

She was far too used to being alone, she wanted to say, but didn't. Instead she told him not to worry, she was fine. And she was, wasn't she? To prove it she ordered coffee and juice and yogurt with fruit and ate it all while leafing through the city magazine the hotel provided, trying to decide what to do with a whole day to herself.

At ten, Sebastian phoned, as promised, to see if she needed anything. She told him no, and thanked him. He was going to visit his son at the hospital, he said, and asked if she would consider coming with him to meet Nicolas. She knew she wouldn't be able to help the boy but Sebastian had been kind to her since she'd arrived; it seemed like the least she could do.

Meer must have dozed off because when she awoke they were already in the hospital parking lot.

"If there's a map in God's house, this spot is marked in blood," Sebastian said.

"What do you mean?" Meer asked, responding viscerally to the disturbing expression.

"This is an unholy place. That Rebecca worked here was bad enough. Then she convinced me to let Nicolas attend the day care and summer camp the hospital built for the doctors' kids. And now he's living here."

"It looks beautiful," Meer said. "What's wrong with it?"

Sebastian slipped into guide mode but with a catch in his voice. "The Third Reich's doctrine of racial hygiene was acted out right here at Steinhof hospital starting in 1938. A program named Action T4 identified medical institution patients deemed unfit to live who were then sent to Linz and gassed. More than thirty-eight hundred from this hospital alone died there."

In the pauses between his words Meer heard birdsong through the open window, and for a moment was surprised that they hadn't stopped singing after hearing what he was saying.

"In one pavilion doctors conducted horrifically painful experiments on children who were then sent to another pavilion to die of malnutrition or disease. More than seven hundred children died that way and their brains and their spinal cords were saved to be used in research—" He stopped, either unable or unwilling to go on for the moment and she was almost sorry when he chose to continue. "But it wasn't just what happened here during the war. What's just as horrible is that it didn't stop when the war ended. Not the brutality, not the callousness. The remains of those children, their brains, the spines…other organs continued to be used in medical research at the hospital until 1978. They were even on display for visiting research-ers. Sometimes, the staff still finds small horrors tucked away in corners of the various pavilions. While Nicolas was at day care here during a school break, a gardener unearthed a child's skull. Who knows how many of the kids playing outside saw that? Six months ago the city finally buried the last of the remains from that terrible time…but who knows what another gardener will dig up one day?"

"Did your marriage break up over the problems with Nicolas?"

Sebastian shook his head. "Two years before. It's rather sordid, I'm afraid." His voice sounded bitter. "Rebecca had an affair with another doctor." The bitterness gave way to wistful reflection. "We didn't make it through that."

"I'm sorry," Meer said softly, and she was, both for him and for asking.

The nine-year-old boy who had Sebastian's honey-colored hair and gray-green eyes was sitting at a table, working furiously, molding dull gray clay into a ball, murmuring words she couldn't hear except as a constant hum.

Looking up from his work, he stared at Meer for a moment but didn't make contact with her. What did he see? A stranger in a long black skirt and boots standing in the doorway? Another nurse come to give him more medicine? A ghost? Nothing at all?

"Six months ago he was a normal child going to school, good at sports, riding his bicycle, playing with his friends…now he's lost." Sebastian spoke openly in front of Nicolas, as if the boy either couldn't hear him or wouldn't understand him. "He lives in an impenetrable shell, spending his days chanting that song and drawing or sculpting the same thing over and over..." He pointed to a pile of drawings. "He only stops to eat or drink or sleep when someone gives him food or puts him to bed."

Meer remembered how she used to sit at the piano for hours trying to find one certain musical sequence on the keyboard. Obsessively testing different combinations of notes, she would sometimes fall asleep there and wake up hours later with the keys pressing into her cheek.

In Nicolas's eyes she recognized the empty look she used to see when she looked at herself in the mirror. She didn't need to play Cicero's memory game to remember how it felt to be taken over by memories that didn't belong to her—

"Was tun Sie hier?"

Meer turned at the voice. The words were in German but the tone indicated the speaker was annoyed.

"Meer, this is Dr. Rebecca Kutcher, Nicolas's mother. Rebecca, this is Jeremy Long's daughter," Sebastian said in English to his ex-wife.

She was lovely, despite the anger that pursed her lips and glittered in her eyes. Her blond curls trembled as she shook her head. "Sebastian, I was clear, I thought, on the phone." She spoke with a British accent. "I'm sorry," she addressed Meer, "but strangers are too disruptive to my son's treatment." The pain on her face was difficult for Meer to look at, reminding her of her own mother's discomfort.

"I don't want to upset you or your son," Meer offered. "Let me go wait in the hall." She turned to Sebastian. "I don't want to ruin your visit."

"No, please, Meer. I want you to spend some time with Nicolas." Then he addressed Rebecca. "Nothing else has helped. Why not let her spend a few minutes with him? She might have some insight. She's been where he is."

Nicolas's murmuring increased in volume, becoming more of a

droning than a hum. The doctor looked over at her son and watched him for a long moment, then she spoke to Sebastian. "It's not fair to press me so hard on this. Please, don't stay too long."

As the door shut softly behind Rebecca, Sebastian knelt down in front of the boy and started whispering to him. Nicolas didn't react but Sebastian kept at it, stroking his hair, smiling—the expression on his face a heartbreaking combination of love and desperation.

Nicolas's eyes were large and troubled, as if he was watching battles being fought and wars being waged. As if he was witnessing horrors that were shaking him to the bone. He didn't look directly at his father but he did lean toward him; on some subliminal level he craved what Sebastian offered.

"This is how my son lives now."

Meer wasn't sure if Sebastian was talking about the surroundings or the boy's mental state. "For how long?"

"About two months. Rebecca had been dealing with him at home, as difficult as that was and then…" His mouth contorted with fury and turned into one straight angry line. "He slipped deeper into this state and it became obvious he needed constant care." He broke off, took a breath then continued. "I was willing to bring him to my apartment and give him that care but Rebecca insisted this was the right solution and got his other doctors to agree, of course. Being on staff here, she was able to make special arrangements to let him stay as long as the bed isn't needed and since the psychology wing is now eighty percent outpatients, it's unlikely he'll ever be asked to vacate the room."

It was the mention of the room that forced Meer to take her eyes off the child and look around. She focused on the pile of drawings Sebastian had pointed out before and now she took in that horror, too. One after another, every one of the monochromatic childish sketches were done in shades of black, gray and brown. Not a single bright color had been used. And next to the stack were three putty-colored clay busts. Each drawing and sculpture depicted the same subject: a little boy's face—not Nicolas—a very different looking child—eyes alive and wide in terror, mouth open in a silent scream.

"Nicolas, does it make you sad to be with this little boy all day?" Meer asked.

He didn't answer.

"You said he speaks English?" she asked Sebastian.

"Yes, or at least before all this he did. Rebecca's mother is British, her father is German. Nicolas spent summers with her family in Surrey."

"I think you are a very good artist, Nicolas." Meer tried again.

The boy was rocking himself back and forth in his chair now, still mouthing words that Meer couldn't make out.

"Do you know what he's saying?"

Sebastian nodded solemnly. "Yes. Rebecca brought in a woman who can read lips. It's called dovening in Yiddish. Our son is saying the Jewish prayer of the dead."

"Are you—"

He didn't need to hear the rest of the question. "No, neither Rebecca nor I is Jewish. As far as we know he's never been in a temple in his life. There's not a very big Jewish community in Vienna."

Meer didn't know Sebastian that well, but she could tell from the way he was pressing his lips together that there was more he wasn't saying.

"Nicolas?" Meer sat down very close to him. "I know how it feels to remember people you've never met and places you have never been. It all seems so real to you but no one else can see them or hear them. Is that what it's like for you?"

She waited for a response but he ignored her and continued chanting. She was moved by how much grief she could hear in the sounds he made.

"If you want I could tell you about the little girl who lived inside of my head…the way this little boy is living inside of yours. I couldn't draw her though. She played piano and I kept trying to play the song she played. I could almost hear it. Almost. But never quite."

Meer was surprised how easy it was to talk about her past with the silent boy whose consciousness seemed to be trapped in another time and place. Einstein had written: "Reality is merely an illusion, albeit a very persistent one." Meer always thought she'd been living the proof of the opposite. Illusion was her reality and always had been. The same way it seemed to be for Nicolas. She stayed for a few minutes more telling him about how scared she was when the dreads took over and how she could never find the outer limits of her terror.

"My parents didn't know what to do with me either." She tried to make her voice light as she whispered. "You'd think sometimes they'd realize how much pressure they're putting on you, wouldn't you?"

Still no response.

"I could sing along with you if you sang a little louder, if I could hear the tune."

Finally, realizing that even if he could hear her, he wasn't listening, she stood up, ran her hand over his head, smoothing down his hair, and in a soft voice, said goodbye. "If you'd like me to come back, I will. It would have made me feel better if I'd known someone understood what I was feeling and how really awful it was."

As she stepped away, Sebastian came over, put his arms around his son and kissed his forehead. He stayed like that for a few seconds and Meer turned away, not wanting to intrude. She wished she could tell Sebastian that holding Nicolas like that helped, except she knew that for her, nothing helped. No one's arms had been able to pull her out of the freezing cold hell when she slipped into it.

Before they left the room, Sebastian walked over to a shelf above the bed where there was a radio and turned it on. A Sibelius symphony filled the room. "Now, we can go," he said to Meer.

* * *

Outside, Sebastian led her down a small path. "Do you mind walking?"

Mostly because he wanted to and she ached to assuage some of the pain in his eyes if she possibly could, she said it was fine.

"I saw you turn on the radio in your son's room," she said, returning to the only subject, she was sure, that he could focus on now.

"Nicolas always loved listening to music. Even when he was a tiny baby. I think that's when I was the happiest... when my son sat, listening to music I made for him."

"Do you still play for him?"

He nodded. "He doesn't seem to hear me but his chanting seems to adjust to the rhythm of what I'm playing. I've arranged for the nurses to play the classical music radio station for him, and when I have a performance that's being broadcast they're very good about putting it on and telling him it's me. I keep hoping that one day the music will reach him."

"The power of music..."

"Is there anything you noticed about Nicolas that's similar to what you experienced?"

"I wasn't that lost."

"Your father thinks he's having what Malachai Samuels calls a past life break."

She nodded. "He describes it as a dam collapsing. Too many memories flooding in, overpowering the mind."

"Is that what you think happened to you?"

"No. I had a slow trickle of false memories that I created myself."

"Your father introduced me to Malachai Samuels via e-mail and since then I've talked to him twice over the phone. I wanted to pay him to come here and work with Nicolas but he told me it's hard for him to leave the country now."

"Not anymore. In fact he'll be here tomorrow, coming for Wednesday's auction. Maybe you can convince your wife to let just one last stranger in."

They'd reached a small pond encircled by tall pine trees that scented the air with menthol and cast cool blue shadows. Picking up a pinecone, Sebastian threw it into the pond with surprising ferocity, and it hit the silvery calm surface with an angry splash. The impact sent a series of concentric circles rippling outward, each ring growing larger and larger until it vanished.

"Did he help you?"

"Not to figure out what was happening, no. But he did teach me to keep the attacks at bay and stop them from paralyzing me."

She tripped on a branch and Sebastian reached out to keep her from falling. She was aware of the momentary pressure of his fingers on her arm.

"Where are we going?" she asked.

"I thought since we're here, I'd show you the church that Wagner built. It's beautiful. Probably the only thing worthwhile in this whole detestable place."

While they continued on, she tried to answer the rest of his questions about what it had been like for her when she was a child.

"You must have been very scared," he finally said with so much empathy it made her throat hurt.

I still am, she almost said. But that would be saying something she wasn't sure she wanted him to hear. Or wanted to admit. Even to herself.

Chapter 27

The Celts were fearless warriors because they wished to inculcate this
as one of their leading tenets, that souls do not become extinct, but pass
after death from one body to another...

—Julius Caesar

Vienna, Austria
Sunday, April 27th—3:00 p.m.

Sebastian stood in the small square and pointed to the stone staircase and street beyond it. "Up there is the Mölker Bastei where Herr
Beethoven lived for a time."

On the way back to town, Sebastian, who was depressed after his
visit with his son, asked Meer if she still wanted to see the Beethoven
house that she'd been interested in the day before. She was reluctant
to take up more of this man's time but he insisted it would be as much
of a distraction for him as it was for her. Now, as they climbed
toward it, Sebastian fell into guide mode.

"Beethoven lived in over forty apartments in Vienna, moving so often because he was so messy and noisy he kept getting evicted. This is one of the few residences open to the public. A few others are just outside the city."

Like every serious student of music, Meer knew the basics: born in Germany, Beethoven spent most of his adult life in Vienna. Despite a significant hearing loss that ultimately led to deafness, his infirmity didn't mar his genius and he composed some of his greatest symphonies without being able to hear them clearly.

Looking at the long row of attached cream-colored identical buildings, her eye was drawn to number eight, which flew an Austrian flag. Staring at the freshly painted facade, Meer searched for spots where history seeped through. Her eye was drawn to one set of eight-over-eight paned windows on the sixth floor.

"This is what I love the most about Vienna," he said as they kept climbing. "Streets where nothing has changed in over two hundred years. This is almost exactly how it looked when Beethoven lived here."

A pigeon landed on the building's pitched roofline. Then another. Until there was a twittering audience watching their progress.

"In his diary," Sebastian continued, "he wrote that every afternoon he'd go for a long walk because he thought so much better when he was on the move. I picture him charging out the front door, coattails flying behind, disappearing down these steps. Already quite famous by the time he lived here, people on the street would recognize him and point him out. 'That's Herr Beethoven, the composer,' they'd whisper as he strode by."

The words on the plaque on the front of the building were in German but Meer recognized Beethoven's name and the dates of his residence there.

"Most people make the gigantic fuss over Mozart," Sebastian said. "Vienna has made him the hero of the city. There's even a chocolate candy with his picture on it. I understand he was, what's the expression, a true native son, born in Vienna. But like you, I prefer Beethoven."

Had she actually told him that or had he simply intuited it because she'd chosen his house to visit?

"Why?" she asked.

"He had every reason to give up his hope and his music but he persevered. He faced the worst thing a composer can face and it made him stronger. He went further than everyone before him and influenced all those who came after. He wrote music that mapped the soul."

"Mapped the soul," she repeated, wanting to remember the phrase.

Sebastian held the door open and Meer walked inside. The vestibule was dark and small and there was nowhere to go but up the staircase. She started climbing. *Twenty-one, twenty-two, twenty-three.* When she realized she was counting the steps she stopped but was at it again without realizing it only a few seconds later. *Fifty-four, fifty-five, fifty-six.* At the sixth landing, Meer stopped.

"How did you know we're here?" he asked from behind her.

"Didn't you tell me the apartment was on the sixth floor?"

"Did I?"

The door to the left was painted white like all the others, except beside it was a plaque etched with Beethoven's name and a set of dates. Sebastian pulled it open and held it for her.

The jarring brightness of the whitewashed walls bewildered her as strains of the *Moonlight Sonata* emanated from inside and reached out to welcome her. Meer hesitated at the threshold, carefully wiped her feet first, then stepped inside.

Sebastian hadn't followed her in. He was still standing in the hallway with a curious expression on his face. Meer followed his glance. He was staring down at the spot where she'd wiped her feet on the doormat.

Except there was no doormat.

Something was wrong with the air inside Beethoven's apartment; it smelled of fake pine disinfectant instead of wax and wine and bread baking in the apartment next door. Even the walls were the wrong color—instead of such a clean, bright white, they should have been more yellow.

Meer wandered from room to room examining the exhibition cases that housed Beethoven artifacts, studying the portraits of his contemporaries, street scenes of Vienna at the turn of the nineteenth century, handwritten scores, programs from musical events, even his shaving mug and hearing trumpet. When she reached the case with his plaster life mask she stared at Beethoven's face—not handsome but imperious and vigorous with broad cheeks, a strong chin and a wide forehead. She stared at it so long she became self-conscious and looked around to make sure Sebastian wasn't watching her, but she was alone, waiting, as if communication across the centuries was possible.

In the next room, she stood in front of the maestro's piano. It was so easy to imagine him hunched over the keyboard, the black and ivory keys dancing as he coaxed elaborate melodies from them. Meer started to shake as chills racked her body and her head began to throb. The room shimmered and became translucent. The familiar metallic taste filled her mouth and made her teeth hurt. Her back throbbed. Music filled her head and, dizzy with the sound of it, she expelled a long breath and felt a deep and debilitating emotion rise out of the depths of her subconscious.

Chapter 28

"Your fingering is off. Try again. Move faster, as if the wind is chasing you." Beethoven's voice was too loud—he couldn't hear himself well enough to modulate it.

Margaux tried to concentrate...but these days she was always thinking about what she was doing—how terrible it was and how necessary. Was the plan working? Was Beethoven starting to trust her? Was Caspar worse or better? She felt as if she hadn't taken a deep breath since Caspar had left almost nine months before.

"Much better. But try again. Faster still. Feel more wind."

She moved her fingers faster. Then faster. And then she was making music. It wasn't right that she had to discover a passion for the piano during an act of duplicity and deception.

Finished, she looked up from the keyboard to find Beethoven nodding at her.

"Yes, yes. It's wonderful how quickly you learn. Beauty and talent. You're doubly blessed, as am I, to have you as a student."

His flirtatiousness was so sincere it disarmed her.

"Thank you," Margaux said, remembering to look at him when she spoke so he could read her lips.

"And your husband…he was even more blessed."

Moved and truly grateful, she put her hand on his.

"I have often thought about what I've missed by never being married. But whatever I gave up in one way, I gained by having time for more noble pursuits." There was pride in his voice but also a lonely echo and Margaux didn't remove her hand.

After Rudolph Toller had admitted he'd given Beethoven the flute that legally belonged to her in the hopes the composer would be able to decipher the ancient instrument's music, the British major, Archer Wells, had come up with a scheme.

Margaux would take piano lessons from the maestro, which would put her in his home and give her access to steal the flute once he had figured out its song. Then Archer would buy the flute on behalf on the Rothschild family whom he'd contacted and were so anxious to own it they'd offered enough to fund Caspar's search party.

But the plan depended on Beethoven accepting her as a student, and that worried her.

"Margaux, how could he refuse you? How could any man?" Archer had asked, flirting. The compliment had made her think of Caspar, feel his breath in her ear as he'd whispered to her the last time they'd gone to the opera—*you're the loveliest woman here, do you know that?*

Archer's eyes lingered on her décolletage as he continued, "Beethoven adores having beautiful female students. Especially when they come bearing money. Since July, he's lost two of his three benefactors. First Prince Lobkowitz, who had serious financial setbacks, and then Prince Kinski, who fell off his horse and died." He reached out and in the air drew a line following the swell of her flesh where the neckline of the dress ended.

This, too, she would endure. For Caspar. Anything for Caspar. While other women changed men like costumes, she was interested only in moving all the mountains in India to find her husband and bring him home. And to do that she needed Archer and the money the Rothschilds were offering in exchange for the flute and its music.

The hour lesson ended and Margaux proposed supper—she'd gotten into the habit of bringing the maestro's favorites when she came to study: good wine, cheese, fruit and bread.

"First the wine," he said. "And bring it here, I thought I'd play something from my new symphony for you."

Margaux brought a full glass to the piano. She was still horrified at how sloppy he was, eating and drinking everywhere but at the table, leaving glasses and plates on the bench, under it, on the piano lid itself. Even his chamber pot was sometimes in plain sight. As disgusting as his behavior was, Beethoven's music made it possible to ignore what was so base and mundane about him. It elevated him.

He took the wine with his left hand while with his right he teased out a few notes on the keyboard. Greedily, he emptied the glass, put it down and began to play with both hands. His music dipped and soared and caressed and soothed and aroused all at once, and she was moved.

Finished, he sat staring down at his hands on the keys and spoke without looking over at her. "Life has been a little brighter to me of late since I have mingled with you. I think you can have no idea how sad, how intensely desolate, my life has been during the last two years. My deafness, like a specter, appears before me everywhere, so that I flee from society and am obliged to act the part of a misanthrope, though I hope you see by now, I am not one by nature."

"I'm honored. More than I can say."

He didn't hear her so she lifted his chin so that he was looking at her and repeated her words. Beethoven smiled and Margaux knew at that moment her plan was going to work.

"Should we have something to eat?" he asked, suddenly full of energy.

On her way to the table she passed the window, glanced out and noticed a man standing in the shadowed recess of a doorway across the street. Even in profile the sharp nose and slightly stooped shoulders were familiar. Stepping back a few inches to make sure he wouldn't be able to see her if he looked up, she peered into the encroaching twilight. Was it really her husband's partner? Then he turned and she saw Toller's hollow cheekbones and half-dead eyes. How had he discovered her plans?

It wasn't that difficult to figure out, really. Foreign ministers of the five great powers and all their minions were gathered in Vienna to define the future of Europe; every one of them was so paranoid about the others, spying was now as much a national pastime as dancing the waltz. Everyone's valets, butlers, maids and menservants were capable of espionage. Garbage was sold at premium for the scraps of notes that could be salvaged from the potato peels and beef bones. A shopping list from the Tsar's household went for more money than a silver service on the chance it was a coded communiqué.

Toller could easily have hired someone to follow her and keep track of her appointments without her ever noticing. Not in the crowds these days. Not with all the people who visited her salon at night. But would she be able to accomplish her task under Toller's watchful gaze? Was her plan ruined?

Setting the table, her hands trembled and dropped a knife. She looked over. Beethoven's hearing was slightly better today and he'd noticed. His eyes questioned her but she just shrugged. Maybe she should just tell him the truth and offer to pay him more than what Toller had offered for Beethoven's translation of the notes. Would the Rothschilds' offer cover what the Memorists were paying Beethoven and pay for the expedition and search party?

Margaux cleared a chair for herself and then went to do the same for Beethoven. Lifting his coat off the second chair she felt the rough wool in her hands and noticed how worn it was: fraying at the edges, missing buttons.

"You should have a better coat."

"I do. But when I go out for a walk and don't care to be disturbed I wear that old one and a hat that casts deep shadows over my face. Disguised as such a poor man, I can observe without being observed and the world is mine to explore."

Maybe she could borrow the coat and the hat to leave with tonight so Toller wouldn't notice her. It was worth a try. Caspar used to have her dress as a young boy when traveling was dangerous and she was good at changing her stride to mimic a man's.

The last article on the seat was a tan-colored chamois shirt and as she touched it the soft leather fell away and she was looking down at the treasure she hoped was going to be the key to saving her husband; her personal holy grail.

Being married to Caspar had put her in a rare position to learn what men learned. Studying with him, reading the books he read, her interest in foreign cultures, legends and mythology developed to match his. She shared his dreams about finding treasures hidden under layers of dead cities and lost civilizations and had long imagined finding one of the fabled memory tools.

During their twelve years of marriage, he'd taken seven trips to India, which had cost them dearly; all of her dowry and his inheritance had been spent, leaving them almost impoverished. But he'd been certain he was getting closer to their goal with each trip. He'd lived to find one of the memory tools and either he'd died acquiring it or was going to die if she couldn't use it to save him.

Beethoven approached to see what was keeping her so preoccupied.

"Ach. I am supposed to keep that away from prying eyes," he said, picking it up.

"No, please. I know what this is," she said, whispering in a combination of awe, relief and excitement, forgetting Beethoven couldn't hear her when she spoke softly.

"What? What did you say?"

How inconsequential and fragile the flute seemed. So old and brittle it looked as if it would break if she even breathed on it. Barely six inches long and less than two inches around, it was uneven and slightly bowed with a series of seven holes spaced evenly down the center. And covering the entire surface were carvings. Caspar had written about the strange artwork in his last letter, even sketching some of the designs but she wasn't prepared for how complex the engravings were.

"What did you say?" Beethoven asked again in frustration.

She looked up. "Caspar told me it was thousands of years old...maybe even older than the Bible... Finding it was the pinnacle of his career. Do you know what the flute's supposed to be used for?"

"Yes, Herr Toller explained that its music is purported to induce past life memories." Running his forefinger over the marks, lost in the incoherent lines and squiggles, he shook his head in awe at the idea. "Imagine that. It's an idea that has fascinated me for a long time—since I first read the translated scriptures brought back from India."

"And have you figured out the flute's music?" If he said yes, all this scheming would soon come to an end and she would be able to mount the campaign to find Caspar. At last.

"They think I should be able to." Beethoven frowned as he stared at the flute, displeasure on his face. "But I haven't even found a starting point to interpret all these markings. You can't imagine how many times I've wanted to take the damn thing and fling it at the wall—it's so fragile, I'm sure it would shatter to bits but at least then it would stop taunting me and jeering at me. Making a fool of me."

Archer had been clear that the Rothschilds would only pay for the flute if it came with its song. The object alone was worth nothing to them. Keen students of the Kabbalah, the family was anxious to explore their past lives. The irony that their emissary was encouraging her to break a commandment so they could delve more deeply into their religious convictions wasn't lost on her.

"Did your husband believe?"

"Once he told me that maybe in a past life he hid the tools himself and this time he just needed to remember where he put them. I don't know if he was teasing or not, but he certainly believed it was his destiny to find them." Margaux was ashamed at the tears that came to her eyes.

The maestro moved closer, reached out and clumsily touched her shoulder. "It's a terrible thing to lose someone you love."

She nodded.

"By all rights this belongs to you, doesn't it?"

Yes, she wanted to shout. *Yes, and this will be so much easier when the time comes, if you give it to me instead of making me take it from you.* But her only response was to nod.

"Perhaps you would like to hold it. It might make you feel closer to the man whose heart is still in yours." Beethoven put the flute into her hand.

Like many women, when she was a young girl Margaux had been taught to play the pianoforte and study composition but she had no affinity for music and practicing was a chore. Except now, as her fingers curled around the chalky bone instrument, she shuddered. For the first time in her thirty-five years, she heard music in her head, coming from inside of her, music of its own will and volition, music that she wasn't writing but that somehow was already written in the deepest recesses of her mind. It was beautiful and frightening at the same time. She needed to isolate it, remember it, tell him about it, but as she tried to hold on to its cadence and tone, it slipped away.

"You look like you've seen a ghost," Beethoven said as he picked up the bottle and drank from it directly as he was wont to do.

"No, not seen a ghost."

The expression on her face caused him to stop midaction and give her all of his attention.

"I've heard a ghost."

Chapter 29

Outside the Dorotheum auction house the next morning, the armed uniformed guards controlled the snaking line of potential bidders and curiosity seekers waiting to see the "Beethoven Gaming Box," as the press had dubbed it. Meer gave her name to one of the guards and was allowed to bypass the line and go right inside, which was a relief because not having slept well for the second night in a row, she was overtired and didn't feel well. Didn't feel like herself. When she'd been getting dressed and glimpsed herself in the mirror it had been like staring at a stranger. She wasn't connected to the woman who looked back at her with pained, haunted eyes. Except Meer knew it wasn't possible for her to be feeling the desperation and sorrow of a woman who'd lived over two hundred years before.

The lobby was crowded and Meer had to wade through the mass of people. "Your name will be with the guards outside and I'll be waiting for you in the main viewing room," her father had told her the night before when he'd called from Switzerland. He'd stayed on later than he'd expected because sadly, Dr. Smettering had died. Now there were two murders being investigated.

Meer walked among chairs, couches, armoires and tables covered with small objets d'art, and strained to find her father's head over the crowd. As a little girl, his towering height reassured her she could never get lost. Or at least any more lost than she already was.

When she finally spotted him, he was gesticulating toward a display case with a graceful sweep of his hand and lecturing to a circle of people who appeared absorbed by his words. His hair looked grayer than she remembered and there were inky shadows under his eyes. How old was he? She had to think. Sixty-six? No, a year older. She felt a throb of anxiety deep in the pit of her stomach. Her mother died before she turned sixty. But her father was healthy. Of course he'd look worn out…the last forty-eight hours had been filled with trauma.

She leaned against the wall, not wanting to approach him with the group there or see the gaming box for the first time with a dozen strangers looking on. Or was it for the first time?

Einstein once said he believed it was possible to occupy two spaces at the same time but in different dimensions. Her father had tried to use the quote to counter Meer's arguments against reincarnation. At the time she hadn't been swayed even though the scientist, who had loved music and studied violin and been so sensitive to the wonders of the universe, was one of her heroes.

Now, she rethought the concept. Since she'd wiped her feet on a doormat that wasn't there but that she had seen as clearly as her own feet, Meer's concept about her false memories had developed its first crack. Nothing in all her learning about memory and reality could explain that one small action.

Did Einstein's theory also mean there could be a transfer of consciousness from one material form to another? From a human in one time zone to another human in a different time zone?

"Hello." Sebastian sidled up to her and tilted his head toward where her father was still holding court. "Have you seen it yet?"

"I didn't know you were coming today," Meer said, feeling a curious mixture of pleasure and anxiety.

"I don't have a rehearsal till this afternoon and I didn't want to miss a chance to view a true Beethoven relic."

"It appears you weren't alone." She gestured toward the crowd.

"This is a major discovery. Everyone's curiosity is aroused. Especially because of Antonie Brentano. It's not just music, it's love." He offered a warm smile that shouldn't have disturbed her but did.

"Before I forget," Sebastian said, and reached into his pocket and pulled out a small white envelope, "these are my house seats for a private concert being given on Thursday night. I'd like you and your father to come. While you're here you should see Vienna all dressed up at least once. She's quite amazing."

"Thank you. What's the event?"

"A gala performance for an international association of top-level security firms with dignitaries and government officials coming from all over the world."

Taking the envelope from him, she slipped it into her bag.

"You and your father will need to stop by the hall in advance and have your pictures taken and your passports scanned to activate the tickets. The security for the event is staggering."

"What will you be performing?"

"The *Eroica.*"

"So you'll have a solo in the third movement?"

He nodded.

"My father loves that symphony, he'll be thrilled."

"Does he know you're here?"

She was about to say that she wanted to see the box without a crowd around her but didn't. First, thinking he wouldn't understand, then afraid he'd understand too well and that disturbed her more. Meer heard her name.

"Meer, sweetheart, I'm so sorry." Her father took her in his arms. She felt the familiar rub of his cashmere jacket on her cheek and smelled the ever-present verbena cologne. With him holding her a beat too long, she wondered if he was offering solace or taking it.

Turning to Sebastian, her father shook his hand. "It was a real comfort to know you were taking such care of my daughter. Thank you."

"My pleasure. I'm sorry about both your friend and your house-keeper."

"Two useless deaths." Jeremy shook his head. "The funeral for Ruth is this afternoon. Karl will be cremated." Checking his watch, he frowned. "Has been cremated. Both gone, and for what?" Jeremy was quiet for a few seconds, despite the cacophony all around them. Meer wondered if her father was praying. Like her mother, Meer was always astonished when she glimpsed the depth of his spirituality. It never seemed to fit the brave adventurer who traveled to faraway places, tunneled behind the Iron Curtain when it still existed, was shot at and recovered treasures. But today he seemed ordinary and almost frail. Someone who needed his faith.

"I'd like to go to Ruth's funeral with you," Meer said.

Jeremy smiled sadly. "Thank you, sweetheart, but it's not necessary."

"I have a rehearsal this afternoon or I would—"

Jeremy interrupted. "No need to explain, Sebastian. You've done enough." Straightening up, he threw back his shoulders as if he was shaking off the melancholy, and the powerful man Meer remembered reemerged. "Now," he said, looking at his daughter. "Are you ready to see your box?"

As Jeremy ushered them through the crowd he explained this was supposed to have been a minor auction, but between finding the Beethoven letter and the robbery it had turned into a media circus.

"I've arranged for tighter security and am moving the auction itself to a larger venue on Wednesday. We should have moved the viewing to another room, too." Finding a group congregated in front of the exhibition case, Jeremy subtly made room for Meer and Sebastian to step up to the plinth.

In the showcase, the gleaming wooden box was open, revealing the velvet-lined compartments holding various gaming pieces and decks of cards. A mirror allowed the viewer to also see the box's elaborate top. Meer fixated on what she saw in that mirror: a silver oval with fancy etched scrollwork, flowers, birds, the initial *B*.

Yes, she'd seen all this in Malachai's office in the catalog photo but that had been a facsimile, not the three-dimensional manifestation of her imagination. She stared at it hoping the real box would help her remember when she'd seen it before. Not in some past life, as her father and Malachai suggested, but at some prior point in her own life.

But nothing came to mind. Her only reaction was to notice that the decks of cards were similar to a pack in Malachai's collection. When she was a child she always asked for that deck as soon as she arrived and played with it during her sessions. There was even a game that she'd made up with those cards. What was it?

Using a key on a very full ring, Jeremy unlocked the cabinet. "Let's take this to a private viewing room so you can have some time alone with it."

As he began removing the box, Meer stepped up and, almost in a trance, reached out for a deck of cards and then started searching through it. Unaware of the room around her, she was only conscious of the stiff cards in her fingers as she counted the hearts in the deck, checking they were all there and that there were no duplicates. This was the same game she played with Malachai's cards.

"Meer, wait till we get into a private viewing room," Jeremy insisted.

A loud, intimidating ringing ripped the moment apart.

"Was ist das?" she asked her father, frightened by the noise, not even realizing she'd asked in a language she didn't speak.

"The fire alarm," Jeremy shouted over the noise. "Probably a glitch. It happens—"

The smoke came quickly; billowing clouds rising upward and outward, reaching out for her. For all of them. The alarm continued shrieking. Jeremy was coughing. Meer's eyes stung. Then she was coughing too. Unexpectedly, tears came to her eyes and spilled over. People were screaming and the alarm bells continued shrieking. In the chaos, someone ran past and pushed her. Losing her balance, Meer put out her hands, trying to feel for support, but there was nothing to hold on to and she went down, hitting her shoulder on the edge of the showcase. A crack of pain shot through her and its intensity, mixed with the voluminous acrid smoke, made her gag.

She knew she might be hurt but couldn't worry about that now…had to save the box…needed to get up and find it and protect it from the fire. Groping blindly she found the edge of the pedestal and grasped it, prepared to feel it burning hot but it was cool. How could that be if there was a fire?

That's when she realized there was no heat and no smell of a fire either. She didn't have time to try to understand. All that mattered was keeping the box safe because she was certain it held the clues to where the memory flute was and she needed it to save her husband. Somewhere, sick and alone, Caspar counted on her. Thrusting her hands down into the case she felt for the box. Right. Then left. The case wasn't that big. There was nothing in it.

The wind and the rain were so loud but she could hear a man was calling out to her, shouting at her to stop. Except she couldn't. Her horse responded to the pull of the reins and took off, galloping. The woods were deep here and he'd have trouble following her. He was a brilliant horseman but she had the advantage; even in the rainstorm she knew these woods, he didn't. Then the sound of a gunshot rang out.

No, it was not a gun, only the fire alarm. What was going on? The smoke was clearing but her eyes were still tearing and it was hard for her to see clearly. Then the outlines and shapes started to turn into people and furniture. Furniture? People? Where were the woods? She'd been riding in the woods trying to get away from terrible, imminent danger, trying to save the box.

"Are you all right?" It was her father helping her up, his face wet with tears.

"Do you have the box?" she shouted over the noise.

Before he could answer, one of the guards rushed over, yelling loudly. The man's face was flushed and his cheeks were wet with tears, too. Every second more smoke cleared, revealing other guards helping people who'd fallen and ushering them out of the room. Everywhere pieces of furniture were overturned and objets d'art lay broken on the floor.

"What are they saying?" Meer shouted. Even in her own ears, her voice sounded hysterical.

"There was no fire, it was tear gas," her father said. "This...all of this...must have been a staged distraction."

Meer grabbed his arm. "What happened to the gaming box?"

"It's gone."

Chapter 30

At frequent intervals on the tree-lined road David drove by shrines to Christ or the Virgin or other saints that he didn't recognize. If only the painted plaster effigies really could protect from danger or assuage pain the way so many believed. He'd been something of an observant Jew before, but now all he believed in was the presence of evil.

Arriving at his destination four hours after leaving Vienna, he parked the rental car, got out, stretched his long legs and looked around. It was dreary under the gray sky. The lush countryside had given way to spindly trees, footprints of long-dead gardens and a looming chateau that appeared to be in desperate need of restoration. This place must have been impressive at one time but now yellow paint flaked off the outside of the building and dozens of the sienna roof tiles were missing.

Hidden in the middle of the southern Moravian countryside, an hour's drive from the closest town, Moravsky Krumlov was an unlikely museum for the most valuable artwork in all of the Republic and an even less likely place to meet with a liaison from an underground terrorist cell.

Inside the entryway, where it was even damper than outside, the walls and floor were in worse shape than the building's exterior. After buying a 50 Kc ticket, David followed the signs to a staircase that creaked as he climbed it. Before he was allowed to enter the first gallery, a woman wearing a red kerchief handed him two dark brown felt bags. Without speaking, she demonstrated that he should put them over his shoes, which he did. They made walking slippery. Inside the first gallery a group of children all in stocking feet sat cross-legged, listening to a young woman who lectured to them in Czech. Surprisingly, they didn't fidget or whisper as they stared at the heroic canvas that took up the whole wall. His eight-year-old, Ben, wouldn't have been able to sit there so still, with his socks on, he would have been impelled to go floor skating across these wide wooden planks.

Opening the English version of the flyer he'd picked up at the ticket booth, David read about the painting the children were engrossed in.

Twenty feet wide and thirty-two feet high, this mural illustrates the first chapter in the 1000-year-old history of the Slav nation.

In the center of the canvas, under a starry sky, the figures of Adam and Eve cowered and hid from ghostlike, fearsome figures atop horses, spears at the ready, galloping toward them. Deep in the background a village burned, the orange-red flames glowing like sunrise. According to the pamphlet, there were twenty of these heroic paintings on display, all created by the Art Nouveau painter Alphonse Mucha.

As instructed by his contact, David walked through the galleries, examining each of the paintings as if they indeed interested him. He was not to approach anyone. At the right time, they'd find him. He'd reached the second to last room without anyone making contact and was about to walk out when the lights flickered off. Then, just as quickly, flickered back on.

David entered the last exhibition room where, dwarfed by its size, he regarded the only remaining mural: a triumphant ensemble piece, full of victory. His older son Isaac would have wanted to dissect the symbolism, discuss the ways in which the artist had created the sense of hope with specific colors and explore every inch of the painting with his father. Ben would still be off, sliding across the room.

David wanted to put his fist through the canvas as if it were the painting's fault he was thinking of his children. This was just a romanticized picture of war, and peace, of death and triumphant life.

Behind him he sensed someone had entered the gallery and turned to see a young man walking toward him holding a black nylon knapsack.

"I think you left this in the other room." His accent was thick but the words were clear enough.

"How stupid of me," David said out loud. It might very well have been any man's reaction to leaving his pack behind. "The lights…?" he offered by way of explanation but it came out as a question.

"Yes, the lights." The other man was about twenty with acne on both cheeks and stringy black hair hanging to his shoulders. His jeans were ripped, his gray sweatshirt rumpled but his trainers were clean. "It was just a fuse, they said. You must have been worried to have left this."

"Yes." Reaching out David took the proffered knapsack. It was light. He knew from his research how potent Semtex was and how little he needed. All it took to blow up Pan Am Flight 103 was 200 grams. At least in the paintings here at the castle the enemy was painted in dark tones and came at you with brandished swords so you had a clue who was who. David shifted the backpack to his right shoulder. Everything that was wrong in the world weighed less than a pound and was in this backpack.

"You should be more careful," the messenger warned.

Was there subtext to this? A message? David couldn't translate the inscrutable expression on the young man's face. He was waiting, his eyes challenging David, his smirk admonishing him. *Naive amateur,* the look said. The transaction, David realized, wasn't completed yet.

"I want to give you a reward. For finding my bag."

"I won't say no." The man smiled sincerely as if this was all very normal.

David had prepared the bills the way he'd been instructed; four one-hundred-euro notes enclosed in ten-euro notes. There were no cameras but in case anyone happened to be watching they'd only notice a ten. So little money to destroy so much. "Please accept this as a thank-you."

While the young man stuffed the money in his pocket in front of Mucha's last heroic mural, David walked out of the gallery thinking how the painting's gargantuan shadow cast the messenger in darkness, and that he could use that image in the article he was writing about this saga. He even knew where it would appear: at the beginning of the end.

It was drizzling outside and David dreaded the long drive ahead of him on unfamiliar roads in the rain in a rental car that should have been retired ten thousand kilometers ago. Opening the door, he slid in behind the steering wheel and gingerly put the knapsack on the passenger seat. This wasn't the time to look inside the pack in case he was being followed, but he couldn't hold back.

David didn't know what he'd expected. Brown wrapping paper? A manila envelope? Anything but navy foil imprinted with frosted cakes with white candles. The irony wasn't lost on him. It was a birthday party that had started this journey, and explosives wrapped up like a birthday present that would end it.

Chapter 31

The Memorist Society had only been open for fifteen minutes when Dr. Erika Alderman arrived to have lunch with Fremont Brecht and found him already in the clubroom and glued to the television. "You need to see this. The gaming box was just stolen," he said without bothering to greet her.

On the screen Jeremy Logan stood outside of the Dorotheum auction house, being interviewed by a reporter explaining that a smoke bomb had apparently been used as a distraction while the thieves got away with the antique. Behind him police cars and fire engines continued pulling up to the scene with lights flashing and sirens shrieking. Meer stood off to her father's side; her chin-length dark hair was tousled and her wide eyes looked haunted. There was dirt on the collar of her white shirt and a black button was hanging by a thread from her blazer.

"Damn it, Fremont," Erika said. "How many close calls must we have before you do something about what's going on here? Someone is spying on what we are saying."

"You're forgetting about the article in the newspaper. The Beethoven connection made both the letter and the box worth stealing."

"But three robbery attempts in three days and two people dead over Beethoven relics? I don't think so. Someone out there is very ruthless and determined, and I think it's because they know something."

"We will just have to be more ruthless and more determined," he said. "Don't worry. I have no intention of anyone owning the gaming box but us. I've said that from the beginning."

"How can we get it if it's no longer for sale?" Erika was confused.

"We find out who stole it," Fremont said matter-of-factly. "And then we'll steal it back."

Chapter 32

At Global's temporary offices on the second floor of Vienna's main concert hall, Bill Vine watched a red circle slowly moving across a section of Moravia, Czechoslovakia on one of six computer screens. On a second screen, there was another red circle holding on the western tip of Yugoslavia. On a third, the dot was stalled in central Slovakia.

"No, we don't have any info yet on what kind of explosives were purchased in any of these transactions. I should have that information for you later this afternoon," Vine said, reporting to Tom Paxton, who reacted impatiently.

"But we're seeing all the purchasers?"

"Yes. And following them, without any problem."

"What do you make of the fact that there's been no activity for six days and suddenly three transactions occurred almost simultaneously?" Paxton asked.

"It suggests a shipment came in as much as anything else. Or it could just be a coincidence."

"I don't believe in coincidences."

"Neither do I," said Vine. "Except when they are coincidences."

"How soon will you be able to get people in the field to start following these bad boys on the ground too?"

"They're on their way and we should have everyone covered within two hours, three at the latest."

"Too long."

Vine didn't react to the criticism. "We don't get the addresses of the drops, Tom."

"For what they're getting paid, all these suppliers should be giving us that too."

"Requires too much communication with us. Don't underestimate the coup you've pulled off here. Bribing the enemy's no small feat. Even if we don't know yet if any of these purchases are headed our way, it's one helluva insurance policy."

"You're sure there won't be more than a three-hour wait? I want *people* on their tails, not just machines."

"I'm sure."

"Is there anything else we need to worry about before we move on?" Paxton asked.

"Nope, nothing," Vine said, without any indication that he'd heard the question a thousand times before.

Chapter 33

Jeremy took Meer to his doctor, whose office was only a short car ride from the auction house. While they sat in the waiting room, she perused a magazine, unaware of what she looked at. Her mind was filled with too many kaleidoscopic images for any new ones to make an impression. The last forty-eight hours had been filled with shocks and memories that couldn't be her own, but felt just like her own. She knew that was why false memories were so insidious; they masqueraded as authentic recollections.

Once the doctor saw her, the examination was brief. He assured her—and then afterward in the waiting room assured Jeremy—that the bruises blossoming on her left arm and thigh weren't serious.

"Now, why don't you let me give you a quick exam, Jeremy," Dr. Kreishold suggested.

"You're far too conscientious. I'm fine."

"Jeremy, let me just look you over—" the doctor insisted.

"If anything starts to hurt, I'll be back for a bandage, I promise," Jeremy interrupted.

"Come on, Dad, you should be examined too," Meer said.

Jeremy kissed her on the forehead. "I'm fine—don't worry about me, sweetheart. They examined me in the hospital in Switzerland after the attack. I'm all right."

As they walked out of the office and into the dark hallway, Jeremy told Meer that while she'd been in with the doctor, Malachai's secretary had called. "She booked him into your hotel. If you're not too tired, he'll meet you in the lobby at six and the two of you can come to my house for a quiet dinner. So you should get some rest now," he added.

"Aren't we going to Ruth's funeral now?" She ignored the fatherly concern.

"I told you—it's not necessary for you to come."

"I want to, for your sake." She paused. "Ruth died because of me, didn't she?"

Jeremy stabbed the elevator button again, once, then twice. "No, of course not, why would you—"

"If I didn't have a connection to that gaming box, would you have been so interested in it? You find old Torahs, menorahs, Haggadahs and Kiddush wine cups. What kind of Jewish artifact is a gaming box from 1814?"

The elevator arrived with a groan and the door opened slowly.

"This is much bigger than you know, sweetheart."

"And I can't know if you don't tell me."

Her father nodded and looked away. "You're right."

While they walked toward his car, Jeremy started at the beginning and told her about the call from Helen Hoffman. Despite Meer's irritation, her father's raconteur style, full of details and curious asides, was as compelling as ever and she had a sudden memory of him sitting by the side of her bed at night and telling her about his most recent adventure. His voice filled the silence when she was a child—the silence she feared and hated because it was in those quiet spaces between words that memories and music she couldn't quite catch hold of or make sense of scared her with their insistence.

Meer knew how emotional these finds were for her father. People who did what her father did weren't just on a treasure hunt to find and preserve objects, they were reclaiming their heritage. "We owe it to the memory of those who came before us to discover what they left for us to find," he'd once told her, and she'd heard the pride in his voice. She always loved her father, but she liked him the best when he talked about his work.

Jeremy eased the car out of the parking spot and at the next corner turned into the traffic. As they crept ahead Meer watched yet another section of the city reveal itself while she listened to her father describe seeing the gaming box for the first time.

"It was a shock. I'm sure you can imagine just how bizarre it would be to walk into a stranger's house to examine a holy relic and see something that had so much significance to me and to you. There are no accidents of fate," he said. "Every act has a reaction through lives, though time. Déjà vu and coincidence are God tapping you on the shoulder, telling you to pay attention, showing you that you are walking in the footprint of your own reincarnation."

"You've always been so sure…"

He nodded.

"Why?"

"Faith."

She shook her head; for her it wasn't a sufficient answer.

"And now, just like Malachai, you're convinced the music—my music—has some connection to the flute that Beethoven wrote about in the letter?"

Jeremy looked surprised. "How do you know what was mentioned in the letter?" Then, realizing, he shook his head. "Malachai told you, didn't he? I'm sorry. When I told him, I should have asked him not to tell you about it. I wanted to show it to you myself when you got here."

Meer let that explanation stand. "What, exactly, does the letter say?"

"That the box holds the clues to where the flute was hidden." His voice sounded resigned as if this was a conversation he wished he could avoid.

Meer shuddered. The image of Beethoven holding the flute was impossibly clear and the burden of finding it weighed on her shoulders. Except it wasn't *her* burden. Her husband wasn't lost and sick. Her rising panic and urgency to find him was a manufactured emotion. And then Meer realized something tangible that really was urgent. "Do you believe the person who stole the letter from you and Dr. Smettering also stole the box and now is looking for the instrument?"

"Yes. A story broke here in the newspaper on Friday about a Beethoven letter being found in the gaming box, which is reason enough for someone to steal both of those objects. But I think they're after the flute."

"Did the article go into those details?"

"No. And I didn't discuss them with anyone other than my fellow board members and Malachai."

"But then how...?"

"There are hundreds of reincarnation scholars, musicologists and archaeologists around the world, not to mention members of the Society here who know about the memory tools and the history of Beethoven's connection to an alleged memory flute." Jeremy's fingers clenched around the steering wheel. "Either whoever was responsible for stealing the letter also stole the gaming box, or the contents of the letter reached someone else who organized this morning's theft."

They'd stopped at a light. To the right was a stone church with spires reaching high into a cloudless blue sky. As they waited the bells began to chime, the ringing reverberating inside Meer's body. "Why did you send the catalog and the drawing to me through Malachai? Why didn't you call me and tell me what you were involved in and warn me?"

He didn't answer.

"Did you call Malachai after I left his office to find out how I'd reacted?"

"Of course, because I wanted to make sure that you were all right. I knew it was going to be a shock."

"I don't want be your guinea pig."

"You're my daughter. All I've ever wanted to do was help you and protect you. That's all Malachai wants too."

"And in the process use me to prove your theories."

"Reincarnation is not my theory or his."

"You act as if it is."

"It's part of my belief system."

"A part of your belief system that you want to prove."

This was as blunt a conversation as Meer had ever had with her father on this or any subject. The last forty-eight hours had provoked it.

"Meer, sweetheart, you've always had it backward. Before you started hearing the music, I was never very religious. Yes, I searched out lost pieces of Judaica but I was an antique dealer. I went to temple on the high holy days but out of routine and respect to my heritage. I'd never studied Kabbalah. I didn't even know how important the concept of reincarnation was to the Jewish faith. I learned about all of this after you started to have problems."

"So you did it all for me?" she said more sarcastically than she'd intended.

"To understand, so I could help."

"I'm sure you think that."

"Did you ever see a movie called *Total Recall* with Arnold Schwarzenegger?"

Meer looked at her father with surprise. "No."

"The character Arnold plays can't trust his memories—can't tell what's real or false. When he's asked what he wants, he says, 'to remember,' and when he's asked why he wants to remember he says, 'to be myself again.' That's all I want for you. To remember, so you can be all your selves again."

They sat in silence for the next few minutes until Jeremy reached the Praterstrasse and Meer noticed the familiar Hebraic signage on some of the buildings. This was where she'd wandered on Saturday night. "Where are we?"

"The old Jewish ghetto. Most of it has been restored by Jews who've moved back to Vienna," he said as he turned off the main street and drove down a narrow lane. Glancing over at her, he asked: "Why, what's wrong?"

"Nothing, I'm fine."

Jeremy pulled into a parking spot. Without waiting for him, Meer got out of the car, turned right and started walking down the block.

"You don't know where—" He broke off to hurry and catch up to her just as she stopped in front of the nondescript building at 122 Engerthstrasse. "How did you know this was where we were going?"

Chapter 34

Live so that thou mayest desire to live again—that is thy duty—for in any case thou wilt live again!

—Friedrich Nietzsche

Monday, April 28th—1:25 p.m.

"This is where the Memorists have been meeting since they formed in late 1809," Jeremy said as the intercom buzzed and he opened the heavy door. Holding it, he waited for her to precede him but she didn't make any move to go inside. Shivering, tasting metal, she was aware the buildings on either side of her were becoming translucent.

"Are you all right?"

"Fine." She tried to make her voice sound as normal as she could as she fought back the dreads.

"What's wrong?"

With a burst of effort, Meer stepped over the doorstep and into the anteroom. Behind her, the door closed and the loud click echoed in the antechamber. Her legs felt as if they were weighted down and each step was a terrible effort but she followed her father across the black-and-white marble-tiled floor, through the doorway under the middle arch and into the Society's main room.

Last night, while she'd been standing on the street, she'd imagined all of this: the elaborate ceiling with its tiny mirrors that appeared to be twinkling, the extravagant decorations, the stone Buddhas.

Despite a lifetime of trying to remember, despite being hypnotized dozens of times and learning different meditation techniques, she couldn't grasp how she'd apparently seen across the years to the inside of this building and a time long gone.

An imposing silver-haired man who walked with a slight limp approached and Jeremy introduced Meer and Fremont Brecht to each other.

"I'm so sorry for the trouble you've had since arriving in Vienna," Fremont apologized in a cultured, slightly accented voice. Regardless of his girth, he was extremely well groomed and dignified. He indicated a grouping of cordovan leather club chairs and they sat down. "Did you have any time to examine the gaming box before it was taken?" he asked her, not bothering with any small talk.

"A few minutes."

"Was there anything that struck you as unusual in its appearance?"

"What do you mean?"

"Did you have a reaction of any kind to it?"

How many people had her father told about her affinity for the box? Who else besides Sebastian and Fremont? Had they all sat around playing a guessing game about whether or not it would trigger past life memories for her? She looked over at Jeremy but either he couldn't read the accusation in her eyes or chose not to.

"Everything happened too quickly," she said to Fremont.

He asked her something else but she wasn't listening. The longer she sat there the worse she felt. Meer couldn't get enough air in her lungs and she was so cold. Noting her discomfort, he stopped mid-sentence and apologized. "What's wrong with me, this has been a trying morning for you, and here I am putting you on the stand and demanding you give me your testimony. Would you like some lunch?"

"No, thank you—"

"Coffee or tea?"

"Tea, yes," she said. Maybe having something hot to drink would help her stay centered.

"And for you too, yes, Jeremy?" Fremont asked.

"You look very troubled," Jeremy said to Meer after Fremont left for the kitchen.

Meer laughed sourly. "As if there's no reason to be troubled? Please stop taking my emotional temperature, Dad."

Being here was so disturbing…the room was familiar but at the same time so many things were wrong. Like in Beethoven's apartment, the lighting here was far too bright. And she couldn't smell the paraffin or Cassia incense. Worst of all was the sadness and an ineffable longing that overwhelmed her. This was Caspar's world.

"Meer, tell me what's happening."

She didn't know how to explain, so she said nothing.

"Forget the tea, you need some water right now."

Meer put her hand out, about to ask her father not to leave her alone, except she knew that would open her up to more questions and she didn't have any answers. She let it flutter back into her lap. Whatever was happening, Malachai had taught her how to deal with it. Moving her fingers on an invisible keyboard in her lap she tried to play a complicated section of Rachmaninoff's "Rhapsody on a Theme of Paganini" that had no emotional memory for her. Usually this exercise required so much concentration it broke any anxiety surge. But not this afternoon. Meer couldn't stay with it because the other music demanded her attention and exacerbated her sadness. Old music…familiar music…and just when it seemed as if she might capture it finally…it flitted away, remaining just out of reach.

"Here's your tea," Fremont said, offering her a steaming mug.

Chapter 35

Finished filling up the rental car with petrol, David locked it and walked into the small store to get coffee. He needed to refuel, too. Stress kept him up most of every night—stress or nightmares—and by midafternoon he was always exhausted. The coffee was hot and bitter and, sitting in the car by the side of the highway, he drank it as if it was medicine. Something else that used to be enjoyable…now meaningless. When was the last time he felt real pleasure? Before the birthday party. Tasting blood, he realized he'd bitten the inside of his cheek.

After he finished the coffee he opened the knapsack, pulled out the package wrapped in foil imprinted with birthday cakes, put it on the floor of the passenger seat and then slowly and methodically inspected the knapsack.

He'd been cautious in arranging this buy but terrorist cells were not known for their honorable practices, and Paxton had been too smug. It only took him five minutes to discover a tracking device imbedded under the rubber tab on the end of the zipper like a small and vicious insect.

Over the years, David had cultivated relationships with criminals, convicts and members of underground extremist networks on all sides of every issue. He'd ferreted out secrets, sharing relevant ones with the world, holding others in abeyance for the right story at the right time. On assignment with fellow reporters over beers in bars when they were all far from home and exhausted, they'd argue the question of whether a free press encouraged or discouraged crimes by making them public. Regardless, their job was to expose the truth and David had done that job well enough to have three Pulitzers to show for it. Getting those stories he'd often been at risk. But never like this.

At least his arrangements to buy the Semtex were handled anonymously, which meant Paxton and his team at Global weren't tracking David Yalom, but rather a delivery of Semtex to a man who'd used a false identity. So on one front he might still be safe. But there was still Abdul to consider. Had Hans Wassong told the Palestinian anything or had he been acting on his own with plans to collect the bounty after the act was done? David had expected that he might run into adversity on this journey but so far he might have underestimated who would deliver the most dangerous threats.

An encroaching storm smudged the line that differentiated the hills from the horizon. The presence of a tracking device in the backpack suggested the absence of anyone in the near vicinity watching him. In such an isolated area, a tail would have been too easy to spot; the electronic trace was smarter.

Leaving the backpack in the car, David grabbed his empty cup, got out of the car and walked toward a refuse bin. Just as he passed a parked navy sedan that had a map opened on the dashboard, he tripped and the cup went flying, the dregs of the coffee spilling. Bending over, David was hidden from sight for a few seconds. When he stood he was holding the coffee cup, which he pitched into the wire mesh can.

Two minutes later he turned the key in the ignition on his rental car and pulled out of the lot and back onto the road. As he headed toward Vienna he imagined Paxton's men glued to a ground-penetrating radar screen watching a blip of light, riveted by the indicator, so pleased with themselves that they had their target in sight.

For the rest of the drive he checked his rearview mirror often to be certain no one was following him, almost wishing more than once that someone was and that they'd stop him and save him from the black bubble of rage before it made its next appearance.

Chapter 36

"It's not an accident that Sigmund Freud coined the phrase 'death mania' while living in Vienna," Jeremy told his daughter as they reached the gates of the Zentralfriedhof cemetery and he paused for a second, taking a deep breath before entering the city of the dead. "The Jewish section is this way." He pointed into the distance. They'd come directly from the funeral service, which had been well-attended and heartbreaking.

On both sides, the lane they walked down was bordered with fifteen-foot-tall arborvitae trees standing like feathery pyramids and through them Meer glimpsed the manicured lawns, sculptured monuments and the rising roofs of mausoleums. The air was rich with birdsong and the scent of evergreen. "This is a beautiful place," she whispered, surprised.

"Yes, quite different from other cemeteries in other countries, isn't it? Vienna's always had a preoccupation with death—dressing it up, writing music to it, commemorating it in art...there's even a museum devoted to it."

"What's in a museum devoted to death?"

"Grave-digger tools, coffins, funeral sashes, urns. The art of the undertaker through the ages. One of my favorites is the life-saving bell that's buried with you. If you find yourself being buried alive you can make sure your mourners hear you.

"Here we are," he said as he opened a rusty gate and she followed him into a rundown and overgrown area. Many of these tombstones had collapsed and fallen to rubble. Weeds overwhelmed whatever shrubbery had once been well tended. Compared to the rest of the cemetery, this was a slum.

"Why is it like this here?"

"There are several separate cemeteries sharing this one giant central space—Catholic, Protestant, Russian Orthodox and Jewish. All but the Jewish section have received uninterrupted care from the children of the children of the children of the dead." Jeremy stepped off the path to avoid pieces of a fallen tombstone. "Barely three thousand Austrian Jews even survived the war," he continued, "and afterward none returned to Vienna. So for more than sixty years, no one's been here to pay the rent on these graves or take care of them. Recently the government, partly in thanks to the effort Fremont Brecht's made, has pledged to restore our cemetery. What he's done for Austrian Jewry is astonishing. Fifteen years ago he was a well-respected public figure from a good Catholic family. And then he published a memoir called *Our Secret History* about Austria's deep-seated anti-Semitism and his own hidden Jewish heritage."

"How did he hide being Jewish for so long?"

"He didn't know until then, until his father died and he found out his birth mother, a Jewess, had died in childbirth and his father had remarried a gentile widow four months later. If not for the second marriage that covered up the past so conveniently, Fremont might have been sent to the camps when he was a boy."

"What was the reaction when the book came out?"

"It was a scandal. Shook a lot of people up. As he'd feared, there was a serious anti-Semitic reaction but it only made him more determined to work for Jewish reform, acceptance and restitution. And he has, tirelessly."

"But?"

He looked at her, questioning.

"You're not saying something, Dad. I can hear it in your voice."

Jeremy shrugged again. "It's a bone of contention between us. He believes keeping a contemporary and progressive face on modern Judaism is important in a country still accused of having anti-Semitic leanings."

"And you?"

"I think he's doing us a disservice. Our mysticism is an important and respected part of our religion."

They'd arrived at a cordoned-off plot where a recent grave had been dug but other than the gravediggers standing off to one side, smoking and waiting for the end of a service that had not even begun, no one was there. Jeremy spoke to them while Meer inspected the names and dates on decrepit stone markers nearby.

"We're too early," he said when he came back. "I'm always too early to burials. Afraid to keep the dead waiting, I guess." He looked around. "Come, we have time for me to show you where the great composers are and sculpture along the way. Maybe even some birdwatching. More than twenty-five species live here."

Soon they were out of the shambles and back into the extravagant landscaping. "An artist named André Heller called this place an aphrodisiac for necrophiles. Even for all its macabre attention, I think the way the Viennese deal with death is healthier than the way we deal with it in America," Jeremy said. "There, they try to sanitize dying. Bury it, no pun intended, as if it's something so dark and secretive it shouldn't even be examined. Here in Vienna it's the opposite. There's even a term for a beautiful corpse—*Schoene Leich.* It's an obsession that goes all the way back to the Hapsburgs and the crazy ideas they had about how to be interred. I'm afraid I'm being too morbid."

"You are, but what did the Hapsburgs do?"

Jeremy gave his daughter a wry smile. "Some call it the divide-and-conquer burial strategy. Their bodies are entombed in the Imperial Crypt in Kapuzinergruft church. Their intestines are in urns in St. Stephens. And their hearts are interred in small silver jars in the Herzgruft."

"The heart crypt?"

"You've heard of it?"

"Their mummified hearts are there?"

"Yes. It's a tourist destination. Not one of the major ones, but it draws the curious. Did you read about it?"

"I must have. Why are their intestines and their hearts separated from their bodies?"

"It started in the early 1600s with an emperor, I think Ferdinand IV, who wanted to lay his heart at the feet of the mother of God—"

"I'd like to see it," she interrupted.

"I might be able to get you in before it opens to the public tomorrow morning but I won't be able to go with you."

"I'll go by myself, it's fine. You know, I'm all grown up now and don't really need a babysitter."

"Actually, you do—two people are dead," he whispered harshly. "Inspector Fiske doesn't have a single lead. Serious professionals are at work here and they haven't made any mistakes. At least none that

the police have found. You have to promise me you won't go anywhere alone."

Meer's inclination was to argue, but she didn't.

"Maybe Sebastian can go with you. Or maybe I can rearrange the
time of my meeting to be there. I'll ask him. Maybe Malachai will
want to go, too. Especially if I can arrange for a private visit."

"How many babysitters do I need?" She smiled.

"No, I was just thinking that he'd like to see it."

On either side of them, taller evergreens cast dark, long
shadows over them.

"I didn't know you spoke German," Jeremy said after a long pause.

"What? I don't."

"You did this morning, when the fire alarm went off."

She shrugged. "I must have picked it up since I've been here."

"And on a whole block of buildings you knew exactly which one
was the Society."

"How could I? I've never been here before."

"This time."

"Dad." She spoke softly, making an effort to keep the rancor from
her voice, not completely succeeding. "Let's not have this conversation. Not here, not now."

"Sweetheart, you can't keep pretending the—"

"I'm not pretending. I've made a choice about how I want to live
my life so we can skip the lecture about the wheel of souls and the
angel of forgetfulness and the divine sparks of light and all the other
mystical reincarnation theories from the Kabbalah. You and Malachai
can talk about it when you see each other and I'm not in the room."
Even though she wasn't as certain as she usually was, Meer had fallen
back on the way she'd always responded to this argument, using half
her own words and half her mother's. It was the same fight she listened
to her parents have when she was supposed to be asleep and they

thought she couldn't hear them. Meer wondered how exactly she'd paraphrased her mother because her father looked so disquieted.

"Your mother made quite an impression on you, didn't she?" he said. "I wish I could convince you that great peace comes with believing."

She was about to disagree but he stopped her. "No, you're right. Not now. We should get back for the ceremony. If we take this path I can still show you what I brought you here to see."

The sound of their individual footsteps on the walkway marked the physical and emotional distance between them and they continued on in silence for a few hundred meters until they reached a small plot of grass with an iron grill in front of it. Surrounded by conical evergreens, the white obelisk reached skyward, simple and yet majestic. On the frontispiece was a one-word name in gothic black letters. The sorrow stabbed quickly as Meer realized she was looking at Beethoven's gravestone. Her mouth was dry and so were her eyes, but she felt sad and hollow.

Her father waited a few minutes and then said, "We should go now."

Passing stone markers as they walked back, Jeremy pointed out Johannes Brahms' and then Franz Schubert's resting places.

As they passed the beautiful monuments to lives lived and people lost, Meer noticed the occasional bunch of flowers in front of a grave—usually at the resting place of someone famous. Her mother had once told her that a person never really died as long as someone still loved them.

"All the great Austrians are buried here. Architects, politicians, artists, writers—quite a few Memorists here too. I think if we stay on this path we might pass..." Her father stopped at a monument of a male angel with beautifully detailed wings. "Yes, here it is." The grief on the statue's face was so genuine, Meer was riveted by him and the way his hand rested on the tombstone he guarded, as if it were a living being he loved, not an inanimate object.

"Whose grave is this?" she asked.

"The wife of the Society's most important founder," he said, then read the inscription on the tombstone. "Margaux Neidermier, 1779–1814. A world of memory will forever sound in this one mournful, golden chord."

Chapter 37

"Be careful," the client on the other end of the phone warned him for the third time.

Paul Pertzler was annoyed. Since he'd been hired, this client had lectured him as if he were a clumsy oaf. He'd stolen the Beethoven letter and the antique gaming box but he couldn't be trusted to touch the precious items? Moving the camera, he aimed it away from the box onto an empty section of the wall, careful not to reveal anything identifying.

"I've lost the picture." The voice on the other end was restrained but frustrated.

Smiling to himself, Pertzler just waited.

"Are you there? I said I've lost the picture."

Pertzler thought about cutting the computer connection that allowed him to speak to the buyer and simultaneously show the item.

"What are you doing?" the voice demanded.

Even paying top dollar didn't buy his employer the right to be rude. "Where's the camera?"

Repositioning the camera, Pertzler angled it back on the gaming box. "Computer glitch, so sorry."

"I've seen enough of the outside, let's go inside," the client said. "We need to check that everything's intact. Give us an overview first, if you will."

Pertzler panned the contents, slowly moving the camera over each small compartment.

"Now, please show us the whist markers close up."

Pertzler stared down at the various gaming pieces without any idea which ones were whist markers. He didn't like the buyer's attitude and would prefer not to ask what whist markers looked like.

"Those chips made of mother of pearl. To your right."

Moving the camera right, Pertzler zoomed in and wondered if the "we" that the buyer used was a figure of speech or a ruse to give the impression there was a group involved instead of an individual. Pertzler knew better than to indulge in speculation like this. He was good at his job because he didn't get distracted wondering about irrelevancies. Except he'd made mistakes on this job. Two people were dead. A shame for several reasons but especially because the dead attracted the authorities in a way that stolen goods didn't.

"Now, show us the cribbage board, that's a scorekeeping device for a card game that dates back to the 1600s. We didn't see it in the overview but it should be there. It's probably made of bone or wood and has many holes in it."

"I think this is it, no?" Pertzler adjusted the light so it illuminated the left corner and then moved the camera across the surface of an ivory object yellowed with age.

"Wonderful. Now there are four decks of cards, with gold edges. Can we look at each one of those more closely?"

One after another, Pertzler focused the camera on each deck.

"I'm afraid this is going to get a bit tedious, but I need you to go through each deck with us. Show us the front and back of every card. We're going to be freezing the frames and keeping them as static shots."

"It's your time. You've paid for it."

The buyer was amused and chortled. "So we have, so we have."

The process took the better part of the next two hours and was, as his client suggested it would be, laborious.

"All right then," the client said finally. "We're done."

"Where would you like your items delivered?"

"For now we'd like you to hold tight to both the gaming box and the letter you found in Geneva. Is that possible? We expect you can keep it as safely as anyone else."

Pertzler specialized in marital assets recovery. Typically, that meant stealing jewelry and artwork back from husbands who preferred their exes not keep all the spoils, or wives who wanted a family heirloom to remain on her side of the family. It was highly unusual for a client, or the group of clients, to ask him to keep possessions.

"For how long?"

"A week. No more. We would also like to know if you also do surveillance work?"

"I do, yes."

"We are going to need you to start right away."

They discussed money, agreed to a price, and then the buyer described who they wanted followed and how and when they'd be calling in for updates as well as a number to call in case of emergencies. "Leave a message, if it's necessary to get in touch with us."

"What would constitute an emergency?"

"Use your judgment."

After ending the marathon call with that enigmatic coda, the client hung up. Pertzler rose from his desk and stretched the way his cat did after waking up from a long sleep in the sun. She sat watching him from the couch. A black cat with white markings. The apartment smelled musty from all the cigarettes he'd smoked while he was on the phone and he opened the window, standing there for a few moments, watching the sun sinking below the horizon. This time of day always depressed him and he went into the kitchen and cut a thick slice of a chocolate cake he'd bought the day before but his cell phone rang just before he could take the first bite.

Pertzler had two phones, one on which he accepted incoming calls but never used to call out and the other, which he used to call out but never shared the number.

"Hello?"

"Hi. Are we still going to the cinema tonight?"

Pertzler recognized Klempt's voice. No salutations were necessary. It was safer this way for both of them. A brief discussion ensued about what movies were playing. The two men decided on the seven-o'clock showing of Alfred Hitchcock's *Rope* and planned on meeting at the theater a half hour before to get a beer at a nearby tavern.

It was the kind of conversation no one paid attention to if they happened to overhear it but if someone had been listening and checked the movie theaters they would have discovered there were no Hitchcock films playing in all of Vienna that night. So there would be no way to figure out which theater the two men were meeting at, if they were meeting at a theater at all.

They didn't, in fact, meet at a theater, but at the Hummer bar. If they'd said they were going to see a Godard movie they would have met at the bar called the Guess Club II. If they'd chosen a Fellini film it would have been the Fledermaus and so forth. There were ten bars coded, so they could avoid being seen at the same one too often.

Klempt was already nursing a beer when Pertzler arrived.

"I got a call about a freelance job," Klempt reported after some small talk. A computer hacker and corporate espionage specialist, he and Pertzler worked together often, availing each other of their specific expertise.

"Will it pay well?"

"Very well."

"You want another?" Pertzler asked, noticing Klempt's empty tankard.

He checked his watch. "My wife...I'd better not."

Pertzler made a joke about his friend being under his wife's thumb and the two laughed.

Only there was no wife. It was more code they'd perfected over the past fifteen years of working together. If they erred on the side of being too careful, it served them well.

Out on the street they headed toward the same subway station and only then, after they were both sure they weren't being followed, did Pertzler ask about the job.

"I have a client who would like to hire you to find something that has been lost," Klempt said.

"Lost?"

The light changed and even though there was little traffic, they stopped at the curb.

"Interesting word, no? The client said lost. I questioned him and asked if it had been stolen. He said he preferred lost."

"Sounds like a fruitcake."

Klempt shrugged. "Lost. Stolen. It doesn't matter. I need you to steal it back."

"How much?"

Klempt named a substantial five-figure sum.

Pertzler nodded. "Do you have a photograph?"

Klempt pulled an envelope from his pocket.

"Good night," Pertzler said, taking it and walking off in the opposite direction.

Fifteen minutes later, back in his kitchen, Pertzler opened the envelope and found page 16 from the Dorotheum auction house catalog. All the information he needed was written in the margins but he wasn't reading the words, he was staring at the photograph.

Page 16 showed an antique gaming box, circa 1790. The very same one that he had been hired to steal last week.

That he had stolen. And that was in his living room, right now.

Chapter 38

As the silver-and-navy Smart Car sped along the Graben, Inspector Alex Kalfus, dressed in civilian khaki pants, white shirt and a blue windbreaker that had seen better days, navigated with his right hand while smoking with his left. There was a Van Gogh portrait hanging in Amsterdam of a farmer who had the same curious expression on his face, Lucian Glass thought. Amazing how much of a man's soul could be captured in rough strokes and applied color. There was a rough scar on Kalfus's neck running from behind his ear down to his collarbone. So, the Austrian detective was a traveler on the same rough road Lucian had been stuck on his whole adult life.

Hanging a left, Kalfus drove into traffic, cursed and blew smoke out the window but the wind pushed it back into the car and Lucian inhaled it. He wanted to bum a cigarette off the Austrian, could already imagine how satisfying the first drag would be…except all it took to be a smoker again was one cigarette.

"I'm coming up to a corner," Kalfus prompted.

Checking the monitor built into the briefcase open on his lap, Lucian directed him to take a right turn at the next light. "As long as this surveillance equipment's performing properly," he added.

After landing that morning, Lucian had hooked up with Kalfus and together they'd waited an hour for Malachai Samuels to arrive from New York. From the minute the reincarnationist walked off the plane, picked up his luggage and got into a limo, the two lawmen had been tracking him. Lucian preferred working with his own team but the Austrian government had insisted this was the only way they'd allow the FBI to work on their soil.

"And now a left," Lucian said.

Kalfus made the turn. A few blocks later another left and then a right. "I know where he's headed now. This is the way to Jeremy Logan's house which makes sense since you said he'd come here to see what Logan found."

"And lost," Lucian agreed.

For the last hour Lucian and Kalfus had filled each other in on the actual criminal activity and suspected criminal activity that had put them both on the same case.

"How did you plant the bug?" Kalfus asked.

"We had a few men take over airport security during the hours before the flight and when Samuels went through the screening process, one pulled him out of the line to check out why he set off the machines—which bought us some time. While he was being inspected, an agent inserted the transistor chip inside his billfold."

"He won't find it?"

"It's microscopic and hidden inside a seam."

"You have been doing surveillance on this man for how long now?"

"Nine months."

"So even if Langley's techniques are state-of-the-art, their efforts to find any hard evidence against Malachai have failed?"

"Not *their* efforts…*my* efforts. It's been my case and I'm its last lone crusader."

"Why haven't you given up by now?"

"The man is a psychologist and amateur illusionist. He understands how to misdirect and manipulate. It's more than just making coins disappear or disguising himself, he tricks everyone. I refuse to allow him to trick me."

"Has he been calling many people here in the last few days?"

"Jeremy Logan several times and your ex-minister of defense, Fremont Brecht, twice. We think Brecht and Logan are members of the same Society. The Memorist Society. A small, nonpolitical organization with no criminal associations as far as we can determine. Originally it was formed as an offshoot of the Freemasons."

"Here in Vienna?" Kalfus sounded miffed that the American was telling him something he didn't know about his own city.

"There's no reason for you to be aware of it, it's deep under the radar."

"And how does all this relate to this weekend's murder and the robberies?"

"Based on what we heard on our phone taps, the Society was going to bid on the gaming box and Malachai was negotiating to go in on that purchase with them, in exchange for unlimited access to the object. But it's possible he was only saying that to get information from them and that he was behind the robberies. If that's true, then following Malachai could lead us to the antique and the letter or to whoever has them. If it's not true, we know he wants them and has the money to buy them on the black market if they're for sale, which could also lead us to the antiques or whoever has them."

"You seem certain one way or another he's connected to what's gone on here."

Lucian nodded. He'd seen determination in Malachai's eyes that was almost maniacal but he didn't say that. Looking away from the monitor, he glanced out the window at the passing buildings, wondering what it would be like to actually spend a few hours being a tourist here.

"Instincts are important," Kalfus said.

"What do you have so far in your investigation?" Lucian asked.

"Many details. Many suppositions. No tangible evidence. No mistakes on the thieves' part," Kalfus complained.

"No obvious mistakes, you mean."

Kalfus shrugged. Lucian noted the Austrian did that often and wondered if it was the way he got rid of the uncertainty that every law enforcer and investigator lived with.

"The question I've never gotten a good answer to is how come it's so easy for us to see those mistakes in retrospect?" Lucian said.

"Self-deprecating? It's not a personality trait I associate with American FBI agents."

"Left up ahead."

Conversation came to a halt as Kalfus reached the corner, turned and they both watched the black Mercedes at the end of the block as it slowed down and parked.

Kalfus shifted the car into idle in front of number 59: a white stucco house with black shutters, while in front of number 83 Kirchengasse, a uniformed chauffeur got out of the car, went around to the passenger side, opened the door and helped the passenger out.

The front door opened and a tall man with tousled hair walked down to the curb to greet his visitor. "Is that Jeremy Logan?" Lucian asked.

"Yes."

Logan put his arms around Malachai then Meer stepped forward and embraced him.

Kalfus put the car into Drive and slowly made his way down the street toward number 83. "That's Jeremy's daughter, Meer Logan," Kalfus explained. "The gaming box was pulled out of her arms during the tear gas attack."

"Do you have surveillance tapes of what happened at the auction house?"

"There are tapes but the smoke bombs make it impossible to see anything helpful."

Kalfus hadn't told him if Meer was hurt but Lucian didn't bother to ask. By now they were driving by and Lucian could see her clearly. She didn't look physically hurt but he had the distinct impression that she was even more troubled than the last time he saw her.

It must have been the jet lag that made him suddenly more tired than he could remember feeling for a long time. A bone-tired exhaustion that he imagined would take years to recover from. Kalfus was asking him something that required a response but Lucian had no idea what the Inspector had been saying for the last minute or two. That must have been the jet lag, too.

Chapter 39

Sitting in the living room, Jeremy poured wine while he briefed Malachai on the details of what had transpired, starting with the robbery in Geneva and ending with the one at the Dorotheum. Malachai listened, sipped from the cut-crystal glass, nodded and then when Jeremy finished, asked Meer, "Now, tell me what's been happening to you?"

She hesitated.

"It's understandable that after all these years of not believing, what's occurring is disturbing, but it will help if you can talk about it. Meer, tell me."

She recounted what transpired then and also what happened during the second episode when she was with Sebastian in Beethoven's apartment. And then what happened at the cemetery.

"Did you already know the woman in the memory lurches was named Margaux before you found the tombstone?" Malachai asked.

She nodded.

"Margaux's husband found the flute in India and then died there," Jeremy explained.

The icy bands were encircling her, tugging at her, trying to pull her into their vortex. Meer put her head down in her hands and felt a tsunami of sorrow come over her.

"No!" Meer almost shouted. "He's alive. In India. That's why I need to raise the money. To fund a search party to find him." She missed Caspar. Missed a man whose name she never knew before Sunday. A man she would sacrifice everything for if she could just find him and save him and bring him back to her.

Then from a distance she heard her father's voice breaking through.

"Malachai—stop. Look at what this is doing to her."

"This is important, Jeremy. She's remembering."

"No!" Jeremy raised his voice in anger but Malachai ignored his friend and was talking to her again.

"Margaux, what's happening?"

She made an effort and reached down into the blackness to find the answer. "Beethoven had the flute and was trying to figure out the melody from the markings carved into the bone."

Even from inside the icy fog, Meer was surprised. The carvings were the key to the song?

"Do you know if Beethoven found the song?"

It was dark again. A familiar darkness worse than any of the memories. When she was a child, this was the darkness that surrounded that one memory that repeated over and over—a woman on horseback wearing a man's coat, racing through the woods in a storm while being followed. She could hear the sounds of the horse's breathing and the rain and smell the wet wool of her coat. But then the scene would fade to black and leave her enveloped by this same force field of sadness.

"Margaux?" Malachai asked.

"Enough, Malachai," Jeremy insisted.

Malachai half turned to respond. "If this flute really does still exist and if we can confirm Margaux Neidermier was studying with Beethoven at that time—"

"You don't have to bother Meer for that. I can confirm she was a student of Beethoven's during 1814. I searched through a database of his letters when we came back from the cemetery this afternoon and she's referenced several times."

The cold was disappearing and the shivering stopped. Meer was listening to her father explain about Margaux's studying with Beethoven.

"Did you find out anything else about her?" Malachai asked.

"I don't have access to the complete letters. The database only gives me highlights but she first appears in a letter dated September of 1814."

This was what it had been like when she was a child and under their constant scrutiny—a discussion topic and not a person at all. She stood up. "I can't listen to any more of this now. I need a break."

"Of course you do," Malachai said. "We all need a break."

Meer heard the concern in his voice but she also heard the hope...always hope. She looked at her father. Despite himself, the same hope shone in his eyes.

Chapter 40

Monday, April 28th—8:50 p.m.

Monday, April 28th—8:50 p.m.

"I can't see how far down the shaft goes." The American's words echoed in the underground chamber.

David sucked in his breath. What was going on? There hadn't been any music coming from the concert hall tonight: no performance, no rehearsals. Only the occasional scurrying of a rat or a rock falling. And now suddenly these voices were reaching him down in the crypt from men who sounded as if they were deeper and closer than could be possible.

"Let me send down a probe," a second voice, also American, responded. "See if we can hit bottom."

Were these men working for Global Security? Part of Tom Paxton's effort to look for trouble before it showed itself? How far down were they?

David glanced over at the cage he'd brought into the cave with him tonight and the three rats he'd already beguiled into the trap.

"Any luck with that reading? What's going on?" the American called out.

David pulled on the heavy gloves. If his plan worked the rat would offer an explanation for any infrared patterns that might show up on Global Security's monitors. He knew from his interview with Paxton that their GPR system was not only generations more sophisticated than the ground-penetrating radar first used in the Viet Cong tunnels, but the most sophisticated equipment available. The basic methodology was so commonplace now everyone used it, from crime scene investigators searching for graves to construction companies investigating sites before building. Of course Paxton, a man obsessed with winning, would have the most advanced system available. In every news story David had written about the security business, in the war against terror, Global was consistently far ahead of the rest in innovation and results.

"This shaft must go down into some sewer system," the American called out. "I'm past twelve meters and still dropping."

David looked at his watch. Ten to nine. Why were those bastards still working? But he knew the answer—because that's what Paxton demanded.

"Can you get down any deeper and shine some light down there?"

"The opening's too narrow," the first man's voice echoed. "No way."

David imagined the man trying to lower himself down the shaft that ran perpendicular to where he was hiding. But he'd looked through the cracks and knew it wasn't even large enough for a child to fit in. From what Wassong had told him and from the blueprints David had found, it was part of an archaic turn-of-the-century heating system, long ago abandoned but still in place.

Reaching into the cage, he grabbed one of the rats and shoved the vermin through the narrow crack in the rock wall that separated his hiding space from the shaft. David could hear the rat scurrying up the wall. He waited.

"I'm getting a reading here that I don't like." The American sounded alarmed.

David imagined the Global employee noticing the activity on his monitor and checking his diagnostics. They were seeing the rat. He was sure of it. But what if the system had other sensors? Could it be detecting the Semtex he'd picked up in Czechoslovakia? No, he reasoned, he was using the older type that had virtually no radioactive material they could detect.

"You sure there's no way you can shimmy down any farther?" one American called out to the other.

David opened the cage and pulled out another rat: the biggest one this time, and as he did, the creature sank his teeth into David's hand. It didn't tear through the glove but he still felt the pressure of the sharp little fangs. He didn't waste any breath cursing it as he released it; he owed the rat only thanks for playing its part as a diversion. He wondered if on Thursday night when the last notes of Beethoven's symphony rang out, any of the rats would survive.

Chapter 41

The virtues we acquire, which develop slowly within us, are the invisible links that bind each one of our existences to the others—existences which the spirit alone remembers, for Matter has no memory for spiritual things.
— *Honoré de Balzac*

Vienna, Austria
Tuesday, April 29th—9:20 a.m.

Across the street from the Riding School, the Hofburg's complex of high baroque imperial court buildings dwarfed the nondescript fourteenth-century church where they were headed. The line was very short; only about ten people were waiting for the crypt to open its doors to the public at 10:00 a.m.

Meer and Malachai, who'd walked over together from the hotel, bypassed the queue and continued toward Jeremy, who stood with Sebastian just outside the front door. It was strange that Sebastian kept showing up, even though her father had said he'd ask him to come.

Spotting them, her father waved. He'd arranged for a private tour before the church opened and now that they were all there, ushered them inside.

The Gothic structure's exterior didn't prepare Meer for the elegant interior. Light streamed down from immense brass chandeliers, illuminating the enormous hallway, naves and aisles, and a tiny monk who was slowly approaching. Jeremy introduced Brother Francis, explaining that the monk didn't speak English.

Following the brown-robed figure, the group crossed the church and entered the Loreto Chapel, a diminutive whitewashed space. The ceilings here were arched but lower, the altar simpler and unadorned. The light-toned pews looked more inviting than the darker ones in the main sanctuary and Meer thought that if she were someone who prayed, it would be easier to reach out to God in this intimate space.

To the right of the miniature altar was a seven-foot skeleton painted on a darkened wall who appeared to be guarding two iron doors decorated with crowns and swans. Brother Francis waited beside this grillwork for the group to assemble. As Meer stepped up an invasion of cold air blew around her. Through the bars she saw two shelves lined with dozens of silver chalices and urns shimmering in the light flooding through the windows. The heart crypt.

Brother Francis fit a black key into the lock, and then had to force it to turn as if the entryway was reluctant to allow anyone through. Finally, with a sweep of his arm, he gestured for them to enter as he doled out facts about what they were seeing.

Jeremy translated: "There are fifty-four hearts here. All from the Imperial Family..."

The urns shone brightly, glints of silver refracting off their rounded bodies, mesmerizing her. Everything else in the room was unimportant; these urns were what she had come to see. Her father had just told them all how many there were but Meer started to count them again. Not sure why.

One. Two. Three. Four. Five. Six. Seven. Eight. Nine.

The ninth urn appeared to shine more brightly than all the others, she thought, as she stared at it and stopped hearing anything her father was saying. She had to figure out how to get closer to it, even though she didn't have any idea why or what she was looking for.

"Do you speak any English?" she asked the monk—although her father had told her otherwise.

"English? Not good, no," he said in a heavy accent.

Meer nodded. She needed to be sure. "No English?"

Brother Francis shook his head.

Meer walked to her father and pointed to a plaque on the far right of the top shelf while she whispered a question, low enough not to interrupt the monk's continued recitation. When Brother Francis finished talking, so did Meer.

Jeremy was a few seconds late in translating but somehow had managed to hear what both the monk and his daughter had said. "The first heart here belongs to King Ferdinand IV of the Romans. It was placed here on July 19th in 1654. The last heart belonged to Franz Karl of Austria, and it was placed here on the 8th of March in 1878."

Moving as close as she could to the shelf, Meer counted once more to be sure, from right to left, stopping again at the ninth urn and straining to read the inscription carved into a small brass plaque beneath it. In German, all she could make out were the words *Marie Theresa* and the date *1696*.

The diminutive silver urn sat on ball feet. Around its rim were three rows of hearts, the point of one fitting in the space where the two halves met on the one below. Hearts all around. The object was slightly lopsided and in some places there were faint dents. *The ninth urn*. The deck of cards she'd had time to examine from the gaming box had two nines of hearts in it. *An extra nine of hearts.* What did it mean? Did all the decks have double cards? Would she ever be able to find out?

"Do you think they got the idea to do this from the Egyptians?" Meer asked her father. Her voice sounded a false note but she hoped no one noticed. Jeremy began answering and then his voice faltered. He stopped speaking. And then he fell to the stone floor.

"Dad?" Meer dropped down to her knees next to him, grabbing his wrist to take his pulse. "He needs a doctor," she cried.

"*Dringlichkeit, dringlichkeit,*" Sebastian shouted, and the monk rushed off.

Chapter 42

Meer's terrified expression morphed into one of deep concentration as soon as the monk ran off to get help. She couldn't waste a second explaining what was happening to Sebastian or Malachai so while they worried over Jeremy's supine form, she got up and rushed over to the ninth silver urn on the top shelf and without any deliberation opened it and reached inside. There was no time to inspect the mummified relics that were almost four hundred years old, no time to be concerned about desecrating the remains of this royal personage.

What was left of the human heart felt like a piece of dried fruit, shriveled and leathery, but under it, Meer's fingers found something smooth and chilly. Tiny. She didn't think about what it was or what she was supposed to do with it. Didn't stop to be amazed that she'd intuited there was something waiting there for her.

Slipping the object into her jeans pocket, she returned to her father and dropped to her knees slightly to the right of Sebastian, not sure if either he or Malachai had noticed what she'd done.

A few minutes later the paramedics rushed into the small room and set about saving her father's life.

Chapter 43

Parked on the street, inside the small silver-and-black car, Lucian Glass and Alex Kalfus watched the sequence of events outside the church: an ambulance pulled up, a monk rushed out to greet it and paramedics hurried inside.

Lucian ached to run inside and see for himself what was going on. Used to moving around on a case, he hated just watching but he wasn't on home turf and this was the best he could get the Austrian authorities to agree to. As he watched, he realized he was unexpectedly and surprisingly anxious. While Kalfus stayed on the phone trying to get information about what was happening, the medics exited the church carrying someone on a stretcher. Sebastian and Malachai accompanied them.

"Can you see who they're carrying? Jeremy or his daughter?"

"Not from here," Kalfus said, still holding on his call.

Then the church doors opened and Meer walked out, her skin pale, her black hair in disarray.

Kalfus clicked his phone shut. "Jeremy Logan collapsed. Early indications suggest a heart attack."

Sirens screaming, the ambulance took off and a policeman helped Meer into a waiting squad car that took off almost immediately, leaving Sebastian and Malachai standing on the sidewalk beside the distraught monk. The men exchanged a few words and then walked off together.

Lucian watched them stop at the taxi stand on the corner and get in line behind an elderly woman carrying a large bouquet of tulips. It only took a minute until she got in her taxi and another pulled up. The two men got in. As their cab pulled away Kalfus pulled out after it. "I'm going to guess we'll be going to the hospital now."

"And I'd guess you're right. What I'd really like to know is what they were looking at in there. Can you call in someone to stay on Malachai's tail if he does go to the hospital so we can come back here and talk to that monk?"

"Should be possible."

"My next two questions are, who is the man halfway up the block in the blue Mercedes who's been watching the church along with us and will he be joining the entourage to the hospital? Correction. Three questions. And if he does, who in particular is he keeping tabs on?"

"What man?"

Lucian wasn't proud that he'd noticed the man reading a newspaper in his car and Kalfus hadn't. In fact, he'd prefer if Kalfus had spotted him first; it would give Lucian more confidence in his new partner. "He pulled up right after we did," Lucian explained, "just parked and then stayed in his car. He made two phone calls, checked his watch and then read his newspaper. He continued checking his watch every three minutes as if he was waiting for someone but I'm pretty sure the only person he was waiting for was whichever one of the group inside the church he was following."

Chapter 44

Tuesday, April 29th—9:49 a.m.

The monk remained on the street, watching the procession of ambulance and police cars disappear. He hardly noticed the man in the ordinary gray suit, until he came right up to him. "Excuse me, Brother," he said in German as he held out a badge and identification card.

The monk glanced down at the silver shield that identified the man as a member of the state police, and nodded.

"I'd like to discuss what just happened here."

"I've already talked to the police," Brother Francis said in a bewildered tone, confused by how many officials were involved in the small emergency.

"Yes, I know that, and I'm sorry but I'm from the Department of Antiquities and I also need to make a report since this is a national site."

With resignation the monk repeated what he'd seen. "A man had what seemed to be a heart attack in the chapel."

"What were they doing in the church before it opened?"

"Like everyone else, they came to visit with God and to see the crypt."

"I'd like to look around the crypt if you don't mind."

"It was a medical emergency. There was no altercation, no accident, nothing to do with the chapel."

"I'm sure it was. Now, if it wouldn't be too much trouble could you show me where this happened? And please keep the tourists out until I'm finished. I'll be gone in a few minutes."

Reluctantly, but not sure he had any choice, the monk led the policeman through the main church across the nave, into the Loreto Chapel, over to the disconcerting skeleton barring the way to the entrance, and then into the inner chamber.

Like many natives of Vienna, including members of the state police who he was impersonating, Paul Pertzler didn't know as much as he should about the tourist destinations in his native city and didn't know why this chapel was important.

"Could you explain what I'm looking at? And as you do, please point out anything out of place or missing. Take your time, Brother."

"This vault belonged to the Imperial Family. These are their remains." Pausing, the monk walked up to one of the shelves, focused on a specific urn, reached out, moved it slightly to the left and back a half an inch.

"Their ashes are in those urns?"

"No, their hearts."

"Hearts?" Pertzler repeated, staring at the small silver urns. "How long have they been putting their hearts here?"

"Since the early seventeenth century."

"And when was the last heart buried here? Is it even buried? What do you call it?"

"The last heart was *placed* here in 1878."

"How many are there?"

"Fifty-four hearts."

Pertzler made a note. Then he remembered something. "Is Beethoven's heart here?"

The monk looked startled but answered confidently. "No. Only members of the Imperial Family."

"But something about my question struck you. What is it?"

"It's funny you would ask about Beethoven. One of the members of Mr. Logan's party asked about him too."

"Who? Which member of the party? What did he ask?"

"The man from America asked if there was a record of Beethoven having anything to do with this church."

"And is there?"

"Yes," the monk said proudly. "The connection comes through one of Beethoven's closest friends—his student and his principal benefactor, the Archduke Rudolf, youngest son of the Austro-Hungarian Emperor Leopold II. He gave Beethoven rooms in the royal palace to rehearse and perform. What not many remember is that the Archduke was also a priest, and as this church is part of the Hofburg, it was one of the places of worship where he held mass. Because of that connection, Beethoven, who spent a lot of time at the palace, performed sections of his 'Missa Solemnis' here two years before he'd completed it. When he did finally finish the piece in 1823 he dedicated it to Rudolf and inscribed the manuscript with the words, 'From my heart—to your heart.'"

"Yet more hearts."

"Many hearts," repeated the monk, smiling a little.

"Now back to this room and the urns. Are you sure you don't notice anything missing or out of place?"

"Nothing missing. Nothing out of place, no."

"Why did you move that one when we came in?" He pointed.

"It was off its mark by an inch."

"Is it possible a member of the Logan party touched it?"

"I don't think so."

"Could you check? Could you look inside?"

The monk frowned. "The mummified hearts are considered holy."

"I understand. But I'd like you to look inside."

The monk hesitated.

"It's necessary, Brother."

Crossing himself first, the monk walked back up to the shelf and lifted the lid of the ninth chalice and peered inside.

Pertzler came up behind him and looked over his shoulder at the dark brown mass: a rotted heart nesting in its silver casket. What were Logan and his daughter doing here in the Heart Vault? What was he missing?

Chapter 45

As Meer traveled from the elevator down the long hospital corridor checking the numbers on the doors of the rooms, she tried not to look inside as she passed. She didn't want to spy on strangers suffering in their sickbeds, helpless to shut their doors if nurses had left them open. Their fear and distress would stay with her for days if she glimpsed it because she knew too well what they felt. Though she'd only been nine, the long weeks she spent lying, immobilized in a bed, unable to protect herself from the prying eyes of the people passing by her room, were seared in her memory.

The door to room 316 was open wide enough to reveal a white-coated doctor standing beside her father's bed. The woman's back was to Meer so she couldn't see the expression on her face but her tone sounded serious—too serious for a situation her father had manufactured on the spur of the moment.

"Excuse me," Meer said from the doorway.

The doctor turned, annoyance clearly visible on her face, and said something in German that Meer didn't understand.

Jeremy sat up straighter in the bed, spoke to the doctor in German and then to Meer. "Come in, sweetheart. This is Dr. Lintell. Dr. Lintell, this is my daughter."

Now the doctor offered a smile. "Hello," she said, extending her hand.

Meer shook it and asked, "How is my father?" Even though she knew nothing was really wrong, she needed to keep up the charade.

"We need to run some more tests."

Surprised, but trying not to show it, Meer looked over at her father. "Tests? Why?"

Jeremy smiled. "Even though the doctor thinks it was just an anxiety attack she wants to torture me a bit more."

Meer didn't understand. She and her father had planned his attack in the crypt during a minute-long whispered conversation after she'd realized—suddenly amazingly known— there was a clue buried in the crypt and where it was. She'd asked her father if he could distract the monk so she could search for it. A panic attack, her father had whispered back, and she'd understood. He'd done it before, and it had been one of her favorite bedtime stories…how he'd outsmarted a border guard in East Germany by faking a heart attack that was then diagnosed as a panic attack. All without arousing suspicion.

"He told you he's had panic attacks before, hasn't he?" Meer asked the doctor.

The doctor nodded.

"How many tests do you have to give him for anxiety?"

"Actually we need to rule out some other possibilities, too." She was very brusque. Not cold, but not offering up one word more than was necessary. Meer wasn't sure if this was a Germanic trait or a bad bedside manner.

There was a third possibility too.

"Dad, is there something really wrong?"

He laughed in that reassuring way of his that made the most monumental problem appear under control. That laugh was one of the things she missed the most when he moved out of the apartment when she was twelve. That laugh, and the relief she felt when she swam in its wake. "No, sweetheart. There's nothing really wrong. The tests are all routine, isn't that right, Doctor?"

The doctor responded to him tersely in German. And he replied, but also in German.

All her life Meer had hated secrets. Her mother used to catch her listening on phone extensions, hiding behind doors eavesdropping, always trying to find out what they weren't telling her. There was so much they hid. So much her own mind hid from her. Images and sounds wrapped up in blankets of fog, memories just beyond reach.

Meer wondered if it was her imagination but her father seemed frailer here, as if the last hour had sucked the energy out of him. After the doctor left she was about to question him again but was interrupted when Sebastian and Malachai came in.

"Are you all right? What happened in the crypt?" Sebastian asked.

"You were with the doctor for a while," Malachai said. "What's the prognosis?"

Jeremy explained that Meer needed some time to look inside one of the urns and he'd faked the attack to draw attention away from her. "Even so, I have to stay for some tests. I'm at that age when they won't just let me out of here without making sure every part of me is working right. In the meantime, we need to figure out what Meer found, what it means, and what we need to do next."

Meer understood why her father included Malachai in this effort but not Sebastian. She glanced over at him and found him watching her and met his eyes. Once again she felt that push-pull of being both drawn to him and repelled at the same time. Comforted to see him. Frightened that he was there. She turned to Malachai. "What did you say?"

"I asked you what you took." His ebony eyes were gleaming with anticipation.

Reaching into her pocket, Meer pulled out the object she'd extracted from the ninth silver chalice in the Heart Vault. No more than an inch long, it was made of tarnished metal, silver perhaps, pitted with black. She examined the small tube that had a hole in the top and one notch on the side. There were no other markings on it and it was cold to the touch, a cold that traveled through her fingertips, up her arms, down her neck, across her back. As she shivered, the small object trembled in the palm of her hand.

"What is that?" Sebastian asked.

"Did you know you were looking for a key when you went down there?" Malachai asked.

"No. I had no idea."

"Do you have any idea what it's for?" he asked.

She shook her head.

"We have to figure out what the key's for but we aren't going to be able to do that from here," Jeremy said. "Sebastian, are you free today? Can you help?"

"I have to go to the Musikverein for a rehearsal for Thursday's performance but not until seven."

Jeremy was perplexed. "I don't have tickets for Thursday night?"

Sebastian explained and then looked at Malachai. "If you'd like to come also I think I can get one more ticket. I'd be pleased to have you as my guest. We're doing Beethoven's *Eroica*."

"I'd love it," Malachai said enthusiastically.

Meer wasn't listening anymore. Hearing the maestro's name she was visualizing his tombstone yesterday. And Margaux's.

"Are you remembering something?" Malachai asked.

Meer heard the desperate searching in his voice, the leitmotif of her childhood. Malachai and her father, trying to sever what they believed was the membrane that kept her past from spilling into her present. "You've worked with thousands of children," she said to him. "Haven't they given you enough chances to find the proof you want?"

"A memory tool would be validation of a very different kind."

"If there really is a such a thing, how would it work?" Sebastian asked. "Do you imagine the sound of the music will be enough to bring back someone's memory?"

"That's what the legends claim," Malachai answered. "Either the music or the vibrations made when the flute is played."

"And if there was an actual physical way to manipulate time like that would it work with the more recent past too, or just the deep past?"

Meer understood what Sebastian was asking, even if Malachai didn't. He was wondering if the flute might be able to help his son, Nicolas. She could tell from the shift in his voice, the desperation under the words. Sebastian was scavenging for information that might enable him to help his child. She wished she could aid him too but she was thirty-one years old and hadn't yet been able to help herself.

She shivered and this time the cold was like a blizzard of emotion, freezing her own heart. The taste of metal filled her mouth. Her father and Malachai and Sebastian were shimmering as if they were no longer solid forms. *No, not here, not now,* she thought as she tried to stop the images from forming in her mind, but they were coming too fast and with too much force.

Chapter 46

Vienna, Austria
October 18th, 1814

Across the room the Tsar caught Margaux's eye and smiled disarmingly. There were two men standing in front of him but the monarch towered over them, so while they believed they had his full attention, he was able to play his eye games with Margaux.

Even though the salon buzzed with conversation and the string quartet's delightful music, nothing lessened the underlying note of sadness that played for Margaux no matter where she was, what she was doing or who was flirting with her.

The more lovely the moment, the more aware she was of Caspar's plight and the more desperate her mission became. How much longer could she afford to wait? Day after day, she visited Herr Beethoven and witnessed his continual inability to decipher the memory song while Caspar languished in some unimaginable monastery on another continent. How ill was he? Would he survive until she raised the money? How long would it take to find him? She took a breath, deep and disconsolate, and let it out slowly, wishing she could give in and cry instead of standing so straight and making this effort at control. If she could stop loving her husband she would. Give it up for a day without worry, without the fear of what would happen to him if she failed. But she couldn't stop. Neither loving him nor trying to save him.

The Tsar, one of the richest men in the world, was glancing her way again, his gray eyes intent and inviting. She returned his gaze.

If Major Archer Wells wasn't authorized to purchase the flute for the Rothschilds without the score, perhaps the Tsar could be tempted by the idea of the object's magic. Now. Before it was too late. She fought her rising panic. Double-dealing was dangerous but grief tempered her fear. Now was not the time for retreat; she'd spent too many days setting up this meeting.

Margaux's lovely home was filled with clever and important people, fine food and charming music. It was all a patina. The threads that held the partygoers' polite masks in place were fragile. Everyone in Vienna had an agenda and a plan for how the reapportionment of Europe would work best for them now that Napoleon was in exile. To the victor had gone the spoils, and now that the victor had been vanquished they were all arguing about how the spoils would be doled out. Despite the lofty talk about doing what was best for all nations, each country was ultimately concerned only with its own interests. So even here tonight, at what purported to be a totally social gathering, nothing was as it seemed.

Margaux looked at the Tsar again, responding not with the flirting she knew he expected but with a straightforward glance. She was betting the best way to play this game was not to play it at all. The power of the unexpected. One of the lessons Caspar had taught her along with a hundred others. So she held the Tsar's gaze with a cool indifference, and from the intensity of his returning glance it appeared nonchalance intrigued the man no one dared treat with anything less than reverence.

Picking up two crystal glasses of champagne from a tray her servant passed around, Margaux crossed the room and delivered one to the Russian monarch, not only interrupting his conversation but ignoring the men with him. A handsome man with light auburn hair, the monarch wore the uniform of a field marshal and the many elaborate medals and thick gold epaulettes on his green coat caught the candlelight and gleamed as brightly as any queen's jewels. Most women would have hung back at first, tried to be charming about the intrusion but she wanted to ensure the Tsar knew just how different she was.

It hadn't taken much to pry the Tsar away. He agreed to her suggestion of a stroll in the garden with an intimate smile and the offer of his arm. Outside, where the moon and the lanterns cast the intricate paths in seductive shadow and the blooming night flowers scented the air with sweet smelling perfumes, the monarch—who had a reputation for being a Lothario—leaned in close to Margaux and thanked her for rescuing him from a boring political argument.

"It was my pleasure. I'd been wanting to talk to you all evening." As did most people in Vienna that season, they spoke in French.

"Ah, so you have an agenda of your own. Nonpolitical, I hope. I've had enough of that for one night."

"It is political but not the kind of politics you were discussing."

Alexander smiled more intimately still. "How clever. I never tire of politics of the bedroom."

"We've all heard about your spiritual marriage. Is it really true?"

"You take me by surprise. That's a serious subject and here I thought we were having a frivolous conversation."

"Do you mind?"

"Not at all. Are you a student of mysticism?"

"My husband is, and I learned from him. He's talked to me about many things, Your Excellency, including the idea that two people can communicate with each other through prayer, no matter how far apart from each other they are."

They'd reached the center of the mazelike gardens. Here among the rose bushes was a stone bench that the Tsar brushed off for her. Once they sat, they were instantly hidden by pruned boxwood bushes so thick they functioned like walls.

"Yes, that's what it's like for us."

"There are three of you involved in this marriage?" she asked, already knowing the answer, having grilled two ladies-in-waiting to the Tsarina yesterday and paid them off with jewelry she could ill afford to lose.

"Yes. We support each other with our hearts and our souls."

"Is your spiritual wife here with you in Vienna?"

"She's my own wife's lady-in-waiting. Countess d'Edling. Maybe you've met her?"

"I haven't had the pleasure," Margaux said as she searched Alexander's eyes, looking for a spark so she'd know if she should make the joke that was on her lips or stay away from making light of the situation. The Tsar's expression was intensely serious.

So her spies had been right. His mystical interests were not sexually motivated but deeply held convictions. Everyone knew he believed Russia had been ordained by God to execute Napoleon's downfall and then help organize the security for all European nations. So when his country did, indeed, prove instrumental in stopping the French Emperor, Alexander took it as confirmation of what he had to accomplish next. That mission was the reason he was in Vienna. He believed it was his destiny. But Alexander's efforts to annex Poland and move Russia's border several hundred miles west concerned the other heads of state at the Congress because the Tsar's mystical beliefs made all of his reasoning suspect.

They'd fallen silent. Around them insects hummed. From inside her apartments came the murmurs of conversation and strains of the chamber orchestra's music. It was cooler out here but she didn't pull her shawl up around her shoulders because she knew the moon made her skin glow and that the Tsar was looking at her bodice even while he discussed philosophy.

"It impresses me that you are so generous with your soul that you'd share it with a woman who shares hers with another man."

The Tsar laughed. "You mean the Theosophist, Schilling?"

She nodded.

"It was actually after meeting with him that I decided I wanted to be part of his union. You should hear how eloquently he explains the ways in which the spirit is superior to the flesh. Of all of us, he enriches the marriage. There is a fourth too, Baroness Kruedener. They are my phalanx of angels."

Margaux did know, but feigned interest and surprise. Everyone knew. The Tsar's spiritual marriage was a joke to most of them. "I heard that Schilling is a friend of the poet Goethe. Have you met him also?" she asked.

"No, but I'm familiar with his work."

"Do you know about Goethe's beliefs in reincarnation?"

"I do."

"And do they interest you also?"

"Of course. Do you believe in past lives?"

"My husband does, Your Highness."

"Ah, that's right. The explorer. He was lost in India, wasn't he? On some kind of treasure hunt."

As Margaux told the Tsar about the flute, he was wholly absorbed in what she was saying. She was concentrating so hard on tantalizing him with her offer that neither of them noticed the flicker of a shadow on the path as someone approached.

"So this artifact belongs to you now."

"Yes," she said, "in fact I've been approached by the agent of a powerful family who wishes to buy it from me."

"Why don't you show it to me first," the Tsar said. "I'd like to see it before you sell it to anyone else."

Chapter 47

Meer resurfaced—that's what it felt like—coming up for air having been underwater for too long. It took another minute for her to connect to where she was and who she was with and remember what had been going on before the lurch began. Someone was talking. Her father. What had he just said? How long had she been lost in the daydream? A daydream? What an inappropriate word for the hallucination she'd just experienced. But there was no word for a nightmare that you experienced while you were wide awake, was there? Or the residue of real grief she felt for a man she didn't know and would never meet.

Malachai's eyes were on her. Understanding, offering comfort, and curious. It was too soon to tell him or her father the details of what had just happened or that she no longer believed she was having false memories. Not until she had some time to absorb the disturbance. Yes, that was a better word, *disturbance.* The forcing away of her present, the inexplicable replacement of people and places for a memory that felt like hers, even though she knew it couldn't logically have any connection to her.

Meer concentrated on what her father was saying.

"Please, I want you all to go now. There's a puzzle to piece together and you can work on it at my house and let them fuss over me in peace. You need to figure out what the key is for."

"I can't leave you here," Meer said, unable to let go of the nagging feeling that he was hiding something about his condition. "What kind of tests do they want to run?"

"I'll make a deal with you," Jeremy said in his most reassuring voice. "I'll tell you, but then you have to do what I ask."

She half smiled, despite herself. He always negotiated. "Okay."

"I am fine but I did have a very minor heart attack ten months ago. I take medication for it and it's not serious but the doctor thought she detected a slight irregularity on the EKG today and wants to run some additional tests to make sure everything's completely fine. At the most I'd need my meds adjusted."

Scared, she searched his face. He smiled, took her hand. Was he really all right? She thought back to ten months ago...trying to remember if she had talked to him then, if she had missed any clues? "Are you really all right?" Her voice trembled a little.

He nodded.

"Why didn't you tell me before?"

"It was a very mild attack. It happened and then it was over. Nothing to tell."

Looking over at Malachai she asked, "Did you know?"

"Yes."

One look at Sebastian and she didn't have to ask him. "You told a stranger and not your daughter?" Meer accused her father.

Getting up, Sebastian walked to the door, mumbling that he had to make a call. Meer was glad he was leaving but Jeremy stopped him. "You don't have to go on our account."

"I really do have a call to make. I'll rejoin the argument in a few minutes."

Jeremy smiled, Meer didn't.

"This isn't funny," she said to him. "Why would you keep your health issues a secret from me?"

"I made a choice based on what I thought would be the best thing for my daughter."

"I'm an adult."

"That doesn't change the fact it's still my prerogative to choose what I burden you with. I don't want you to take on my medical issues and worry about me the way you had to worry about your mother."

"How could I not worry about my mother? She was dying. Are you dying?"

"No, of course not. That's not what I meant, and you know it."

"What do you think will happen to me if I know the truth? Don't you have any faith in me?"

"I've always had faith in you," Jeremy said in a voice subdued by emotion. "From the very first time you ever gripped my finger in your little hand."

"If you had any faith in me you wouldn't try to control what I know and what I don't."

Chapter 48

They were all sitting at the round dining room table in Jeremy's house and trying to make sense of the clues they'd amassed, Meer's memories and information Sebastian was looking up in books from Jeremy's library or on the Internet.

"You mentioned a staircase in the Society," Malachai said. "Where did it go?"

"It was a hidden staircase that led to an underground vault," Meer said. "I think Caspar must have told Margaux where it was because she knew where to find it, but the flute wasn't there."

Talking about the memories now—with some distance from when she'd experienced them—was easier than she'd expected. This was like recounting a scene from a movie or a chapter she'd read in a book.

"I wonder if it's still there? I never heard about a hidden staircase," Sebastian said curiously. "But I haven't been a member that long. Where in the building was the staircase?"

Meer closed her eyes and concentrated. "Inside a closet in what I think must have been a library."

"And down that staircase is the vault?"

She nodded. "In a small room with stone walls and a door with iron bars."

"It sounds medieval," Sebastian said.

"Anything else about being down there that you remember?" Malachai asked.

"No, there wasn't much that mattered once she found out the instrument wasn't there."

"I'd like to focus now on what you noticed when you were in the auction house looking at the gaming box," Malachai said to her. "You said there were two nines of hearts in one deck and both had been slightly damaged. Do you remember how you noticed the aberration? Were you looking for something?"

She answered the last part of his question first. "I must have been but the only reaction I remember is the one I had when Dad first told me about the Heart Crypt. At the auction house I was so stunned at seeing the box..."

"I can imagine," Malachai said with a hint of what sounded like envy. "I'm certain even if you don't remember it, you were drawn to the deck of cards for a reason. Like you were always drawn to the cards in my office when you were little..." He paused for a moment to think about that and then continued. "Were you curious about any of the other items in the chest? Did you feel a sense of urgency while you were looking at them? Did you focus on any of the other game pieces?"

"I don't remember."

"What about anything to suggest there were other clues in the gaming box?"

She shook her head. "I don't know but even if I did, the box is missing."

"Yes, it is. Let's turn our attention to Jeremy's copy of the Beethoven letter. He said it mentions a metaphorical key. Sebastian, can you find that section and read it to us...or maybe it would be helpful if you read the whole letter. There might be something that would otherwise have been elusive but will now be obvious," Malachai said.

Sebastian found the letter and glanced at it for a moment. Even though it was a copy, seeing the words written in the maestro's hand, he was moved and he took a moment before he began to read.

"'Dear Beloved.'"

As he listened, Malachai reached into his jacket pocket and pulled out a well-worn deck of cards. Their presence was no surprise to Meer, who was used to his habit of shuffling when he was deep in thought. The soft slapping noise, rather than being a distraction, was like a musical accompaniment to the words Sebastian was reading.

"'Having been able to decipher the music and having experimented with it, I've seen firsthand how extremely dangerous it is. Much too valuable and dangerous to put in the hands of men who want to use it for nefarious gain. At the same time too valuable to mankind to be destroyed. So I have chosen to tell you three, lest the secret be lost forever.

"'Herewith are the clues to where the flute is hidden.

"'The gaming box holds the heart of the puzzle, and the key to that puzzle is yours, Rudolf, to find.

"'Once found, Stephan, you will be able to unlock the treasure because it is already in your possession.

"'As for the music, Antonie, you alone will understand this. I've done the only thing I could with the music and have given it to our lord and savior. The same who sanctified and blessed our love.

"'One more note. Antonie, if you find this letter by happenstance, please put it away, forget you read it and don't try to decipher it or attempt a treasure hunt on your own at any cost.'"

Sebastian put the papers down on the table. "And it's signed with his initials."

Meer reached for the letter and looked at it, not sure why since she couldn't read German, but the scrawling curves and lines moved her. Across the centuries she imagined the man who wrote these words struggling with something he didn't understand. That she still didn't understand.

Malachai didn't waste any time on an emotional reaction and was already reasoning out the cryptic instructions. "Well, clearly Beethoven didn't divulge the hiding place of the flute in the letter itself. Was there any question Beethoven died under suspicious circumstances?" he asked Sebastian. "Do you know?"

"Not then, no. Although there were always rumors. Recent tests done on his hair prove he was indeed quite ill but interestingly it seems the medicines that he was taking might have hastened his death."

"So there's a possibility the individual letters Beethoven left for these men were never opened and the fact that this letter was still hidden in the false drawer suggests that no one ever found it. Thus one might assume no one ever found the flute either." Malachai had stopped shuffling the cards at some point during the reading of the letter but now began anew.

"The monk mentioned the Archduke Rudolf this morning in the crypt, didn't he?" Meer asked.

"Yes, and it's well documented that he was one of Beethoven's closest friends, as was Stephan von Breuning whose son, Gerhard, was very important to the composer in the last year of his life and—"

"Maybe there's something in Beethoven's papers or letters," Malachai suggested, interrupting, excited by the idea. "Where are they?"

"Didn't my father say he had access to them on his computer?" Meer asked.

"Yes, but he can only read extracts online," Malachai reminded her.

"Where are the actual letters?" he asked Sebastian as he stood up. "We need to see them. As soon as possible." He was putting his cards back in the pack. "Are they here in Vienna?"

Chapter 49

David walked out of the National Library in the same section of the old city where the Heart Crypt was located, and descended the steps, distracted by a woman coming up in the opposite direction. What was it that made him pay attention to her? The way the sun made the auburn highlights in her dark hair dance? Her unnaturally straight back as she climbed the steps? The intensity of her gaze? The closer she came the more he felt pulled toward her. He wanted to stop and figure out what it was about her that was so arresting but he needed to keep moving. He shouldn't even be aboveground during the day where he could be spotted with the concert looming so close.

As she passed him he looked away but she'd been close enough that he could smell her fragrance. It wasn't the same perfume his wife wore but it reminded him that he'd once had a wife whose skin was always warm to his touch and whose eyes had always smiled for him.

And then while he was seeing her in his mind she turned into a grotesque mask of charred flesh.

No, not again. He didn't want to see it all again. Couldn't bear it to see it all again.

Hurrying, David reached the bottom of the steps and headed toward the Kolhmarkt. This last effort had reassured him there were no drawings or maps of the tunnels among the city's records. And that was good. If David couldn't find any details, neither could anyone else. There were a hundred other things that could go wrong between now and the night of the concert but at least a blueprint left in some archive wouldn't lead Paxton's men to him. If he could feel happiness, he thought, he might be happy that this was almost over, but David couldn't exactly remember what happiness felt like.

His pace accelerated. He needed to get back to the crypt, away from these memory triggers. The woman on the library steps had disturbed him even more than he realized. Tonight, he decided, when he went back underground to the tunnel beneath the music hall it would be to stay there with his rats until the night of the concert, and then long, long after it.

Chapter 50

Tuesday, April 29th—1:44 p.m.

The violin's cry was driving Tom Paxton nuts. Music even in the background was distracting but it was necessary to them to have an office inside the music hall. "Where are we with the Semtex tracking?" he asked Vine. "Damn it, if you haven't had any luck, make some. We only have two days left. Way too close for comfort, my friend."

They were seated at a table covered with papers, coffee cups, glasses and a few laptop computers while Alana Green and Tucker Davis conferred over a computer screen at a desk shoved into a corner where there was barely room for it. The one window in the room faced into an alley that offered almost no ambient light and by itself the hanging brass lamp with its mediocre lumens wasn't enough to brighten the gloom, all of which added to Paxton's sense of impending disaster.

"We have three of the buyers under heavy surveillance—not anywhere near Vienna by the way. Two of them bought Semtex and the third—"

"I know all that—what I don't know is what we're doing about the fourth buy," Paxton interrupted. "Why didn't your contacts tell you they'd arranged another sale? What damn good does it do us if we don't even know how many buys we need to track?"

Vine didn't even bother responding but continued explaining what he did know. "Yesterday, for about a half hour, we were able to track the fourth buy to a hotel here in the city. And we just found out that it seems to have been coming from a room registered to one of the press."

"Who's the reporter?"

"David Yalom."

"Shit. He'll do anything to protect a source. I've known the guy for years and he's fearless. Meeting with a known terrorist wouldn't faze him, especially after what he's gone through. Can you ask Kerri to call him and ask him to come in and talk to us, and in the meantime also put a tail on him to see who he's talking to and what he's doing?"

"Will do."

"You said you only caught the signal in his room for a short period of time. What happened to it?"

Vine only hesitated for a fraction of a second but Paxton was all over him.

"Are you saying you don't know?"

"We lost it."

"How do you lose a tracking device?"

"We followed it from the hotel to the subway and then lost it."

Paxton got up and walked around the small room, inspecting every computer screen he passed while the melancholy violin solo tested his patience. "We should have been able to read signals at the subway level, shouldn't we?"

"Yes. That's what makes no sense. We're still investigating."

"And what about this area?" Paxton pointed to one of the screens that showed a darkened area under the concert hall. "Tucker, you said you couldn't get a reading past a certain point in that shaft. Is that right?"

"Right. We haven't even been able to ascertain how deep the shaft goes but it's so narrow—not even two feet wide—that we're not focusing on it."

Paxton took a deep breath, trying to ease the tension gripping his chest.

"Well, I'm focusing on everything within five blocks of the concert hall now that we might have missing explosives. Bill, get on the phone and find out if anyone has even the most rudimentary next-level test model GPR that can get us a deeper reading—"

"Nothing out there exists that we don't have." Vine cut Paxton off somehow, managing not to allow even the thinnest vestige of aggravation in his voice although he'd had this conversation with his boss several times in the last few hours.

"Then we're vulnerable. We're unprepared. And that's unacceptable." Paxton put extra emphasis on the first syllable of unacceptable so the *un* was almost its own word.

"You don't need to tell me. Regardless, the machines you are asking for don't exist."

Kerri walked in with a tray of fresh coffee, bottles of water and a plate of cookies and had to shove papers out of her way to put it down. Just as she did, Paxton responded to Vine by banging his hand on the table and shouting, "Fuck that."

China and silverware clattered.

"Getting angry isn't going to get us deeper readings or find that fourth tracking device," she said as she twisted open a bottle of water and handed it to him. "I think you wanted this about four screams ago."

There was an imperceptible shift in Paxton's expression as he took a long drink. Coming up for air he looked over at Alana Green. "Can you show me the tunnels you already have mapped leading into and out of the area?" His tone was back to even, his drawl was smoothed out and everyone in the room relaxed a little. But only a little. This was still what it had been from the beginning: a high-level security situation. Thursday's concert was a target. There was no other way to look at it. No smarter way to look at it. There may or may not be a terrorist threat but Paxton's plan was to operate as if there were.

Green hit some keys on her keyboard and pulled up a series of computerized graphics illustrating the underground world she'd been charting since arriving in Vienna. Paxton and Vine were riveted to the screen, as was Kerri, but Tucker Davis was still working on his own laptop. Since he'd announced his wife was pregnant, Paxton had noticed Davis had been preoccupied a couple of times and that made him nervous. He couldn't afford for a senior member of his team to be lax about any part of this job. "I think we need to get more men down there," Paxton said.

Tucker's head was still down.

"Tucker?"

"What?"

"I said I think we need to get more men down and search all that uncharted terrain."

"Okay, I'll get more men on it."

"But? I hear a but in your voice."

Tucker hesitated; no one liked giving Paxton no for an answer.

"What is it?"

"We're on top of fucking Roman ruins that no one's ever excavated. There are entire cities down there that we couldn't find, even if we had dozens of teams and months to work. Why didn't we know about this before we bid on this job?"

"None of that matters now," Paxton snapped. "If you can't get the job done, tell me and I'll find someone who can."

Kerri looked up sharply at the tone and the threat in Tom's voice. She was the only one who really got him. But there were too many other sparks right now; far more dangerous ones he had to make sure didn't burst into full-blown fires. "Is there anything we need to worry about before we move on?" He threw out the signature line and then added a coda. "As if we don't already have enough to worry about."

Chapter 51

Tuesday, April 29ᵗʰ—2:30 p.m.

After spending an hour at the library, Malachai hurried off to keep a prearranged meeting with Fremont Brecht at the Memorist Society and Meer sat with Sebastian in his car and called her father. If he was finished with his tests, Sebastian had offered to pick him up and drive him home.

"They're not done with me yet," Jeremy told her. "It seems as if I might not get out until tomorrow. What did you find out?"

Cradling the phone between her chin and shoulder Meer looked out the window at the busy street and told her father about the letters they'd found, including one from Beethoven to Stephan von Breuning that referenced various instruments the maestro had given him as a gift for his young son. "I copied the end of it. This is what Beethoven wrote: If, my friend, my own music continues to be played, and my reputation continues to grow after my death, this silver flute and oboe will have added value for your son. He will have instruments of mine from the past that can give him pleasure in the future if he learns to play them and unlock their treasures."

"Lots of innuendo there," Jeremy mused.

"Except it refers to a silver flute. Not an ancient bone flute. We didn't find any obvious clues to where Beethoven might have hidden an ancient flute."

Jeremy laughed. "Sweetheart, if they were obvious they wouldn't be clues."

For the next few minutes he quizzed her about the content of the letters and then pointed out a pattern she and Sebastian and Malachai had all missed. "Sounds like he wrote about the woods a few too many times. Tomorrow once I'm out of here, we're going to have to make a study of the areas he might have visited during 1813-1815."

Once Meer got off the phone she asked Sebastian where Beethoven had lived that was close to the woods.

"Mdling, Penzing, Dbling, Heiligenstadt..." he listed the towns.

Meer didn't know what she expected. They were all just foreign sounding words to her.

"Jedlesee and Baden," he finished.

"I don't know where to start."

"Well, Baden literally borders the Vienna Woods."

"Can I take a train there?"

Even though it was almost four, Baden was a popular destination and that afternoon it was crowded with tourists. Sebastian, who didn't have a rehearsal that day, had insisted he come with her. He studied the map at the town's information center. "It's only a short distance from here to the entrance to the woods."

"That's fine." Meer was wearing jeans and her black leather blazer and boots with low heels so she wasn't worried. She relished the idea of trekking through the woods and stretching her legs.

"Would you give me a moment? I need to call and check on Nicolas. I do every afternoon around this time."

"Of course." Meer walked a short distance away and looked down the street at the picturesque town that seemed frozen in the past, giving it a storybook feeling. Sebastian joined her only minutes later, looking troubled.

"Is he all right?"

"I don't know. I didn't get through, which is unusual. I left a message though. The nurses are usually good at calling me back."

"Tell me about the town," she asked, hoping to distract him, and he gave her a hint of a smile that suggested he'd noticed her effort.

"I don't know much. Baden has been a rich resort for the people of Vienna for centuries. In Beethoven's time, they arrived with their servants and their china services, their music and their paintings and left it very cultured."

Sightseers made their way in and out of stores on either side of the street, but Sebastian led Meer across the epicenter, past a fountain and to the right while keeping up a running commentary. "The ancient Roman-built baths here rise up from springs rich with sulphur and lime. When they were rediscovered in the 1700s they became famous for their restorative properties and it was those baths that first brought Beethoven here. His doctors recommended the waters as a cure for his hearing and stomach problems."

"Of course, it didn't help."

He shrugged. "Nothing worked for any length of time. He was a very sick man but he composed well here. He loved the forest." He pointed to the lush green hills rising beyond the town. "Those are the real Vienna woods. After we see the house we can walk through them if you like. We still have at least two hours before dusk."

"Yes," she answered immediately, despite the slight shivers that ran down her arms. Something was wrong. The air shimmered; the cars were becoming translucent, the people walking down the street looked different. She steeled herself against the unwelcome onslaught.

Sebastian must have sensed something, because he stopped and put his hand on her shoulder. "What is it?"

Meer was afraid to say anything. Afraid too, she realized, of the drastic wave of cold wind that blew her long lavender-and-navy lace dress around her legs at her ankles...

Crossing the road to the maestro's house, Margaux overheard two men gossiping about the Tsar Alexander's showdown with Prince Metternich. Apparently the day before, the Austrian representative at the Congress had accused the Russian monarch of excessive spying and the Tsar had threatened to pull out of negotiations over the Polish Grand Duchy of Warsaw, which remained one of the most problematic areas. Alexander had desired the territory for years, but Austria and Prussia were both vying for the old Polish kingdom. If the news was true and the Tsar stormed off and left Austria, it would destroy Margaux's plans to sell him the flute. Hurrying on, ever more anxious to reach Beethoven, she was about to enter his house when she sensed someone watching her again. Was it Toller or someone he'd sent to spy on her? Trying not to be obvious she turned and called out a last-minute instruction to her coachman and noticed the sudden movement of a man's shadow shifting on the street as he ducked into a doorway to avoid being seen.

Meer forced herself back. To Baden in the present. Like breaking free from thick ropes, it took all her effort. The first thing she did was look down to check on her jeans and boots. Yes, the lavender dress was gone.

Each time one of these memories overwhelmed her, her anger increased. Uninvited, they mocked any illusion that she was in control of her own life. She couldn't prevent them and couldn't make sense of them. All she could do was collect the varied sequences and hope that at some point they'd tell a cohesive story and then maybe leave her alone.

Glancing around, getting her bearings, she noticed a movement to the left. Was someone hiding in the doorway of a building across the road? Was someone following her in the present as well as the past? Or could something she'd sensed in the here and now bleed over into her unconscious?

"Are you all right?" Sebastian asked as he took her arm and led her to a bench. "You have that expression again, like you saw a ghost. Let me get you some water."

She started to say no but he was gone before she could stop him. Sitting on one of the numerous white wooden benches in the Kurpark she barely noticed the carefully laid out rows of trees and the precisely landscaped gardens. There were people around her talking and birds singing to distract her from the strange sense she still had that she was being watched.

Sebastian returned offering a bottle of ice-cold water and nodding toward the violinist. "He's not bad." While she drank, they listened for a few minutes and then he asked, "You're still shaken up, aren't you? Maybe we should skip the sightseeing."

"Hell, no. We came all this way. I want to see what's inside the house and what the woods are like."

"You believe there's something out there, don't you?" He nodded toward the hills. "Waiting for you to find it?"

The sky was a clear cool blue without any clouds. "I don't know what I believe. That's what makes my father so unhappy."

"Nothing about you makes your father unhappy, Meer. Don't you see that—the way he looks at you, speaks to you? You're his joy."

On Sebastian's face, Meer saw his parental suffering. His son's long, drawn-out illness weighed on him, and she wondered how similar this was to what her father had felt. "You want me to find the flute so you can play it for your son, don't you?" She finally voiced what she'd been thinking. "That's why you're so devoted to helping me, why you befriended my father?"

"Your father befriended me."

"Because of your son, though."

"You're saying that as if it's wrong of your father to help me and wrong of me to want to help Nicolas. Of course, that's how I met your father...looking for a way to try to bring my child back. Is that a bad thing?"

"No, I'm sorry." She was confused again. One minute she saw him in a dark haze, the next with it lifted.

"But yes, if—when—you find the flute I want to play it for my son. Wouldn't you? Don't you want to play it and finally find out the rest of what you're remembering?"

"You're that sure that if the flute exists it works?"

"No, but are you that sure it doesn't?"

"I'm certain only of my uncertainty. After a long time of search-ing, I've accepted that."

"Until now?"

She shrugged. She just didn't know.

He stood so close to her she could smell his ginger-and-orange scent and again felt the need to get even closer and also to stay away.

"How far is Beethoven's house from here?" she asked, anxious get there. To get to any destination even if it was yet one more maze.

The small building at Rathausgasse 10 was a sandy pink color with green window shutters. Two stories high, it had a sloping roof, and the waving flag and plaque next to the door were similar to those at the Beethoven house in Vienna.

Upstairs, a group of tourists filled the foyer and Meer glanced at Sebastian in dismay.

"We can wait a few minutes until some of them have gone, if you'd like."

"Yes."

But it turned out the group was leaving so only a minute later Sebastian and Meer went inside and over to the desk where a teenage girl wearing earbuds and nodding to her personal music was selling tickets. Here, as at the apartment in Vienna, there was almost no security and overly relaxed students managed the property. Strains of Beethoven's music filled the room and while Sebastian bought the tickets, Meer wondered what music the girl preferred to this glorious sonata.

Meer stood on the threshold of the first room, which was dominated by a Broadwood piano. Facing the windows, its mahogany surface gleamed in the late afternoon light. It took Meer five steps— steps that began hesitantly but ended with a kind of authority, as without any vacillation she walked toward it and sat on its bench.

She didn't look back to see if anyone was paying attention. If the young woman came over and chastised her, she'd get up. But this was a once-in-a-lifetime chance and she had to know what it felt like to play one of the maestro's own pianos. To hear what music sounded like to him—when he could hear it.

Lifting the plastic cover over the keys she put her fingers on the yellowed ivory and began. The piano had obviously been kept tuned and she was surprised at how differently this two-hundred-year-old instrument played from the ones she was used to. There was more power and feel to its sound, less control, less sustaining power and it seemed she could do more with its loudness and softness.

Finishing the *Moonlight Sonata,* she let her fingers improvise on the keyboard.

Suddenly the music seemed to be playing itself, her fingers moving on their own. The song sucked the air out of the room. Out of her chest. It dipped and soared and caressed and soothed and aroused and carried her up into the nighttime sky where she flew in the stars, on the wings of this sound, on the notes of this song. It was the melody—the same melody—she'd been hearing for all of her life but had never been able to grab hold of.

"What is that you're playing?" Beethoven asked.

The maestro sat close to the piano with his head resting on the wooden body: the only way he could hear some days was to almost be inside the instrument.

"I don't really know. It's only a fragment. And I'm not even sure it works. It just arrived."

He smiled. "Yes, it's like that sometimes. As if you are a conduit for the music of the planets. Now, play it once more," he insisted.

She complied, used to him by now, no longer surprised by his gruffness. It was a relief to be here, playing for the maestro, waiting for the music to quiet her mind but there was so much to think about, work out and plan. The Tsar was interested in buying her treasure, but would he even still be in Vienna by the time she got up the courage to steal it from Beethoven? What was stopping her? Well, for one thing when she'd told Alexander about the possibility of the memory song, the Tsar offered three times as much as she'd get from Archer. And what would Archer do if he found out she was going to sell to someone other than him? What if Toller guessed what she was trying to do and recalled the flute? Where would she get the money for the expedition to find Caspar then?

After she completed her little ditty, Beethoven asked her to play it yet once more.

It was an odd musical composition, simple and atonal to the point of being disturbing, but it had been in her head when she woke up that morning and she'd been so anxious to play it for Beethoven that she'd ridden out to Baden where he was taking the waters.

"I'm not sure if you wrote that or it wrote you," Beethoven finally said after asking to hear it a half dozen times more. Then, without explanation, he went to the china cabinet and pulled out the chamois-wrapped bundle. He unwrapped the soft suede, revealing the yellowed, ancient bone flute. Margaux hadn't known he'd brought it with him to Baden.

"I think the music you've written might work on the flute..." He answered her question before she asked it. Then, putting the bone up to his lips, he played her first three notes, but tentatively, as if he were expecting something cataclysmic to occur. When nothing did, he played the next phrase and then the next. Eighteen notes. He tried again, playing the music from the beginning straight through to the end without hesitation. Finally putting the flute down, he turned to Margaux. "Noting happened," he said in a defeated voice. And then noticed she was silently weeping. "What is it? What's wrong?" he asked.

But she couldn't tell him, couldn't speak because she was remembering. Remembering something she had forgotten. Or something she'd never known.

The music was inside of her now. It lifted and soared and crashed and then built up again to yet another crescendo, bringing with it images of another time and place that made no sense to her. A place unlike anywhere in Europe that she'd ever seen.

Margaux saw a hot sun and a wide river. She felt a deep sadness, and saw many women weeping around a blazing fire, all of them wearing robes, not gowns. Mountains towered over the landscape.

Then the scene vanished and Margaux saw Beethoven again, staring at her with a disconcerted look in his eyes. She noticed the way the sun was shining in the windows. There was something important about the light, as if it were shining to show her something.

She followed one beam, watched dust motes dancing. There was knowledge in the gleaming. Years and years of knowledge collected in the energy that was coursing through her. More than she needed to breathe, she needed Caspar with her now so she could tell him about this amazing discovery of his and the power it held. More than anything she wanted her husband to share in this painful yet excruciatingly beautiful truth about light and time and circles and repetition, and who we are and why we are here.

"What is it, Margaux?" Beethoven asked. "Why does the music affect you so?"

But she couldn't tell him. She was still inside the light, traveling on the vibrations of the dissonant song Beethoven had coaxed from the ancient flute. She was remembering back in time.

Chapter 52

Indus Valley, India—2120 B.C.E.

Stealing from the dead was a crime, stealing the dead themselves was a sin, but her desolation was stronger than her fear of the punishments, so Ohana hid behind the trunk of the tree as the sun set the river on fire, shielded her eyes and waited for the funeral service to end.

The combined cacophony of lapping water, bells clanging and cows mooing couldn't cloak the widow's bitter wailing; Ohana's painful reminder that she had no right to be here at Devadas' Asthi-Sanchayana ceremony, that there was no one she could turn to for solace, that her mourning was the last secret in a series of secrets she would have to keep.

Yesterday, two men on their way to morning prayers had found Devadas's body by the riverbank, the flies buzzing around her lover, already attracted by the pool of blood that seeped from his head gashes. Other than Devadas's brother, Rasul, who pressured the lawmakers for an investigation, no one seemed to care who the killer was or how to find him. The two brothers, instrument makers by trade, had been labeled as heretics for claiming certain music played on their flutes and drums could heal and soothe. They were a threat to the old customs and much reviled in the town. And now one of them was dead.

As the wailing intensified the wind picked up, and Chandra, Devadas's wife, gasped as some of her husband's ashes blew on her. Stunned, she stopped sprinkling his cinders with milk to touch the powder on her cheek with her fingertips. A fresh tear fell from her eye, leaving a track in the dust.

It was hypocritical the way these women were carrying on. Devadas's wife had exiled him from her home a year before because of his rebellious ideas. His own father had called both his sons insurgents. Yet now they were all prostrate with grief.

While the women continued to wet down the pyre, a second, more violent, gust blew ash into Devadas's eldest daughter's face and she coughed as some of the debris got in her mouth. She spit once. Twice. A third time. If it had happened to her, Ohana would have accepted the ash gratefully as if it had been a sacrament.

"Now the water, hurry," Devadas's elderly mother admonished, talking her three granddaughters through the next step of the ceremony. "Hurry, before the wind blows him away."

Once the girls emptied the second jug and there was no water left, Chandra took up the scarred wooden staff and sifted through the muddy mixture separating the bones from the ash. Like a ragpicker the older daughter collected the bigger, wet cinders—the residue of his flesh and muscle and sinew—filling an earthenware bowl with them, and his youngest daughter picked up the bones that were no longer hot.

From her hiding place, Ohana watched Chandra take the bowl and throw the ashes into the rushing river while the others gathered around the bones and waited. Even though they were not supposed to show grief, all but the old woman continued wailing.

"He is traveling by the Path of Light," Devadas's mother admonished. "Many tears," she said, "burn the dead."

Each of the seven women tied the fruit of the *brhati* plant to her left hand with a deep blue thread the color of the night sky and a red thread the color of flowing blood, then one by one they stepped up onto the stone pyre, wiped their hands with *apamarga* leaves, then closed their eyes and stood in a circle, swaying to the river's music.

"Arise hence and assume a new shape," the matriarch intoned. "Leave none of the members of your body. Repair to whichever place you wish—may Savita establish you there. This is one of your bones; be joined with the third in glory; having joined all bones be handsome in person; be beloved of the gods in a noble place."

As the women washed Devadas's bones one last time, Ohana shivered remembering the feel of them, covered by muscles, pressing against her body. It was wrong that they were allowed to mourn him in the open and she had to hide in order to honor him.

Chandra filled a terra-cotta urn with the bones and then took it over to the sami tree. Stretching, she hung the urn from the highest branch she could reach.

Finally, the women left.

Ohana watched them growing smaller and smaller in the distance until they were gone. The sun slipped below the horizon. The moon would not rise for hours. A gray wash settled over the evening as the air chilled. The water still lapped the shore but the bells were silent and the women's crying was too far off for her to hear anymore. This horrible day was at last over. The death ceremony was almost complete, except for one last visit when, two days from now, the women would return to take down the bones and bury them.

Knowing she was veiled by the twilight, Ohana crept up to the tree, reached into the urn and felt all that was left of her lover, this calcified measure of one man. Her hand came out clutching what she'd come here to get. Smooth and pale, the bone glowed almost incandescently in the evening light. Then, holding it close to her breast as if it could speak to her, as if it could save her, as if it could offer solace, she crept away into the lonely night.

Chapter 53

He saw all these forms and faces in a thousand relationships become newly born. Each one was mortal, a passionate, painful example of all that is transitory. Yet none of them died, they only changed, were always reborn, continually had a new face: only time stood between one face and another.

—Herman Hesse, Siddhartha

Baden, Austria
Tuesday, April 29th—4:20 p.m.

Meer sat at the piano in Beethoven's apartment, her fingers resting on the keys, feeling the music's reverberation. She was so cold but that didn't matter in the face of trying to figure out what had happened. Time had just warped back on itself twice. She'd been sitting here as Margaux—on the day Margaux had first heard the flute music and disappeared inside of it—and then she'd remembered a more distant past. Had she just glimpsed not only one previous life but two, centuries apart?

Music had been the trigger but Meer couldn't remember the actual song—only the sense of it.

"Did you recognize it, what I was playing?"

Sebastian looked at her, confused. "You weren't playing, Meer. Not anything that resembled music. You played a C note. Three times. And then you just sat there with your eyes closed for twenty, thirty seconds."

"No, I was playing. I could hear it."

He shook his head. "Just the C. You're shivering so badly. Let me get you—"

Margaux *had* found the memory song and played enough of it on the piano for Beethoven to have figured it out and played it for her on the ancient flute. It had worked, had stimulated her memory of an even older story about a man whom she had been desperately in love with, who had died, whose bone she had stolen.

"Why are you lying?"

"Meer, you weren't playing any music. I wouldn't lie. Think of what the memory song might mean to me. To my son."

The cold was pervasive. Standing up, she walked past him, past the girl at the desk. With the same strange assurance she felt when she sat down at the piano, she strode down the hall as if she knew exactly where she was going. The small bedroom contained a single bed dressed with a thin, coffee-colored blanket, a chest of drawers, a basin for water and a coat hanging on a hook. Without any trepidation, Meer lifted the heavy wool coat off its hook and slipped her arms into it. This coarse garment was warm. Warm enough to stave off the shivering that, despite the weather, overwhelmed her.

Stuffing her hands into the pockets she found a small hole in the left one. Reaching down, holding the hem by the corner, she scrunched up the material so her fingers could get to the bottom where a coin had been trapped between the lining of the coat and the outer shell. They always fell there, she thought, smiling to herself. But there was something else stuck in the lining, too. The nib of a pen, stained with dried black ink.

What was she doing wearing Beethoven's coat? The young girl who sold tickets would call the police if she found out someone had disturbed the exhibition. Meer felt guilty; working in a museum herself she knew how sacrosanct every item was. Taking the coat off, she hung it carefully back up on the hook.

Everything was the same as it had been before she'd come in here except for the strange idea that taunted her now: she'd once worn this coat as a disguise to hide from someone who'd followed her.

Chapter 54

As she and Sebastian hiked up the hill and into the densely wooded mountains, everywhere Meer looked she saw another postcard image: a herd of goats grazing in a glen, a rough-hewn stone wall and a scenic overlook dangerously hanging above a thirty-foot drop, offering an expansive view of the town below. The vista was exactly how she'd imagined it earlier when Sebastian first mentioned Baden.

"You can look all the way out there but no one can look up and see you," he said softly.

Meer was surprised to feel his hand on her shoulder.

"You're getting too close to the edge. The overhang is unprotected. People have fallen."

"Death in the Vienna Woods," Meer said. "Johann Strauss would be distressed."

"Especially since the waltz was known as the flight from death.

But there's been more than enough tragedy here for someone to write that version, too. Mayerling's not far. You know about that?"

She shook her head.

"The Archduke Rudolf of Austria and Hungary and his mistress, Baroness Marie Vetsera, committed suicide a few kilometers away at his hunting lodge. He was married and she was only seventeen. The building's a convent now but locals say the lovers' ghosts haunt these hills."

"My father wasn't kidding when he said people are preoccupied with death in Vienna. That's not the first time you've brought up ghosts. Do you believe in them?"

"I never wondered about ghosts or life after death before Nicolas—" he broke off and checked his watch. "We should keep going. There's only about an hour of good light left."

As they walked away from the overlook Meer veered right as Sebastian took the left.

"No, it's this way," he called out.

"Can't we take this route?"

"I don't know that way. This is the main trail. I don't want to get us lost."

"We won't get lost."

"How do you know that?"

Meer shrugged. "Can we just see what's this way?"

They climbed for a few minutes more, and after another turn in the road, arrived at a small yellow, three-walled hut. An almost life-sized wooden Jesus affixed to a large cross hung on the back wall behind a rough stone altar flanked by statues of Mary and Joseph.

Meer stared at the shrine in the middle of the woods as if it were an apparition.

"I've seen this place..." she whispered as she walked into the shadows of the structure, knelt down and ran her hand along the edge of dirt where the ground met the wall. Closing her eyes, she tried to see backward through time again, but couldn't. She had no idea what this place might once have meant to her. Even so she kept running her hand over and over the dirt as if she would be able to divine some message from the ground.

"Meer, what are you doing?"

She turned to Sebastian to explain and saw a deer run by, followed by a buck. Their hooves cracked small branches and crumbled layers of dried leaves.

Sebastian asked again: "What are you looking for?"

"I'm not sure but I think—" Her voice had dropped in register and was as low as the dark blue-greens of the conifers casting shadows all around them. "Margaux... helped him...she helped Beethoven hide the flute and the music. I think she might have hidden one of them here."

Chapter 55

Baden, Austria
October 18th, 1814

At a brisk pace, Beethoven strode up the pathway toward the gardens outside the hotel. As he walked and talked he kept rolling and unrolling the score he held. Margaux was amazed at his stamina. She knew his stomach and head hurt. His energy level was low and he'd complained about being tired.

"I have written much music that has made me proud. But that was when I was younger. Now I know how much more the music needs to do. I have given up so much. Even made a deal with my God to forgo all earthly riches, a wife and children, if only I could go on creating the music.

"I have lived up to my side of the bargain but God has not lived up to his. The struggle to create has not gotten any easier. If anything, only more and more obstacles are thrown my way. And now this music from the Devil that you've brought to me out of your dreams and that ushers forth such dangerous visions... I won't unleash this on anyone. I can't."

She touched his arm so that he would look at her and be able to read her lips. "Where are we going?"

"I need to think."

"Why did you bring the music? You're not going to do anything to the score, are you?"

He ignored her questions and all she could do was struggle to keep up with him. Margaux was alarmed. Although he'd been able to work out the complete memory song, she couldn't remember any more than those first three notes.

Passing through gardens, they continued climbing the hill into the woods and were deep into the forest by the time they came to the small chapel with the crucifix, rough-hewn stone altars and statues of Mary and Joseph.

Sheltered from the wind, Beethoven opened the score and read it over. "I don't know what to do with this unearthly music," he muttered. He was still studying it when the storm came upon them without any warning. A fierce wind blew the rain in, splashing the score, making the ink run.

"Put it under your coat," she shouted, and mimed to his coat pocket in case he couldn't hear her over the thunder. But he didn't see her, was too busy looking around...searching. Suddenly he rolled the score into a tight cone and wedged it in the narrow space between Christ's body and the wooden cross.

"It will be safe here at least until tomorrow," he told her as a new crack of thunder reverberated though her. Lightning lit up the forest and through the sheeting rain she thought she saw someone out there watching them, but couldn't be sure.

Was it Beethoven's secretary, Schindler? Had he followed them there? Was it Toller? No, she was no longer in the past. She wasn't Margaux anymore.

Meer was staring at a man wearing a dark mask and pointing a gun at her.

Chapter 56

The terror coursing through her made it almost impossible for Meer to speak. The man holding the gun wore a dark slicker, its hood up. Frantic, she looked around for Sebastian…and then saw him on the ground, unmoving, lying behind the altar beneath the crucifix.

"You're going to wind up like your friend over there unless you give us what you found up here." The man whispered the words harshly in a thick German accent but she understood every syllable.

"What did you do to him?"

"Your friends, your father…we can keep going with this game, hurting everyone you know and love until we get what we want."

"My father? Is he all right?"

"For now, yes. But how he winds up is up to you."

She didn't even hesitate. "What you want is there." She pointed to the cross.

"Get it."

It was only four steps to the crucifix. Reaching up, feeling between the wooden body of Jesus and the flat surface of the cross, Meer's fingertips found what felt like the edge of a sheaf of paper. She'd been searching in the wrong place before. It wasn't buried in the ground. It was up here. She pulled it out.

Insects had eaten through the paper, mold had attacked it. Only a few random marks and the nauseating stench of rot were left. Meer lifted her head up toward the hut's roof to escape the overwhelming scent. Drops of rain came though the cracks in the two-hundred-year-old structure, hanging for a second and then falling, one and then another splattering her on the forehead and cheeks.

Was she really holding what had once been Beethoven's score of the memory song, written in his own hand? He'd gone to so much trouble to convince everyone he'd never found these notes. No longer here to protect what little of his work was left, she could. Moving her hands a half inch, she positioned the score under the rain that dripped through the cracks in the ceiling.

The few still viable marks blurred as the rain fell and the ink ran.

The man in the ski mask grabbed the disintegrating clump out of her hand and looked at it. For one second he wasn't focused on her and that second was enough for her to run.

Chapter 57

Tuesday, April 29th—5:56 p.m.

In the teeming rain, the forest had become treacherous and it was impossible for Meer to get her bearings or recognize any landmarks as she ran. All she knew was that she had to keep descending, and if she could manage that she'd find her way out of the woods. She had to get Sebastian help.

She tripped on tree roots, vines and twigs but she kept getting up and soldiering on down the mountain all the while listening hard, knowing that just because she couldn't hear her assailant over the sound of the rain didn't mean he wasn't there.

Did the man in the slicker want her or just the papers? Was she actually getting away or did he know the forest so well he was waiting for her up ahead? Was her running putting Sebastian in more danger? If the man had taken off after her, maybe she should double back and help Sebastian?

A burst of lightning illuminated her surroundings for a brief second at the same time her foot hit a patch of mud. Sliding, she reached out for a root or a rock, but found she was clutching at nothing but air—and was still falling.

Finally, Meer grabbed hold of an exposed root. She lay in the dirt, tasting it, smelling it, for what seemed like a long time. All she knew was that no one stood over her, there was no gun poking her in the side, no one was screaming at her to get up and move. Finally, she accepted that if someone had been following her, they would have found her by now. Her legs, arms, chest and back all ached.

Crawling to the base of a pine tree about five feet away, she used the trunk to stand up. She was in pain but Sebastian needed help.

Except what was the best way to help him? Go back up to him or head down to the town and get the police? She wished she knew how badly he'd been hurt. Unsure with every step that this was the right solution, she started back up toward the hut.

She'd only been moving for a few minutes when she saw the glow of a searchlight through the trees to her right.

The gunman had found her.

Frantically she looked around for someplace to hide and in the semidarkness made out what looked like a large clump of bushes. Was there space to crawl inside them? Could she reach their shelter without making any noise?

Slowly she inched forward through the mud, careful to keep checking the ground for branches lest she come down on them and make any noise that would give her away. And then she heard something—it sounded like someone calling out her name. She stopped moving, listened, peered through the trees.

"Meer?" It was Sebastian with a group of policemen, and they were searching for her.

Once the police ascertained she didn't need to be taken to the hospital they offered to escort her to the station so she could answer questions while they secured the scene but she insisted on going with them back up to the hut. Sebastian was adamant about accompanying her.

This was her last chance to search for any remnants of the music she'd been hunting for her whole life, that she'd miraculously found and then lost only minutes later.

As they made their way through the soggy forest, she and Sebastian filled each other in on what had happened. The police suspected he had been chloroformed because all he remembered was coming to, lying in the mud, in the rain. When he was able to get up he started searching for her, finally working his way down to the town and eventually to the police.

"I was afraid that if I kept looking in the woods I'd wind up going in circles and keep missing you," he said. "Did he get the music?"

"He got a handful of pulp but no music."

"You have it then?"

"There were only a few musical notations left and not in sequence. They washed away in the rain."

"But you saw them first, didn't you? You saw the notes?"

"There was so little left to see. And it happened too fast. I wasn't thinking straight. But maybe some of the shreds of the paper are still up there. That's why I have to go back. To see if there's anything at all left. Once it gets into police custody we might never see it again. Anything I can take back to my father that could be examined and dated might be of use. There must be infrared techniques they can use to pick up vestiges of faded ink."

Reaching the shelter, the officers cordoned off the hut and the surrounding area. The old chapel with its fading plaster statues couldn't just be a dead end. The music couldn't be gone forever. But she couldn't even get inside to see if anything was left.

What should she do? Her father had spent his life hunting down hidden Torahs. What would he do if he were here? Once he'd told her that there was always a point when the clues would seem to dry up and he'd feel utterly lost and then he'd rely on faith. In the moments when he wanted to curse, he forced himself to pray, to remember that there was a purpose to everything and in those prayers he always found the strength to keep going.

She'd never prayed before but no one would know that. Neither would they know that she was Jewish and that even if she did pray, she wouldn't kneel. But now, without asking the police for permission, Meer walked around to the crucifix, knelt down in front of it and bowed her head.

"Miss Logan..." the inspector said softly.

From this vantage point she could look for shreds of paper without appearing to do so.

"Miss Logan..." he said again, but she didn't lift her head, hoping he would allow her these few moments of devotion.

The stones hurt her knees, which were already sore from the fall, but she remained frozen, her eyes scanning the ground, not thinking about what she'd do if she found anything or how she'd pick it up without anyone noticing. But it didn't matter. There wasn't anything left. Not a shred. The paper must have completely disintegrated in the rain and, with it, every last hope for discovering the elusive music that had haunted her for most of her life.

Chapter 58

Tuesday, April 29th—7:50 p.m.

During the question-and-answer session with the soft-spoken inspector at the police station in town, neither Meer nor Sebastian said anything about the parchment she'd discovered. Sebastian improvised that they'd been in the woods on a Beethoven pilgrimage when they'd been mugged. When the time came, he looked through his wallet and told the policeman the thief had taken over a hundred and fifty euros and a gold signet ring off his right hand.

After an hour the inspector apologized profusely for what had befallen them in his town and said they were free to go. He told them he would be in touch if they found any of the stolen items.

Inside the car, Sebastian locked the doors and sat for a moment as if trying to gather the strength to turn on the ignition. Not until he'd driven out of town did he speak and then it was in a low voice filled with remorse. "I feel responsible for what happened tonight and don't know what to say other than I am so very sorry. With everything that has already happened, how could I have been so cavalier? You are in terrible danger, Meer. You have to be careful. We have to be careful."

"I didn't take it seriously enough but when we were in town before we walked into the woods, I sensed if someone was watching us."

"They must have followed us here from Vienna." He rubbed his temple.

"Are you all right?"

"I suppose I hit my head when I fell." He waved it off. "What matters is that Beethoven hid the music and you found it. Not by chance or by accident, you knew exactly where it was. You probably know where the flute is too."

Meer shook her head. "I don't."

"Not consciously, but you must."

She didn't want that to be true; it was hard to accept that she was unable to remember what she couldn't forget. The damned conundrum that had shaped her life. "Come on, the flute could be anywhere."

"Not really. There was a clue to where the music was in the letter, now that we can look back. 'I have given it to our lord and savior. The same who sanctified and blessed our love.' It's clear now. The little chapel in the woods must have been one of Beethoven's trysting places with Antonie. Beethoven hid the key in the Heart Crypt and left a clue to that in the letter. So it follows that there's a clue to where the flute is."

His cell phone rang. Meer couldn't understand the ensuing conversation but she had no trouble recognizing the anxious tone his voice took on.

"My son isn't well," he told her after he hung up. His hands clenched the wheel and the intensity drained the blood from his knuckles. "It's pneumonia, which can be dangerous for anyone, but even more so for him because he's so unresponsive. Let me drop you off and then—"

"Isn't the hospital on the way back into town? I'll go with you and get a taxi from there."

They were traveling over a hundred miles an hour and Meer reminded herself that it was all right to go that fast—until the rain started up again. First it was just a few droplets splashing on the windshield that the wipers took care of, but then the shower intensified. So for a few seconds the road was clear, then it blurred again. Swish. Clear. Blur. Swish. Clear. Blur.

There weren't any other cars on the road and without ambient lights, Sebastian's headlights only offered visibility a few yards ahead. He took one sharp turn. The next was more harrowing. It wouldn't make any difference if she asked him to slow down; he had to get to his child.

Chapter 59

Meer didn't need to speak German to know that the hospital orderly was blocking Sebastian from going in and seeing his son. In the ensuing argument, Sebastian never raised his voice above a fierce whisper. Was that in deference to the other people on the floor or was he circling down deeper and deeper into silence the nearer he was to rage? No matter how close Sebastian moved toward the guard, the man remained even-tempered and even-toned. Several times the orderly referred to "Doktor Kutcher" and Meer surmised that Sebastian's estranged wife had given the order to keep him out. Finally, Sebastian made a move as if to turn around and give up, and then suddenly lurched forward, successfully pulling open the door to his son's room, leaping inside, disappearing from Meer's sight.

The guard rushed in after him.

Through the glass panel, Meer watched Sebastian reach his son's bed and bend down just seconds before the guard approached and put his hand surprisingly gently on Sebastian's shoulder. He tried to shrug it off but the orderly held tight and using his other hand, spun Sebastian around. Meer stepped away as Sebastian emerged from the door, his shoulders rounded in defeat.

"How is he?" Meer asked as they walked toward the elevator.

"Physically? He's holding his own, which in this case is a positive sign. Thank God. But as you could tell, it seems that I am no longer allowed in to see him. I have been in the process of trying to get an injunction—I think that's the right word—so Rebecca can't prevent me from bringing specialists to see Nicolas but it seems she got one first. Now *I* need *her* permission to see Nicolas. Me. His father."

"Didn't she call to tell you he was sick, didn't she expect you'd want to see him?"

"No, she didn't call me, the nurse did. I don't know what Rebecca expected. The orderly said that she left instructions I'm not to be let in unless she's here."

"Maybe if you called her she'd change her mind."

For a second there was some hope in his eyes, and he asked her to wait while he returned to the nurses' station.

Meer sat down in a green leatherette chair, thinking about how many thousands of pained and worried mothers and fathers, husbands and wives, children and relatives and friends had sat there since the early twentieth century when the hospital was first built. And then she remembered what Sebastian had told her about the experiments performed within these walls during the war.

"The nurse called her and she lowered herself to talk to me instead of going through other people. She says she's had it with the 'voodoo' I'm trying out on him and doesn't trust me to see him anymore if she's not there," Sebastian said. He sat down next to her and slumped in the chair. "Bringing you here over the weekend was the breaking point, it seems. And now that he's sick, she doesn't want anyone to impede his recovery. But he's lost inside, and he can't fight the pneumonia if he's not here. Why can't she understand that?"

Meer put her hand on his arm, and even through his jacket she could feel how tense his body was. "I don't know the laws here but in America, getting an injunction without just cause is almost impossible. Sex offenders are about the only people who can be stopped from seeing their children. You should call your lawyer."

He looked at his watch. "Would you mind if I called now? I don't want to wait till I get home and it's even later."

"No, it's fine, of course, go ahead."

She walked down to the other end of the hall where there were windows that overlooked the woods where they had walked on Sunday. In the dark there was very little to see but pale moonlight shimming on the pond. Leaning her forehead on the cool glass, she shut her eyes and thought about what a long strange night it had been. A long, strange and sad night.

"There's nothing he can do about it tonight," Sebastian said when he returned. "Or even this week. Fighting her injunction will take time. The possibility of filing the papers and being heard in less than two weeks seems to be nonexistent."

"I'm sorry," Meer said.

He glanced back at his son's room where the orderly stood guard. "Give me one more second and then we'll drive back."

Meer noticed that this time Sebastian didn't exhibit any animosity or anger in his body language. The guard wasn't completely relaxed as he listened, but he did tilt his head to the side as if he was commiserating. Finally Sebastian reached into his pocket, pulled out a pen and a card, wrote something down and held it out. The guard stared down at it but then took the card and moved to the right, clearing the door and allowing Sebastian a sight line into the room. For a full minute he stood there, immobile, staring at his son through a wire-reinforced glass panel.

As they headed back down the hall toward the elevator again, Meer was aware of how labored Sebastian's step had become.

"What did you give the guard?"

"My phone number. And a promise to reward him for calling and keeping me informed. Every time I leave here I feel as if I'm abandoning my son to that black forlorn space in his head where he's living. If it is even living."

"Certainly Rebecca hasn't tried to blame you for Nicolas's state, has she?"

"No. But you believe, even though it's foolish, that you are a man and that you are strong and that you should be able to protect your child from everything. From *every* thing. And when you don't, when you can't, you feel like a failure, consumed with only one thought—there must be something *I* can do."

Chapter 60

Sleeping in the crypt on the dirt floor with only his jacket as a pillow had actually been easier than sleeping in the ugly room at the pensione. For the first night since David could remember he hadn't been haunted by the familiar and hideous PTSD dreams that were his nemesis. Instead a very different vision had woken him up. The images had been very vivid; intense but fragmented. He'd been in terrible pain but at the same time felt a deep satisfaction that he'd done the right thing.

Standing, stretching, he took some supplies out of his knapsack, then drank a bottle of mineral water and ate a hard-boiled egg— consumed them mechanically as if they had no taste or texture but were just sustenance. That last morning, Lisle had made him eggs. He'd been in a hurry, but she'd insisted. It was his son's birthday morning—they'd all have breakfast together—no. He had to stop doing this. It was not helpful anymore. He was taking care of it now.

Action fueled by rage was better than helpless pity. His family was not going to have died in vain. The Bible talked of an eye for an eye. What he was doing was that and more.

A ragged scratching noise startled David and as he spun around he put his hand on the hilt of his Glock.

But it was only one of the half-dozen caged rats scraping its sharp nails on the metal bars of its cage. David considered his companion rodents who survived in the world's cesspools. But wasn't the whole world becoming a cesspool? Several of the rats were scratching at the bars now as if they sensed that their captor was thinking about them. They were impatient but they'd have to wait…

David had found that waiting down in the crypt wasn't as difficult as he'd imagined. So much of his anxiety over the last few weeks had come from the fear he'd be discovered before he'd accomplished his task.

He only had a few more hours until the concert hall came back to life and Paxton's men would return to continue their explorations. It was easier to stay awake when there were noises above him. Concentrating on them gave him something to do. The rats had stopped scratching and it was too quiet now; quiet enough to fall asleep again…even on the ground…here on the dirt…

Standing on the shore of a rushing river with tall snow-capped mountains filling the Indus Valley horizon, he breathed in air sweetened with the fragrance coming from flowering trees. An older man wearing a light-colored robe was screaming at him bitterly, threatening him. But he wasn't scared of the elder. The woman with sea-green eyes was in danger because of this man and he had to do something to save her.

David woke up with a start, surprised that the dream had returned. He felt an overwhelming sense of impending doom.

Chapter 61

I know I am deathless. No doubt I have died myself ten thousand times before.
I laugh at what you call dissolution, and I know the amplitude of time.

—*Walt Whitman*

Vienna, Austria
Wednesday, April 30th—9:15 a.m.

Jeremy Logan looked more exhausted than he had the day before and when he told Meer and Malachai that he wouldn't be leaving the hospital that morning or probably even that afternoon, she wasn't surprised but she was worried.

"I'm running a slight fever. Something I'm sure I picked up here in the hospital yesterday. The longer you stay in a hospital, the sicker you get."

"How high a fever?" Meer asked.

"It's nothing serious but because of the episode that showed up on the EKG, the doctors want to keep me under observation a little longer. Damn their efficiency. Now, I insist you stop asking about my health and tell me everything you've found out since yesterday."

The only part of the trip to Baden and finding the mess of parchment that once must have been the memory song that Meer left out was the attack in the woods.

"Let's not worry about what we lost," Malachai said when she finished. "We'll figure out the song once we've found the flute. That's what we should be concentrating on. It's clear from everything we've read that von Breuning must have had the flute even if he never realized its value. Fathers leave their estates to their sons, especially in the nineteenth century. Did Stephan have a son? Did his son have children...did the family stay in Vienna? Maybe some old man has it still and doesn't know what it is."

"He had a son, yes. Gerhard von Breuning," Jeremy said. "In fact, Gerhard wrote one of the few firsthand accounts of knowing Beethoven. I'm certain the library has the book." He looked at his watch. "But it doesn't open till noon on Wednesdays."

"Isn't there a bookstore open now?" Meer said.

Jeremy stared at her. "I don't want you involved anymore."

"Too late for that."

"Let the people who know how to handle dangerous situations do their job."

"At this point we're only talking finding a book and seeing if it offers up any more information."

Meer could tell her father wasn't convinced so she gave him something she knew would satisfy him. "Malachai can come with me." Hesitating, she wondered if she was reading her father wrong. Maybe this was about him. "Unless you want me to stay here with you."

"Yes, but only because it will keep you safe. Certainly I don't want you to stay here for my sake."

"I feel like I have to keep looking, Dad," she said, lifting her hands and letting them drop.

Jeremy smiled. "There's an answer to every question even if it's elusive. The Kabbalah tells us that there's a level of our souls where we all connect to all the world's accumulated knowledge. Jung agreed, just used different words and called it the collective unconscious. It manifests itself in an inner voice we all can hear if we listen deeply enough. You hear that voice. You've always heard it. Now you have to trust it. Just promise me," he said with a smile, "you'll be very careful."

There was no way Meer or Malachai would be able to find the book or read it since neither of them spoke German so Jeremy called Sebastian, apologized and asked for one last favor.

The scent of leather and ink, glue and oil greeted them when they walked into the used bookstore off the Graben. A middle-aged woman with thick black hair looked up from her perch at a drafting table. Around her were pots and razor blades, papers, soft cloths, books in various states of repair, along with a battered copy of Gerhard's memoir, which she handed to Sebastian.

As he scanned the pages, Meer noticed the circles under his eyes and felt sorry that he'd been pulled back into her crisis when he had one of his own to deal with.

After only a few minutes he closed the book and handed it back to the shop owner, thanking her.

"What did you find out?" Malachai asked over the sounds of the traffic once they were back out on the street.

"When Stephan died, Gerhard von Breuning inherited his father's estate, which included dozens of items that had belonged to Beethoven."

"Was he specific?" Malachai asked.

"Many books, several metronomes—a new invention at the time

that Beethoven had been involved with—a dozen conductor's batons and several musical instruments including a piano, two violins, an oboe and two flutes."

"Did he describe them in detail?"

"No."

"We need to find out what happened to Gerhard's estate," Malachai said.

Meer suddenly felt her father's presence, almost as real as if he were standing there with them. Everywhere she'd been for the last two days, she'd pictured him making the journey with her and offering advice on how to proceed. She should have told him that in the hospital this morning. He would have liked knowing. When she went back later she'd tell him what it had been like in Beethoven's apartments, both here in Vienna and in Baden, to sense his presence so strongly.

Thinking about the apartment on Mölker Bastei she'd visited on Sunday she had a strong feeling that there was something she'd seen there she needed to remember now… but what? It had only been three days ago.

While Malachai and Sebastian continued talking, Meer concentrated on playing Cicero's memory game. Picturing herself in Beethoven's apartment, she walked through the foyer…noticed the piano…circled the room…read the legends beside every item and artifact…and then she remembered exactly what she'd seen. What she'd read on the legends beneath each and every item in the house and why it mattered so much now.

"I know what happened to his estate and where those instruments are," she said.

Chapter 62

Wednesday, April 30th—11:30 a.m.

Silently counting the all-too-familiar number of steps, she mounted the staircase to Beethoven's Mölker Bastei apartment. Malachai and Sebastian followed as, without hesitation, she went straight to a violin in a case where, just as she remembered it, there was a card describing the instrument and giving its provenance in four languages. The three of them read different versions at the same time but both the English and German legends ended with the same information: the violin was a gift of the Gerhard von Breuning estate and was one of seven original instruments belonging to Beethoven and on display at the composer's residences in Vienna and Baden.

"Except we've been here and there and didn't see a bone flute," Sebastian said.

"No. And you wouldn't," Malachai said. "It's hidden. Beethoven said so himself in his letter to Antonie. Maybe Meer's silver key will open its hiding place. Beethoven wrote that both the Archduke

Rudolf and Stephan von Breuning had all the necessary clues even if they couldn't see them."

"And if von Breuning left his son everything that Beethoven gave him and Gerhard left everything to the state and the state put all those objects on display in Beethoven's apartments…" Sebastian connected all the dots in his mind. "You think that hidden amidst all these objects there's a flute made of ancient bone?"

Meer wasn't listening to their conversation. The lights enfolded her, separated her from herself so that she was at once in this moment and outside of it, watching and trying to communicate with the woman on the other side of the divide who knew exactly where the ancient flute had been hidden. Her back ached; the metallic taste filled her mouth. Meer didn't hear a voice giving her the answer to the puzzle, or see a ghostly figure pointing the way. Suddenly there was just knowledge she possessed that she hadn't had a few seconds ago.

Crossing the room she paused in front of a second glass case. Inside was a silver oboe more than two feet tall and two inches across. A white oblong card described the instrument in four languages but Meer didn't need to read the English version. The only words she cared about were the same in every translation.

Gerhard von Breuning.

Chapter 63

Like a flock of birds descending, the rooms suddenly filled with dozens of small noises that all together created a great flurry. Glancing at the door, Meer watched a harried female teacher trying to corral a bevy of kids. The same college student who'd been sitting at the front desk selling tickets followed them in, beginning a guided tour.

"Bad timing," Sebastian muttered under his breath as the three of them watched the group gather in front of the piano. As the guide spoke, she gestured to a painting on the wall. "Except I think we can make this work in our favor. Stay here." Leaving Meer and Malachai by the oboe cabinet, Sebastian went up to the guide. She appeared fascinated by what he was saying, nodded twice, and then gestured for him to follow her. Together they approached the cabinet and, using a ring she took out of her jeans pocket, the young woman tried first one and then a second key. Pulling the hasp lock apart, she opened the lid, reached inside, gingerly extracted the silver oboe and handed it to Sebastian, as if she were making an offering. He examined it with an expression of reverence on his face; one that Meer was sure was sincere. He was holding an instrument owned by one of the greatest composers of all time, the instrument he himself played in the Vienna Philharmonic.

Behind them and beside them, the children milled around and when one started chasing another, the ticket taker excused herself. Calling out, she gestured for them to gather around her in front of another case in the far corner of the room.

"How did you get her to give you the oboe?" Meer asked incredulously.

"I told her who I am and showed her my ID from the Philharmonic," Sebastian whispered as he set about carefully examining the instrument.

Meer glanced over her shoulder at the children, who were all riveted to the Beethoven death mask, which she'd examined herself three days before. As the young woman explained what it was and how it was made, a hush fell over the room. It was a haunting object, not so much because of what it looked like but rather because it had been made within hours of the maestro's death. Even a photograph would not seem as real as the bronze sculptural sepulcher of his soul. Meer's heart ached and she felt a stab of grief.

"Look at this." Sebastian's voice was low but insistent. They closed ranks around him and each peered down.

On the underside of the oboe was a group of silver hallmarks. Meer knew a fair amount about them from working in her mother's antique store on weekends and summers. Handling so many silver objects she'd memorized many of the most popular but she'd never seen this particular grouping before. Then she noticed something she never had seen before on a maker's mark: a small hole. Cleverly hidden in the midst of the engraving was a pin-thin opening. Her fingers went to the chain around her neck.

"Yes, we have to try it," Sebastian urged, figuring it out at the same time.

"Now? Here?"

"Yes," Malachai's voice insisted.

She glanced up first at the children who were moving on to the next room with the ticket taker and then she checked the young woman's counterpart at the front desk who typed away at his computer.

"Now, quickly," Malachai persisted.

Fingers shaking, Meer lifted the chain out from under her shirt, leaned over and slipped the tiny silver key into the keyhole. She'd wondered since she'd first seen what she'd pulled from beneath the mummified heart what lock could be this small. Now she knew.

The mechanism gave as softly as a butterfly sighing and she let the chain and the key fall back as she tried to open the oboe. How many years had it been since this hinge had been exercised? Gently, she pried the two halves open, forcing the instrument to give up its prize. Gazing down at the contents of the slim silver tomb, Meer recognized what was nestled there from a place deep, deep inside her soul.

It was so delicate and brittle-looking she was afraid to even touch it. Very gently she lifted it out of its hiding place.

"Quickly, give it to me," Sebastian said.

She was confused. Which instrument? Before she figured it out, he reached out, took Beethoven's silver oboe from her and snapped it shut.

"Put that in your bag, quickly, Meer," Malachai said, nodding at the bone flute.

Meanwhile Sebastian had taken several steps away from both of them and put the silver cylinder up to his lips. Not Beethoven, but Pachelbel's *Canon* filled the room. It seemed appropriate to Meer; this was music that Beethoven would have heard, Pachelbel having been a composer who'd also moved from Germany to Vienna almost a hundred years before Beethoven did. The children, their teacher, the ticket taker guide and the young man at the computer all focused their attention on Sebastian and the sweet and sacred sound that he brought forth from the oboe.

Hands trembling, Meer opened her bag and slipped the bone flute inside.

Sebastian finished the piece, accepted an enthusiastic round of applause and with a flourish returned the oboe to the ticket taker, who replaced it in its repository without showing any undue curiosity. Wasn't it lighter without the flute inside? Or hadn't she paid attention to its heft in the first place?

Done, the woman locked the cabinet and thanked Sebastian who in turn thanked her for the honor of letting him play the instrument. Then, nodding at Malachai, he put his arm around Meer's shoulder and gently led her out of the room and out of Beethoven's house.

Chapter 64

None of them spoke as they walked down the stairs until they were out on Mölker Bastei and then Malachai and Sebastian proceeded to have a totally innocuous conversation about other Austrian cities within driving distance that were worth visiting.

Meer soon realized they were obfuscating in case someone was following them or listening to their conversation with wireless microphones. She stopped paying attention. All that mattered was whether or not they were in danger.

Crossing the street, they entered a park. Meer noticed mothers watching their children and elderly people sitting on benches. A woman called out to a dog. Where was Sebastian taking them? A couple strolled by holding hands. A little boy zoomed by them on a bike, so close she could feel a *whoosh* of air as he passed.

Suddenly Sebastian gripped Meer's shoulder and he steered her to the right. Exiting the park, they continued on down the street toward the corner where a tram waited.

Sebastian sped up, pulling her with him. They were almost at the corner. The tram's door was closing. Sebastian's grip tightened. He was going to try for it. Not sensing Malachai on her other side, she glanced over. He wasn't keeping up with them. He wasn't going to make it. She wasn't sure she'd be able to either. What if the door shut on her bag? The flute could be crushed if—

Sebastian jumped on the tram, turned and lifted Meer up and through the door just as it closed behind her. Dazed but unhurt, she looked around the car at the standing-room-only crowd.

"Hold on to me," Sebastian said.

"But Malachai?" She strained to look out the window but the tram had already pulled away from the corner. "Will he be all right?"

"He'll be fine," Sebastian said, speaking softly. "We'll call him as soon as we get to where we're going. It's better this way. Three of us together were too easy to notice."

"But we can't just—" Then she realized what he'd said. "You did it on purpose?"

"Are you all right?" He ignored her question, his eyes telling her this wasn't the place to discuss it. "Did I pull your arm too hard?"

Meer shrugged, not telling him how much it hurt. "Where are we going?"

"To get lost," he whispered, so low she wasn't sure she'd heard him right.

She almost told him that she already was lost and had been for a long time. But like the pain, she didn't want to admit it, and she wasn't sure why.

Chapter 65

Wednesday, April 30th—2:08 p.m.

Swinging 200 feet above the ground in the enclosed space of the Ferris wheel's red cabin, Meer looked out over the city sprawl. "This is crazy."

"It was our best chance. The way the two trains were sitting there, even if someone had followed us from the tram stop, there wouldn't be any way they could have seen us get off the first train and onto the second one."

"And now?"

"And now we're waiting. Catching our breath. Letting the sun set."

"And then?"

"A hotel."

"You mean a different hotel?"

"Yes, not the Sacher where you're registered. We'll find someplace else."

"When can we call Malachai? And my father? We have to let my dad know what's going on."

"Once we get to the hotel."

The cabin swung in the wind and Meer felt her center of gravity shift.

"I remember this scene from *The Third Man*," she said. "We studied that movie for its zither score in a film scoring class I took at Juilliard."

"That's what everyone remembers, the zither and this scene."

"It was a frightening movie, but Vienna really is a frightening city, isn't it?"

"Yes, behind the facades of these elegant buildings are ugly secrets and dirty shadows. Like a beautiful woman holding a gun behind her back."

His voice crawled on her skin and she glanced away from him and down at the miniature city below them.

"What was that famous line from the movie about this view?" she asked.

"It's one of my favorite movies. By the time they're here, Holly Martins knows all about the diluted penicillin and that Harry Lime has destroyed people for his own gain. The corrupt man as metaphor for the corrupt state. Sitting in one of these cabins—looking out at this same view, Lime tells Martins to look down and asks him if he'd feel pity if any of those dots stopped moving forever? 'If I offered you 20,000 pounds for every dot that stopped, would you really, old man, tell me to keep the money? Or would you calculate how many dots you could afford to spare?'"

"That's not the line I remember."

The wind picked up outside and the cabin swayed back and forth. Sebastian smiled and she saw something of Orson Welles's character's devilishness in his eyes as he recited the line: "'In Italy, for thirty years under the Borgias, they had warfare, terror, murder, bloodshed, but they produced Leonardo da Vinci, Michelangelo and the Renaissance. In Switzerland, they had brotherly love. They had five hundred years of democracy and peace, and what did that produce? The cuckoo clock.'"

"That's it. We used to play a game at Juilliard. What would you give up to create something brilliant and timeless?"

"We've all played a version of that game."

Or what would you give up to save someone you loved? she thought but didn't say as the car started on its downward cycle with a hard jerk. They were returning to earth, the people on the ground getting larger, and then there was a clap of thunder as the clouds broke open and fat, heavy drops streaked the windows. Minutes later, the car came to a stop.

"All safe now," Sebastian said.

Chapter 66

Sebastian paid the taxi driver, got out, offered his hand and helped her exit. Her back had stiffened up and she needed the assistance. Despite steeling herself not to, she winced with the exertion. It was only drizzling and there was no reason to rush but they hurried across the street and quickly slipped through the frosted glass doors of the Thonet Hotel. Both of them were stressed and anxious. They'd spent the afternoon at the Prater, making sure they weren't being followed, trying out alternative plans for what to do and where to go.

The eighteenth-century villa's ancient wooden beams, old stone floors, vaulted ceilings and six-foot-tall leaded glass Gothic windows had been restored so that the modernized space exuded character. Mozart's Symphony No. 25 in G Minor played in the background and the air was scented with apples and burning wood. Under any other circumstances, it would be very pleasant here.

Sebastian nodded toward a small seating area where maroon velvet club chairs nestled around a roaring fire.

"Have a seat, let me see if there's any room at the inn," Sebastian said, smiling.

Watching his tall figure cut across the room as he headed over to the reception desk, she wondered at his calm demeanor. A few minutes ago he'd been just as jittery as she was. Which Sebastian was real? Meer's anxiety level accelerated at the thought that she didn't know him at all. Not really.

Her internal metronome kept swinging wildly from the sense that everything would work out to the certainty that disaster was imminent and she should take off and run away now, even from Sebastian. Meer had suffered free-floating anxiety before, first when she was a child and then again in college and knew the symptoms: sweating, trembling and a racing heart.

Five minutes later the manager opened the door to room 23, a junior suite painted dusty blue that had high ceilings, parquet floors and large double windows overlooking the church across the street. And in front of those windows, almost as if it waited for Meer, was a shining black lacquer Bösendorfer piano. Its surface was like satin. Its keys gleamed. The instrument was begging her to sit down and play.

For the first time in four hours Meer put her handbag down, actually let go, placed it on the piano bench and sat down beside it. Placing her fingers on the keys, she shut her eyes and sat there quietly, just feeling the smooth ivory.

Somewhere behind her, Sebastian talked to the hotelier but Meer wasn't paying attention to them or thinking about the priceless treasure in her bag as she began to move her fingers about the keyboard. She hadn't chosen the *Appassionata* Sonata as much as it had chosen her. Nothing mattered in that moment but the blanket of sound that blocked all her thoughts, chased away her physical awareness of herself, picked her up in its arms and flew her away, soared with her into another plane where there was only sound. Rich, full, rounded-note sound.

Meer only became aware that Sebastian was talking to her when he put his hand on her shoulder but she didn't want to return to the moment, she wanted to—no, needed to—finish at least this one piece. Afraid the piano was the bridge to her nightmares, she'd avoided it for so long but now that she couldn't escape her memory lurches anyway, there was no reason to hold back.

Finished, she lowered her head and listened to the last notes lingering in the air, to the metamorphosis from sound to silence, from timbre and tone to only vibration. She didn't feel any less worried when she stopped, but she was better prepared now for what was coming next, as if the music had fortified her.

With a sigh, she pulled her bag toward her. It was time. Opening the oversized leather satchel, she reached inside, felt the handkerchief she'd wrapped the flute in, and pulled it out. The thin object was covered in the cotton, inert, yet her fingers experienced something living, with potential. Not unlike how the keyboard had felt to her.

"Meer? You haven't heard a word I've said for five minutes. Are you all right?" He sat beside her and put his arm around her shoulder. "You're shivering." He stroked her hair as if she were a child in need of calming. "I'm afraid for you. Look at you—and you're just holding it."

"That doesn't matter. This could mean so much to so many people. Including you. What if this is the one thing that could pull Nicolas out of the abyss?"

He leaned in, kissing her lightly on the lips. To Meer it felt as if he were transferring fire from his mouth to hers, that where he'd touched her would be indelibly scarred and she pulled back lest he scorch her more.

"I need to do this," Meer said. "I can't be scared of it." Unfolding the handkerchief, she exposed the flute and they both stared down at the ancient human bone engraved with hundreds of complicated, exotic symbols.

Chapter 67

They were still studying the flute and its mysterious markings when the rain started to beat harder on the windows. The thunder was so loud the building vibrated with each new crack. Sebastian drew the drapes and returned to where Meer was sitting on the couch. And then the lights went out.

The darkness was immediate and complete. Meer was aware of Sebastian getting up; she heard him knock something over and curse under his breath, and then she smelled the distinct odor of sulphur.

Suddenly candlelight glowed, illuminating his face and the part of the room where he stood. Light from another time and place. It might have been the nineteenth century. This could be Archer Wells holding the candelabra. But it wasn't, Meer reminded herself, as Sebastian walked over to the phone and lifted the receiver.

"No dial tone but this is a remote. It wouldn't work in a power failure. I don't know if there's a wall phone in the suite. Did you notice?"

"No, but there's usually one in the bathroom."

He was gone for a few moments and then called out: "Yes, you're right."

She heard him dialing, talking in German, and then he returned.

"There's a blackout in the whole area. None of the trams or subways are running either. Something to do with the storm. I'm going downstairs and get more candles."

At the door, about to leave, he hesitated, walked back to her and sat down next to her. "You understand this has nothing to do with us. No one knows where we are, but don't open the door for anyone, all right? I'll take the key."

Meer had a sudden memory of being in the dark like this with him before. Of him standing just this way in a doorway some other time. Of him asking for a different promise.

No, not him.

"You're seeing a time before, aren't you?"

She nodded.

"And am I there?"

"No, not you."

"But someone connected to me?"

"I'm not sure," she equivocated.

"You don't want to find out, do you?"

"No." She realized it only as she said it. Realized more, too, but didn't say it.

"Whoever he was he did something terrible to you, didn't he? Did he hurt you? Is that why sometimes it seems as if just as you're going to open to me you shut down?"

"Maybe," she whispered.

"I've learned from your father and from Fremont Brecht that we're here to do it right this time. We come back within the same circle of people and are given a chance to do it better. Not to make the same mistakes. I would never hurt you, Meer. Just the opposite. I want to help you and keep you safe." He reached out and brushed her hair off her forehead in a tender gesture.

Her conflicting emotions warned her to stay away from him and at the same time to give in to him. When she did neither he gave her a heartbreaking half smile that surged through her.

"I'll be back in a few minutes. All right?"

She nodded.

While he was gone, Meer sat in the semidarkness. What she and Sebastian were experiencing was what her father had told her about. What ancient sages, followers of Pythagoras and Jung, early Christians, pagans and Kabbalists had identified as being connected to what was known as same soul consciousness. People are part of one great cosmic awareness, her father had tried to explain in different ways over the years. And souls who'd bonded in several lives over time and grown together through the millennia were eventually able to communicate with each other without words through that awareness. When she was old enough to understand it, she'd thought it was a hopeful concept. Even an amazing, magical idea. If it was true, the longing and loneliness plaguing so many people would be eradicated. But she never had truly believed it.

Putting the flute up to her lips, Meer tentatively blew a C note. The bone was so brittle and fragile-looking she was afraid it would shatter with the effort. The sound was awkward, trying but failing to become music. Again she played the note and waited but nothing in her rose up and presented itself. What had she expected? In her memory lurches Archer only wanted the flute if it could be delivered with the song. Without that the instrument was a curiosity, nothing more. Even *with* the song it might be nothing more.

The candelabra Sebastian had left on the table near the piano cast flickering shadows on the walls and in the half light Meer studied the flute.

One of her favorite paintings at the Metropolitan Museum of Art was a melancholy nocturnal scene by Georges de la Tour, called *The Penitent Magdalene*. In it a slight, brown-haired woman, her face turned away, sat in a darkened room where a single candle burned, its image reflected in an ornately framed mirror, drenching her in its mystical light. There were castoff pearls on the table and gold necklaces and bracelets dropped on the floor. In her lap, her hands clasped a skull.

In this candlelight, the flute in Meer's hands took on the same mysterious color and portentous glow as the human bone in the painting.

Studying the hundreds of black markings engraved into the cylinder, she struggled to find just one that was familiar, but none were. Whether they were a long-lost language of ancient hieroglyphics or meaningless symbols, she didn't know or remember from any of her memory surges. But she did remember how it felt in her hands before...somewhere in time when she'd first touched this slim bone, when she stole it from an urn hanging on a tree by the side of a sacred river in a land she couldn't even name.

The object measured six inches long and was less than two inches around: too small to be Devadas's ulna or radius, femur or tibia, but it could be a piece of any of them.

Devadas?

Across all the years, she'd suddenly and inexplicably remembered the name of the man who had once held her in his arms, and it was as familiar as the elusive music she'd been almost hearing since she was a child.

She whispered it out loud: *"Devadas."*

Closing her eyes, Meer struggled to remember more of the memory surge that had presented itself to Margaux in Beethoven's house in Baden that had something to do with a burial scene and this bone, but there was only the chaos of thousands of gossamer cobwebs connecting one time to another. Somewhere at the center of the perplexity was the certainty that the marks were ciphers that translated into the memory song.

Casper Neidermier and Rudolph Toller were right about that. Beethoven was right too.

Meer needed to call her father. These were manmade marks: an archaic alphabet of sound. Maybe he'd know something about them. Maybe they were connected to the Gematria, the reading of the Hebraic words and letters translated into mystical numbers, a holy language that he'd been studying most of his life.

Chapter 68

Wednesday, April 30th—9:15 p.m.

"You shouldn't have phoned your father but at least there's no possibility of anyone tracing the call if it went through the switchboard," Sebastian said. "You can't phone Malachai either. What if his hotel room phone is tapped? People other than us are desperate for what's sitting next to you."

One by one Sebastian lit the candles he'd brought upstairs, and as the room became brighter the scent of paraffin intensified, imbuing the air with an aroma that for Meer, harkened back to long-lost memories. He came and sat down next to her.

"Wouldn't you kill for the chance to find the memory song and to finally remember the whole story behind all the fractured images that have been torturing you since you were a little girl?" he asked. The depth of sadness in his eyes was almost intolerable to look at.

He didn't know her well enough to even guess at how far she'd go to quiet her memories. It was Nicolas he was thinking of, Nicolas in his hospital room, dissociated and disconnected, drawing the haunted face of some lost child and chanting the Jewish prayer for the dead.

"If I talked you through it, would you try to hypnotize me?" Meer asked.

"You don't have to, I know how. When Rebecca wouldn't let me bring a hypnotist in to see Nicolas, Dr. Alderman, a member of the Society, taught me." He hesitated. "You're kind to do this for me."

"For Nicolas," she corrected.

There was every reason for the session to be a success. Sebastian's voice was a comfortable and comforting timbre and the instructions he gave were similar to those that Malachai used. The lighting was soft—thanks to the power outage and the candles—and there was no noise to distract her and prevent her from entering a deep stage of relaxation.

Except there was a vise on her consciousness keeping her in the reality of the hard-edged moment. After trying three times, Sebastian stopped. "I don't think this is going to work," he said. "You're not relaxing."

Getting up from the couch, she went over to the piano where the flute rested on the velvet-cushioned seat glowing in the candle's light.

"I'm sorry," she said without taking her eyes off of it.

Sebastian walked into the bar area, opened the small refrigerator and pulled out a bottle of wine. "It's still cold," he said. He poured two glasses and brought one to her. "You have nothing to apologize for. Come, sit down with me. We have the flute. We'll figure out the rest."

As she sipped the wine, she stole looks across the room at the ancient bone instrument, as if willing it to give up its secret.

"Have you ever wondered what triggered Nicolas's breakdown?"

"I have an idea, but there's no way to know for sure."

"You think he saw the child's skull the gardener dug up at Steinhof?"

Sebastian nodded. "Nicolas was there…all the children were… playing outside. I think Rebecca believes so, too, but whenever I tried to talk to her about it she became irrationally defensive— as if because it happened on her turf it was her fault…" He stopped talking and looked off into the distance. Picking up the bottle, he refilled their glasses, and for a while they sat there in silence.

An hour later, Meer woke up still sitting on the couch. In her head was the music she'd been hearing all her life. She recognized the tune, as if she'd always known it. She opened her eyes and smiled, thinking that she was finally going to be able to play the song and then all this would be over. But in the few seconds between having her first conscious thought and opening her eyes, the memory of the music faded.

"You fell asleep," Sebastian said from the table where he peeled an orange. "One minute you were sipping the wine, the next your eyes were closed." He gestured to plates of cheese, bread, sliced meats and fruit. "I brought up some food. You must be hungry."

She wasn't but knew she needed to eat something so she managed half the orange and some cheese.

"For safety's sake, even though it's unlikely anyone was able to follow us, we should probably take turns sleeping," he suggested.

"Well, I already had my nap. You go ahead."

After Sebastian retired to the bedroom, Meer brought the flute over to the coffee table. As the hours passed, she sat vigil over the instrument. Finally, unable to resist, she examined it once more, scanning up and down the lines of engraved markings, not focusing on any one of them but visually playing with all the shapes.

Through the window, the full moon shone through the gap in the drapes onto her lap, onto the flute, casting the bone in a bluish light, making the incisions appear even deeper than they were. Shutting her eyes, she touched them with her fingertip. One after the next. Tactually discovering each shape.

Meer sat like that for a long time, listening to the occasional sound of a car *whooshing* down the rainy street, touching her treasure, trying not to think, sleepy, almost dozing…

Her finger moved around and around one shape. Sleep… easy, dreamless, quiet sleep was at the center of the circle she touched. Once more around and Meer was certain she'd find the end of the dream and finally be able to rest. Everyone would be able to rest. Not just her. Not just now. Everyone. For all time. Around and around. One circle. Another circle. Three. Four. Five. Six circles. Another. Another. Nine. Ten. Ten circles. One inside the next.

Meer looked down. Her finger was tracing a deeply engraved circle close to the mouthpiece. It wasn't just a simple circle but several tiny carved circles, a series of tight concentric circles, ten in all.

She remembered this symbol. Had seen it before. But where?

Playing the memory game, she went through an exercise of seeing the circles in her mind, then widening out as if she was stepping back and saw them on a gray metal disk and then widened out again and again and finally was in her mother's antique store twenty-five years ago.

The elderly man with the droopy white mustache, gold-tipped walking stick and heavy German accent showed Pauline Logan a clock he wanted her to buy from him.

"Clocks like this were only made for a hundred years," the man said. "Music clocks, they were called. Very entertaining. Very popular. So popular even master composers wrote music for them. Listen if you will. This piece is very lovely. Beethoven wrote it just for these clocks."

The music that emanated from that ancient timepiece was Meer's introduction to classical music; the first piece that wedged its way into her consciousness. Every day for as many months as the clock was in the store, Meer would sit and watch the minutes move forward while she waited for the clock to play its magic music on the hour. It was the only antique in the store that she'd cared about and had cried bitterly when it was sold. As recompense, her mother had offered to give her piano lessons so she could learn to play the music herself. But she hadn't been able to play the Beethoven piece and she never stopped missing her clock. And it had been *her* clock. She'd learned every inch of it: the face, the steel flutes, the casing, the inner workings and the maker's mark engraved on the back of the face.

The same mark she was looking at now.

Ten concentric circles.

And exactly like that maker's mark there were small perpendicular lines marking these circles, too. Little nicks. Meer was sure, even though it had been so long ago, that they were in the same places; certain that everything about these circles on the ancient bone flute was identical to those on the back of the clock that had introduced her to music so long ago: to Beethoven's music.

It happened instantly, without warning, without the cold embrace she was used to. There was no sense of time flattening out or turning over on itself. She simply knew how to find the memory song. In her mind's eye she performed the magic: cut the symbol of ten circles in half and, as if they were made of string, laid them out horizontally into ten straight lines.

Ten lines with small marks on them in various places. Not an arbitrary abstract design but a perfect musical staff, and on each of the lines were marks that she now understood as notes.

C-G-D-A-E-B-F#-C#-G#-D#-A#-E#.

She studied the familiar musical sequence and so many different things she'd read, and her father had told her, and her teachers at Juilliard had taught, all coalesced. This was the Circle of Fifths Pythagoras had identified over 2500 years before, tying harmonic relationships to the human energy system. The fifth was also the interval found in most sacred music and said to harmonize human energy. Pythagoras had used music compositions based on this interval to heal illness, to effect mood changes. It was said that through exploring his past lives he'd discovered a constant: a universal life form inhabiting and connecting all living things: vibration. Everything, he said, from a grain of sand to the stars, was in a state of constant vibration.

As if she was reaching out into that collective unconscious that her father always talked about, and plucking the information like a grape from a cluster, she understood that these twelve notes that Devadas's brother, Rasul, had engraved on the bone flute were his memory song in honor of a truncated life. A song he wrote to soothe the young girl Ohana, who had brought him her lover's bone, whose heart had been cut down the middle and separated into before there was tragedy, and after. A song to help Ohana remember that before there was a death there had been a life, and before that life a death and that there would be a life after this death too. The circles would continue on without end and everyone who was once connected would be connected again.

Chapter 69

Wednesday, April 30th—11:03 p.m.

Lucian Glass and Alex Kalfus pulled up to the Sacher just after Malachai's cab dropped him off and the two of them watched him disappear through the hotel's front door. They'd trailed him all day, from the hospital early that morning to a bookstore with Sebastian and Meer, then to the Beethoven house and then into the Rathaus garden where the three of them had parted ways.

It was easy enough for the agent and the policeman to stay on Malachai's trail even when he was out of sight thanks to the tracking device still in place. But the team following Meer didn't have a tracking device, and after she and Sebastian jumped on the tram they'd lost her.

"If you don't mind, I'd like to wait a while and see if Meer returns," Lucian said to Kalfus, who gave him a curious look.

"This isn't just professional for you, is it?"

"It's a case, Kalfus. A case I want to solve."

"Are you personally involved with the woman?"

"I've never met her."

The two law officers stayed on watch until one-thirty in the morning but when Meer still hadn't arrived, Kalfus insisted they call in backup and each try to get some rest themselves.

Lucian couldn't sleep, though, and sat in his hotel room with the television on and the sound off, sketching scenes from the day. One after another he ripped them off the pad before they were finished and let them fall to the floor until there was a pile of almost a dozen. He didn't care about them; it was the action, the movement, and the release of the tension that he craved.

Where was she? And why, as Kalfus had asked, was he taking her disappearance so very personally?

Chapter 70

My life often seemed to me like a story that has no beginning and no end. I had the feeling that I was an historical fragment, an excerpt for which the preceding and succeeding text was missing. I could well imagine that I might have lived in former centuries and there encountered questions I was not yet able to answer; that I had been born again because I had not fulfilled the task given to me.

—Carl Jung

Thursday, May 1st—8:00 a.m.

"Good morning."

The sound of his voice split the silence open, startling her and she jerked up into a sitting position.

It was just Sebastian.

"What time is it?" she asked. "I wasn't supposed to fall asleep."

"There's nothing to worry about. We're still here. So's that." He pointed to the flute. "It's eight. The electricity's back on—would you like coffee? Something to eat? You barely ate last night."

"Does the hotel have room service?"

"They have a buffet downstairs, but I can ask them to bring up something. What would you like?"

"Coffee. Toast. Some honey for the toast. If they have eggs, I'd like some and juice too."

When he came back from ordering he told her the manager was going to send someone up with the food right away. "It shouldn't take long."

"I need to call my father and find out if he's all right. And Malachai."

"All taken care of," Sebastian said. "While you were sleeping I checked on Nicolas from the pay phone down the street, then called both Malachai and Jeremy. Your father was still sleeping. The nurse said he was resting comfortably and that his fever had dropped during the night. I asked her to tell him you'd be there later this morning. I assume that's fine?"

"Yes, thanks. How's Nicolas?"

"Improving. Well, the pneumonia is improving."

When the food came Meer plucked the juice off the cart while Sebastian signed the bill. After the waiter left, Sebastian double-locked the door behind him, the precaution bringing back the edge of nervousness that her sleep had smoothed out.

"That's great news about your son."

"Yes…yes…but he's still in so much danger. Every day that he remains lost inside his head is exponentially worse." Sebastian poured himself coffee. "I'm sorry. I'm just so frustrated. I phoned Rebecca, too, but if she was there she wouldn't take my call. Why is she doing this? I never abused him, never hurt him. When nothing else works, why not try an alternative?"

"I remember how angry my mother was when my father first took me to Malachai."

"He told me he didn't have an easy time of it."

"None of us had an easy time of it." Meer picked up the toast and took a bite. She'd been ravenous a few minutes ago but now the food held no interest for her. A surfeit of memories—ones she wished had faded—flared: the bickering behind their bedroom door at night, the hushed arguments, the icy stillness in the house that kept them all separated and isolated during that last winter. What would have happened if she hadn't told them about the dreads? Would they have stayed together?

"All I know is she's stopping me from trying to do everything I can for my son and I am not going to let her." He stood. "I'm going to take a shower."

Once the door closed behind him she was sorry she hadn't told him the amazing news that she'd uncovered the memory song. Wasn't he the reason she'd worked so hard last night? To find the song so he could play it for his son and help him the way no one had been able to help her? Yes. Of course, but after so many years of searching for the music through the fog of endless dreams and half-waking nightmares, she wasn't quite ready to give it up and give it over. She needed to hear it just once by herself. Last night she couldn't play it for fear she'd wake him up, but he wouldn't be able to hear her now over the sound of the shower.

Holding the ancient piece of bone gingerly in her hand Meer waited to hear the water's steady pounding and only then put the crudely crafted instrument to her lips and arranged her fingers.

Covering one of the holes she blew air into the cylinder and played a C, a G and then a D. The notes sounded rough, a primitive call brought up from the earth, a tone that contained rain and smoke and fire and cold that filled the room and then slipped outside and encircled the city and the country and then the planet, going wide into the galaxy. So disturbing and complicated were the first three notes, Meer put the crude flute down. Throughout history people had played those same notes on a wide variety of instruments. So it wasn't just the notes but these particular vibrations that were different. She could still feel them in the room and how they were taking a longer time than was usual to dissipate. Were these the binaural beats her father had talked about?

The steady shower reminded her that she had a limited amount of time.

She had to do this now.

Trying again, she blew with more confidence, holding the C note longer, and then played the second note, this new sound mingling with the restive tone already lingering in the air and the third and the fourth. The beats of the blended music verged on difficult and unqualified noise.

She stopped playing. This wasn't a game. Not a theory on paper. *Beethoven was right.* She played the next two notes and the next. An unholy blackness settled on her. A treacherous miasma. An awful preamble but she had to do this…get it over with once and for all.

Meer started at the beginning of the song and blew out the first note again, and then the second and then—

"What are you doing?" Sebastian asked.

Chapter 71

He stood in the doorway to the bathroom, a towel around his waist, his hair dripping. The strong shoulders and delineated muscles in his arms and chest were tensed. "You figured it out?"

She nodded.

"Play it for me, please."

"We don't know what it can do."

"I don't care about that."

"Beethoven was so convinced of how dangerous this was he went through an elaborate ruse to hide—"

Sebastian cut her off. "Beethoven lived over a hundred and fifty years ago and you don't know for sure why he hid anything."

"I do know. He was sure the song was a malevolent force. He'd heard it. He knew what it was capable of. He was right."

"That's not in the letter. He never explained that."

"But I know it. Don't you believe me?"

"If I didn't believe you would I have come this far? Would we even be here? Did you really figure out the song? Please, Meer. I won't hold you responsible for anything that happens to me, just play me the song." The plea in his eyes was even more desperate than the one in his voice, and she wished she could help him but she'd experienced memories without being prepared for them. Trying to run away from them had almost crippled her.

"Not without knowing what the full ramifications of your hearing it might be. Not while we're alone. Not while we're still in danger. Help me get out of here with the flute…get me to my father and Malachai…and then together all of us can figure out what we need to do next."

Sebastian started to interrupt her again but she wouldn't let him. "I know you want to play the music for Nicolas—and I want you to be able to do that. Nothing would make me happier than if the music works and brings him back but we need to do this safely. I can't risk hurting him or you. I'll go on blaming myself forever."

Sadness overwhelmed her as her last words lingered in the air. She *had* been blaming herself forever, for much more than one lifetime, but why? And as soon as she asked herself the question, she knew the answer. *His death had been her fault.* But whose death?

Meer closed her eyes and searched the inestimable blackness until she finally saw the outline of a man. But who he was and who she had been when she was with him wouldn't come into focus. Only the sickening horror that someone she'd loved had died because of her, and somehow this flute and its music were connected to that tragedy.

Chapter 72

Thursday, May 1st—9:00 a.m.

Nine hours after leaving the same spot the night before, Lucian Glass met Alex Kalfus in front of the Sacher Hotel at 1010 Philharmonikerstrasse.

"According to our backup team, which has been trailing Meer Logan, she never returned during the night," Kalfus told him when he got into the car at nine-fifteen.

"Can you find out from the hotel housekeeper if her room was used overnight? It is possible that your men missed her."

Kalfus bristled. "Not likely." But he made the call. "They are sending someone to the room," he reported back.

While he watched the hotel entrance, Lucian sipped his second cup of coffee of the morning with the devotion of an addict, hoping the elixir would do more than the first had to shake him awake.

"The *fräulein's* bed was not slept in and the towels and service in the bathroom showed no signs of being used. Not even a washcloth," Kalfus reported.

"I think we should call the hospital and find out if Jeremy Logan had a visit from his daughter yet this morning—and let's see what we can find out about Sebastian Otto's whereabouts while we're at it."

The voice on the other end of Kalfus's phone crackled back to life. *"Ja?"* He listened, nodding, and then turned back to Lucian. "So, Jeremy only had one visitor last night and that was Malachai. The hospital's record coincides with ours. He arrived at five o'clock and stayed until visiting hours were over at eight."

Lucian checked his notes anyway. Malachai had left the hospital at 8:05 and taken a taxi to the Memorist Society where he stayed for three hours and fifteen minutes and then left at 11:22 with Fremont Brecht. The two of them got into Fremont's chauffeured car, which dropped Malachai off at the Sacher Hotel at 11:52.

"Phone calls?"

"Jeremy Logan received one call last night and another this morning."

"What time?"

"10:15 last night."

"From where?"

"The call went to the general switchboard and wasn't traced. The one this morning came in at 8:15 but Jeremy was sleeping so the call wasn't put through—but it was traced and originated from a phone booth in the Spittleberg area."

"Isn't that near Jeremy's house?"

"Yes."

"Maybe she stayed there last night. Or in a hotel in that section. Could you get a patrol car to canvas the hotels in the area?"

Kalfus was about to make the call when he pointed to the front of the hotel. "There he is."

Both men watched as Malachai stood outside, perusing the street.

Kalfus turned the key in the ignition preparing to pull out. Lucian knew they had to follow Malachai and not wait for Meer but he was angry with his quarry for choosing now to leave. Except he didn't leave. Not yet.

"There's something about the look in his eyes, as if he's always planning two steps ahead," Lucian said.

"I can't decide if it makes him look intelligent or guilty."

"Both, and he's much more guilty and much more intelligent than you'd guess. The man hasn't taken one misstep in nine months."

"Well, certainly not one misstep while he's been here. Visits with friends, a meeting at an archaeology society, out to dinner…all seemingly innocent." Kalfus shifted into Reverse but Lucian stopped him.

"No, sit tight, he's just going into the café next door."

Seconds later, Malachai could be seen through the restaurant window and as he studied the menu, Lucian studied him.

"Whatever happened in those woods in Baden," Kalfus said, "is it possible that Malachai was responsible, even though he wasn't present? Do you think any of these robberies or attacks have been Malachai's doing?"

"It's possible."

"Probable?"

"I'm not sure. Meer Logan is one of the few people Malachai's shown any genuine affection for."

"Do you think that his feelings would prevent him from going after what he wants?"

"No, but I don't believe he would have to hurt her to get what he wanted. If she had it, she'd give it to him." Lucian paused. "No one wants Malachai to be guilty more than I do but he was instrumental in bringing Meer here—he wanted her to look at the gaming box and hopefully glean important clues from it—so why would he arrange to have the box stolen before she really got a good chance to study it? Nothing is straightforward with him, but Meer *is* the only link to where the flute might be and what the memory song is. Would he put her in jeopardy if she's his best chance?"

"Who would?"

"Someone who doesn't believe in reincarnation and just wants the objects for their monetary value." Lucian finished what was left of the bitter coffee as a waiter in the traditional black suit and white apron served Malachai his breakfast. "Or someone who wants us to think that."

"I'm not sure I follow." Kalfus frowned, confused.

"I'm not either." Lucian gave a halfhearted laugh. "How much do we know about Sebastian Otto?"

"Absolutely nothing to make us suspicious. He's a musician with the Philharmonic here. Plays the oboe. Thirty-eight years old. Never has had any dealings with the police. Divorced, one child, age nine, who has been suffering a mental disorder for the last six months."

"A son?"

Kalfus nodded.

So that was where Lucian had heard the name before. He was annoyed that he hadn't remembered sooner. About three months ago Malachai had received a phone call from Sebastian Otto, calling at Jeremy Logan's suggestion, to ask if the reincarnationist could come to Vienna and see his son. Lucian had remembered the call because of how frustrated Malachai had sounded when he explained he couldn't make the trip.

"Sebastian believes that his son is suffering from some sort of past life crisis," he told Kalfus. "There's more than one connection here."

Watching Malachai read through that morning's newspaper, Lucian wondered what else he'd forgotten that might be important now.

Chapter 73

Thursday, May 1st—9:39 a.m.

"I have some bad news," Bill Vine said as he rushed into the make-shift office at the concert hall, slamming the door behind him.

Paxton stood up, ready to spring into action.

"The signal we've been tracking out of Czechoslovakia, to Vienna and then to Durnstein has been taking us on a joyride. Apparently our buyer found the little gift we put on the knapsack and attached it to the underside of a car belonging to a couple from St. Mary's, Georgia, who had the bad luck to visit the Moravsky Krumlov on Monday. He's a lawyer and would-be novelist; she's a Mary Kay executive. We've run them through every computer system we have and they are who they say they are with no connections to any known terrorist group. She grew up in St. Mary's and her family practically owns the town. He's been on the city council for ten years. Brother, are they brand-spanking clean."

"So now we know the tracking device was on a holiday and the device we lost in the subway was the damn Semtex," Paxton said. "And we still don't have a clue where that disappeared to, do we?"

It was a rhetorical question. They'd been obsessed with locating it since it dropped off the radar two days before and everyone knew they didn't have any idea where the Semtex was.

"I thought we were using a global positioning system that would prevent this very thing from happening. You guaranteed it."

"As long as the tracking device wasn't taken out of range."

"Well, how did someone get it so fucking high in the sky or deep in the ocean that we didn't watch him on his way there to do it? Where's the device, Bill?"

"We don't care anymore."

"What the fuck are you talking about?"

"We're wasting time now, Tom. It doesn't matter where the hell the device is, we can't find it. We can't waste time looking for it. All we have time to worry about now is that no one with that block of Semtex winds up in the vicinity of this building."

Paxton glowered at his employee. "And what are we doing to make sure that isn't happening? We're going to have top brass from twenty-five countries and every branch of our own government including the fucking Vice President—"

"We're fine," Bill interrupted. "We're in good shape. We've had men combing through the tunnels under this place for days and have air traffic control on alert. We've doubled the teams. If anyone's above us or below us, we'll find them."

Chapter 74

While the hot water beat down on her, Meer played the elusive music in her mind. After a lifetime of not being able to grab hold of it, now she couldn't let it go. Seemingly disparate information connected the flute's music to the rest of her life, almost as proof that she was meant to make this discovery one day.

She remembered being in the hospital after the spinal fusion and her father showing her a book with a drawing of the Tree of Life in it. All circles. Had all of these circles separated by thousands of years come together for her now? And why her?

She quickly finished washing her hair with the hotel-provided shampoo. She wanted to get to the hospital as fast as she could and talk to her father and have him explain some of those lessons she'd always been too busy for. Stepping out of the shower stall, she put on one of the hotel's thick bathrobes and wrapped a towel around her head.

"I'm anxious to get out of here—" she was saying when she walked into the suite's living room expecting to find Sebastian eating his breakfast. But he wasn't there.

She walked over toward the open bedroom door and stood outside. "Sebastian?"

No answer.

Maybe he'd gone downstairs to pay the bill, to arrange for a car, for any one of a hundred reasons. Tightening the belt around the robe, she padded back into the bathroom to finish drying her hair and get dressed, playing a childish game with herself: when she finished and went back outside he'd be there.

Chapter 75

Thursday, May 1ˢᵗ—10:20 a.m.

Malachai walked out of the restaurant, walked the five steps to the front of the hotel, nodded to the doorman and waited while he hailed a cab.

Following at a safe distance, neither Kalfus nor Lucian was surprised when they arrived at the hospital.

They'd just settled in for another interminable wait when Malachai came back outside after only five short minutes, looking distraught and confused. It was the first time Lucian had seen him with his mask askew and not in total control.

"Something's up. Call the floor. Find out if Logan's all right."

Malachai was just getting into a taxi when Kalfus said, "Jeremy Logan left the hospital about ten minutes ago against his doctor's orders."

"Was he alone?"

"No, he was accompanied by a man."

"And from the looks of it Malachai didn't know a thing about it and was expecting his friend to still be in his room. We have a problem, Alex. We're going to need backup. We have to find Logan. Fast."

Chapter 76

Thursday, May 1st—10:42 a.m.

Sebastian was still missing. None of the reasons Meer had come up with would explain why he'd been gone more than forty minutes. Unless, no…after everything he'd done for her… Something must have happened to him. Unless he was so angry she'd refused to play the memory song for him, he'd walked out in frustration and was sitting in some café stewing. So what should she do now? Go to the hospital on her own? She had Inspector Fiske's card in her bag. Should she call him? No, not the police. What could she tell him he'd even believe? Besides, he might want to take the flute away from her as evidence and she couldn't take that chance. Her father and Malachai had to see it before anyone else did. She'd ask the concierge to call her a taxi and go to the hospital.

Sitting down at the desk, Meer wrote Sebastian a note. Just a few lines, telling him where she was going. Then she started to take an inventory of the room—a habit of her mother's she'd picked up—

except she'd come here with nothing but what she wore and the pocketbook she carried. There wouldn't be an errant bottle of cologne or vial of pills by the side of the bed. Everything she had that mattered was across the room on the piano bench where she'd left the flute beside her purse when she went to take a shower.

She bent to pick it up. Yes, the bag was there. But the flute wasn't.

Maybe Sebastian had put it inside her pocketbook before he'd gone out in case housekeeping came in while she was showering. Frantically she emptied her bag onto the floor. But it wasn't there either.

Halfheartedly she checked the rest of the room, almost certain the flute wasn't going to be there and was in despair when the suite's doorbell rang. She rushed toward the living room. As she reached the door she heard a man call out, "Fräulein Juska?"

It had to be Sebastian using the name they'd checked in with. He'd apologize and tell her where the flute was and explain that—

Meer jerked open the door without looking through the peephole. A man wearing a bellman's uniform with the hotel's insignia on his breast pocket held out an envelope. Suddenly Meer remembered Sebastian's warning from the night before not to let anyone in, to be suspicious even past logic. This man might be the assailant, might have knocked out the real bellman, stolen his clothes—she slammed the door in his face and threw the lock, the clicking loud in her ears.

"No—please—I'm very sorry," the man on the other side of the door said in awkward English. "Herr Juska asked me to deliver to you this note at ten-forty-five."

"Will you…will you slip it under the door?"

"Certainly."

Dear Meer,

Your father was going to have a procedure this afternoon. His heart's worse than he's let on and he was finally going to tell you when he saw you this morning...but he's missing. No one knows where he is. It's imperative he's found and returns to the hospital.

I think I know where he is but I need your help. Please, do what I ask without calling the police yet. Once I explain... then you can call them if you want. Come as soon as you can. Just walk to the taxi stand on the corner and give the driver the address: Engerthstrasse 122. Ring the bell when you get there. I will see you on the video camera to let you in. Hurry.

Sebastian

Chapter 77

Thursday, May 1st—11:22 a.m.

Standing across the street from the police station at Deutschmeisterplatz 3 on the busy Schottenring, Malachai weighed his options. He didn't know what to do and that wasn't a feeling he was used to. All he knew was that there was no way he could conduct a proper search for either Meer or Jeremy by himself. Not in a foreign country where he barely spoke the language. And there was no time to hire anyone. There was too much at stake to risk anything but a full-out effort with the local authorities. There were simply too many questions he didn't have answers to.

Who else knew that Meer found the flute yesterday? And Jeremy? What had happened to his friend? Had he found out Meer was missing and checked himself out of the hospital to try to find her? He'd do anything to save his daughter; endangering himself wouldn't be of any consequence. But who had he called? The nurse said he'd left with a man. Maybe Sebastian? But Sebastian wasn't answering his cell phone.

Despite the traffic, few car horns honked and the morning was deceptively lovely. There were red and purple flowers in the pots in front of the clothing store next to the station house. On the other side of the street the early nineteenth century building showed off a sculptured frieze of Pan playing his pipe.

Everywhere in Vienna there were monuments to music. This particular one being on this particular corner would seem to be a coincidence to anyone else but not to him. He'd spent the last thirty years refuting coincidences.

If he didn't walk across the street and through the large glass doors to file a report, he could be endangering both Jeremy's and Meer's lives. That they were *both* missing couldn't be chance. But by making the report he would certainly be opening himself up to scrutiny he didn't want. The circumstantial evidence would be against him yet again. It didn't take a leap of imagination to construct the argument the FBI and Interpol would make: for the second time in less than a year an ancient artifact worth hundreds of thousands of dollars that could challenge the belief systems of millions of people and many scientific precepts had been stolen, and Malachai Samuels was not only at the scene of the crime again but was also close friend of the missing persons involved.

Except weren't there hundreds of people who would want the item besides him? He could name several himself. It wasn't about money for Malachai and he doubted it was about money for whoever else was involved at this point. He knew the limits of his own conscience, but how far would the board of directors of the Memorist Society go to get the flute?

How badly did Fremont Brecht want to prove reincarnation? Last night he said he'd hired someone to find the gaming box but his contacts hadn't been able to locate it yet. Was he lying? Had he found out that Meer had discovered the flute? Had he kidnapped her?

How desperate was Dr. Erika Alderman to prove the potential of binaural beats?

She'd been studying the idea of harmonic resonance for the last thirty years. He'd seen determination flare in her eyes last night when she talked about proving her theories and establishing her place in the scientific community.

And for all Malachai knew there were other Memorists he hadn't met who coveted the flute. Certainly by now there were dozens of people who would know what he'd known all along: if there was any chance of the flute and the memory song being found, Meer Logan would be instrumental in that discovery. Conversely, if anything happened to her, any chances for access to the flute would disappear.

In his life, the opportunity to actually prove the existence of re-incarnation would not come that many times. It had already slipped out of his grasp once. He couldn't allow it to happen again. But willingly talking to the police?

He imagined Detective Barry Branch back at home smiling smugly at hearing the news. The baby-faced member of New York's Finest who'd been the investigating officer on the memory stones case from the beginning would reopen that case, and Malachai would be under intense investigation once again. Except there was no evidence to use against him. None found to date. None that they would ever find.

The steel handle was cold to the touch and the glass door was heavier than he expected. Inside there was so much activity no one even noticed him until he'd been standing at the front desk more than five minutes. Finally, the officer on duty turned to him and, in rudimentary German, Malachai explained that he needed to talk to an inspector who could speak English.

Waiting on an uncomfortable wooden bench, Malachai pulled out a deck of cards and shuffled them, letting the slapping sound soothe him. Not paying attention to how many times he performed the activity, he went over and over what he would tell the police and what he'd keep to himself. It was important to be prepared and only give as much information as necessary.

The story he'd offer was that he'd come to Vienna to meet with his old friend Jeremy Logan and inspect the treasure Logan had found. As head of the Phoenix Foundation he had many reasons to do that.

The cards moved so quickly they blurred.

Maybe he shouldn't stay. He wasn't used to vacillating and was annoyed with himself that he was second-guessing his decision. Besides, having come this far, if he didn't report Jeremy and Meer as missing and left now, it would be even more suspicious; he'd already given his name to the officer on duty. Clumsily he mixed the deck and the cards flew out of his hand and spilled onto the floor. The last thing he wanted to do was get down on his hands and knees and pick them up, but the only alternative was to leave them there like litter.

"Dr. Samuels? I'm Inspector Kalfus. You asked for someone who could speak English. How may I help you?"

Chapter 78

Wipers swept back and forth on the taxi's windshield, sluicing away the steady rain. Meer's hands were clasped together so tightly she hurt herself. Nothing about the trip so far felt familiar until the driver turned the corner onto Engerthstrasse and up ahead, through the rain, she saw the stone columns of the Toller Archäologiegesellschaft.

Walking up the steps to the Memorist Society's building, she saw a bright yellow sign affixed to the gate—it showed the symbol of a door with a large X through it. Despite the obvious *do not enter* warning and the fact that the Society didn't open till after noon, Meer pressed the doorbell.

Thirty seconds passed. She pounded on the door. Sixty. She rang the bell again. Ninety seconds. Leaving her finger on the buzzer, Meer wondered how Sebastian knew where her father was. And why had Jeremy left the hospital if he needed a procedure? Would she and

Sebastian find him in time? Her mind had been churning the same questions since she'd run out of the hotel.

Why wasn't someone answering the door?

Suddenly a sickening thought occurred to her: she didn't know Sebastian's handwriting. Maybe the note wasn't from him at all. What if the people who attacked her in the woods and knocked Sebastian out, who were probably responsible for stealing the Beethoven letter and the gaming box and for Ruth's and Dr. Smettering's deaths, were behind this ruse too? Maybe they had Sebastian and her father and the flute.

A creaking hinge alerted her as the door opened quickly, and before she could protest or look to see who it was an arm reached out and grabbed her, pulling her inside into a dark, shadowy foyer.

"Thank God it's you. Is my father here?" she blurted out as soon as she saw that it was Sebastian.

"Yes."

"Is he all right?"

"Yes, I'll take you to him."

Meer was skeptical.

"You're sure he's all right."

"Meer, he's fine. I promise." He looked right at her and she felt safe and then instantly frightened as if she were hearing two different beats, one in each ear.

"He's this way." He gestured to the gloomy interior and she followed him inside.

"The flute's missing, Sebastian. Do you know where it is?"

"Yes."

"That's all? Yes?"

As they passed into the main room where it was even darker, Meer's anxiety increased. The first time she'd come here with her father she'd had a toxic reaction; the air was rife with affliction and tragedy on Monday and it was worse today, so thick she thought she might choke on it.

"The flute's safe. I'd never let anything happen to it." His words echoed along with their footsteps on the marble floor.

"I don't understand…why did you take it? And why did you leave without telling me?"

"There was no time to waste. I'm sorry about this. About everything." There was so much pathos in his voice it broke through the alarm she was feeling.

As they left the inner sanctum and kept walking, Meer asked him why there was a no-entry sign outside the building.

"The majordomo received a call this morning that there might be a gas leak in the sub-basement so he alerted the staff and told them not to come in until notified."

"There's a gas leak and my father's here?"

"I told you, he's fine."

They'd reached a large oak door that Sebastian held open for her. Stepping into the book-lined library she spun around, looking for Jeremy but saw only empty chairs, yards of carved wooden shelves, intricately pattered carpets, a suite of stained-glass windows.

"Where is he?"

"This way." In the corner he flung open another door, revealing a small walk-in closet. Cartons were stacked at one end, double shelves lined the opposite wall. As he reached out Meer knew even before he did it that he was reaching for a hidden handle, and when a section of the wall swung out, she rushed to the access and looked down into a gaping black hole, smelling a surge of damp, dank air.

She knew this place. Remembering the cloaked entrance and the details of what lay beyond it, she was lost for a minute between now and then and tried to grab hold of a tangible memory.

"We're going down into the catacombs, aren't we? Why?"

"All the Society's valuables are down there...all the historical papers," he explained as he pulled a cord illuminating a deep descending spiral staircase and she hurried down the same staircase she'd seen in a memory lurch. Meer's shivering started with sudden intensity and she had to put her finger between her teeth to stop them from chattering. Remaining in the present was urgent; she couldn't allow memory to overtake her now.

Eight, nine, she couldn't keep herself from counting the steps. Eleven, twelve...there were going to be fifteen steps, she thought, and yes, the fifteenth step was the last.

Sebastian flicked another switch. Weak light showed the way through a twisting tunnel. Hearing rustling, she spun around.

"Just mice, they scamper when they hear movement," he said. "It's not much farther, I promise." The kindness and sympathy in his voice reached out to comfort her, but nothing except seeing her father would alleviate her anxiety.

Proceeding through the low-ceilinged passageway, she noticed niches carved into the stone walls, each containing a dusty skeleton but she wasn't shocked. She remembered them, anticipated them, from Margaux's journey down here. They'd looked at her with their eyeless, unwelcoming stares before.

Up ahead she saw footprints in the dirt. Three sets. Not all were going in the same direction. She remembered, from that distant morass of confused images and ideas, that there was an exit down here.

"Be careful you don't slip, it's muddy," Sebastian said considerately, altering the distance between centuries. "We're here," he announced as they came around a last turn.

The vault room, barricaded like a prison cell with iron bars, stood at the end of this hallway. Inside a bare bulb descended from an ugly black cord that twisted down like a snake hanging from the ceiling and shed its harsh light on her father, sitting on the floor, his back up against the wall.

Chapter 79

"Thank God." Jeremy Logan was enormously relieved to see Meer and Sebastian. His voice was weak and he was pale; there was no doubt her father was unwell.

"Meer, did they hurt you?"

"They? No. I'm fine but you should be in the hospital. Are you hurt?" She turned to Sebastian. "How are we going to get him out of here?"

He held up a key: old and worn and made of brass. Like so many other things related to this place, it looked familiar. "I have the key," Sebastian said. "I was on my way down here when you rang the bell. Meer, you can stop worrying now. Everything is going to be fine."

Meer took a breath, tried to relax. It was all going to be fine now that she and Sebastian were there.

Sebastian swung the cell open and Meer rushed inside to help her father, who had stood up but seemed to be shaky on his feet. Jeremy opened his arms to hug her and even though his grasp was weak, it reassured her that she'd found him in time. He really was all right. They could get him to the hospital now.

Jeremy looked over the top of her head to Sebastian. "What happened to you?" he asked, concerned. "Did they hurt you? I can't remember anything after——"

"Dad, how did you get here?" Meer interrupted.

"Sebastian came to the hospital this morning and said you'd been tricked into coming here, thinking I was here and in danger but that it was a trap and that you were the one in danger. We rushed over together and almost as soon as we walked into the building I was knocked out. When I came to I was locked in this damn cell, not knowing where you were or what I could do to find you."

Meer's shivering resumed as she desperately tried to make sense of what he was telling her and comprehend its implications. Without looking for it, her father found her crescent-shaped scar and he rubbed her back.

"You took my father from the hospital." Meer spun around and accused Sebastian. "Even though he's scheduled for a procedure today you brought him here and endangered his life? What made you think I was in trouble? I don't understand."

"You haven't been here all along?" Jeremy asked Meer. Now he too was confused.

"No, I was at the hotel when——"

The sound of the iron door closing shocked Meer into silence and the click of the key turning in the lock punctuated the moment. Meer and Jeremy looked away from each other and through the bars at Sebastian, standing on the other side of the cell.

Chapter 80

Thursday, May 1ˢᵗ—11:39 a.m.

Her mind took in what the locked door meant. Sebastian had been helping her since her first morning in Vienna. At what point had that changed? When had he started to exploit her? Using her father, he'd distracted her and led her right into this trap without her questioning his motives. But why would she have? There'd been no indication he was anything other than what he seemed. Incredulous that she had been so wrong about him, she searched Sebastian's face, looking for an answer. They had been too in sync for too many days for their connection to suddenly disappear now. And in this one thing, he didn't disappoint her. He replied to her unasked question.

"If you had only played me the song this morning...none of this would have happened. Please, play it now," he said, holding out the flute to her. "That's all I want."

This moment was what she'd been running away from all of her life. Not the music. Not the rain. Not the dreads. But the inevitability of her own failure. She'd misjudged Archer Wells long ago and had misjudged Sebastian now.

"You figured out the song?" Jeremy asked his daughter.

"Last night," she answered without taking her eyes off Sebastian.

"Is it the same music you've always heard?" Jeremy seemed amazed and focused on her discovery, despite the danger they were in.

"Yes. That and more. All the ideas you tried to talk to me about— the Tree of Life, the overtone series, binaural beats…they're all connected to the music and its vibrations. You were right about everything."

His eyes lit up with pride. "That's all I ever wanted. To help you. To teach you something that would help you live your life."

This is what she needed to remember about Sebastian, that he was a parent who would do anything to help his child, including threaten that same relationship between Meer and her father. But first she needed to know how wrong she had been about him.

"How far back does this go? Did you steal the Beethoven letter? Take the gaming box from the auction house?"

"No, of course not. I'd never hurt anyone or steal anything."

"Until now?"

"I don't want to now. I don't want to steal the flute, I just want to play it for Nicolas."

"How are you going to do that? You're not even allowed in his room anymore."

"I can work that out."

Meer had an idea. "If you let me, I'll go to Steinhof and I'll play him the music. If we leave now we could be there in less than an hour. We can free him from the past, Sebastian. We'll just drop my father off at the hospital and go see Nicolas."

"Rebecca won't let you see him."

"I can convince her. I know I can. I know what's wrong with him. I can explain it to her."

He shook his head. "She won't talk to you. She won't even take my calls anymore." His voice was strained with emotion.

"Then how are you going to play it for him—"

"I've made an arrangement," he interrupted.

"You're taking too great a chance here, Sebastian. What will happen to Nicolas if you wind up in prison? Believe me, you don't want to be separated from your son. Nothing's worth that."

"Nicolas deserves this chance, and I'll do whatever I have to to give it to him. To save him." Sebastian moved closer to Meer so that he could reach through the bars and touch her, so that she could feel his breath on her face. "And you'll tell me the notes to the song because you'll do whatever you have to to save your father, won't you?"

"How dare you! How dare you use my daughter like this?" Jeremy's neck muscles were attenuated and Meer could see his pulse beating under his pale skin.

"Meer, please, tell me the notes. I promise if you do you'll both walk out of here untouched." Sebastian held the flute out toward her and in the muted light because of the slight tremble of his hand, it looked as if it were a living thing.

Her heart lurched at the sight of the ancient instrument originally created to bring comfort and sustenance now being used to cause pain, confusion and chaos.

"Meer, don't do what he's asking," her father pleaded. "Even for my sake you can't betray a promise you made that goes back hundreds of years."

How did her father know about the promise Margaux had made to Beethoven to help him hide the flute? The question would have to wait till later; Sebastian had turned away from them, crossed the narrow passage in two strides and leaned down over an old heating unit nestled into an alcove that still cosseted a few Roman bones. It took a few tries but finally he managed to twist the black circular handle to the "on" position.

Beside her, Meer was aware of her father's too-labored breathing. "What is he doing?" she whispered.

"Turn off the gas, Sebastian," Jeremy called out. "They'll find out you did this and you'll wind up in jail, and that won't help you or Nicolas."

"Not if I come back and open the door later and let you out." Sebastian twisted the black wheel open further, the strong hiss of the escaping gas its own warning.

"That's not necessary. Sebastian, turn off the gas. Meer, give him what he wants." Jeremy's voice was rife with defeat.

"I'll shut off the gas *after* I have the notes to the song. There's more than enough time. Meer? The song?"

Sebastian took a pen and paper from his pocket and waited. He was close enough to the door again so that she could reach out and take the pen from his hand. Or the key to the cell from his pocket where she'd seen him put it just a few minutes ago.

"I figured out the key to the song late last night," she said to her father, hoping he'd understand her clue.

"You can tell him all about it later," Sebastian said.

"The key," she continued talking to her father, "was right in front of me the whole time and—"

"Meer!" Sebastian interrupted.

She had no choice, could only hope that Jeremy had understood the message she tried to communicate. Glancing down at the flute, even though she knew Pythagoras's Circle of Fifths by heart, she slowly read off the twelve notes secreted away inside the concentric circles. She was trying to buy her father some time to make his move.

Beside her, she heard him gasp, recognizing the sequence.

"And then another C," she said to Sebastian, "as it starts again."

Sebastian looked up from the piece of paper in his hand. "How do I know that these are the right notes?"

"They are, I wouldn't lie to you. Not with my father's life at stake. Will you let us go now so I can take him back to the hospital?"

"Once I'm certain." Sebastian quickly reached back through the bars and plucked the flute out of her hands, put it up to his lips and started to play the memory song. C, G, D...

Meer began to shiver.

Sebastian played an A and then an E.

Her teeth were chattering.

The sound emanating from the bone flute was the musical accompaniment of her life. Pervasive and absorbing, tantalizing and hypnotic. It hadn't caused an actual memory lurch last night... Maybe the person who played it couldn't be moved by it—the way she was being moved now—as the music swelled deep inside of her. Familiar and terrible and very beautiful.

It was working. She was remembering.

The thunder clapped so loudly it sounded as if the sky were breaking apart. Margaux's horse reared up but she held on. Through the sheets of rain she could just make out the other horse coming closer. Digging her heels into her horse's flank, she urged him on, while at the same time she reached into her coat pocket and wrapped her fingers around the gun's cold metal handle. As long as she had her pistol, she'd be safe.

"No," Meer said, putting her hands up to her ears. "No, please."

The rider came up on her right side, his pistol already drawn. "You little fool," Archer Wells said, just as another clap of thunder filled her ears. "We have an arrangement and I'm holding you to it."

Fumbling, Margaux pulled the pistol out of her pocket, trying to stop her hand from trembling, and aimed it at him.

"No, please, stop!" Pain coursed through Meer like liquid fire. She didn't want to remember like this. Not here and not now. But she couldn't halt the onslaught of images.

Jeremy couldn't know exactly what was causing his daughter to suffer but it was obvious it had to do with the music, music he'd desperately wanted her to hear her whole life. But she was in too much pain. He couldn't stand it. He grabbed for the flute through the bars instead of the key, frantic to stop him for Meer's sake.

Sebastian shoved him hard enough for Jeremy to trip backward and fall, smacking his head on the stone wall.

Stuck halfway between the past and the present, Meer couldn't move fast enough to get to Sebastian and grab the key from his pocket. By the time she reached out, he had already backed far away from the door. Behind her, she heard her father moan. She spun around.

"Daddy..."

He didn't answer. She tried again but he still didn't respond.

Sebastian's footsteps echoed as he ran down the hallway away from them.

"Daddy?"

No response. She put her head on his chest and listened.

"Daddy?"

Sebastian's footsteps were as faint as her father's heartbeat.

"Daddy?"

This time his eyes flickered open and he gave her the smile that still promised protection and comfort. "I'm okay...just thinking things through." He paused and coughed. "We have to get ourselves out of here. I think he left the gas on, Meer. He never shut it off, did he? Go look...you'll be able to tell by how much of the shaft is exposed."

"You're right. Oh, God, you're right."

"We can't stay here."

And then Meer remembered she had a phone. How could she have forgotten and wasted the last few precious minutes? Getting up, she searched the small area for her bag and found it discarded in a corner. Her relief was palpable. The solution was so simple. Reaching inside she pulled out the small silver phone, opened it and waited for the signal to catch. The clock showed that it was almost one o'clock in the afternoon.

One bar. Two bars. Everything would be fine now. So simple. Then the bars disappeared and the *no service* message popped up.

"No!" She shut it off and restarted it. Watched the phone try to connect and then fail again.

"We're too far down," Jeremy whispered hoarsely.

Chapter 84

The sound of the alarm startled everyone except for Bill Vine, who took the earsplitting, shrill ringing in stride as he opened his cell before it rang, anticipating the call reporting on the reason for the alarm. "Fill me in fast," he said, and held the phone slightly away from his ear so Tom Paxton could listen in.

"Appears we've got a security break at the back entrance and we're in lockdown," Alana Green reported. "The mantrap's operational. We're secure."

"Is this a fire drill or the real thing?" Vine asked.

"I'm trying to find out," Green answered. "I'll get back to you as soon as I know something."

"Fuck," Paxton muttered once Green disconnected. One real security break and he could—and would—call off the concert, but if he acted too soon and it turned out to be a false alarm it would be bad for business. Standing over Vine's shoulder, Tom watched as his second-in-command typed instructions into his laptop, bringing up pictures of each entrance, inspecting them and calling out information as he did. Everyone else in the room had frozen, listening to the vitals. "Front main doors, secure." Pause. "Ticket holders' side entrance secure." He listed them all, not finding anything amiss until the stage entrance cameras. "Got it," he called out.

Paxton leaned down and inspected the scene displayed on Vine's computer more closely. Or tried to. There was a flurry of activity, making it hard to see anything but a mass of men converging on a locked-down mantrap.

"There's someone in there," Vine said. They all crowded around and watched as a dozen guards, all armed with assault rifles, escorted a young man out of the locked-down door system.

"What's Green doing? Get her back on the phone. I want to know what's going on," Paxton barked, and reached for his seventh or eighth cup of coffee. "We are less than three hours away from two thousand, eight hundred people descending on us, waving their tickets in their hands."

Vine's cell phone rang just as he was about to dial. "Tell me." Again he held it slightly away from his ear.

"No breach. It was a musician," Green explained. "Sebastian Otto. Principal oboe. Originally he weighed in without his instruments but today walked through with them. The monitor kicked in when the numbers didn't match the stats on the biometric card. Stupid mistake. His cases should have gone through security on their own."

"No one thought to stop the guy from walking in with his instruments? That is a basic error, Vine. Who's down there? Change whoever is in charge. Right now." Paxton wasn't screaming, but it might be better if he was. The low, angry words were more alarming to the people who worked for him. "How do we know that those instrument cases aren't a part of some plot? We're still missing a Semtex buy. Get them inspected."

"All the instrument cases are being inspected. And Otto is being checked out as we speak. I'm watching it on the screen. No problem. Intact and clean."

There was a collective sigh of relief in the war room.

But Paxton's concern level remained as intense as it had been minutes ago. "This orchestra's given us problems from the beginning."

"But every one of them has checked out," Vine responded. "This wasn't serious, just stupid."

"At this point I don't care which it was. Let's go, I want to have a conversation with the illustrious conductor." About to exit the make-shift office, Paxton stopped and looked back at Kerri. "Are you coming with us?"

"Not yet, too much to do here. Twenty-two VIPs were added to the guest list in the last hour plus the Vice President confirmed and I have an entire team working on getting them all cards."

"Can you find someone else to do that?" It wasn't really a question.

Kerri asked her assistant to take over for a few minutes and followed her boss out of the room and down the hall.

The concert hall spread out before them, the deep crimson seats filling the auditorium. Dozens of musicians milled around while others sat in their seats playing for the conductor, who sat on a stool, listening with his eyes shut. For several minutes the rich sound continued, multiple instruments melding into one concordance. Then the group held back as the Principal oboist hurried onto the stage and launched into his evocative solo, not stopping even as Paxton's group approached. Sebastian Otto's playing didn't falter for a second and in no way did he acknowledge the new audience. But the conductor did. Leopold Twitchel pushed his thick, black-framed glasses up on his bald head and spun around with a deep scowl on his face. "This is not an open rehearsal, Mr. Paxton."

"I don't care if it is or isn't an open rehearsal. We can't secure the building if we don't have your cooperation. And clearly, we still don't have it. Walking in with instrument cases...refusing to follow instructions...this isn't working."

"I've explained to you already. These men and women are artists. There are no strangers in our midst. You don't need to treat us as if there are."

"Not strangers to you, perhaps, but as far as security risks go, you're all strangers to me. Whenever you get a body of diplomats of this magnitude together there are security measures that have to be observed, and to do that effectively we must have your help. Get your team to follow the rules. *All* the rules."

"You're interrupting a rehearsal." Slipping his glasses back down onto the bridge of his nose, the conductor returned his attention to his oboist. "We can start at the beginning of your solo if that's all right with you, Herr Otto."

Suddenly, Paxton's words exploded out of him, eclipsing the sound of Otto's instrument. "If you won't comply, we won't fucking have a concert! That's a call I can make, and one I'll make if I have to."

The oboe's flourish added an unexpected and coincidental punctuation to the outburst as Paxton strode out of the hall.

Chapter 82

The Memorist Society
Thursday, May 1st—3:46 p.m.

Meer was having trouble breathing. The gas was making her sleepy, dizzy and nauseated. Her father was in worse shape, his breathing even more shallow and labored. They'd been down in the catacombs for hours.

"When you were walking toward me, when Sebastian brought you down here, I could hear your voices." His speech was so weak.

"Yes?"

"You said something about this place. That Margaux knew there was an exit down here. Do you remember?"

Meer nodded.

"Do you know where it is?"

"No. It was just a sense I had, like all the other goddamned half thoughts."

"There's not much down here but this vault, Meer. If there's an exit somewhere..." He started to cough, and its intensity frightened Meer.

"Didn't you tell me the other day that...that Margaux had seen all the plans for this building?" Jeremy asked when he could catch his breath.

"She did. I didn't."

"The last time I saw you...in New York...you told me that you're building a suite of rooms in the Memory Dome based on Cicero's memory game... How does it work?"

She was confused. "Why are you asking about this now?"

"Indulge me." He smiled.

"Let's say you wanted to memorize a speech. You'd start by choosing a building that's familiar to you..."

"For instance, this building."

She nodded. "You'd walk it a few times in your mind, studying specific rooms or areas so they were very clear to you and then, breaking the speech into separate parts, you'd connect each to an object in a room. When you want to remember the speech, you walk through the building in your mind's eye and, seeing each object, you'll be reminded of that part of the speech."

"Try it," he whispered urgently. "Picture yourself walking through the front door and into the lobby. Go slowly, look around. Do you see anything?"

"No."

"All right. Keep going then. Go into the clubroom. Look around..."

Meer kept at it, trying to virtually tour the building and connect to a memory.

"Go into the library."

Her voice lifted a little in astonishment. "Yes. Caspar showed Margaux the hidden door in the plans and told her the building had twelve doors. That two were hidden doors and part of an escape route...the door in the closet was the first one...the other is down here."

"Where?" His voice was barely a whisper.

Meer tried to open her eyes but the gas was making her so tired it was a huge effort. Beside her now, her father had slumped down against the wall, half lying—half sitting. Taking his hand, she was shocked at how cold it was.

"Daddy?"

No answer.

"Daddy, please…"

But he didn't respond.

Margaux preceded Toller into the underground tunnel beneath the Memorist Society and when she came to the vault where she assumed her husband's treasures were kept, found the iron bars locked. Using the keys around his neck, Caspar's keys, Toller opened the lock and then stooped to enter the crypt. Once inside he walked to the right corner, counted up eleven stones and pressed on the twelfth. With a scrape, the stone released. Toller removed it, revealing a hollow where in the shadows she could see an iron key and a metal strongbox.

"This is all we have, Margaux," he explained, opening the box and pointing down to a booklet of copper sheets, verdigris green with age. "This document, written in some kind of ancient Sanskrit we can't read, supposedly lists a dozen memory tools, explaining what each one is and how it works. Other than the flute I gave to Herr Beethoven, this is all your husband and I found and all I brought back from India. Meager treasures, indeed. Beethoven has had no luck with the flute and implied that it is as inscrutable as this booklet. All in all I'm beginning to believe the entire expedition was a failure."

As Toller replaced the box his torchlight flickered over the key, and she asked him what it was for.

He glanced over his shoulder. "Our back door. You never know when the government will come knocking and we'll have to leave without them seeing us go."

Yes, Caspar had told her he'd required the architects to build a second exit out of the building and that there had been a natural one through the catacombs. Margaux looked in the direction that Toller had indicated and saw a keyhole partially hidden in a crevice between two stones on the west wall.

The gas was so heavy it was hard for her to move, hard for her to stay awake but she had to. She forced herself to stand up, to put one foot in front of the other.

Counting up from the floor, she found the twelfth stone, pressed on it with all of the strength she had left and felt it give. Drawing it out, she peered inside the crevice and found a metal box and an iron key.

She was having such a hard time making her limbs move. Every second that passed, she felt more ill. Shaking from the lack of oxygen, she had trouble fitting the key into the lock on the west wall. It took three tries. Once she managed to insert it, she struggled to turn it. Nothing happened. She couldn't make it move. Why was she making all this effort? She was so tired, all she wanted to do was sleep. Holding the key with both hands to keep it steady she tried it again, and this time heard the mechanism release and the hinges scrape as a portion of the wall opened like a door.

Air, stale but clean air, waited for her. Gasping in huge gulps of it, she peered into the darkness. Illuminated by the cell's ambient light she could see a twisting set of stairs heading upward. Where it led didn't matter as much as the air mattered. She gulped twice more and felt some strength returning. Going to her father, she gripped him under his arms and struggled to drag his inert body closer to the opening. "Breathe in," she whispered. Then louder. "Breathe in." Then shouting, "Please, breathe in."

His eyes were still closed; he wasn't responsive.

She took a huge gulp of air into her lungs and started CPR on him.
Nothing.

Again.

Nothing still.

Once more. This time he took a breath. It was shallow and not
enough but it was a start. Watching him take in the air and expel it,
she tried to figure out what to do next. Perhaps if she pulled him into
the tunnel there would be enough clean air for him to be all right long
enough for her to take the exit and find him help on the other side.

What should she do? Leave? Stay with him? Was the gas affecting
him more than her because of his condition? Had he hurt himself
when he'd fallen against the stone wall? Had he suffered another
heart attack from all the stress?

Maybe she didn't have to leave him. Maybe if she yelled loud
enough someone out there would hear her.

"Hello?" she screamed.

"Hello?" came the reply.

Chapter 83

Thank God, Meer thought. Someone had heard her, someone who would bring help—but then the single word repeated again. *Hello.* And again more softly. *Hello.* And then she knew it was only a pitiless echo.

"Dad?" she whispered, this time not waiting for the answer. "I need to get help… I'm only leaving you for a little while…it's the only way… I promise I'll be back as soon as I can…"

She didn't realize it at first but she was using the same words her father had used when she'd had her accident in Central Park, twenty-two years ago. After the impact with the speeding cyclist sent her flying into the air, her father was there when she came to, leaning over her, telling her not to move, that he needed to get help. Meer could still remember how warm his tears were as they fell on her cheeks. *"I need to get help,"* he'd said. *"I'm only leaving you for a little while…it's the only way… I promise I'll be back as soon as I can…sweetheart…I promise."*

"I need to get help," she said once more. Even though his eyes were closed, he nodded and the corners of his mouth almost lifted into a smile. And then he sighed, and in that one exhalation of breath she felt a vibration that engulfed her and calmed her and gave her courage.

Stepping into the cool void that stank of dampness, mold and rot Meer started climbing. In the paltry light that filtered down from cracks in the ceiling, she slipped on the stone steps and broke through spiderwebs that brushed her face. Reaching the top she found herself in a small chamber with no discernible exit.

The grate in the ceiling was a cruel tease. It was not only too high for her to reach, it was too high for anyone to reach. It couldn't be the exit she'd come this far to find. Except there didn't seem to be any other egress. What reason would the Memorists have had to protect the exit to this passageway if it didn't lead somewhere?

Inspecting each of the surrounding stone walls, she brushed away years of dirt and broke her nails digging in the crevices, looking for something like the keyhole down below in the Society's vault room.

It wasn't until she worked her way to the third wall that her efforts proved productive. Under the filth were crude markings: circles with squares in them and squares cut on a diagonal to imply triangles. Staring at the runes, trying to make sense out of them, Meer noticed one that wasn't a symbol drawn on the stone but an actual rusted iron ring: a handle protruding from the rock.

The metal's rough edges ripped at her skin and cut her flesh as she tried to turn it but it remained frozen in place. How many years had it been since anyone had used it? She tried again but her hands were bleeding so much her skin slipped on the metal and she couldn't get a good enough grip. Taking off her jacket she wrapped it around the ring and made another effort, twisting her whole body this time, feeling something in her back protesting but ignoring it, and this time she managed to turn the handle slightly. Gripping it more tightly, she made another effort and managed to turn it a full 180 degrees. The tired hinge gave and the door opened into yet one more crypt and Meer was overwhelmed by frustration. Like the nesting Russian dolls that her father had once brought home from a trip to find a Torah, this mystery seemed to have led to nowhere but a smaller crypt.

Narrow bands of leaded windows at eye level let in what looked like daylight. Looking around in disgust all she saw was the detritus of another catacomb: more bones and skulls, tumbled together like refuse, filling the space, leftovers of lives long past. And then she noticed a shadow on the opposite wall. Something had to be casting it. Stepping forward, she tripped and fell. Her stomach churned as she felt bones crunch beneath her.

The shadow led her to a false wall with a staircase behind it. It was an easy climb; dry and less steep. Only a dozen steps and she reached a door that swung out…easily this time. Warm air, imbued with the scent of resin, enveloped her. Stunned, Meer looked around.

The cathedral's tall ceiling soared above her. Colored light streaming down from the elaborate stained glass windows fell at her feet. Hearing the murmur of voices, Meer spun around and found two priests talking quietly beside a confessional booth.

Running toward them, the words spilled out of her in a rush. "I need help."

Chapter 84

Musikverein Concert Hall
Thursday, May 1st—4:22 p.m.

In the operations room at the back of the concert hall Tom Paxton scanned the bank of monitors showing the hall's strategic exits and entrances, as well as all the areas Global's team had designated as "at risk." Other than the false alarm, nothing had happened to suggest any suspicious activity. Four and a half hours from now, this would be over and Global would be swimming in contracts and on the upside of financial stress.

A few feet away from him, Kerri talked on the phone and checked names on a list of the attending press corps. Clicking off one call, she made another, listened to it ring, waited till it went to voice mail and then clicked off again.

Paxton read the look on her face and asked: "What's wrong?"

"The press are all checked in except for David Yalom, and he's still not picking up his cell."

"I don't care how good his answers were on Tuesday about protecting his sources. On Monday he meets with someone carrying enough Semtex to blow up an airplane and now he's MIA? Tonight's concert isn't something he'd miss, unless he was following a bigger lead."

Kerri frowned. "Let me find out if he picked up his press pass."

"You also might want to call some of the other reporters and check around," Paxton ordered. "When was the last time anyone saw him? He's infiltrated too many damn terrorist cells for his own good. His entire family was blown up because of his reporting, for God's sake. Where is Ahmed Abdul?"

"Which is why I don't think this is connected to us," said Vine, who'd been listening to the exchange. "From what I've heard he's still a target, and it's likely he was followed to Vienna and is being set up."

"Killing his family wasn't enough revenge?" Kerri asked.

"And why now?" Paxton asked.

"He went underground for a long time and has been very careful about not being seen," Vine answered. "This is the first time he's surfaced for any length of time."

"Almost as if he was using himself like a target." There was so much sympathy in Kerri's voice that Paxton shot her a questioning glance.

"I want to assume it is connected. I know explosives move in and out of Eastern bloc countries on a daily basis but this buy moved into this city, this week, and showed up in the vicinity of this particular reporter, and now he's missing. I don't like the coincidences. We all know a journalist like Yalom makes for a great hostage. When it's one of their own, the media go crazy. Damn it, Vine, if Yalom is really missing…" Paxton's jaw muscles clenched. "Has there been any chatter intercepted from Interpol or any other major government agency in the last two hours?"

"You'd be the first to know it," Vine said.

"Let's make double sure. Then triple sure."

Activity resumed at an accelerated pace, exacerbated by the increased tension in the room. Paxton stared at the monitor showing the empty stage as if he'd find the answers they were looking for there. He had the power to shut down the concert but he had to be one hundred percent sure before he took such drastic steps. Vine was right. Explosives did move all the time. And because Yalom was here to cover ISTA didn't mean that was all he was doing here. He glanced at Kerri, who, sensing his eyes on her, looked over at him. Pencil poised, phone in hand she was ready for whatever request he was going to make. Paxton motioned toward the monitor. For the first time he wondered about the concert he'd been paid to protect. "You're the music lover, you've heard the rehearsals? How good is this going to be?"

"We're in Vienna, and this is the Vienna Philharmonic playing one of their most beloved composers. A once-in-a-lifetime experience for a lot of people."

Chapter 85

The Memorist Society
Thursday, May 1st—5:47 p.m.

While the medics worked on her father, Meer stood in the small space with her back up against the wall feeling the rocks pressing into her. Why was it taking so long for them to turn to her and tell her he was fine, that they'd gotten here in time, that he'd had another attack but he'd be all right?

Another minute passed. Then another. Finally one of the medics stood and wearily walked toward her. Too slowly, as if this was an effort for him. At the same time she saw the others getting up. Why were they stopping?

Three steps and she was by her father's side, holding his hand, waiting for his fingers to curl to meet hers.

"Daddy?"

Meer looked down at him but couldn't see his face, didn't understand at first that tears were making her whole world invisible.

"His heart…" the medic said.

None of the words made any sense.

"…was too weak to…"

Someone gently put a blanket around her shoulders. "You're in shock and you have to stay warm," she said. "Let me help you up. We need to move your father, now."

"Where are you taking him?"

"To the hospital."

"But I thought…" Meer's heart banged against her rib cage. "He's alive?"

She saw the reaction in the woman's eyes. "I'm so sorry, no. We need to take your father to the hospital for the autopsy."

"My father's Jewish," Meer protested. "Autopsies are against our religion. I need to talk to a rabbi." She noticed the woman held her father's watch and wallet. Suddenly his things and being able to hold them was all that mattered to her.

"Can I have those?" Meer asked.

"I'm sorry, we have to give them to the police. They're waiting outside. You're going to have to talk to them about the autopsy and about your father's personal items."

Chapter 86

The light in the cave never changed. It was eternal night no matter what time of the day it was but David was watching the clock carefully. The concert would be starting in approximately an hour. He sensed a kind of elation bubbling up from deep in his chest. The sadness, grief and rage were, at last, almost over. His fingers caressed the small suitcase beside him: regulation size to fit under the seat in a commercial airliner, with wheels and a retractable handle for easy portability. Sometimes on the first night of a trip he'd find a note tucked into the front pocket from one of the kids. A child's block letters: *I miss you already. Hurry home.*

No hurrying home now to a house that no longer stood. To kids who were blown up into the night sky, never to come back to earth.

Now the only item in the suitcase was his rain slicker, a little thicker than normal since it was wrapped around a four-inch-long brick of putty that he'd picked up in Czechoslovakia on Monday: four hundred grams of somewhat malleable Semtex 1A. Half of this amount was all it had taken to blow Flight 103 out of the air. But the concert hall was bigger. This should be the right amount of the IRA's favorite explosive to expose the guts of the building to the stars shining down from the sky. All for just four hundred and forty euros, the cost of two very good bicycles for his sons, or a gold bracelet set with turquoise birthstones for his wife, or a new set of woodworking tools for his father.

In the silence before the symphony, David unwrapped his slicker, exposing the two halves of the red block that would have looked like Play-Doh to his middle son.

When he'd inspected his purchase on Monday it had been whole but he'd cut into it to check for another of Tom Paxton's bugs and, sure enough, had found one. Tossing that device onto the subway rails, he'd thought about Global Security Inc. and how with that one flick of his wrist, he was almost single-handedly dooming the company. Especially after Paxton had been so clever and bribed all those separate arms dealers to inform on their buyers.

But he didn't feel sorry for Paxton. At the rate the man was expanding his empire, David guessed Paxton didn't know that the Israeli security company he'd purchased three months earlier had been the one that had failed to protect David's family.

Unzipping the suitcase's outside pocket, David reached in and pulled out the rest of the paraphernalia he'd need: a battery pack and a det cord the thickness of a pencil, which would set off the blasting cap, which in turn would set off the Semtex. All he would have to do was stick the cap with the cord rolled around it into the explosive.

The assemblage looked like one of Ben's science projects but he couldn't think about that now.

David practiced the actions he'd be taking in approximately seventy-six minutes—the length of time it would take to play to the end of

Beethoven's heroic Third Symphony, depending, of course, on this particular orchestra's pacing and the length of time between movements.

David had timed his efforts to the moment in the symphony when the minor key music of the third movement comes back in the middle of the triumphant major key third movement. He didn't just want an ending, but an elegant ending. So during the final coda, when the last notes of the monumental piece rang out, David would activate the detonating cord using the wire connected to the battery pack. With the current applied, the assemblage would become a short circuit, turn red-hot and explode. *Like a lightbulb burning out,* was the way a top security analyst had explained it to him years ago when David was writing an exposé of terrorist tactics in one of the many Gaza Strip uprisings. Like the light burning out the lives of his wife and each of his children and his parents and his aunts and uncles and cousins. Caressing the wires as if they were strands of his wife's heavy raven hair, for a moment he could almost imagine the scent of the lemony lotion she uses—used—to counteract the arid desert air.

With a start, David looked around. He'd heard something. A sound. Close by. Not music. Not rats. Not a human voice. It was coming from the air shaft. He heard it again. The sound of rocks crashing. Or a wall collapsing. And then faraway muffled shouts. A disaster? Or an expedition? None of the questions mattered anymore. Only the answers did. And only time would give those up.

Chapter 87

"His name is Sebastian Otto," Meer said, getting the words out of her mouth as fast as she could as if that would take away her nausea. "He locked us in and left. Left with the gas turned on, and I know where he is…where he's going. To see his son at the Steinhof hospital. Nicolas Otto. Sebastian thinks he can help his son…that's why he killed my father…" She wanted to cry, could feel the tears just behind the words but she needed to tell them what they needed to know so they could find Sebastian. To arrest him. For doing this.

While Inspector Schmit called in the information, Inspector Krantz helped Meer into the patrol car, explaining he needed to take her to the police station for her statement and then apologizing for the intrusion.

"No. I want to go to the hospital. To stay with my father."

"All right, we can find a room at the hospital and talk there," Krantz said as he started the car.

Schmit hung up and turned to Meer. "We have men on the way to Steinhof."

"Do we have a description of Herr Otto?" Krantz asked his partner as he drove off.

From the back seat she could see Schmit's neck turn slightly red. "Would you mind, Miss Logan?" he asked.

She described Sebastian and as soon as she was done tried to picture her father's face. Not the way he looked on the gurney as the medics pulled the blanket over him—gray and inert—but any other time—a day in New York when they were having lunch and he was telling her about finding one of his Torahs. But his face eluded her.

Swallowing her emotions, she looked out the window at the passersby on the street. The rain had stopped but the sidewalks were still wet and most people were carrying dripping umbrellas. Three jean-clad teenagers all wearing earbuds were talking to each other on a corner. An elderly woman holding a light blue shopping bag with gold letters on it walked beside a mother pushing a baby carriage that had a red balloon attached to its handlebar. The traffic was heavy and the police car traveled slowly, so slowly they were going at the same speed as the balloon. For two more blocks, Meer watched the red dot instead of the ambulance, and then the traffic eased and they sped off. Twisting around, she kept her eyes on the balloon as it got smaller and smaller until it was completely invisible. When she could no longer make it out at all, a new wave of sadness crashed over her. Putting her fist up to her mouth, she forced the sob back.

Krantz must have noticed her sudden movement in the rearview mirror because he said: "We are almost there. Is there anyone you need us to contact?"

"Malachai Samuels."

"Is he back in the States?"

"No. Here. At my hotel."

He made a note. "Anyone else?"

There must be but she couldn't think of who. Couldn't think at all. She kept seeing her father lying, unmoving, with the medics surrounding him.

The car veered to the right into the emergency entrance of the hospital where five ambulances were parked. Meer didn't know which one carried her father's bo— She couldn't even think the whole word. Jumping out of the car, looking at the five identical vans, she panicked.

Sensing her confusion, Krantz came around to her side. "Your father is already inside," he said, offering his arm but she shook her head and preceded him toward the double glass doors.

The antiseptic smell hit her as soon as she entered the lobby. Now that she was inside, she didn't know where to go and looked around, lost.

"We've secured a room where we can talk. Please come this way," Krantz said, after he gave her a few moments alone with her father's body.

In the middle of a round table was a bouquet of drooping daisies in a glass vase and half a dozen pieces of a child's puzzle. Inspector Fiske, the officer she'd met almost a week ago after the robbery and Ruth's murder, was waiting, writing in a notebook when she walked in. His sad, basset-hound eyes looked up at her sympathetically. "I know this is a very hard time for you," he offered.

She nodded. Spoke quickly. It was too soon to hear condolences. "Am I under suspicion?"

"No."

Krantz and Schmit were standing behind her, not sitting down at the table. "Then why are they standing by the door? Making sure I don't run away?"

"I'm not worried about you running away. They're there to protect you."

"Isn't it a little late for that?"

Krantz tried to hide his reaction by writing something in his notebook, but Meer had noticed how he'd recoiled.

"But we *were* following you," he said.

She was startled. "Why?"

"We caught the report about what happened in Baden to you and Sebastian Otto and put a detail on you, which you managed to slip right after you left Malachai Samuels—and his police detail—in the park and jumped on a tram."

Meer could feel Sebastian's fingers gripping her arm and pulling her onto the moving vehicle. At the time she'd believed him when he'd said he was trying to evade whoever had attacked them in the woods, whoever wanted to use her to find the flute. She'd believed him when he'd lost Malachai in Rathaus Park by accident. But now she knew better. By grabbing her like that he'd managed to separate her from Malachai and the police following them. Was that the point when Sebastian had gone from helping her to trying to do whatever he had to do to get what he wanted? Or was it, as he'd told her in the vault, when she refused to play the song for him early this morning?

Schmit's phone rang and he answered it. Meanwhile Krantz asked Meer another few questions about the timeline of what had happened in the vault under the Memorist Society but she stopped halfway through her answer when she heard Schmit say Sebastian's name on the phone.

"What is it?" she asked Krantz.

"I don't know what—" He'd just started to speak when Schmit snapped his phone shut.

"Sebastian Otto isn't at Steinhof. He hasn't been there since the day before yesterday but he called the nurses' station a half hour ago. Our men are looking for the nurse he spoke to. Seems she's on break."

Meer thought about Sebastian as a father...thought about her own father...the adventurer who fired guns and got arrested and smuggled treasures across borders...who would have done anything to help her. Broken any law. Committed any crime.

"Inspector, there's a special concert tonight at the Musikverein. I think it's going to be broadcast, is that right?"

"I think so, yes."

"Can you find out for sure?"

His forehead creased in consternation. "Why do you want to know?"

"Please..."

Over his shoulder he asked Fiske, who answered in English. "Yes, it will be broadcast."

"What time is it now?" She'd lost her watch in one of the tunnels.

"Almost seven," Krantz said.

"We have to go. That's where Sebastian is. I have to talk to him...to stop him."

Chapter 88

David Yalom's fingers rested on the detonating device, playing with it as if it were the ring on his wife's finger that he used to twist around and around when they sat in a dark theater watching a movie or listening to a concert. There were people he knew by name up above him in the hall who would not survive the blast. Tom Paxton and Bill Vine, plus dozens of other executives and heads of government agencies from every country in the world— so many of whom he'd interviewed and written about over the years. They were in their seats now, listening to the performance, having no idea what the grand finale of Beethoven's Third would be like tonight.

At 9:50 p.m., David's computer would e-mail a series of articles he'd composed to three major newspapers simultaneously. The manifesto he'd been working on was a confession no one would ignore. The basics that he learned in journalism school so long ago—the who what where

when and why of the bombing of the Vienna ISTA Conference—
would be delivered in the crisp prose he'd always been known for.

Only those left behind would be able to judge if David's sacrifice
was worth it.

The first movement ended and there were a few beats of silence
and then the glorious symphony filled the underground cavern again,
drowning out David's beating heart and the rats' scratchings.

David imagined that in the audience each of his children and every
member of his family was sitting on the plush seats, programs discarded on the floor or scrunched in their hands, faces rapt, eyes half
shut, listening. In less than an hour the explosion would both destroy
him and resurrect them. He would become memory as they were
memory now and they would all be together again in the past. He
felt very close to them now. To his end and their end. His nerves were
untangled and smoothed out for the first time in months; the music
had calmed him, the music and the knowledge that even if they were
to find him now he'd have enough time to press the detonator.

He only needed a few seconds.

And that might be all he had because the men chasing him were
nearby. One layer of stones and one shaft of light nearby. David had
guessed they were Paxton's men because they spoke English with
American accents but he couldn't be certain. The men could have
been hired by Abdul to track him to these underground caverns.
They were close though. That he was sure of. He could hear them
in the shaft, getting closer and closer to his hiding place.

He was actually rooting for them to be Tom Paxton's men and half
hoping they would find him and outsmart him. Prove that this time
their mousetraps were as good as they said they were. Prove they'd
improved since their failure a year and a half ago. At one time, David
had been impressed by the brash American so convinced of his own
ability and he wished, just once, the good guys could win.

Chapter 89

The mayor, Herman Strauss, and his very much younger wife, Annabelle, sat in the front row. Toying with a covered button on the sleeve of her ruby evening dress, which had been chosen in homage to the ruby and gold concert hall, she was busy looking around. While she noted who was there, who they were with, and what they were wearing, her husband listened intently to the music. She was bored. Bored with the music. Bored with the endless events. Herman hadn't taken her to this many official functions when they were dating, but now it seemed as if that was all they ever did. And if she heard once more how much his dear departed wife had loved classical music she was going to spit.

Strauss was indeed oblivious to his wife's boredom. The Austrian sat at attention in his red velvet chair, proud of his Philharmonic and the superlative job they were doing. He noticed that many of the dignitaries from other countries seemed more than appreciative; they looked astonished. Strauss was sure that even people who couldn't care less about classical music had to be moved, despite themselves. He knew something spectacular was happening tonight, that this wasn't an ordinary performance. Didn't everyone in the audience suspect it?

The chairman of the ISTA conference, Stan Miller, sneaked a look at his watch. It wasn't that he wasn't enjoying the music; he was. Every aspect of this concert had been sublime, from the conductor's powerful emotional virtuoso performance to each orchestra member's flawless playing. This evening, coming at the end of a grueling four-day conference, was truly a celebration of how far ISTA had come in the post-9/11 years in instituting new security measures. But he didn't feel well. Something he'd eaten at the dinner wasn't agreeing with him. He'd popped heartburn pills before the lights had dimmed but they didn't seem to be doing a very good job. Trying to refocus his thinking away from the fire in his chest, he examined the faces of the orchestra members.

Two rows behind him, Gerta Osborne, a well-known and celebrated Austrian opera singer, felt the large diamond earrings pinching her earlobes and cursed that she couldn't take them off. Beside her, the lovely young tenor she'd brought with her sensed her discomfort and turned to smile at her. She delighted in the gossip that she'd taken him for a lover—gossip he'd perpetrated even though it wasn't true because it made the spotlight shine on him. And that could only be good for his career. Gerta knew that and took advantage of it. It was only good for her career, too. She was seventy-four and he was forty years her junior. The idea was delicious and fit her larger-than-life image.

As the head of the American National Security Commission, Edward Fields knew this conference was a very important event and felt it had gone well. He'd been impressed by some of the new concepts in security that he'd seen. The only fly in the ointment was the woman sitting beside him. All he wanted to do was pull Ellen Grant's icy blond hair out of that French twist and unbutton her severe black evening suit. He found it unbearable that this was going to be their last night together before he went home to Washington and his wife, and Ellen went home to her family in California.

Dr. Erika Alderman sat next to Fremont Brecht, who had invited her to the concert. His invitations were among the few she ever accepted anymore. Relationships, family, food, hobbies—everything in her life had been subordinated to her research. She fell asleep worrying about it and woke up to the last thought she'd had before she'd closed her eyes. But when Fremont invited her to concerts she always said yes. Not because she enjoyed the music—in truth she found listening to music tedious—but she was fascinated watching the people around her being affected by what they were listening to. How they relaxed and their body language changed as the music cast its spell over them was research. A concert like tonight was an experiment—albeit on a larger scale than she was used to—and with better-dressed subjects than she typically worked with.

Malachai Samuels tried to enjoy the concert but was preoccupied by the two empty seats beside him. He hadn't heard from Meer since yesterday when they'd been separated in the Rathaus garden and no one had contacted him with any information on where Jeremy Logan had gone or with whom, even though Inspector Kalfus, whom Malachai had talked to that morning had taken his cell phone number and assured him that he would be in touch.

By five that afternoon he'd become frantic. For hours he'd been calling Meer on her cell and Jeremy on his, but neither of them answered. He'd finally called the inspector but had only reached his voice mail. He'd left a message but that did nothing to alleviate his panic. Where was Jeremy? Meer? Did Meer still have the flute?

There was only one person who might know but Malachai didn't have any way to get in touch with Sebastian Otto, except to come to the concert and talk to him when it was over. So he'd changed into his tuxedo and used the ticket that Otto had supplied him with earlier in the week, and here he was.

Chapter 90

Thursday, May 1st—7:51 p.m.

At the door to the concert hall the Global Inc. security officers had stopped Meer and the two city inspectors accompanying her and for the last ten minutes two men in one set of uniforms argued with two men in another set. Every minute that went by brought them closer to the end of the second movement. Meer knew there was an oboe solo coming up in the third movement. She'd remembered him telling her that the nurses at Steinhof always played his concerts for Nicolas. That had to be his plan. To play the flute during his solo so Nicolas would hear it in his room.

"What's taking so long?" she asked Fiske, urgently.

"They won't let us in without top-level confirmation of who *we* are." He was furious. "The security for this event is so tight, not even police are allowed in."

"We can't get in?" There was panic in her voice. "Does that mean there are no police inside?"

"No. There are police inside. And more outside." He gestured to the vestibule and the mantrap. "It's *us* getting inside that's an issue. Or convincing anyone here that there is a reason to interrupt the concert in order to prevent a member of the Philharmonic from playing a flute. Their position is that they will detain him after the concert. It's hard to argue with them, Fräulein Logan."

"We *need* to stop him from playing," Meer insisted. What had Malachai told her once? The past lives you remember first are those that ended in the most violence or tragedy. If Sebastian played the music for all the people in the hall it could be horrific. She explained this as quickly as she could to Fiske, but he only nodded, unconvinced, she knew.

"No one can go in without special numbered holographic tickets and your name appearing on the master list," he told her.

"But my name should be there. Sebastian invited me. My father and I stopped by late Monday afternoon to be verified. Tell them that."

Before he could, the security guard responded to Meer with a proper British accent. "Miss Logan, I do have your name here and I have a copy of your United States passport—all I need now is your ticket."

Pulling out her wallet, Meer searched but it wasn't there. Had Sebastian also taken this while she was in the shower? She looked up to explain and was momentarily distracted by the scene on the closed-circuit television to the right of the mantrap showing the full orchestra in a close shot. Meer had no trouble picking out Sebastian. He played with an expression of intensity she remembered from her years at Juilliard. He was one with his instrument, no boundaries between him and the oboe. There was no past and no future now, no memory except for memory of the notes. His heart wasn't beating to its own rhythm anymore but to the beat of the symphony.

"I don't have my ticket," Meer told Fiske. "I forgot...my father had both of them. Do you have his wallet?"

"No."

"The medic took it out of his pocket in the tunnel—didn't she give it to you?"

"No, but let me see what I can do."

Fiske hurried over to Krantz, who listened and headed outside. Less than two minutes later he was back. First he gave Meer Jeremy's watch, which she slipped on and felt the cold stainless steel embrace her wrist. Then he handed her a brown leather wallet, its edges worn to unraveling, its compartments bursting with cards and slips of paper and slit at the seam. Why would he have such an old…and then she realized she'd given him this wallet for his birthday the year she was twelve, the last year he'd lived at home. Her mother had taken her shopping at T. Anthony on Park Avenue and waited patiently while Meer inspected all the different styles before choosing this one. That night at dinner, Jeremy unwrapped his gift, thanked her with a kiss and promised her it would go around the world with him. That he'd always have her with him because he'd have her gift with him. Always with him. Until today.

Glancing up at the closed-circuit television again Meer concentrated to find where in the score they were. It would be time for the oboe solo in eight or nine minutes. Opening the wallet, she searched through the bills, the credit cards, then started on the bits of paper, startled by a photograph of a little girl sitting at a grand piano, a beatific smile on her face. The edges of the photograph, like the wallet itself, were worn away. Shoving it in her jeans pocket she kept looking, until she finally found the small pristine white envelope with the name of the concert hall printed in the corner.

"Here." She thrust one of the holographic tickets at the guard.

"Your name?"

"I already gave you my name. Please, this is urgent."

"There's protocol that—"

"Meer Logan," she said.

Glancing at her father's watch, seeing the seconds pass, listening to the symphony, she figured there was now less than five minutes before the oboe solo. Before Sebastian was going to take the irrevocable step of putting the ancient flute up to his lips, play a simple string of notes and possibly send God knows how many people into a maelstrom of fear and grief and tortured memory without any preparation or warning.

"Please hurry!" Meer begged the guard and then heard a sound ominous only to her: the last section before the solo. At this rate she wasn't going to make it in time to stop Sebastian.

Chapter 91

Thursday, May 1st—8:01 p.m.

"David Yalom hasn't made any phone calls from his hotel room or ordered any room service since yesterday afternoon. The manager at the hotel finally called me back. He had to track down the head of housekeeping to get the reports. His 'do not disturb' sign has been on the door since about two in the afternoon when he also left a 'do not call' order on his phone," Kerri reported.

"That's not good news. Call the police. Ask them to check out his room ASAP," Paxton said. "He could still be there. Hurt or worse."

"The symphony will be over in less than a half hour—" Kerri started.

"I'm not sure this has anything to do with the symphony," Paxton interrupted, "but the man is on a known terrorist hit list and we might be the only people who know he's missing."

She nodded and opened her phone.

Paxton looked around for Vine but didn't see him. Hurrying out of the makeshift office he found his number two man monitoring a checkpoint at the end of the hall near the stage entrance.

"Where's Tucker Davis?" Paxton asked Vine.

"Supervising all the teams we have crawling though those fucking underground labyrinths."

"Good. We've got less than twenty minutes left to this symphony and I want them working till the last round of applause," he whispered so as not to alert anyone nearby. He knew all too well how easy it was to start a panic and that was the last thing he wanted in an enclosed space holding over two thousand people. But even more important, he was concerned about image management. He didn't want anyone from ISTA thinking he wasn't completely in control.

"All the activity they've identified is related to an infestation of rats that live—"

"Fuck the rats," Paxton interrupted. "I know this is a long shot and I know there are miles of tunnels down there but we have Semtex missing and a reporter missing. If David Yalom is being held hostage under this venue, we need to know about it and empty out the theater fast."

Chapter 92

Thursday, May 1st—8:02 p.m.

On the stage Sebastian, holding his oboe with one hand, reached inside his tuxedo jacket with the other and extracted a small, fragile instrument from his pocket. The orchestra was playing the last measures before his solo. No one was yet focused on him. Unobtrusively lowering the oboe to the floor, he brought the flute up to his lips, waited a beat and then looked up and over at Leopold Twitchel.

In deference to the conductor, he'd start at the right moment; give the maestro and Beethoven that much respect.

Twitchel pointed his ivory baton at Sebastian and as it quivered in the air, his eyes narrowed. Sebastian knew he'd noticed the absence of the silver-and-black instrument he expected. Arching his eyebrows, Twitchel silently questioned his principal oboist.

Sebastian ignored the conductor's glance. He no longer cared what his maestro thought. Focused on another goal, he only cared that the thousand euros he'd promised the male nurse at the Steinhof hospital when he called him earlier were enough to ensure that the radio in his son's room was on as usual and tuned to the station carrying this symphony in its entirety, and that what he was about to play would reach Nicolas's ears. The flute felt brittle in his hands. Dry against his lips. Positioning his fingers he pictured the notes he'd written on the staff as Meer had dictated them.

Chapter 93

Thursday, May 1st—8:03 p.m.

David watched as a brick fell out, a crack in the airshaft opened wider and a substantial splash of light spilled in. Flattening himself against the wall, protected by an outcropping of stone, he watched as another brick fell. And then another. As much as he'd prepared for this, he was still caught off guard. David had never believed in the inviolability of this crypt. But none of that mattered now. He still had time and surprise on his side, even if they did break through and find the chamber.

Trying not to breathe or make any noise, David carefully and slowly moved his explosives out of the path of light. Inch by inch, he pulled each component back into a darker corner of the crypt.

"Don't move," a man shouted. "I have a gun."

David had timed his efforts to the perfect moment in the symphony but could he wait that long? Holding his breath, he listened to the Americans who'd broken through the brick cistern on the far side of his hiding place. Everything would be decided in a matter of minutes...it all depended on his last decoy.

"I have a gun!" the American shouted again. "Don't move."

Releasing the remaining rat in the cage and cursing himself for not catching more of them, David watched the rodent scurry across the rutted dirt ground.

"Damn it, Tucker. It's just more of those damn rats," another voice shouted.

A beam of light caught the rodent as it darted to the west wall and slipped through a crack.

"I think we should head back up. This is a wild-goose chase," the man said.

"Wild rat chase," the other joked.

Laughter between the men echoed in the chamber but it seemed slightly farther away. Were they retreating? It sounded like they might be. David sat in the dark and listened intensely. He wasn't sure how long it took for the men to leave because from his hiding place he couldn't see anything and the music overwhelmed the now faint sounds the two men made. The question was should he wait for his marker in the fourth movement or do this now? Could he still afford to wait? What if Paxton's men hadn't given up? What if they were just lingering? To be this close to his goal and fail because he wanted an elegant ending—wanted to detonate the device precisely at the end of the concert... Did that make sense? No, there was no reason to hold off. He reached out for the wires.

Chapter 94

Thursday, May 1ˢᵗ—8:04 p.m.

As soon as Meer arrived at the auditorium's entrance the usher stepped in front of her, barring the way. Ignoring him, not caring that he was trying to stop her, not giving a damn about interrupting the concert, she reached for the door handle with authority. But of course he put his hand out, keeping the door closed and in a hushed but harsh tone informed her she couldn't enter during a performance.

She knew that. It distracted musicians. Any movement once the concert was in progress could throw a performer off track. But that's exactly what she wanted to do. Listening to the man responsible for her father's death, Meer heard him blow the first note of the song that had been haunting her since she was a child. An ancient and strange sound filled the auditorium. The vibrations reverberated off the walls and ceiling, dazzling and absorbing. Otherworldly. Not music. Not noise. Not anything anyone had ever heard. And it was affecting her.

Dizzy, Meer put her hands up to her ears, trying but failing to block the sound. Swaying, she fought to regain balance. Her bag slipped from her shoulder, its contents spilling out on the carpet. Bending over, she began retrieving the items and, courteous despite himself, the usher leaned over to help her. Which was just what she'd counted on.

Taking advantage of his kindness, Meer straightened up and quickly lunged for the door. She opened it, slipped inside and sprinted toward the stage.

Chapter 95

Thursday, May 1ˢᵗ—8:07 p.m.

Few audience members guessed anything was occurring, but the orchestra knew something was awry. The conductor—baton in midair—was immobile. Never at a loss on a stage before, Twitchel simply stared at Sebastian while he debated what path to take, surprised to feel a wave of sadness overtake him.

The floor below Twitchel was dissolving. He wasn't on solid ground at all anymore but was treading water. Icy, cold, black water under a black sky. No moon. No stars. Around him, pieces of his ship floated by: broken pieces, broken lives. Screams came from close and far away. As captain of the ship he was responsible for their crossing and now he'd be responsible for their deaths. The cries of the passengers slipped into a pattern; their terror was its own song, music he knew he would hear throughout eternity. The freezing water was turning warm; his limbs were too heavy. He wouldn't mind drowning, he thought, as long as he didn't have to hear the horrific symphony of screams anymore.

* * *

As Meer edged up to the stage her vision went in and out of focus and the dark auditorium phased into a night sky.

Margaux could smell her horse, the pine trees and the fresh scent of the rain. The wind was blowing so hard Beethoven's borrowed hat had flown off and her hair whipped her face, stinging her skin. His coat, soaked through with cold rain, was heavy on her shoulders now. Just hours ago, the disguise had seemed like such a good idea.

Archer Wells was as wet as she was and was breathing heavily—at least she had the satisfaction of making him work to catch up with her.

"You'll never use that," he smirked, nodding toward the pistol in her hand. "You could betray me, yes, that much is clear. But kill me? I don't think so."

If Caspar were there he'd knock this man off his steed and beat him to the ground to protect her. How wonderful it would be to have her husband back and to have him take care of her again but that was a lost dream now. The night before, the Tsar had informed her that Caspar was, indeed, sadly, dead. The story that he was alive somewhere in the Himalayas had been an fabrication contrived by Archer Wells to induce her to steal the flute and the memory song and sell them to him. It had been an elaborate ruse, right from the beginning.

"There are spies everywhere, Archer," Margaux said. "Remember? You told me that. Well, the Tsar has his spies too and he found out about your lies. You're not going to get the flute, no matter what you threaten me with."

The Tsar wouldn't be getting the flute, either. Margaux wasn't selling it to anyone anymore. She was determined to deliver the gaming box—complete with its clues—to Antonie Brentano as Beethoven had asked.

Her husband had died finding this ancient talisman. Danger surrounded it as this night was proving. She wouldn't allow it to bring anyone else to harm. That would not be Caspar's legacy. So help her God.

With the flute up to his lips, Sebastian played the deceptively simple notes, and as the brittle and sublime sound pervaded the hall and saturated Meer's mind, pandemonium broke out around her.

Screaming and crying, not understanding the terrible images, smells, sights and sounds overwhelming them, one person after another was affected. Meer tried to stay in the present but kept slipping back, back to the forest, sitting atop her horse, the rain beating down on her. Her hand no longer shook. She held the pistol steady, pointed it at Archer, and tensed her trigger finger.

Chapter 96

Thursday, May 1ˢᵗ—8:12 p.m.

Tom Paxton stood in front of the monitors, not consciously paying attention to the music. He was about to ask Bill Vine about how the underground effort was going, when he suddenly felt as if the air was pressing down on him. A terrible pressure behind his eyes forced them closed. The images he was envisioning made no sense.

While his soldiers set fire to the village, William Moore entered the hut. Inhaling a stink that permeated the small room, a stink that was ripe with sweat and warm, fresh blood, he choked back bile. Two pairs of eyes were staring at him from under the table in the corner of the shack; a woman and a small boy who cowered and whimpered. A half-dozen apples knocked over in the melee were strewn at their feet, red like blood against the gray stones. The fire in the grate smoldered. The room would soon grow cold as the winter winds blew through the thin walls, but the woman and the boy wouldn't care, they wouldn't even know; Moore wouldn't be leaving them alive. The boy was too small to be of any use and the woman would only be trouble but first…he'd been fighting this war for King Henry IV for a long time and hadn't had a woman in weeks.

Ripping off her pathetic shift, he was disappointed by the small, flat breasts and the pale nipples. He wanted handfuls of flesh and rosy red buds to squeeze, not this meager offering. Her fingernails raking his cheek were more surprising than painful. Not many women fought back, and he laughed.

The boy was crying loudly so Moore kicked him, sending him sprawling. Despite fear of reprisals, the woman shouted at him to stop, not to hurt her son. He slapped her hard across the face, leaving a red welt, which excited him. An instant later wet spittle landed on his chin. He would fuck her and strangle her at the same time just for that, and made a move to mount her when the acrid and harsh smoke from outside caused him to start coughing. Cursing, Moore ran out of the hut, abandoning the woman and the child, not looking back.

Outside, his soldiers were setting fire to more huts and laughing as men, women and children, chickens, dogs, horses and pigs ran from the flames. A crippled woman grabbed hold of Moore's arm and screamed, "Save her, save her!" pointing to a young child crawling out of one of the huts as fiery beams came crashing down around her. The life of one child was of no importance to him. They had to take this town and move on to the next. Casualties were expected. He tried to deflect the woman but she wouldn't give up. She clung to his leg, trying to force him to help. "Save her."

William Moore laughed, kicked her off and moved on.

* * *

"Tom? Tom? Something's happening!" Kerri shook Paxton. Trying to get him to focus on her. To answer her. But his eyes were fixed on some distant point. He clearly didn't hear what she was saying or feel her fingers digging into his flesh.

Chapter 97

Thursday, May 1ˢᵗ—8:13 p.m.

In the audience, Annabelle Strauss climbed wildly onto her seat and stood up. "Help me!" she shrieked as she waved her arms above her head. Beside her, the mayor attempted to calm her but she reacted as if he were a stranger instead of her husband.

Gerta Osborne, the elderly opera singer sitting on the other side of the aisle, stared up at the concert hall's domed ceiling, pointing to something or someone only she could see and screaming that it was coming "too fast…too fast…too fast."

Stan Miller stumbled through the row of other audience members, tripping on their legs as if he were blind. They cried out—fended him off—but couldn't stop him; he was desperate to get away from whatever was chasing him, even if it was only in his imagination.

On the stage, the conductor rolled on the floor, reaching out into the air where there was nothing to hold on to.

The principal violinist used his instrument to swat at his own arms, chest and face as if he were being eaten alive by a swarm of insects.

The female harpist, head in her hands, heaved with deep, wrenching sobs.

Erika Alderman was riveted to her seat, watching the audience members disassembling around her. She knew exactly what was happening. She was close enough to the stage to see her fellow Society member. Sebastian was playing the memory flute, and its tones were sending most of the audience into paroxysms of painful memories. She turned to tell Fremont, to share the amazing news that her hypothesis about binaural beats was being demonstrated all around them, but he wasn't in his seat anymore. In the confusion, she hadn't even noticed he'd gotten up. Where could he have gone? Had he been affected? She should go look for him but didn't want to leave the performance and miss witnessing any of the living proof that was establishing her theory.

Another audience member observed the melee, also immune to the music. Malachai Samuels' mind flooded with astonishment. Why did Sebastian have the flute? How had he learned the music? Had Meer figured it out? And more important, why was he doing this? Amazed by what was occurring, he studied people in the audience as they moved from the present to the past, unprepared for their journeys or their destinations. Finally, he stood. Whatever else happened, he had to be there when Sebastian finished his song, to get the flute.

As he worked his way to the front of the auditorium he saw Meer trying to do the same an aisle away. The two of them were the only ones not moving en masse toward the exit.

Meer didn't even notice the people in her way; it was the onslaught of her own devastating memories that was making it so hard for her to move faster. Trying desperately to hold on to the present, she felt the last vestiges of it dissolve around her, melting in the sounds Sebastian blew through the flute.

* * *

Margaux forbade her hand to shake as she kept the pistol pointed at Archer.

Unafraid of her, so sure that she wouldn't have the nerve to use the gun, he ignored her and nudged his horse closer and closer until he was near enough to reach out for the straps holding the gaming box to her saddle.

"No!" she cried out, pulling on the reins and backing her horse away.

"You stupid fool. Don't you understand what a mess you've made? A mess I have to clean up. I know the box has clues in it. Give it to me and I'll still pay you what I promised. If you don't, I won't hesitate to use this." He brandished his pistol. "How's that for incentive?"

In the hall, Malachai felt panic escalating around him. Fear, hysteria and hallucinations immobilized everyone, making it impossible for them to perform simple equations. Stay? Go? Run? Where? Drop to the ground? Go forward? Even those, like him, who weren't affected, weren't sure what to do; the terror was too pervasive. As he kept moving steadily forward through the chaos, he saw the wild fear in people's eyes and heard their unholy cries as the song played on. But absolutely nothing happened to him.

The surging crowd pulled Meer back to the present again. She was caught up in the maelstrom of people shoving each other as they tried to escape, not understanding what she understood: that as long as they could hear the music, the pain and the memories would continue to bombard them, that even out in the lobby the assault would persist. Each brittle high note after another propelled them all deeper and deeper into netherworlds where the light was hundreds or thousands of years old.

Chapter 98

The air moved in waves around him, its current trying to drag David away from where he was and what he had to do. From one moment to the next, he existed in two alternate realities. Trying to secure a place in either, he was lost between them. What was happening?

He needed to set off the Semtex now but something was wrong with his coordination and his vision. He couldn't concentrate on anything but the sound that wrapped around his head and pulled so tightly he felt as if his brains were being squeezed out through his ears and nose and eyes.

Was this some new technology Paxton had created to drive rats like him out of the tunnels? Except as terrifying as the sound was, it was also beautiful. As frightening as it was, it was also tempting. He needed to attach the last wire to the battery pack and then press the det cap but he had to stop…no, he had to listen…he couldn't protect himself… the music was seducing him…drawing him into its circle.

Chapter 99

Indus Valley, India—2120 B.C.E.

Without a moon, the terrain was treacherous but Devadas had no choice. He had to travel during the night in order to reach his destination in time. Tradition required that all sacrifices be made at sunrise. So in just a few hours, Sunil would lay his daughter Ohana upon the stone altar and with great ceremony slit her throat from one side to the other, giving his virgin daughter up to the gods.

As if the gods wanted human sacrifice.

For the rest of the night, as he trudged through the countryside, Devadas tried to come up with an argument to talk Sunil out of his plan. Searching for any line of reasoning that might change the mind of a man so mired in superstition and the old ways. Why would Sunil listen to him? As one of the village's seven holy men, Ohana's father thought Devadas and his brother, Rasul, were heretics.

But when they played certain songs on the instruments they crafted, the listeners *were* healed and soothed. The tones from their flutes and drums *did* ease complaints like sleeplessness, pain and nervousness. If their own father hadn't been one of the holy men, the two brothers might have been run out of the village. Instead a small cult had formed around them while rumors about their practices raged. Radical thinking and alternative forms of healing were suspect; the brothers were too controversial for their elders.

But since what they offered helped even if it put them in danger, they'd decided to live with the risk. It was worth the threats to see the look of suffering fade from a woman's eyes, or feel a child's forehead cool. Even when Devadas's wife and her family ostracized him, forcing him from their home, giving him the ultimatum that he'd lose his own children if he didn't forsake his healing practices, he couldn't.

Sunil must have seen him approaching from inside the house because he cut him off on the road. "What business have you coming here?" he snarled.

"I request some time to speak with you."

"You don't speak. You blaspheme. And I'm busy. I have preparations to make."

A faint glow of light materialized on the lowest part of the horizon. Devadas estimated that the ritual practice would begin in less than two hours. Staring beyond Sunil at the family domicile, he imagined Ohana asleep on a rush mat in the room she shared with her two sisters.

Rasul had begged Devadas not to make this trip, but he was determined to save his lover. No matter what happened, he owed it to Ohana for what he had taken from her, even if she'd given it willingly.

They had met innocently. Devadas's wife had thrown him out and he had been living on his own at the workshop he shared with Rasul for over a year when Ohana had come to him for help with terrible headaches she suffered.

She came back five times. On the sixth, after he'd soothed her pain with the music, he offered her a cup of tea. They talked as they drank and he came to realize her pain was related to her fears about her upcoming arranged marriage with a man who was off at sea. All young girls were betrothed to men their fathers chose for them but Ohana was rebellious; she didn't want to wed a stranger. Devadas understood—he and his brother didn't agree with the old superstitions either.

As the sun set, they discussed what they each believed. Her mind was so keen and her curiosity was so honest, he was drawn to her. Too drawn to her.

Their dangerous affair had started that day and had been conducted in the shadows. More than once, he'd tried to end it but she'd changed his mind, telling him it would end soon enough when the man she was to wed returned from his voyage.

Then a month ago her intended had drowned, and Sunil read the tragedy as a sign his daughter was destined to be the village's annual barbaric solstice sacrifice.

Did Ohana even know what today was to bring? Was she sleeping peacefully or staring out the window at this moonless sky imagining her death? The thought chilled his heart.

"Please, indulge me just for a few moments, Sunil." Devadas made a great effort to be humble, knowing it was his only chance.

"If you want to walk with me, then fine. I have to collect wood," Ohana's father said as he took off toward the riverbank and the grove of sacred *ashoka* trees that stood by the shore, tall and straight like sentinels. Walking beside the elder, Devadas helped Sunil pick up the twigs and branches he'd need later to burn at the altar. Although it was dark, the melon-colored flowers on the trees glowed as brightly as if they had their own internal light and the air was so heavily scented with their perfume, Devadas felt nauseated. It was said that if you washed the flowers in water and then drank it, you'd be protected from grief. All healers kept jugs of it at the ready.

"Are you still planning on giving your daughter to the gods this sunrise?" he finally asked.

"What business is that of yours? You, whose very name means 'servant of the gods,' dare to question me on a holy day?"

In a few hours, hundreds of people would be coming from far away for the ceremonial welcoming of the new season, but no one was out yet. Devadas knew it was still safe to speak without being overheard.

"I came here to tell you that if you offer Ohana to the gods you'll be insulting them and they will visit their wrath on you and our village." The words were like salt in his mouth but Devadas knew this was the only chance he had to change Ohana's fate.

"And why is that?" The elder man sneered.

"Because the gods require a virgin."

The older man straightened up. His face was set in cold fury. "What are you saying?"

"Ohana isn't a virgin."

"How dare you?"

"I'm telling you what I know as the truth."

Sunil stood as immovable as the mountains on the horizon. "How do you know such a thing?"

"Because I'm the man who has been with her," Devadas whispered, feeling ashamed, not for what he had done with Ohana but for sullying those precious moments by talking about them now using ordinary words.

Water lapped gently on the shore of the Ganges. A single bird flapped its wings as it flew overhead. A dog, in the distance, barked a steady warning.

"My daughter..." Every one of Sunil's words was an effort, each threatening to explode in his mouth. He swallowed and began again.

"My daughter has been promised to another man since she was a child..." He paused, thinking, trying to process the new information. "My daughter was promised to another man and you took her? You, who have a young wife and children of your own?"

How could he defend his actions? Even being exiled from his wife's home, Devadas was still married. How could he explain what it was like to be with Ohana? How he'd felt as if his very soul had been waiting for her from the very beginning of its first incarnation. He could see in the man's eyes that he'd accomplished what he'd set out to do. Sunil believed him. Ohana's life would be spared.

The blow took him by surprise. Sunil was older but had rage on his side. The rock hit Devadas on the side of his head and he went down. Lying on the ground, looking up at the furious man towering above him, Devadas was sure he could take him but a lifetime of instinct kept him from striking out at Sunil. It was in those few moments, while Devadas made the effort to overcome the lessons that he'd been taught—to respect his elders even if he didn't agree with them—that Ohana's father brought the heavy stone down on his head again and Devadas, drifting in and out of consciousness, lost his chance to defend himself.

Unable to move or see through the blood filling his eyes, Devadas sensed this was his end. Here, on the road in the early dawn hours, he was going to die. Through the pain he thought he saw Ohana. Or was he just wishing he could see her? He wanted to tell her that she didn't have to cry, that he'd done this gladly. Given her his life and his love. Nothing hurt him anymore. He'd stopped feeling the rock even as Sunil hit him over and over, venting his rage. All the pain was gone. In its place was the great golden sense that he was saving someone's life. There was nothing more he could offer up. He'd been given a chance to make this sacrifice—maybe had lived expressly so he could die now and save her life. Everyone had a purpose. Understanding that purpose was a gift and he took it with him as he left this life and went into the darkness where the past and the future merged in another dimension.

Chapter 100

Thursday, May 1st—8:23 p.m.

An obese man in a tuxedo was coming at Meer and was going to mow her down if she didn't get out of his way. But there was nowhere to go. The crowd had her hemmed in. He shoved her as he ran by; she fell, smashing her leg on the side of a seat. The pain hit as the next note of the ancient flute split the air. It was glorious and horrible in a way that had nothing to do with ordinary music; the note seemed to shatter into a million sparks of light that pulled her back into Margaux's storm.

There was sorrow in Archer Wells's eyes as he aimed the pistol at Margaux's chest and his voice sounded sincere. "I'm sorry but this whole scheme has taken on ramifications far beyond what you imagined. The British government can't take the chance of this becoming an international incident. Don't you see? If you refuse to steal the flute from Beethoven and sell it to the Tsar now he could become belligerent and leave the conference. The same could happen if you do sell it to him and it doesn't work. I have to take charge of this. If only you had kept to our bargain. When I negotiated with you I made you an honest offer—"

"Based on a lie! You told me my husband was still alive."

Archer ignored her taunt. "Now we run the risk of this becoming a political inferno and I intend to stop that from happening. I must have everything connected to the damned flute and the music. And that includes that box. Give it to me."

"No!" Beethoven had asked her to do this for him and she didn't intend on letting him down.

As she watched Archer's finger move on the trigger, Margaux fired her pistol at him and simultaneously kicked her horse. Pythagoras rose up—partly from the noise of the gunshot and partly from her boot in his ribs—and took off. Margaux let him ride full out, galloping toward the estate. She didn't look back at Archer and had no idea if her bullet had hit its mark or not. She didn't care as long as she got away, as long as she made it to the mansion and handed Beethoven's gift to his friend, Antonie Brentano.

Margaux couldn't see Archer lift his gun in his right arm, despite the throbbing pain in his left shoulder, and take aim at her retreating form.

When she heard the bullet she thought the sound was more thunder. When it hit her and burrowed deep into her side she thought someone had set her on fire. She was aware of only two things—the pain and the thought that before she collapsed she had to reach the main house and deliver the gaming box to protect the secret that Caspar had died for. They'd know how to help her at the house, how to relieve the pain. She just had to make it that far.

A bird sang in a tree behind her. Amazing. To hear birdsong now while she galloped through the storm-drenched forest. She thought about the bird and then about Beethoven. About the flute. About its secret. About her husband. His hand holding hers.

Sebastian took a breath before starting the song over again, and in the beat of silence Meer's mind came back to the present and she found herself sitting on the carpet, sheltered by the chairs. She had to get up and get to the stage and stop him. Around her, the chaos had intensified as people's memories sparked more suffering. Pulling herself up, Meer checked the aisle. The crowd still surged, but she had no choice. She was too dizzy to move but she had to. Margaux was dying and Meer wasn't sure she could go through her death. Didn't know if she would survive feeling the pain of it.

Margaux could no longer sit up on her horse and lay slumped over, holding on to Pythagoras's neck with both hands but she barely had any strength left. The pain was so powerful that she didn't want to stay conscious, except a small part of her mind knew that if she gave in she might not be able to hold on and then what would happen? Would Archer overtake the horse, or worse, shoot him to get to the box?

Gritting her teeth, she clamped her jaw and tried to think about what she would say when she reached the house—the fewest words to explain what was happening—but it wasn't about words, it was about the music that Beethoven didn't want anyone to hear. That was what she needed to warn them about...to make sure they didn't let anyone steal the secret of the music.

Meer fought her way down the aisle, through the crowd, finally reaching the stage where she climbed up onto the proscenium and maneuvered through the throng of the orchestra members, who, like the audience, were in extreme discomfort and duress.

One musician lay on the floor rolling back and forth and shrieking as if he were on fire and trying to put out the flames. Another cowered under his chair, his hands in front of his face, trying to protect himself from an invisible enemy, shouting the same phrase over and over in a language she didn't recognize. Some of the performers were in physical discomfort, others in mental distress. The very few who were unaffected tried to help those who were in worse shape.

Ignoring them all, Meer kept advancing toward Sebastian who, immune to the havoc he created, played on. His eyes were closed and so he didn't see her approach, didn't see her reach out...until he felt the pressure of her hand as she tried to pull the flute away from him.

He opened his eyes, and when she looked into them all she saw was desperation as he held tight and blew the next note. Meer fought to stay present, focused with all her energy on staying present, the pain in her back intensifying with every breath.

"You're done. You can't keep playing it over, Sebastian. You've done as much as you could. Give it to me now."

In her peripheral vision Meer could see a half-dozen police officers making their way onto the stage. Sebastian saw them too, and for one second his fingers loosened on the smooth bone and she was able to pry it from him and slip her hand under her jacket, hiding it. Stepping back she made room for the uniformed men who'd jumped up on the stage and surrounded Sebastian. None of them seemed to notice her. Had they even seen her take the flute? Did they understand that the instrument Sebastian had been using wasn't the silver-and-black oboe on his music stand? She didn't think so. She'd told Fiske but she doubted there had been time for him to alert everyone. Either way she wasn't going to wait and find out.

Putting more distance between herself and Sebastian and the police, she started backing away. None of the policemen followed her: three remained with Sebastian; the rest walked among the psychically wounded, offering help.

Meer was heartbroken. Her father was gone. And it was Sebastian's fault. He'd done a terrible thing to her and her father and to the people in this hall, but he'd also unlocked the secret she'd been looking for all of her life. This—what she held in her hand—was all that was left of Devadas. Was what Caspar had died for. Was what her father had put himself in danger for. No one was going to take it away from her again. She was bewildered about everything except this: in time, over lifetimes, she had been responsible for this object, and now she was its guardian once again. No matter what happened or what it took, she would do the right thing with the memory flute. That was her karma. It had been before. It was again.

Chapter 101

Thursday, May 1st—8:25 p.m.

The symphony had been hijacked and so had David's plan. But there was still time if he acted fast. Except his head felt like it was exploding and there was too much pain. And so much sadness. He thought about the woman with dark hair and almond-shaped green eyes... about Ohana...and her father...and...impossibly...his own death. Tears streaming down his face, he reached for the det cord. He needed to activate it and apply the current to the wire.

Fumbling, he struggled to get control of his trembling. He had to stop thinking about the past, except he could still smell the flowers from the sacred *ashoka* tree and feel the agony of the blows. Could see the older man coming at him with the rock again. Could feel Devadas's horrible pain.

David willed his fingers to pick up the cord but they didn't move. He was lying on the ground, blinded by pain, and then, somehow, surprisingly through the pain, he experienced the joy that Devadas had experienced as he lay dying, knowing he'd saved the life of someone he'd loved.

David's wife had told him once his news stories saved lives. If Lisle was here now, she'd tell him it had never been his karma to cause violence.

Except he couldn't give up now. He had to do this for her, for them. Reaching once more for the det cord, he picked it up, held it and tried to remember what he was supposed to do next. Two steps. There were only two steps left.

The old man brought the rock down again.

No! There were only two steps left, create the short circuit and force the explosion. He stared at the science project and felt a sadness so heavy descend on him he thought he might never be able to get up again. Maybe he could just stay down in the catacombs forever, become part of the rock, part of the ancient burial ground.

Do this, he silently screamed at himself. *Do it now. Get it over with.* He held the wires in his hands. Felt the heavy strands of Lisle's hair.

Who had he been kidding? He'd never been capable of killing anyone. Not even the rats down in the caves with him. But if he didn't do this now, the rest of his life would be an endless loop of loss. If he stayed on and lived out all his days missing them, his family would be gone from him in a more final and aching way than at any time in the last eighteen months.

The rock came down on Devadas's head for the last time.

His hands fell open and dropped to his sides. He saw endless blackness. No matter how many people he'd loved and lost, could he really do to others what had been done to him? Could he be the one to disturb the fragile threads that tied people to each other over time and through time?

Do it. Do it now.

With a burst of resolve, he picked up the wires and the Semtex and the det cap but instead of connecting them to each other, with one great last effort he heaved them all into the shaft, into the same empty channel he'd forced the rats to crawl through, the same hollow that the music had traveled through.

He had to hurry. His computer was set to automatically send his articles to the newspaper in less than an hour. He had fifty-four minutes to get out of there, up to the surface and back to his hotel if he intended to save his own life tonight. The last life he ever would have guessed he'd care about saving.

Chapter 102

Thursday, May 1st—8:27 p.m.

Meer stood stage left watching the police take Sebastian away. There would be time later to try and understand how it had happened and what the ramifications would be of the fact that tonight, here in Vienna, he'd caused thousands of people to remember brutal, horrific experiences from lives they'd lived before. And died before.

More than once, when her father had tried to explain the mystical light of wisdom to her, he'd told her how when we die our souls leave our bodies as pure light that shatters into thousands of fragments, and how each of those fragments returns in another time as another soul. The ultimate goal was that one day all those fragments would be made whole again.

Whose soul inhabited Sebastian's body? Was it really a fragment of the same soul that had lived in Archer Wells? So it seemed. First Archer and then Sebastian had succumbed to base and selfish motives, defiling the promise of the flute. Why couldn't Sebastian have learned his karmic lesson? What was he still working out? And why had so many others needed to be hurt in the process? Had part of her purpose been to give him this chance to do the right thing, repair what he'd done before?

If it was, all she'd managed to do was help him to fail.

An arm gripped her from behind. Strong and secure. The voice was familiar and kind. "I think it's time for us to leave, Meer."

Hearing Malachai's voice she slumped with relief but he kept her supported. "Let me help you. I'll take care of everything now. Just come with me."

"I have it—" Meer showed him the flute.

"I know. Just hold tight and let me get you out of here."

"Do you know what happened?"

"Meer," Malachai whispered, "we need to hurry now. We have to keep the flute safe. You understand that, don't you? We have to protect our memory tool." He chanted soothingly, leading her farther away from the police and Sebastian.

They were in the wings, his arm in hers, when she realized he didn't know about Jeremy. "Malachai—"

"We can't stop to talk now. We must get you and the flute out of here without anyone noticing. Please, just keep walking. All of the exits in the main hall are blocked off so the police can control the exodus in an orderly fashion. We need to use the stage door."

Ahead of them a group of three musicians were running and assuming they knew where the exits were, Malachai followed in their path, leading Meer deeper into the guts of the backstage area. The shouts and screams coming from the hall were muted now and she could hear her footsteps and Malachai's on the concrete. They rounded a corner and were alone. So much quiet after so much noise was disconcerting.

"This way," he said as he took a right in the direction of a glowing red exit light at the end of a long otherwise dark hallway. By the time he saw there were two security guards flanking the oversize metal door, it was too late to turn back.

"We're going through. Don't try to act brave. It's all right that you look shaken up," Malachai whispered. "They expect everyone to be upset. The only thing I want you to do is act as if you're used to coming and going this way. By now I'm sure they all know someone's been arrested and taken into custody. I doubt they're looking for anyone else. Probably just trying to keep the situation calm. If they stop and ask to see what you're carrying, show it to them, tell them it's your instrument, that you're in the orchestra."

Clutching the bone, Meer tried to use Malachai's words to keep her in the present but time was shimmering.

Ohana was running away in the ancient past. Everyone she'd ever been had run away. Always running away. She had to learn to stop and stay. This time she was trying to escape from Sunil's wrath. Clutching the bone, all she had left of her dead lover Devadas, she kept running, not knowing where she was going, only knowing where she had been and that she had to leave there.

"Meer? Meer?"

Time shimmered again. She was with Malachai, backstage at the concert hall in Vienna. Her father had died, not a man named Devadas. From behind her, scurrying footsteps rushed by. Suddenly the hallway was crowded as a group of four dark-suited men escorted a well-dressed couple through the area. Malachai gripped Meer by the wrist and pulled her back, deep into the shadows.

Meer thought she recognized the thin, tall tuxedoed man who was weeping but she wasn't sure. The blond woman with him was trying to comfort him, whispering to him but as they reached the exit, he collapsed and everyone rushed to his side.

"We should stay here," Malachai whispered. "Until they're gone."

"Why? What's wrong?"

"They aren't going to want anyone to see him like that. That's Edward Fields, the head of the American National Security Commission. It would exacerbate the perception that chaos has been unleashed. I don't want them to realize we saw him and detain us. Let's turn around. Go out the front. Give me the flute—if they stop me I'll do some sleight of hand to confuse them."

Meer's fingers tightened around the bone instrument.

"Give it to me," he repeated.

"No. I can't. I can't let anyone else have it."

"Meer?"

"No one."

Chapter 103

The street was illuminated with old-fashioned lamps and Lucian Glass had no trouble seeing Malachai and Meer as they emerged from the concert hall's front doors. Paparazzi, originally there to cover the concert, jostled each other for position, shooting the horrific expressions on the exiting concertgoers' faces. The continuous explosion of flashes lit up the street so that for seconds at a time it seemed as bright as daylight.

Lucian was still haunted by what had happened inside the concert hall when the music turned into human cries. Suddenly there was no air and no space and no time and it didn't matter that he couldn't breathe because breathing wasn't necessary. He was smoke, floating, no longer seeing what was in front of him but visualizing another time and place in some eternal, intuitive way.

He'd been watching Meer make her way up on the stage when she transformed into a different woman with longer, darker hair, wearing

a torn and tattered blue robe…she held a flute…and was crying…
no…it wasn't a flute. Not yet. It was just a small bone, broken off
at one end, and she was handing it to him, telling him she'd stolen
it from the burial site. While she spoke she continued crying and her
face was filthy except where streaks from her tears had made tracks.

Lucian didn't know who the woman was. He'd never seen her
before but he felt as if he'd never *not* seen her. None of this made
sense but it didn't matter. He'd been emotionally and physically mesmerized by the vision.

Watching through an expanse of space that seemed to have no connection to distance as he knew it, he saw a man he was part of and
who was part of him take the bone out of the woman's hand. Then
in quick moving images illustrating different scenes of the same story,
he saw the man—he saw himself—carving seven holes in the bone
and turning it into a flute while the woman slept nearby, close to a
fire in the workshop he used to share with his brother, Devadas.

When the symphony came to its abrupt stop, Lucian was sucked
back into the present with violent force, watching Meer in her black
jeans and leather jacket, Meer with her auburn hair and shocking
green eyes, not Ohana, not the robed woman.

Now as his eyes followed her through the hysterical crowd, Ohana
hovered, ghostlike, beside her. Was it possible to exist in two states
of being? Could he be Lucian Glass, FBI agent working a case that was
breaking open around him and also be alive and aware in another time?

It looked as if Meer was clutching something to her chest and
although he was too far away to tell what it was, he didn't doubt it was
the memory flute he'd seen her take out of Sebastian's hands. Then,
as more of the crowd gushed out of the auditorium like blood from a
wound, he lost sight of Meer. Around him painful screams mixed
with shrieking ambulances and police sirens arriving at the location.

Finally spotting Meer and Malachai again, he also noticed an older man with thick white hair who was moving, catlike, though the melee toward them. It was Fremont Brecht, the head of the Memorist Society. More robust than his age or size suggested; his only sign of infirmity was a slight limp but it didn't seem to be doing anything to slow him down.

Lucian had been with the agency long enough to trust his instincts when he sensed danger. He would have screamed out to Meer and Malachai to warn them if there was any chance they would have heard him but he was too far away. He was cut off by a wall of terror-stricken people. These were the men and women who created foolproof security firewalls in cyberspace, GPR systems, tracking devices, mantraps, and machines to test the air for traces of explosive. Their alarm was exacerbated because they knew too much, understood how impossible it really was to protect anyone and that no lockdown procedure was ever completely secure. Certainly, none of them had any idea that the violent dreamlike images they'd just experienced were their own past life memories. More likely they believed they'd been the victims of a mass hypnotic trance induced by some kind of chemical warfare. But Lucian didn't. He guessed that what Malachai had spent his life trying to verify might very possibly have been proved tonight, triggered not by a sophisticated biological agent but by a handful of notes: a memory song.

And then the crowd broke and in the crazy flashing paparazzi light Lucian saw Brecht pull a gun.

"Meer! Watch out!" The multitude swallowed his scream.

Suddenly Malachai doubled over. Clutching his stomach, he dropped out of sight and Meer disappeared along with him. The crush of people was too thick. Brecht must be after the flute, too. That meant that when he realized Malachai didn't have it, the Memorist would go after Meer. Damn the crush of people. Lucian started shoving his way through.

A heavyset woman was in his way. Swaying on her feet, she was obviously disoriented. Lucian yelled at her to get out of the way but instead of moving, Gerta Osborne froze, panic on her face. And as the opera singer fainted, Lucian had no choice but to dive and try to catch her.

Chapter 104

Thursday, May 1st—8:42 p.m.

Tom Paxton sat alone in the makeshift office, barely aware of his surroundings. He looked at the melee on the monitors but was seeing images the music had induced in him…malignant scenes of a man raping a woman while a little boy looked on… He could smell the fire and filth and hear the screams of the woman underneath him…no, not him…a vicious man in another time. The screams were so horrifying…

And then he realized the screams were real. They were happening now. In the theater. The cries and shrieks of an audience that had come to hear a symphony and celebrate only to be terrorized by an act no one could have anticipated.

"Boss?" It was Kerri.

Paxton looked over, so relieved to see her. "Are you all right?"

"Fine."

"Did anything happen to you?"

"No."

"You're lucky," he whispered.

"Was it awful?"

Paxton nodded, then looked away, back at the bank of monitors.

She walked over to his side and put her hand on his shoulder, surprised to feel his back trembling and even more so to see the tears in his eyes.

"Tom? What happened?"

Paxton heard her, felt her hand, wanted to lean into her and let her comfort him but his attention was drawn to one of the monitors aimed on the theater's front door. There, a swell of people poured out, a wave powered by its own momentum with David Yalom in its midst. The journalist looked how Tom felt. As if he'd been to hell and back. Except in Yalom's eyes there was something else. Even via the mediocre-quality screen, he looked as if he'd found some resolution while he'd been there.

"That's a relief, at least," Kerri said, nodding toward Yalom. "I was worried about him. He's been through enough."

Paxton nodded.

"Tom, I came in to tell you the police want to talk to you," Kerri said.

"Yeah, I'm sure they do."

"They don't know for certain, but there don't seem to be any fatalities."

"What about our team? Has everyone reported in?"

"Everyone is fine."

"Tucker?"

She nodded.

"There was an attack on my watch, Kerri," he said as his voice broke.

Chapter 105

Thursday, May 1st—8:46 p.m.

The lighting director threw a switch and the bank of klieg lights blinded the crowd. The TV crew was determined to interview some of the people who'd been inside and affected by the strange phenomena, and nothing was going to stop them.

From down on the ground, seeing everyone around her surging in hyperrealistic brightness, Meer's panic intensified. She and Malachai were in danger of being trampled. This was worse than what had happened inside the auditorium. There was no chair here to grab hold of. Nothing to hide behind. Getting to her knees, she tried to force him up with her but he was just too heavy and she let go, her hands coming away wet. She looked down. It was blood. Blood? What had happened? He'd been hurt, but this badly? Oh, no, not her father and Malachai on the same night?

I need help.

Almost as soon as she thought it, out of all the thousands of people streaming by, one stopped. It seemed he was holding back the surge of people and clearing some space. Meer was certain that she'd seen him before, but where? She remembered the deep-set brown eyes that were filled with awful sadness. No, it was more than having just seen him before, she knew him. And knew he was barely containing his grief.

He held out his hand to help her up and as she took it, Meer remembered. She'd seen him on the steps of the library a few days ago...as she was going in he was leaving. She understood now what she hadn't been able to then because she hadn't yet heard the memory song.

"Devadas?" she asked.

His eyes widened and a spark of something like hope broke through his anguish.

"We have to get him help," she said, shouting over the crowd. "Malachai's bleeding."

The man she knew only as Devadas reached down to lift Malachai up just as Fremont Brecht, her father's friend and the head of the Memorists, inserted himself between them, separating them, thrusting Devadas out of the way.

The crush of oncoming people swallowed him up. Meer watched him struggle against them like a swimmer fighting a strong undertow but he couldn't beat them back this time and he was carried away from her. *Carried away again*—she thought—*again*.

Suddenly she wasn't sure he'd even been real.

"Malachai's hurt," she shouted to Fremont. "He's bleeding. We have to get him out of here."

"I know. I saw what happened. Do you have the flute?"

"The flute? Yes. But Malachai—"

"Don't worry, first give me the flute—we have to protect it." He grabbed her and his grip sank into her flesh. "Quick."

In the distance a man on a bullhorn shouted instructions as the crowd continued surging. A man tall enough to be visible above the pack broke through and stepped up, pointing a gun at her. Did this man know about the flute, too? Then Fremont grimaced and let go of her, and it took Meer a second to realize the man with the gun was tackling Fremont, that his gun was aimed at him, not at her.

It only took him seconds to secure Fremont's arms. "I've got him," the man shouted in English to two policemen emerging from the mob. "But we have a man down and hurt," the American explained. "Brecht shot Samuels."

"Ambulance on the way, Lucian," one of the Viennese policemen called out.

"*You* shot Malachai?" Meer asked her father's oldest friend.

Fremont's hands were cuffed behind his back but he stood as erect and proud as if nothing had happened, ignoring both the police and Meer's question. She insisted. "Did you arrange to have the letter and the gaming box stolen?"

Fremont's continued silence was tantamount to a confession.

"You're responsible? But why? My father was your friend. He told me he was your friend."

"I had a greater responsibility to safeguard our heritage and keep it from public ridicule," he said with conviction.

"Regardless of who you hurt? I don't understand that kind of responsibility."

"Neither did your father. Jews in the twenty-first century can't afford the wrong kind of attention." The conviction was transforming into rage. "Just as we're losing our stigma as outsiders, if it's discovered we have a memory tool that proves reincarnation, we'll be reviled again as crazy mystical zealots." The rage was edging toward hysteria. "We can't afford to go backward and be outcasts in ghettos—"

Inspector Fiske interrupted, speaking to Fremont in German,

saying something Meer didn't understand. Fremont clenched his jaw and looked away, up at an invisible point in the sky, and then the inspector led him away.

Off to the side, Malachai slumped against the building, holding his ribs with one hand, his eyes closed. The American knelt beside him, taking his pulse. She joined them.

"Malachai? Can you hear me?" she asked.

He opened his eyes to look at her but noticed the American. "What are...you...doing here?" He was in pain but coherent.

"I like Beethoven," the American answered, actually grinning.

"Enough to travel...all the way from New York to catch a performance?"

"Why not? The *Eroica* wasn't playing at Carnegie Hall."

"You're the one who's been following me...on my street...in the car...I know the tricks. You got them to release my passport thinking I'd come here for the flute, didn't you?"

The American didn't answer because the medics had arrived and he'd stepped back to allow them in. But Meer wanted to know the answer. "*Have* you been following Malachai? Why? He hasn't done anything but help me."

"So it seems. At least this time."

"Is he being arrested?"

"Nope, just going to the hospital. And how about you? Are you hurt? Do you need to stop by the hospital?"

She shook her head. "Who are you?"

"Special Agent Lucian Glass," the American said. "FBI Art Crime Team. I'm so very sorry about your father. Will you let me help you, Miss Logan?"

"How?"

"Well, from the way you're protecting it, I'm guessing you'd like to get the flute someplace safe."

"Yes. Someplace safe," she said.

The medics had Malachai on the gurney now. Walking with him as they rolled him toward the ambulance she reassured her old friend that he'd be fine. Lucian followed close behind her. They'd reached the car. The medics moved away from the gurney to open the door. Wincing, Malachai reached out for Meer's hand—the one that held the bone instrument. "It's real, Meer. I saw it work."

"But so many people suffered so much pain...didn't you see that?"

Malachai wasn't listening. "It worked. It worked for you, didn't it? All your frozen memories thawed. You don't have to tell me, I can see it in your eyes. You remembered what you had to, what you've been trying to for so many years. What I couldn't help you remember."

She nodded. "But not the way I was supposed to remember...it was horrible..."

He still wasn't listening. His eyes were looking beyond her. Filled with a longing she'd never seen in them before. A longing that scared her. "I didn't have a single memory." His bitterness was as dark as the sky above them. "Not one."

The medics lifted Malachai up and into the ambulance and then jumped in after him. Through the window Meer watched them worrying over him. He looked so pale. As if he were fading while she watched.

The siren started up and the car pulled out. She was aware that the FBI agent was behind her but she didn't turn around. Keeping her eyes on the vehicle as it drove off, Meer reached into her bag and feeling around found and pulled out the flute. No matter how amazing, it wasn't worth killing for. Wasn't worth dying for. Not bothering to even look down, without any hesitation, Meer raised the instrument high over her head, and in one fierce motion threw it down on the pavement where it instantly shattered into dozens and dozens of shards of old, fragile, brittle bone.

Chapter 106

I am confident that there truly is such a thing as living again, that the living spring from the dead, and that the souls of the dead are in existence.

—Socrates

Vienna, Austria
Friday, May 2nd—11:00 a.m.

The doctor came through the double swinging doors and into the waiting room. "Miss Logan?"

She nodded and stood up, trying to prepare herself for the news. Beside her, Lucian Glass stood too. They'd spent the night in the hospital, in the intensive care waiting room, while Malachai underwent surgery to save his life. Each of them was there for very different reasons.

"He's out of the woods. It's going to take some time but he should make a complete recovery," the doctor reported.

"Can I see him?" Meer's voice trembled with relief that she wouldn't lose him, too.

"He's still unconscious but should be able to have visitors early this evening. He'll be in quite a bit of pain for the next few days."

"At least there'll be one recovery," Meer said to Lucian after the doctor left. She was thinking about her father. About Ruth and Smettering. And Nicolas. While she'd been waiting for news about Malachai she'd checked at Steinhof; Sebastian's son hadn't had any reaction to the flute music. He was still locked in his own world. Both Fremont and Sebastian had been arrested and would each likely wind up in prison for years. There were other casualties, too. The news reported that thousands of radio listeners had suffered horrific flashback sequences and many of them had been hurt. In addition, hundreds of concertgoers had been injured in the chaos and were here in this hospital.

"A complete enough recovery," Lucian said, still talking about Malachai, "for him to try again."

She shook her head. "You're wrong."

"I know you don't want to believe me but he's dangerous. Malachai wants the memory tools and will do whatever he has to in order to get them. I'm still convinced he was responsible for trying to steal the stones that were discovered last year in Rome. Several people died as a result of that robbery, too."

"Do you have proof of his involvement?"

He didn't need to answer. If they'd had proof, Malachai wouldn't be a free man.

"I've known him almost my whole life. Do you have any idea how many children he's helped?"

"One thing doesn't necessarily have anything to do with the other." She stood to leave.

"My partner is downstairs," Lucian said, standing with her. "We've been asked to give you a lift to the cemetery."

"I don't need an escort."

"The FBI would prefer it if you had one, though. At least until the case is officially closed, which should happen sometime in the next forty-eight hours. We won't get in your way."

They went down in the elevator and when the doors opened in the lobby they walked out into what appeared to be a press conference. Reporters, photographers and cameramen crammed around an officious-looking doctor with a dour face who was reading a statement.

Meer and Lucian kept to the edges of the gathering and had almost reached the front door when someone approached her.

"Excuse me."

Meer turned toward the accented voice.

After being swept away in the crowd outside the concert hall, David Yalom had made it back to his hotel room in time to cancel the e-mail he'd programmed his computer to send to his editor. He read each line in the overzealous manifesto as he expunged it and found himself worried for the soul of the man who'd written it.

David had sat up all night thinking about what he'd experienced when he'd seen the dark-haired woman in the crowd who'd called him *Devadas*. He was awake at dawn when his editor called him to request he cover a breaking story: the night before, the Vice President of the United States had attended a concert that had erupted into chaos and had been hurt and hospitalized. There was going to be a press conference at the hospital at 11:00 that morning on his condition and on some of the other VIPs who'd also been hurt in the melee.

"Excuse me, I'm David Yalom—"

"I'm sorry." Lucian Glass protectively inserted himself between Yalom and Meer. "Miss Logan doesn't have any comments."

Meer took in the dark hair and eyes, the notebook and pen. "It's okay," Meer said as she stepped around Lucian so she could face Devadas—no—he'd said his name was David. David Yalom. "I know him," she told Lucian.

Listening to her, David's face underwent a change. Nothing as obvious as a smile, but from one moment to the next, he looked different. As if he'd allowed himself a deep breath finally, and it had almost felt good.

"Thank you for trying to help me last night," she said.

"You weren't hurt, were you?"

She shook her head. "No. Malachai, the man I was with—he was shot—they operated on him."

"Is he all right?"

She nodded.

There was so much to say and no way either of them knew where to begin.

"We should go," Lucian said.

David put his hand in his pocket and as he withdrew it Lucian quickly stepped forward again, instantly suspicious and on guard. David shook his head, silently admonishing him as he pulled out a business card and offered it to Meer. "If you ever..." he started, then stopped, as if he wasn't sure what he wanted to say.

Meer reached out. As she took the card between her fingers she felt the raised letters that spelled out his name and contact information embossed on the smooth satiny stock. Slipping it into her pocket, she kept her hand there, as if protecting it.

Outside, Kalfus sat waiting in the parked car. Lucian opened her door for Meer. Sliding in, she lowered her handbag to the floor, then noticed she'd put it on top of a black notebook, which she picked up to move out of the way. As she did it fell open to an unfinished pencil sketch.

"Let me get that," Lucian said quickly and reached for it.

She looked up at Lucian, then back at the drawing; it was the face of a woman she'd never seen before, except in the woman's eyes she saw herself—her very soul, looking up at her from the page.

Chapter 107

Indus Valley, India—2120 B.C.E.

Ohana woke up with her father leaning over her bed, prying the bone from her grip.

"How could you take this? It's not bad enough that you acted like a whore with him when he was alive. But this? You stole one of his bones?" His eyes glittered like metal, his lips were curled in a snarl.

She'd seen him angry before; he was a stern father, but this was cold fury.

"Please, let me have him back."

His fingers tightened around the white bone. "No. Keeping such a thing you will bring evil down on your head—" spittle flew from his mouth "—and on my house," he said and strode out of her bedchamber.

Jumping up from her bed she ran after him, catching up to him in the courtyard and reaching for the bone. They struggled for a few seconds until he regained control and, brandishing the bone like a weapon, a look of revulsion in his eyes, he held it over her head.

Ohana went from not having had any idea who had killed Devadas, to a possibility that turned her stomach. Tears of shame filled her eyes. Not for what she had done with Devadas but that by doing it she might have been responsible for his death.

"Did you kill him?" She gasped.

The force of her father's hand on her cheek sent her reeling backward and she fell. Pebbles ripped her palms, and a sharp pain shot up her spine.

Her father looked down at her, his lips narrowed in contempt. "How dare you speak to me like this? Go back into the house. Immediately."

It didn't matter that she was disobeying him—she leapt up, grabbed her lover's broken bone and raced through the garden, out into the road—and kept running. Even after he stopped trying to catch her, she kept going, running toward the only place she could think of where she could be safe.

Chapter 108

Dappled light filtered through new leaves in the run-down Jewish section of the cemetery, casting green shadows on Meer's hands and face. Standing alone under a tall chestnut tree, she watched people arrive and gather by the gravesite. Among them she recognized the nine men who, with her father, had made up the minyan that chanted the prayer for the dead over Ruth Volker's coffin the week before.

Today they were here to pray over his ashes. It was against the orthodox Jewish religion to be cremated but Jeremy had stipulated it in his will and late last night, his rabbi gave his blessing and the function had been performed.

"Before I begin today's ceremony," Rabbi Tischenkel said, "I want to tell you about your father's last wishes." He nodded at the silver jar he was holding. "He asked that only half of his ashes be buried here and for you to throw the other half into the Ganges River." The rabbi paused, but before he could continue, Meer interrupted.

"The Ganges?"

"I know. I asked too. He told me that according to ancient beliefs, if your ashes are returned to the Ganges, you get to skip over a few reincarnations and save yourself some time. A shortcut, so to speak." Tischenkel smiled sadly.

The sun reflected off the urn and shone into Meer's eyes.

"Your father also wanted me to tell you to rest your heart about the flute," Tischenkel added.

Meer felt as if across time her father was giving his blessing over what she'd done with the precious instrument. Except...something didn't make sense. "Rabbi, when was my father's will written?"

"About ten years ago."

"Did you witness it?"

"Yes, I did. I was there."

"Was it amended in the last few weeks to add that message about the flute?"

"No, it was in the original. Why?"

"How could my father have known about the flute ten years ago? The Memorists believed Beethoven destroyed it in 1814. It wasn't until my father found the letter in the gaming box two weeks ago that anyone imagined the flute still existed."

The rabbi shrugged again. "I'm afraid it's a mystery to me."

"You're certain he didn't add that in the last few weeks?"

"Yes, I am," he said sympathetically. "It was in the original."

Meer shook her head.

"That's not the answer you expected?" Tischenkel asked.

"No."

Another shrug. "Well, it's one you're going to have to learn to accept on faith. Along with all its ramifications." His smile was enigmatic. "The Kabbalah says if we have not fulfilled our condition during one life, we must commence another...until we have acquired the condition that fits our reunion with God. Maybe your father lived some of this before." He handed her the urn. "I'll tell you when it's appropriate and you can pour half of them in the grave."

Meer took it and shivered. Cold wrapped around her. Too sad, too confused and too tired to fight, she disappeared into the freezing miasma.

Chapter 109

Indus Valley, India—2120 B.C.E.

Ohana had never gone to the workshop without Devadas taking her there. During the day it was where he and his brother made their instruments and at the end of the day it was her trysting place with her lover. Rasul, his brother, was the only living soul who'd known about the affair and he'd never judged or questioned them.

Welcoming her now, he cleared a place for her to sit and then listened as she broke down and, interrupted by intermittent sobs, told him what she'd done and then showed him the bone.

When she finished, Rasul smoothed her hair down and washed her face with cool water from the well and made her drink a thick elixir of honey and herbs. Soon she was tired and he told her to lie down on the straw mat in the corner of the workshop—the same mat where she and Devadas had lain so many times.

When she woke five hours later, it was to an exotic sound. Ohana had spent enough time in worship to know the *kasht tarang* had a hollow wooden tone, that the *manjira* was like bells resonating and that the *bins* gave off reedy notes. These sad tones were different. They rode the breeze and surrounded her and helped her remember Devadas so clearly it was as if he was right there with her, beside her.

And then the song stopped.

Navigating the overcrowded room with its cabinets, shelves of supplies and tables covered with instruments in various stages of assemblage, Ohana found Rasul at the workbench by the brazier, bent over his work, concentrating intensely.

He held a sharp engraving tool over the fire, waited until it turned red-hot and then returned to the intricate detailing he was known for and the reason men came from distant cities to purchase his wares.

Carefully, he finished chasing a groove, laid his iron tool on the table, inspected his work and then lifted the flute to his lips. Almost as if he were kissing it, Rasul pressed his mouth to the body. A low, plaintive whistle developed into a full-toned note. The sound was pure and lucid. Like running water. Or starlight. An enlightened sound. Mesmerized, she stood immobile, then, as she listened, the note modulated. Warbled. Words came after that, soft-spoken words that had body and form and meaning, as if the very heavens were singing to her.

She would never know how long she stood there or how many stories she saw unfold in her mind. The music of the past showed her that she and Devadas had been together before this life in many others.

Rasul's eyes were warm and moist as he extended his hand and offered her the instrument. "The flute is yours to keep for as long as you need its memory song…" he said. "Play it to help you remember that the two of you were together before and will be again. There's no beginning and there's no end. There's only infinite passion. The infinite passion of life."

Ohana took the instrument and brought it up to her breast, and now, for the first time since the Asthi-Sanchayana ceremony when Devadas had been cremated, she felt him close by and was comforted.

Chapter 110

The silver jar was lighter with half her father's ashes in his grave. Meer stepped back as the rabbi motioned to the crowd and ten men stepped forward. One of them was the stranger who'd taken her father's place in the minyan. They gathered around the gravesite and in unison began to pray, not in German, but in Hebrew, the language of prayer for all Jews.

The rich sound resonated though Meer's chest cavity and her heart slowed to the prayer's rhythm. This was the Kaddish vibrating inside of her. The prayer that had been recited millions of times over the dead for the last six thousand years, a tradition intended to give solace and succor as a soul passed from this life and prepared to enter the next. These were the teachings her father had tried to interest her in, that had mattered so much to him and that he had believed in with all of his soul. *His soul.* Had it shattered into those hundred pieces of light he had told her about? Were they waiting now to find another vessel?

Yit'gadal v'yit'kadash sh'mei raba...

The words rose up and surrounded her like a warm wind.

V'yam'likh mal'khutei b'chayeikhon uv'yomeikhon...

She didn't know the words' actual meaning but they resonated inside her the way the memory song had when Sebastian had played it on the flute, but without the fear and panic. It was the same vibration that had engulfed her in the underground chamber when she sat with her father as he lay dying. The same vibration she'd felt when Sebastian's son, Nicolas, had chanted his hymn—this hymn—over and over in his hospital room.

V'yam'likh mal'khutei b'chayeikhon uv'yomeikhon.

As the prayer came to an end, Meer was still thinking about Nicolas: a nine-year-old savant to these words. Had he seen the gardener unearth a child's skull that summer day? Had the souls of the two children—one alive and one dead—connected in a way that caused Nicolas to believe it was his job to mourn that long-deceased Jewish child? Was he lost in that mourning?

The rabbi recited one last blessing.

Meer was hearing his words and staring at the minyan, thinking about Sebastian's useless sacrifice to help Nicolas. A father's dedication to the point of obsession to save his son and bring him back from the land of the living dead.

Chapter 111

Sebastian's ex-wife, Dr. Rebecca Kutcher, sat at her desk and frowned while she listened to Meer's request and did her best not to stare at the nine men who stood respectfully by the window. Each member of the minyan, all in their funereal dark suits and yarmulkes, looked at the doctor with expressions that were so empathetic and kind, they disconcerted her.

"No," Rebecca said when Meer finished. "Everything I've done has been to protect Nicolas from his father's obsessions. Why would I agree to allow you to take strangers into my son's room?"

"I know that what I'm suggesting sounds strange to you. It does even to me," Meer said, trying to think of a way to win over this brittle woman.

Out the window, in the distance, the sun sparkled on the lake, its surface as smooth as a mirror.

"What do you believe in, Rebecca?"

"Science," she answered with no hesitation.

"What about in the gap between where science stops and mystery begins?"

"What has this to do with my son?"

"Have you read any studies on binaural beats?"

Rebecca shook her head impatiently, and Meer knew her chance of winning this woman over was slight.

"There are prayers and mystic rituals going back thousands of years that effect change and help heal both spiritually and physically. They're often words with meanings but they're also sounds that have vibrations. And in the last fifty years there have been studies done that show different kinds of vibrations can affect consciousness." Meer was losing Rebecca, she could see it in the other woman's eyes. "I didn't believe it either but I've experienced it…and it helped me. I was there, Rebecca. Where Nicolas is. All I'm asking is that you allow these men to go into your son's room and chant with him."

The boy didn't look up when the men walked into his room. Nicolas sat drawing, a box of crayons at his elbow. The reds, yellows, bright blues and greens were all still in the container, their points sharp and intact. The ones he used, the grays and the browns, the blacks and the dull taupes, were scattered across on the tabletop, sad, worn-down stubs.

He was drawing yet another version of the boy in the dark passage-way that was identical to the drawings Meer had seen the last time she'd been there. She'd traversed passageways like this one and had finally come out on the other side. Now she wanted to help Nicolas to come out the other side, too. For his sake. His sake alone. Even though Meer understood what had driven Sebastian, she knew she'd probably never be able to forgive him, but neither could she punish the boy for his father's failures. Failures in both the present and in the faraway past.

Under his breath, the boy's singsong words were barely audible but Meer's father's friends recognized what they were hearing. There was no signal, no instant when the decision was made. One moment there was just a thin childish whisper and then a single adult male voice joined in and then another joined in and another until nine voices combined with Nicolas's and the minyan of ten was formed and together they all chanted.

Meer bowed her head, not sure she should watch. Now, not at the concert hall when all hell broke loose; not in Beethoven's house when she realized where the flute was hidden; not at the graveyard when she buried her father's ashes; but *now*, she felt for the first time in her life that she was in the presence of something sacred as the vibrations from the chanting resonated in the hospital room. Was this the sound of myriad pieces of broken, fragmented souls joining together at last?

Meer thought about the love her father had described to her: love that we pass on, that keeps us alive, that makes us weak and fallible when it is taken away and that gives us strength and peace when we realize it can't ever really be taken away but exists always, just transformed.

When Meer had stood at her own father's grave and heard this prayer circling around her, she'd thought of Nicolas and wondered if somehow in his past he'd been a father or grandfather or brother who'd been unable to complete the mourning process for a child. Who'd failed at gathering a minyan and making sure the proper prayers were said. A father or a grandfather or a brother who must have died or been killed, with this unfinished business of grief still on his mind.

Beside her, Rebecca sighed and Meer looked over to see tears and an expression of wonder on the woman's face. The room was silent. The minyan had stopped their chanting. The Kaddish had been said. Nicolas was as quiet now as the others. He sat at his desk, staring down at his drawing, not frantically chanting or moving side to side or sketching. He was absolutely still.

Rebecca went to him, got down on her knees by his side. "Nicolas?" she whispered.

The little boy turned and looked at his mother. There was confusion but also something vitally alive in eyes that had been dead before. He was no longer a child disconnected from himself or the world. Yes, he was pale and looked fragile and would certainly need help but he could see what was in front of him for the first time in a long time and what he saw was his mother reaching out for him and as she gently held him, his hands moved to grip her arms.

Over her son's head, Rebecca looked up at Meer.

"Do you have children?" she asked.

"No."

"Then you can't understand the depth of my thanks."

Meer wondered what Nicolas would remember. What he'd be able to explain about the last six months of his life when he was older, when he was her age, when someone asked him what had happened to him. Would he remember the sensation of today's vibrations in his body, in his blood, in his bones?

Her father would have loved to see what she'd just seen. He'd explain it using theories about the resilience of the human spirit and the human soul, and connect them to his ideas about binaural beats and what Pythagoras believed about reincarnation and mathematics, numbers, sounds and circular time.

With his irrepressible optimism her father would use all this as proof of what he'd always wanted her to understand about her own past and her future.

You see how simple it is? All you have to do—she could hear him say—*is open yourself up to the cosmos as it lays itself before you. See it in all its mysterious dimensions. Without prejudice. Without assumption. There's music waiting for you to write, sweetheart. All you ever needed was the key to open yourself to it. And that key is the wonder of the world. All the songs you could never remember but couldn't forget? You can find them now.*

* * * * *

AUTHOR'S NOTE

As with the first novel in this series, *The Reincarnationist,* there is a lot of fact mixed in with this fictional tale.

The funeral ceremony, musical instruments, culture, customs and flora I describe in the ancient Indus Valley were carefully researched, and I've tried to keep true to what is known.

In almost all cases, dates and descriptions of historical events such as the Congress of Vienna are accurate, as are most of the locales of that beautiful city in which I've spent several months. There is indeed a complex underground world there, rife with tunnels and archaeological treasures. There are several subterranean thermal lakes in the area, though there is not one directly beneath the main music hall, as far as anyone knows. The Heart Vault, the Dorotheum, the museums, Beethoven's homes, the Central Cemetery and Steinhof hospital are all real. Sadly, so is the information about the Nazi experiments done there and the extent to which these experiments were still used and available to researchers.

As far as I know, the Memorist Society doesn't exist, but there were many secret societies in Austria that broke off from the Freemasons—some of which might still be functional.

There is no Phoenix Foundation. The work done there was, however, inspired by the work done at the University of Virginia Medical Center by the real-life Dr. Ian Stevenson, who studied children with past life memories for over thirty years. Dr. Bruce Greyson and Dr. Jim Tucker, a child psychiatrist, continue Ian Stevenson's work today. (These fine doctors are not to be blamed for any of Dr. Malachai Samuels' personality defects.)

There is fascinating research into binaural beats, some of which suggests these tones could offer a portal to past life memories. Sacred music, chanting and repetitive sounds have already been proven to affect the mind and change our perceptions.

The Austrian Orientalist Joseph von Hammer-Purgstall, along with Sir William Jones in England and Silvestre de Sacy in France, was responsible for the great dissemination of Eastern knowledge in late eighteenth-century Europe. In those early days of the Age of Enlightenment the study of Eastern philosophy—including reincarnation—became very popular. Ludwig van Beethoven was in fact among those interested in these doctrines. His own notebooks contain a number of passages from *Bhagavad-Gita,* as well as a quote from William Jones's "Hymn to Narayena": "We know this only, that we nothing know."

ACKNOWLEDGMENTS

The tough thing about writing thank-you notes is that no matter how many people I list who helped with this book, I know I will be leaving out many, so for that I apologize in advance.

To begin, thank you to my friend and agent Loretta Barrett as well as Nick Mullendore and Gabriel Davis of Loretta Barrett Books for so much hard work and excellent advice.

To the whole team at MIRA Books whom I am blessed to have in my corner—especially my amazing editor Margaret O'Neill Marbury, who did so much to shape this book. The idea of writing a book without her or Lisa Tucker and Douglas Clegg seems impossible—I hope the impossible never happens. To Jerry Hooten, who gave me the benefit of his knowledge—if there are any factual errors having to do with security issues and investigative techniques they are mine, not his.

A huge thank-you to readers, booksellers and librarians everywhere, to all my business associates, my friends in and out of the biz. To Doug Scofield, who along with everything else gave me a glimpse into the world of music, and to the rest of my wonderful family for their support and love.

SUGGESTED READING LIST

I have been reading about reincarnation and related subjects for many years and wanted to offer a selection of the books I have found most helpful in writing *The Memorist*.

Andrews, Ted. *Sacred Sounds: Magic & Healing Through Words & Music.* Llewellyn Publications, 2002.

Bache, Christopher M. *Lifecycles: Reincarnation and the Web of Life.* Paragon House Publishers, 1994.

Bowman, Carol. *Children's Past Lives: How Past Life Memories Affect Your Child.* Bantam, 1998.

Chopra, Deepak. *Life After Death: The Burden of Proof.* Harmony, 2006.

Gershom, Yonassan. *Beyond the Ashes: Cases of Reincarnation from the Holocaust.* A.R.E. Press, 1992.

Gershom, Yonassan. *Jewish Tales of Reincarnation.* Jason Aronson, 1999.

Kushner, Lawrence. *Honey from the Rock: An Introduction to Jewish Mysticism.* Jewish Lights Publishing, 1999.

Stemman, Roy. *One Soul, Many Lives: First-Hand Stories of Reincarnation and the Striking Evidence of Past Lives.* Ulysses Press, 2005.

Stevenson, Ian. *Children Who Remember Previous Lives: A Question of Reincarnation.* McFarland & Company, revised edition, 2000.

Stevenson, Ian. *Twenty Cases Suggestive of Reincarnation*. University Press of Virginia, 1980.

Tucker, Jim. *Life Before Life: A Scientific Investigation of Children's Memories of Previous Lives*. St. Martin's Press, 2005.

Wallace, B. Alan. *Contemplative Science: Where Buddhism and Neuroscience Converge*. Columbia University Press, 2006.

Wilson, Colin. *After Life: Survival of the Soul*. Llewellyn Publications, 2000.